AUTUMN'S TITHE

AUTUMN'S TITHE

HANNAH PARKER

COUNTERPOISE
PRESS

AUTUMN'S TITHE

First published in the United States in September 2021
by Counterpoise Press

Identifiers:
Library of Congress Control Number: 2021907955
ISBN 978-1-7367414-1-2 (hardcover) | ISBN 978-1-7367414-2-9 (paperback) | ISBN
978-1-7367414-0-5 (ebook)

10 9 8 7 6 5 4 3 2 1

To find out more about Counterpoise Press visit www.counterpoisepress.com

To find out more about Hannah Parker visit www.hannahparker.com

For Mom and Dad

For Mom and Dad

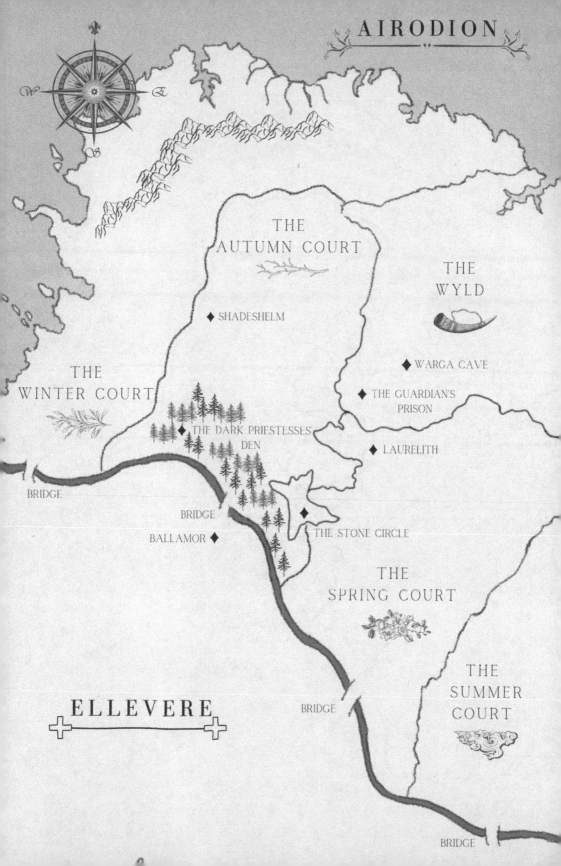

PART I
CEREMONIES AND SECRETS

CHAPTER ONE

Larken pressed the heels of her hands into the cool dough, her body slipping into the dance of bread making. The heavy scent of yeast rose to greet her as she worked. The dough pulled at her and she eased her touch, folding and turning again and again.

Today. Today. Today.

The Choosing Ceremony was finally here. Her hands moved of their own accord, adding a dash of flour, curling into the dough, shaping it. She let the repetition soothe her mind, though her heart still fluttered with anticipation.

One year ago, her dearest friend was chosen to live in the land of the fey. Larken had thought about Brigid every day since. What was it like living with a faery lord? What was it like living in a world filled with magic?

You'll be able to ask her for yourself, soon, Larken told herself. *If she even wants to see you.*

"Hurry up, Larken!" Papa's voice boomed, startling her. "Get those loaves in the oven and come help me with the cookies."

It was only in the kitchen that his voice turned so officious. Had her father been anything but a baker, he would have been absolutely terrifying. Yet despite his broad frame, his huge hands frosted the cookies

3

before him with astonishing delicacy. Larken wondered why he even needed her help, as good as he was.

Larken wiped her hands on her stomach, glad she had put on an apron to protect her Ceremony dress. She had settled on a light blue gown with pink stitching, and while she usually strolled around the village with a coat of flour on, the faery lord didn't have to know that.

Beautiful, immortal, and filled with the grace of the Twin gods, the fey were viewed by humans as near deities themselves. They were shrouded in mystery and even possessed the ability to wield fragments of the gods' magic. Their realm, as mysterious and magical as the fey were, was separated from the human lands by a deep chasm, with only four bridges connecting them.

The bridges only opened for seven days each year—at all other times they were closed off by a powerful magic. The Choosing Ceremony marked the first day that the bridges opened, when the four faery lords would cross their respective bridges and select one human girl each to return with them.

Larken's village, Ballamor, was only a short journey from one of these bridges, making it a perfect place to perform a Choosing Ceremony. The three other human towns closest to the bridges held Ceremonies of their own and were visited by their own faery lord.

Today was Larken's chance to be chosen.

Larken shoved the dough in the oven so hastily she almost burned her hands. She cursed, jerking them back.

"Careful," Mama called, sweeping by with a raisin-studded porter cake. "Forget the cookies, your papa can finish them. Help me take these down to the field." She gestured to one of the wicker baskets brimming with shortbread, scones, and miniature cakes. "Wait! Get your cloak— you'll need it." Mama pushed a strand of her hair back with a flustered sigh.

Mama was always ruffled on Ceremony day. With villagers from the farthest reaches of Ballamor and the surrounding cities pouring into town, there were hundreds of more mouths to feed.

Larken raced up the stairs that connected the bakery to her family's

4

living quarters on the upper level. She grabbed the cloak sprawled across her bed.

Her boot slid on something beneath her. She glanced down—a haphazard pile of unfinished maps stared up at her, the product of her insomnia the night before. Her lips pulled into a frown as her gaze picked up on every line that was out of place on her charts. Brigid would have helped her fix every mistake. But Brigid wasn't there.

Larken had been mapping out the woods surrounding Ballamor when she and Brigid had officially met for the first time.

"What're you doing?" Brigid had asked. Even at ten years old, Brigid had been beautiful. Her dark hair had made her huge blue eyes look even brighter. And even then, they had been opposites. Brigid, willow-thin to Larken's plump frame, Brigid's dark tresses to Larken's mousy blonde.

They were opposites in other ways as well. Brigid had always been so sure of herself, outgoing and talkative, while Larken was quiet and diffident.

"Making maps," Larken had replied, wary. The other children liked to tease her about it. While most of the children her age were playing Faery and Maiden, she was plotting how far away her family's bakery was from the mill where they got their flour.

Papa liked to boast that he was the one who had sparked Larken's love for cartography. He had always gotten lost during his travels to other towns for specialty ingredients. The year he took Larken on one of his trips, they got lost so many times she finally sketched out a chart of the area to use the following year. The hobby had stuck.

Brigid had peered over her shoulder, observing the grid onto which Larken had plotted their entire town. Larken had been toying with it for hours, unable to figure out what was wrong with it.

"That tree there..." Brigid pointed to a tree toward the left of the map. "It should be here." She moved her hand slightly to the right. "It's in front of Da's forge—not to the side." She frowned, noticing Larken's scribbled label. "And 'forge' is spelled with a g, not a j."

"It is a g."

Brigid's eyebrows knitted. "Doesn't look like one."

Larken had giggled instead of taking offense. Brigid was more straightforward than any of the other village children she had met—but she wasn't unkind about it.

They had become fast friends after that. Larken made the maps, and Brigid provided her with helpful insight and artistic skill. She always sketched out the landmarks that dotted Larken's charts. And when the other village children teased her, Brigid always defended her, claiming that one day Larken would be a mapmaker for the Popes themselves.

Larken wondered if her friend would be so willing to defend her, now. Memories of their falling out still haunted her.

Larken pushed down her guilt and the bitter ache of missing her friend. Once the Chosen girls crossed the bridge, they never returned. Larken imagined her reunion with Brigid, seeing her friend's shock and delight that Larken had been chosen. It had been a full year since they'd fought. Surely Brigid had forgiven her by now. But Larken wouldn't rest until she talked to her friend.

Don't get ahead of yourself, a voice in the back of her mind warned. *The faery lord still has to choose you. And he doesn't pick girls who look like you.*

The humans revered the fey for their beauty and elegance. Girls living in the towns that performed the Choosing Ceremonies became obsessed with the idea that the more they resembled the fey, the higher the chances they would be chosen. This theory didn't prove to be entirely inaccurate, as Ballamor's faery lord usually selected the beautiful, wealthy girls that lived in estates outside of town. No one had expected him to choose the blacksmith's daughter, but he had.

Larken pushed open the door to the bakery, the smell of sugar and sweet cream enveloping her.

Papa bustled around, making sure everything was in its proper place. "I've got another batch coming. Those will need to go down to the festival as soon as they cool," Papa called to Mama, pointing to the racks of cookies.

Outside, their cart pony, Snowfoot, waited for them. Larken snuck him a few sugar cubes as she and Mama loaded the baskets onto the cart, and then they were off.

Colorful flags waved at them from windowsills as they made their way down the main road. The doors to the village inn were swung wide, people spilling out into the streets. Wreaths of flowers decorated the doors of the local shops, a nod to the girls participating in the Choosing Ceremony, and to welcome the faery lord.

The lord always brought gifts for the villagers—something that Larken, as well as the rest of the townsfolk, looked forward to. Wine that would cause one to fall asleep to only good dreams. Candies for the children that, once eaten, caused them to feel invisible fingers tickling them. Better still were the special presents given to the families of the Chosen girls: necklaces that never lost their luster, tools that never had to be sharpened. Little pieces of the faery world that showed how dazzling it would be for their daughters once they crossed the bridge.

Once they reached the clearing, Larken helped Mama arrange the pastries on one of the food-laden banquet tables. Already, she could smell meat roasting on spits, glistening with honey and grease. The scent of horses and the clamor of a great many people swept in on the breeze. Children ran by with ribbon sticks, shrieking with delight.

The two crossed wooden beams standing in the center of the field were the crowning glory of the festival. Soon they would be set alight, symbolizing the Popes' blessing of the Choosing Ceremony. Before the Order of the Twins had been established as the one true religion of the human realm of Ellevere, the two burning crosses had stood in every town converted by crusaders.

There were no crusaders now. People either followed the Order, or they were killed. But here in the North, the furthest region of the Empire, whispers could still be heard. Of the time before the Order. Here, they still had a semblance of freedom.

A high-pitched scream made Larken freeze, her hand clutched on a berry scone. Across from her, Brigid's older brother led children around on ponies. His large hands, roughed from long hours in the forge, were gentle as he steadied the ponies' clumsy riders. Brigid's mother was there as well, but Brigid's father remained at home. He had suffered through a debilitating horse-kick to the head a few years prior. Brigid's

7

mother smiled and laughed with the rest, but her shoulders hung low, some invisible mantle draped across them.

Brigid's mother had told her they were happy for their daughter, and still invited Larken over from time to time. Larken didn't see it as anything more than a courtesy. When Brigid had been chosen, Larken didn't just lose her friend—she lost her second family as well. She unclenched her fist, realizing too late that she had reduced the scone to crumbs.

The crowd grew as the day progressed. Rich townsfolk came in from their estates, bringing their splendid clothes and horses with them. Girls dressed in their finest breezed past, and Larken bunched the fabric of her gown self-consciously.

Today was her last Choosing Ceremony as an eligible girl. Girls were presented to the faery lord after they turned twelve and participated until they were eighteen. Larken was seventeen now, and by the next Ceremony she would be too old.

Papa came up behind her, jostling her out of her thoughts. He squeezed her shoulders with his massive hands. Larken was convinced she had inherited her large frame from him, though he looked like a carnival strongman and she more like a powdered doughnut. Still, they both shared round, rosy faces and cheeks, while her upturned nose, short stature, and brown eyes had all come from her mother.

"Dance with me, little lark."

"Papa, I can't. You know I'm about as graceful as a—"

But Papa wouldn't hear another word of her protests. He spun her around the grassy field, both of them trying to keep up with the stringed instruments and drums. Larken's feet dragged at first, betraying her reluctance, but soon the music swept her into its rhythm and her mood lightened. The smell of meat, ale, and sweets was dizzying, and Larken's nerves slowly melted away into happiness.

A jarring weight hit her shoulder, almost causing her to stumble. A tall, slender girl with black hair and a pale blue dress shuffled past. Larken whirled, straining to get a better look at her face.

Brigid. Except it was not Brigid. This girl had brown eyes, not blue, and she was a few inches too tall. The girl mumbled an apology, her eyes downcast. She quickly disappeared into the crowd.

Memories from her and Brigid's last night together swept in before Larken could stop them.

Have you ever wanted to be chosen? Brigid asked.

Of course not, Larken replied. *Why would I? We're going south.*

They planned to leave Ballamor and travel to the South when they turned eighteen; Larken to study map-making, and Brigid to study art.

Have you? Larken asked, unable to keep the smile from her voice. Brigid couldn't be serious.

Brigid bit her lip. *I've—I've been thinking about it more. We only have two more Ceremonies to participate in before we lose our chance forever.*

Bri, you can't be serious. Girls like us don't get chosen.

That's not fair. A crease formed between Brigid's brows. *I could be chosen. My body's changed since we were girls. I have a real chance now.* She gestured to her slim form. Larken recoiled at her words, at the hidden insult within them.

Are you saying that you're better than me now? Larken asked coldly.

Of course not. I'm just saying that there's always a chance. Would it be so bad if I took it?

We have plans to move south, Bri, how could you just give that up?

Because I can't make a life out of a hobby! And neither can you. Brigid clenched her fists. *Can't you understand that? There's nothing keeping me here.*

Larken flinched. *If you truly think that, then you aren't the person I thought you were. You're just like every other girl stupid enough to dream about being chosen.*

Larken shut out the rest of the argument. If Larken was chosen, then they could sort everything out, and everything would be as it had been before. She might get to see Brigid that very night. Her stomach pinched with nerves. Or she would have to wait until after she completed the task for the faery lord.

Rumors about why the fey needed human girls for the task had spread over time. Some claimed that that the fey needed human wives to birth their young, or that they took humans with some great skill to entertain them throughout their immortal lives. Larken could almost believe that speculation as Brigid had been an exceptional artist. Whatever the task was, perhaps she could convince the faery lord that her cartography skills could be of some use.

Don't be stupid, a voice inside her chided. *What use could the fey have for a human mapmaker?*

Evening arrived, darkness draping across the field. Two men set the giant wooden crosses alight, and cheers exploded. Larken closed her eyes, letting Papa twirl her around and around. Streaks of flame from the bonfires flashed against her closed lids. When she opened them, torches blazed, tiny stars against the night.

Once Larken and Papa had thoroughly exhausted themselves, she collapsed on one of the wooden benches. Next to her, Mama spoke with a young woman rocking a crying baby.

"Give him yellow thorn for the cough," Mama instructed. "Mash it into a paste and rub it on his chest—it'll clear it right up." She brushed the baby's fat cheek with her thumb.

Mama had been a healer before she married Papa and began working with him in the bakery. Some of the villagers still asked for her help whenever they couldn't afford the services of Ballamor's true healer.

"Thank you, Maeve—truly," the woman said. "May the Twins bless you and your family. I pray that the faery lord chooses your daughter."

Larken's heart jumped at the words. Mama smiled, but it didn't quite reach her eyes. While Papa had lived in Ballamor his whole life, Mama had come from a town further south. The Choosing Ceremony had never sat right with her. She struggled to see how losing a daughter could be considered an honor. Papa, coming from a family of boys, had never had to participate in the Choosing Ceremony directly until Larken's birth. Her parents both had their doubts—though neither were vocal about them, lest the wrong ears overhear their complaints.

Larken had questions of her own regarding the Ceremony, but she knew she had to reconcile herself to them if she ever wanted to see Brigid again. And while she longed to reunite with her friend, the idea of getting to map out an entirely new world made her fingertips tingle with excitement.

"I have something for you," Mama said with a twinkle in her eyes. She handed Larken a woven flower crown.

It was stunning—white, yellow, and pink blossoms surrounded a base of twigs, looking as if they had grown into a crown of their own accord. All girls eligible for the Choosing Ceremony wore flower crowns, but Larken had never had one this beautiful.

"I love it, Mama," Larken whispered. Wordlessly, her mother placed the crown atop her head.

At a nearby table, children began to cluster around a black-hooded woman. She was one of the younger members of the Black Guard. Pod —Larken thought her name was.

The Black Guard kept both humans and fey alike from crossing the bridges, save for the faery lords and their Chosen girls. Hand-picked and trained in the Popes' opulent palaces, the Guard spent years training for the moment when the barriers between worlds opened. Members of the Guard were the only humans alive educated in faery lore aside from the Popes themselves.

"When the Twin gods created the world, they separated it into two lands, one for each of them to rule," Pod began. "Asphalion would rule over the fey, and Aleea would rule over the humans. But Aleea became jealous of the fey's magic and tried to take it for the humans. Asphalion attacked her, and they fought. The two worlds fell into chaos." She raised her arms theatrically, making the children's eyes widen.

"During the war, four Popes rose to power in the human realm," Pod continued. "They convinced Aleea to beg for her brother's forgiveness. Eventually, Asphalion forgave her, and as a sign of his good will, he allowed four girls, not yet grown and influenced by a woman's guile, to enter the faery realm each year to experience the magic for themselves. He created a task for the fey and girls to complete, one that forced them to work together despite their differences, as he and Aleea had done to end the war."

"What kind of task?" a small girl piped up.

"That is only for the fey, the Popes, and the Twins to know. As well as the Chosen girl, when her time comes. After the task is complete, the girls want for nothing."

The four villages nearest to the bridges were the only ones required to offer their girls up to the fey. People outside of these towns were expected to serve the Popes in different ways. But many of those who lived in cities close to Ballamor entered their girls in exchange for their taxes being lifted. Others entered their daughters to avoid military drafts.

They had nothing to lose. Even if their daughters were chosen, they would be showered with luxurious gifts. And if they weren't, well, they didn't have to pay a cent to the Popes or wield a sword for them.

The whole concept had never sat well with Larken.

"After one of the very first Choosing Ceremonies in Ballamor," Pod continued, "a sister of the Chosen girl, Laila, followed her sibling across the bridge. Laila returned, and spoke of how kind the fey were. She saw the other Chosen girls, and the ones who had been chosen the previous year. Laila begged her sister to return, but the girl refused. She was far too happy to leave.

"But in following her sister into the faery lands, Laila showed that she did not have faith without seeing things with her own eyes. The Popes were greatly saddened when they heard of her disobedience, for they knew she must atone. If not, how many others would venture into the faery realm, disrupting the task and angering the fey and the gods, perhaps even severing the divine bond between our two worlds?"

The children nodded as Pod drew back, her plain features settling into a grim expression. Many of the village children knew the tale by heart, yet they still eagerly awaited what came next.

"The Guard burned out Laila's eyes, symbolizing the blind faith that must burn in all our hearts for the Twins. But Laila gave up her sight happily, repenting her sin and casting doubt from her heart."

And she serves as a reminder of what happens when you disobey the rules, Larken thought darkly. Whispers had spread even as far north as Ballamor about the most recent atrocities the Popes had committed against non-believers in the Twins' name. Larken and her family kept up all appearances of being devout believers, as did all others who wanted to keep their flesh from being burnt on the Popes' pyres.

Pod spread her hands. "That is the tale of how the Choosing Ceremony began, and now you all will be able to witness it for yourselves." Pod rose to her feet, and all eyes turned toward the tree line.

Tingles exploded across Larken's skin, making her shiver. A nervous titter rose up as girls chatted to each other, shifting from one foot to another as they formed a line.

Members of the Black Guard patrolled the line, taking girls' names and ages, comparing them to their records. They kept track of all the eligible girls in the village, ensured that these girls were presented, and punished families that didn't comply. These punishments were rare, however, as so many longed for the chance to be chosen.

A flash of dark hair next to her caught Larken's eye. It was the girl who had bumped into her earlier—the one she had mistaken for Brigid. Larken finally remembered where she had seen her before: she was the butcher's daughter.

Something brushed against Larken's skirts. The girl's hand, shaking madly, had touched her. Sympathy trickled through Larken. Many girls became overcome with nerves at this point of the Ceremony.

Larken took the girl's hand and squeezed it tightly. It was the only comfort she could think to give her. The girl looked at her, and she gave Larken a tiny nod. Larken had held Brigid's hand during the last Ceremony, even though they had both been too angry to speak.

After Brigid had been chosen, Larken had considered trying to cross the bridge to be with her. But even then, it had seemed impossible. The Guard would have stopped her and punished her. And who was she anyway, to think that she was good enough to enter the land of the fey? The faery lord had wanted Brigid, not her.

If she was chosen today, everything would fall into place. Larken would be able to find her friend and make things right. She couldn't stand knowing that the last words they had said to each other had been in anger.

Despite what Brigid had said, Larken couldn't believe that her friend had given up on their dreams for a future together. Brigid understood what it was like to pour one's thirst for adventure and knowledge into pens, ink, and paper. To see the world laid out so beautifully and orderly before her, and the excitement she felt when she looked at the world she had yet to explore. Brigid hadn't meant what she said—she knew cartography wasn't a silly hobby for Larken to occupy herself with. It was a passion. A skill.

The Guard finished their task, stepping away from the girls.

A hush blanketed over the crowd. Larken bit her lip. An evening fog rolled down from the hills, twisting through the woods.

The faery lord emerged from the trees like a ghost, obscured by the mist. He was lithe and graceful, with lightly tanned skin. His auburn hair shone even in the darkness. Though she saw him year after year, his appearance never changed—he always looked to be in his mid-twenties. He was dressed casually enough; a white linen shirt tucked into dark pants and boots. Though his journey must have been arduous, not a speck of dirt touched him. He was beautiful—human enough despite his pointed ears, and yet not human at all.

He halted where the line of girls began, unslinging a pack from his shoulders.

Grass rustled quietly in the wind, and Larken tried not to shiver. A horse whinnied. Her blood pounded so loudly in her ears that she was sure the faery would hear it.

Slowly, he made his way down the line. Her fingers twitched. All Larken heard was the faint rustle of his boots and the loud, frantic pounding in her chest.

Choose me. Choose me. Choose me. Please. I'll do anything.

He was only a few paces away from her spot in line now, and Larken's lungs seized. He examined each girl carefully, eyes drifting from head to toe, holding gazes, studying faces—but he hadn't stopped yet. He could still pick her. She still had a chance.

After what felt like an eternity, yet no time at all, the faery lord stood before her. She was barely level with his chest. The lord was so close Larken could smell him—leaves, apples, and a hint of spice.

She wanted to tell him everything about Brigid, about her mapmaking and how it could be helpful for the special task, but she couldn't form a single word. Panic seized her. Was this truly what she wanted? To leave Mama and Papa behind forever? And what if she was chosen, but failed at the task the fey needed her for?

Larken shoved those thoughts away. She had to make things right with Brigid or she would never forgive herself.

The lord's eyes locked with hers, and Larken found she could not look away. They were as green as a summer forest, with flecks of brown and gold surrounding the iris. The light of the torches set the gold in his eyes on fire.

Larken forgot everything else as he slowly lifted a finger to point. "Her."

CHAPTER TWO

A roar erupted from the crowd, but the voices sounded muffled and far away. Larken had been chosen. It was her, *she* had been chosen. Oh, Twins, she could barely breathe. Dizzying excitement swept over her, her arms trembling.

"Me?" Larken breathed. Her knees were going to give out. The faery dipped his head to look at her again, auburn curls falling across his forehead.

"No, love," he said. "Her."

Larken looked slowly to her right. He hadn't been pointing at her, but at the butcher's daughter. Larken's stomach plummeted. She shook her head. No, *no*—he had pointed at her—this couldn't be happening. Everything she wanted had been firmly clutched in her hands, and then it had slipped away like smoke. The world turned quiet and dark, as if she were looking at her surroundings from the bottom of a lake. Black spots swam at the edges of her vision, the air hitching in her throat.

She would never see Brigid again.

Tears brimmed in Larken's eyes. She wrenched her hand from the butcher's daughter's grasp. Cold enveloped Larken's fingers, their momentary bond breaking. The other girl looked at her, hurt flashing through her features as her brow furrowed.

"N—no, please—" A boy pushed his way through the crowd. She recognized the boy—Roger. It was coming back to her now; he and the butcher's girl had been romantically involved for some time. The girl's name hovered at the edge of Larken's memory but still eluded her.

"Please, milord, we're about to be wed," Roger said. He pulled the butcher's girl to his chest. "She turns eighteen tomorrow, she's too old."

The butcher's daughter reached out a shaking hand toward the lord. "Please, not me. Take someone else."

A gasp ran through the crowd, quiet at first, then followed by louder mutters.

"Take me, milord!" one girl called.

"Or my daughter, take her! I could use the coin!" a man's voice shouted.

More murmurs from the other girls. Disbelief. Anger. How many others would want to go in her place? The faery lord offered her a life of honor and splendor. The Twins themselves had blessed her.

Larken waited for the jealousy to wash over her, but it never came. It felt wrong, knowing what was to come. Once the faery lord made his choice, there was no changing his mind. She gazed at the young couple, buried in each other's arms.

Tearful goodbyes weren't out of the ordinary during a Choosing Ceremony, but Larken had only seen this level of resistance to being chosen once when she was a little girl. Even when Brigid had been chosen, Larken had barely spoken a word, shocked and wounded by her friend's blatant happiness at being chosen.

The faery lord studied the butcher's daughter, his brow knit ever so slightly. A glint of what almost looked like panic flickered in his eyes, but when Larken blinked, it was gone, replaced with calm.

"I'm sorry, truly. But it must be you," he said.

"Please." Tears streamed down Roger's face. "I'll do anything. Just don't take her."

A small girl threw herself into the butcher girl's arms. Another little one came running up—her sisters, Larken realized. The butcher's daughter hugged each of them in turn, then untangled herself from their skinny arms. She didn't say anything, but tears poured down her cheeks.

They tried clinging to her again, begging her not to go, but she pushed them roughly off, sending them stumbling back to their parents.

Larken swallowed. The girl's parents held the children close. Tears glistened in their eyes.

"*Murderer!*"

The word rose like a curse from someone in the crowd. Larken twisted, eyes wide.

A man pushed himself through the throng. His gray hair fell in greasy tangles, an unkempt beard framing the scowl on his lips. An empty tankard hung loosely from his fingers. He stumbled to a halt, using the man next to him to steady himself.

"Murderers. The lot of you!" The man sneered at the faery, then he brandished his mug at the onlookers. "Taking our girls—while the rest of you hand them over like lambs for the slaughter."

A chill ran through Larken. She knew the man—Castor, a former member of the Black Guard. His daughter had been chosen when Larken was only five years old. Though Larken had only been a child at the time, she remembered that the girl had resisted being chosen. Castor had even tried to fight the faery lord to stop him from taking her. After her Ceremony, he went mad with grief and disappeared into the woods near the bridge. He returned for the Choosing Ceremonies, but he had never spoken out this way before. The Guard had stripped him of his position eight years ago on claims that he was spreading poisonous lies about the fey.

"Why haven't we seen any of the girls return after they cross the bridge? The gate opens for seven days each year! You don't think a single one of them would try to come back to see their families? You think they stopped loving us the moment they finished their 'special task'?" His voice turned into a sneer, his thick accent nearly garbling his words.

Larken took a sharp breath. Castor's words dug into her. It was likely that Brigid wouldn't have been able to return in the days following her Choosing Ceremony due to the special task, but what about this year? Would Brigid try to see her? But perhaps Brigid would be too angry at her to return despite the bridge being open.

She had lost her final chance to see her friend. A lump rose in Larken's throat. The weight of never being able to speak with Brigid again nearly crushed her.

"Why does it have to be *her*," Castor demanded, pointing at the butcher's girl, "when so many others would willingly go in her place? There are too many secrets surrounding this blasted Ceremony. Something happened to them. Something terrible. My girl—my girl would have tried to come home. She would have come back to me," he choked.

Someone grabbed Castor's arm, but he shook them off. The old man and the faery lord locked gazes.

"I know the Choosing Ceremony can be a difficult time," the lord began after a tense moment of silence, "but we cherish your girls, and your sacrifice, deeply. Your girls play a vital role by strengthening the deep bond our two races share. Do not allow this man to put fear into your hearts."

Nods and cries of assent swept through the crowd. Two men grabbed Castor's shoulders, trying to pull him back, but he shrugged them off once more—he was stronger than he appeared.

"Pah!" Castor spat into the dirt. "I'll be in my room at the Drunken Trout. If anyone wants the truth, the real truth, you'll know where to find me. The day will come when your deeds come knocking, Faery, and that day will be a dark one indeed." With that, Castor turned and pushed his way into the crowd. The faery lord's face turned white as a sheet.

"Ignore the old fool!" Pod cried. "We all know he succumbed to his grief long ago."

More murmurs rose from the crowd, but they were not in favor of the old man.

Pod turned toward the butcher's girl. "Do not be afraid, child. The Twins are with you."

Larken wanted to believe Pod, but she couldn't get Castor's words out of her head. Brigid couldn't be dead—she couldn't be. But what if Castor was right that something kept the girls from returning even while the bridge was open?

One day, the Popes would send someone to dispose of Castor; she knew it. He was an old drunk, no doubt crazed from the loss of his daughter and isolation in the woods, but talk like that could get you killed. It wasn't as though those opposed to the Choosing Ceremony didn't exist, but no one spoke their dissenting opinions so boldly, especially not to the faery lord during a Ceremony.

"What good does it do to terrify one's children with false ideas about evil fey?" Papa had said once. "It's not as if the girls can choose not to participate."

The Black Guard's record keeping made sure of that. Beyond that, few would risk offending the faery lord. It would mean no more magical gifts, and no more allocations from the Popes. Families were free to leave Ballamor, but most viewed the Ceremony as a gift from the gods. They wanted to participate, as was evident by people from other towns coming to enter their girls in the Ceremony.

The butcher's girl was still tangled in Roger's arms. They whispered to each other, and although Larken was standing close to them, she couldn't hear what they were saying.

The faery lord retrieved his pack, turning to the villagers. He pulled a small wooden chest from within and approached the butcher, silently handing the box to him. The man thanked him, shaking fingers moving to unhook the latch. Dozens of jewels of every color filled the interior— rubies, sapphires, pearls, and stones Larken could not name. They would never want for anything ever again. The fey kept their promises in this regard.

The faery removed two more chests from his pack, giving them to the High-Reeve of Ballamor.

"Send one to your Popes, keep the other for yourself," the lord instructed. The High-Reeve bowed.

Larken hadn't noticed Reeve Hammond until now, as his family and personal guard were clustered around him—still, he was hard to miss. He was a huge man with flapping jowls and a bulging stomach. A ring with a different-colored gemstone sparkled on every one of his fingers. He thanked the faery and gave the chest to his guards, who swept it away. If the need arose, then Reeve Hammond would use it to buy food from further south. And if the need didn't arise…well, then his holdfast would gain another spectacular piece of furniture or his stables a new prize stallion. The town had suffered through many harsh winters in the past, and only once had Hammond ever bothered to buy grain to feed them. Larken suspected things weren't about to change.

The faery lord pulled the remaining chest from his pack, offering it to a woman standing near him. Other villagers drifted closer, eager to see what the faery had brought them. Children swarmed, their chubby hands reaching for the box.

The faery lord lingered, watching as a little girl struggled against the crowd to get to the gifts. She couldn't have been older than three years old. The faery snagged a music box from the chest and handed it to her. A shy smile spread across her lips, and she wrapped her arms around the faery's leg. Larken watched, transfixed, as his eyes turned warm and then distant. The look was gone a moment later as he gently untangled himself.

The lord returned to the butcher's girl. "It's time," he said.

"We were…we were going to be wed," Roger said, his brow wrinkled in confusion.

The lord took the boy by the shoulders. "I'm sorry," he murmured. "But she will be well taken care of." He stepped away.

The girl placed her hands on either side of Roger's face. "I'll be fine. Don't you worry. We'll get through this, all right? We'll be fine." She touched his shoulders, his chest, his hair. She kissed both of his wet cheeks. Finally, she kissed him gently on the lips. Larken looked away, an ache spreading in the back of her throat.

She and Brigid hadn't even said goodbye.

The butcher's daughter wiped her cheeks, turning with her head held high toward the faery lord. He offered his arm to her, and she wrapped her hand around it. They walked back past the line of girls and the crowd opposite them. The crowd cheered and clapped, reaching out to touch the lord and his girl. Roger fell to his knees. The faery and the butcher's girl continued into the darkness. Larken watched until they faded into the trees.

It was over.

"Another Ceremony has ended, but the celebrations have just begun!" Pod called. The crowd roared. "Tonight, we drink, we feast, and we honor the Chosen girls!"

More cheers rose from the crowd. But Larken couldn't tear her eyes away from Roger, still curled in the dirt.

Mama appeared in a rush, squeezing her into a rib-crushing hug.

"I thought it was you," Mama breathed. "I thought he was going to choose you. Oh, Larken…I know you wanted to see Brigid again, but—"

Blankly, Larken stared down at her hands. She hadn't been chosen. She would never see Brigid again.

"Come." Mama supported Larken around the shoulders. "Let's go home."

Flaming torches lined the shops and houses, lighting the way. Her heart thudded dully in her chest. She could focus on nothing but the cold and on placing one foot in front of the other.

But nothing could stop one word from clanging through her head like a bell.

Murderer.

Murderer.

Murderer.

The word plagued her.

Larken tossed and turned, trying in vain to get comfortable. The butcher's daughter…Larken still didn't know her name. Her dark hair, her tall frame. It was as if Larken and Brigid had been together today, standing side by side.

Larken pulled the sheets up to her throat, then threw them off again as sweat began to coat her lower back and legs.

What if everything about the Choosing Ceremony was a lie? What if the girls never returned, not just because they were chosen for some special purpose, but because they were dead?

No, it couldn't be true. The Black Guard couldn't be trained in all things involving the fey and not know the girls had been harmed. Not tell everyone.

The Popes wouldn't allow their citizens to be taken from them and killed.

Flickering images of Castor's outburst danced through her mind. He claimed to know the truth about the fey, and he would know more than most due to his time in the Guard. He truly could have gone mad after his daughter had been chosen. He could just be trying to get revenge on the position he had been banished from.

Murderer.

She recalled the flash of feral panic she'd seen in the faery lord's beautiful eyes. He had been hiding something. She rubbed at her lips, picking at the dry skin. The girls couldn't be dead. They couldn't be.

Maybe some of the girls got injured during their task for the fey, but they weren't dead. Brigid was smart, she could handle herself. This was all probably just a mistake, a misunderstanding.

Don't be stupid. You've known that something was wrong for years—you all have. You just don't want to see it. Larken tossed and turned. *Don't go asking questions you don't want to find the answers to.* But Larken couldn't shake the feeling that if she did nothing, if she tried to forget about the Chosen girls, then she would be doing what the rest of the villagers had been doing for centuries.

She could talk to Castor. Simply see what he had to say. If he spouted nonsense like a village lunatic then, well, she could go back to sleep knowing that Brigid was in a better world and that she had to let her go.

But she needed answers. If Brigid and the other Chosen girls were in danger, she had to know. Larken had missed her chance to be chosen and see firsthand why the girls never came home. So, she would have to find the answers herself. No matter the odds stacked against Castor, she would not rest easy until she'd spoken with him.

CHAPTER THREE

Two men stood nonchalantly beneath the sign for the Drunken Trout. Even in the darkness Larken could make out the sigil stitched above their hearts: a double cross wreathed in flames.

The emblem of the Black Guard.

Their presence was warning enough: stay away from Castor. It appeared to be working, as two villagers approached, but, upon noticing the guards, quickly hurried in the opposite direction. It was clear that Larken wasn't the only one seeking an audience with the old man.

Larken hitched Snowfoot to a post and made her way around to the back of the Drunken Trout. She pounded her fist against the door. Even from outside Larken could smell kegs of sweet cider and frothy ale, along with roast chicken and rosemary potatoes. The aroma was almost as comforting as that of the bakery. Pots and pans clanged, and the voices of the tavern guests provided a low hum in the background. The door swung open, and in the entryway stood Helen, the tavern's owner. She towered over Larken, her muscled arms crossed and glistening with sweat. Helen was a kind woman but knew how to sort out a room of brawling drunks in a matter of heartbeats. She and Larken's father had grown up together.

"Larken! Didn't expect to see you here so late. Has your father sent you for something?"

Larken kept her voice low even though the din from the crowd inside was enough to hide it. "I'm here to see Castor."

Helen scanned the alley before pulling Larken inside. "Don't go around saying that, you hear?" She shut the door quickly behind them. "The Guard told me they'd be standing watch outside, and if anyone was to try and get upstairs who wasn't a guest, I was to tell them straight away."

"It's important, Helen," Larken pleaded. "He might know something about Brigid."

The crease between Helen's brows softened. "Ah. I know you've been missing your friend, but Castor's not right in the head."

"All the same, I need to hear it for myself." She took one of Helen's hands in her own. "He might know something that can put my mind at ease."

Helen sighed. "Oh, all right. But be quick about it. First door on the left."

Larken nodded and hurried up the stairs. She kept an eye on the window, making sure that she didn't draw the attention of the Guard.

Her hand hovered above Castor's door, her breath quickening. Whatever she was about to hear, she wouldn't be able to forget it. But she might not get another chance to speak with him. He might disappear into the woods again, this time for good. If the Guard was so desperate to keep people away from Castor, then they must be hiding something.

She rapped lightly on the door. It immediately swung open.

Castor's scowling face greeted her. "Took you long enough."

Larken stepped inside. "You knew I was coming?"

"I knew someone had to. And anyone who did had to outsmart that lot"—Castor gestured to the window where the guardsmen stood a

25

story below—"or they didn't deserve to know the truth. You're that baker's girl, no?"

"Yes. My name is Larken." She unfastened her cloak. "And you know about Brigid. About what happens to the Chosen girls."

Castor didn't answer for a moment. He crossed the room to the cupboard and pulled out a candle. Larken sat down at a small wooden table. The old man joined her, hunched over in his chair.

"I don't know anything for certain. But I have my reasons for believing what I do." He lit the candle, casting the room in flickering hues. "Be warned, child. I do not tell you this lightly. It might be easier if you go back to bed and forget any of this ever happened. But I want everyone to know the truth—I don't think my mind can take it much longer if they don't." He tapped the side of his skull.

Larken knew she would never forgive herself if she turned away now, no matter how difficult the path that lay ahead. "Tell me."

Castor scrubbed a hand across his face. "It was twelve years ago, but I remember it clear as day. My girl, my Imogen, was taken. I begged my senior officer at the time to allow me to stand watch by the bridge, and he agreed. I waited there day and night, waiting, hoping she would come back to me.

"On the final night that the bridge remained open, near dawn, a faery woman came to the bridge. Only me and one other Guard stood watch. She spoke to us from the bridge, never leaving the stones," Castor continued. "She told us that a great evil lived in the lands of both humans and fey. She said that we all needed to be wary of our rulers, as their power flowed from the Choosing Ceremony and that the Ceremony itself was...corrupted. She told us the girls weren't safe in her world. And that wasn't all."

Castor pulled a cord from around his neck. From it hung a simple gold ring. "She gave me this. It belonged to Imogen." Castor looked away. "It was her mother's wedding band. Imogen wore it everywhere after she passed. She never would have parted with it. And if there was a way for her to come home, she would have. After her mother died, Imogen and I were alone in the world. The only way she would have given up that ring, the only way she would have never returned to me, is

26

if she was dead." Castor's hands twisted in his lap. "The faery woman wanted to warn us. It was as though she were telling parts of the truth, but not all of it. When we pushed her to tell us more, she said she couldn't break her promise and fled back into the woods.

"I told my companion that we had to do something—that the girls could be in danger. That everything we knew as members of the Guard could be a lie. I told him we had to warn the other villagers. But he and I had never gotten along. We had been trained in the same unit, but we'd never seen eye-to-eye. He attacked me, accusing me of heresy."

Larken bit her lip.

"I killed him. I pushed him into the chasm next to the bridge and told the others he'd jumped. They believed me, of course. Members of the Guard have committed suicide before. The Popes' training that we endured was...unpleasant."

Larken had heard as much. The trials the Guard suffered through didn't end in the Popes' palaces, either. Many members of the Black Guard buckled under the pressure of being secret keepers for the realm. They had to live with themselves after they forced heartbroken family members away from the bridge, preventing them from ever seeing their daughters again.

But perhaps the Guard had privileges she had never considered. Since they were so favored by the Popes, maybe they could enter the realm of the fey and not face any repercussions.

"Why didn't you just cross the bridge and see for yourself?" Larken asked.

"You think the Guard hasn't thought of that?" Castor said bitterly. "Because the Popes trained us to be loyal above all else. You cannot believe the tortures we endured. Only a few pass the trials. Those who don't are killed."

Of course, Larken thought. Though the Guard was favored by the Popes, they were still human—and their actions would still be considered a dishonor to the gods. They could disrupt the task as easily as any other human could. But Larken didn't miss the fact that Castor had avoided her question.

"The secrets the Popes and the fey deal in are no small thing."

Castor's eyes darkened. "We fear the Popes' punishment should they discover we've doubted them, or that we'd been disloyal. Do you not know the tales of the burning crosses, girl?"

"Of course," Larken replied. "How does the saying go? 'Nothing burns brighter than a heretic.' But you should know that as well as anyone. It's not as if the Guard hasn't performed burnings of their own."

Castor shook his head. "The Guard's true purpose isn't burning heretics. And it's not to keep people from crossing and upsetting the fey, either. It's to keep the truth from causing chaos."

Cold seeped into her bones. Castor's words made sense. If the faery realm was as bounteous as the Popes and the fey claimed, then humans shouldn't be forbidden from all real knowledge of it.

The Popes said that, aside from the faery lords, the fey were mischievous, prone to pranks that could irritate the humans if they were allowed to cross the bridges. But that seemed like a weak reason to create an entire army.

"But I do know of a few guardsmen who have snuck through and somehow kept their treason from reaching the ears of the Popes," Castor continued. Larken's head snapped up at his words. "They were never gone for long, only a few hours at most. And when they returned, they only spoke of the beauty they saw. None of them saw the girls, but something wasn't right...when they returned, they were different. Stayed different."

"Different how?" Larken's brow furrowed.

"It was like they were in a trance," Castor said. "They spoke of how lovely the faery realm was, how they knew the girls couldn't possibly be in any danger."

Larken blinked. That sounded suspiciously similar to Laila's story.

"The Popes told us about this enchantment during our training even if my brethren saw the need to test that theory for themselves. The Popes said the magic was the very embodiment of faith. That the Twins used the magic to show us that the girls were safe, without us ever having to see it for ourselves. The Popes claimed that only the Chosen girls were immune to its potency. But we were never allowed to share that knowledge with the people."

Larken stilled. "How could an enchantment that makes one *believe* the girls are safe possibly be better than actually seeing the girls for themselves? And what about Laila? Does that mean that she was enchanted, too?"

Castor leaned back in his chair and nodded. "Now you're starting to get it. I believe that Laila never saw the Chosen girls, or her sister."

Larken swallowed. The only explanation she could think of for why the fey and the Twins would enchant the humans to believe that the girls were safe was if the girls weren't safe at all.

"But you never tried to see it for yourself? You never tried to go after Imogen after she was chosen?" Larken pressed.

Even if Castor hadn't heard the faery woman's story until the last night the bridge had been open, he still could have crossed the bridge that night after his fight with his fellow Guard. He had lifted a sword against the faery lord to try to keep him from taking Imogen, for Twins' sake. Even though he would have known he would have been trapped in the faery world for another year, she figured that would have been a small price to pay to see Imogen again. Or he could have tried the year after that. For twelve years he could have tried.

Castor flinched. "No. And it's the greatest regret of my life. I was too afraid. Too afraid of losing my wits in the faery realm and forgetting who I was, forgetting who *she* was. I wanted Imogen to return to me, as she would be able to see through the magic. I was a coward." Castor hung his head.

Larken's brows lifted. He had tried to fight the faery lord himself; he used to be a member of the Guard. Castor couldn't be a coward.

But Larken had only been a child at the time of Imogen's Ceremony, she could hardly remember it in much detail. Had Castor truly fought the faery lord, or had he only unsheathed his sword? He had told his fellow Guard that they had to tell people that the fey were dangerous, had even killed the man when he had refused—yet this was the first time he had truly spoken out against the fey.

"After I spoke to the faery woman and she gave me Imogen's ring, after my girl didn't come back that year or the year after, I knew she was dead. I knew that nothing else would have been able to keep her from me." Castor slumped, his shoulders curling inward. Pity swept through Larken. Castor was alone. His wife was dead, his daughter was gone....

Castor hadn't tried to enter the faery realm because he had given up hope. He had given up on Imogen.

"I knew I had to find answers," Castor said. "I wanted to tell people what the faery woman told me, but I knew I needed more proof. And I didn't want to be killed before I could find out the truth."

"But you were in the Guard," Larken interrupted. "No one knows more about the fey, aside from the Popes."

"Even the Guard doesn't know everything. We know the fey are immortal. We know that they can move objects with their minds, that they can control parts of the earth itself."

Larken's breath hitched. The humans knew that the fey had magic, as evident in the magical gifts they gave the villagers, but they had never been told exactly what aspects of the gods' magic they possessed.

"We know where their palaces are, and that the girls are taken there. And we know there are creatures that roam their realm so monstrous that humans have no name for them."

Her suspicions had been correct. There were dangerous creatures in the faery realm, ones that would cause a lot more than mischief if they ever entered the human realm. Could these monsters somehow be involved in the task the girls had to preform?

"But there is still so much we weren't told," Castor said. "The Popes don't want their secrets getting out. So, I went looking for answers. For four years after Imogen was chosen, I searched, talking with the families of previous Chosen girls, traveling to other villages to see what their faery lord looked like and what kind of girls they picked. None of the girls have ever come back. No matter if they were overjoyed or devastated to be chosen, none of them are ever seen again." Castor ran shaking fingers through his hair. "I visited houses of the rich and the poor alike and dug through the books in their private stores. I found books that should have been burned—and the people who would have been burned alongside them if the Popes ever discovered that those tomes were in their possession. According to those books, the fey also have the magic of deception. And more monsters walk their earth than the ones the Guard were told about. Ancient creatures with dark powers, and a being strong enough to rule over them all."

Even if the Chosen girls were not in danger from the faery lords or the special task, the faery realm itself was more dangerous than the Popes allowed people to believe. A realm inhabited by monsters that the Popes kept secret even from the Guard. Larken felt as though she had pulled a thread from a sweater, and the harder she pulled the more the whole thing unraveled.

"I was banished from the Guard because I went digging for answers. I made myself known as the village madman so I could plant the seeds without being taken too seriously, but it's only a matter of time before I take it too far. Before my bribes and secrets don't keep me safe any longer. Before they come for me. But I've never told anyone all of what that faery woman told me, not until today. I know if I tell the villagers everything she told me, then the Guard will kill me. And I don't even know if anyone will believe me. Or if it's already too late."

Guilt scraped at her for calling him a coward. Yes, it was cowardly not to follow Imogen into the faery realm after she had been chosen, but had Larken not done the same with Brigid? And she didn't know half of the knowledge that Castor did about the fey. And now, as one of the only humans trying to find answers, of knowing some part of the truth from the faery woman, Castor was just trying to stay alive long enough to spread the word.

"Why are you telling me this?" Larken asked. "I know I came to you for answers, but this...this is heresy." Her blood chilled. "Why are you trusting me with this? Or would you have told anyone who came here?"

Castor rubbed a hand down his wrinkled face. "No, girl. I would not tell this to just anyone. I saw your face last year when Brigid was chosen. I remember that look of devastation—I understood. And you probably hoped to be chosen today, right? To be with her again?"

Larken bit her lip, nodding.

"But I saw your face again today when that poor butcher's girl was chosen. When she was ripped away from her lover and siblings. You knew it wasn't right. And when I said my piece, you didn't look at me like I was the village madman. You looked like you'd seen a ghost. You're no fool. You knew there was a chance that those girls could be in danger. I have to be vigilant these days. I have to be on the lookout for those I can trust. You could hand me over to the Guard right now, but you won't. There are those who suspect something is wrong but do nothing. And then there's you, who came here because you needed answers, like I did."

Larken studied Castor, his wrinkled face, his greasy hair. He had no reason to lie to her. Not when it came at such a great risk to him. She thought of everything she had seen so far: the faery lord taking the butcher's girl against her will, the fact that none of the girls were seen or heard from again. The faery woman's warning. Castor's research. Something wasn't adding up about the Choosing Ceremony, and if Castor and the faery woman were correct, it was because the Chosen girls were in danger. Something was keeping them there, keeping them from returning and seeing their families again after they completed their task for the fey.

She had a choice. She could return home, try to forget everything Castor had told her, try to ignore anything suspicious surrounding the Choosing Ceremony. She could leave Ballamor and go south to study cartography like she had always wanted.

But Larken knew she would never be able to forget. She would never be able to move on. Each year that Brigid didn't return would only confirm the suspicion that her friend was in danger—that something was keeping her there. And if Brigid never returned, then Larken would have to carry the weight of her guilt forever.

Castor had tried to find answers, but there was only so much he could do in Ellevere. Castor had been searching for answers for twelve years and look what he had to show for it. His most vital piece of information had come from the faery woman. Real answers could only come from within the faery realm itself. And maybe they could be discovered by a girl who wasn't chosen, who didn't have to complete a special task, one who had nothing trapping her there and who could still come home.

Her stomach twisted into knots. But what could she do? Even

32

Castor, a trained member of the Guard, had been too afraid to enter the land of the fey. Even he had given up hope.

But Larken never had. She had never given up on Brigid, despite her doubts. To say she had completely let go of her anger toward her friend would be a lie, but she still cared for Brigid deeply. She had wanted to be chosen to reunite with her, and though she knew more now, though Castor had warned her, she still couldn't give up on her dream to see her dearest friend again. Now that she knew Brigid could be in danger, that there was something keeping her and the other Chosen girls from returning home, Larken was even more desperate to find her.

Castor had given up hope. But Larken would not give up. Not ever.

Larken would find Brigid and the other Chosen girls. And she would find out what was keeping them there.

"I have to go after her."

Castor shook his head. "There's nothing you can do. You can only live with the truth and try to spread it, as I have. There's nothing you or I can do to stop the fey and the Popes from carrying out their dark contract."

Castor was right. If the fey were hurting the girls with the Popes' blessing, then Larken would stand no chance. If they weren't and she returned, she would lose her sight. Or worse. That was if she got across the bridge at all and made it through the magic that shielded their realm.

But she had to try.

"You said that the lords take the girls to their palaces. Where is the palace that belongs to Ballamor's faery lord?"

"Straight shot northwest. But—"

"I'll head in that direction until I catch up with them," Larken said. "But I'll stay hidden. I'll follow them and try to discover what the special task is. Even if I don't figure it out, they'll lead me to the palace where the other Chosen girls are. I can sneak in, talk to them, and then sneak them out."

A vague plan, she admitted. Larken chewed the inside of her cheek. She was nobody, she had no skills. What could she possibly do to help the Chosen girls? She could go to Mama and Papa for help. They had their doubts about the Choosing Ceremony.

But something held her back. Filling them in on everything would take too much time, time she needed to catch up to the butcher's girl and the faery lord. They knew she missed Brigid, and they knew how badly she wanted to be chosen to reunite with her. They would just view this as a reckless attempt to see her friend again. While neither of them fully consented to the Choosing Ceremony, neither of them had ever done anything to aide in stopping it. Mama and Papa did not understand her need for answers, to know what lay hidden beyond the edges of a map. They didn't understand that Larken had lost everything when Brigid left—her friend, her confidence, her passion. They didn't understand the guilt that slowly gnawed away at her, knowing she and Brigid had fought. They would only try to stop her.

Her fists clenched. Doing something was better than doing nothing. The look in the faery lord's eyes had betrayed him. He was hiding something. And now Larken had heard Castor's story when no one else had.

"I have to try," Larken said. Her mind tore down a darkened path, imagining Brigid hurt during whatever trial the fey asked of her. Or trapped in some palace, unable to leave even if she wanted to. Larken thought of the last words she had ever spoken to her friend, and guilt rose within her like a crushing tide. "And you have to help me."

Castor scoffed. "No. I already told you they'll kill me."

"I can't do it without you," Larken pleaded. "If they catch me trying to cross the bridge, they'll come after me. They could hurt my family… Castor, please. You were a member of the Guard—you're the only one who can help me get past them."

She wanted to beg the old man to come with her, but she knew he would refuse. If he hadn't gone for Imogen, he wouldn't go for her.

Castor narrowed his eyes.

"There's a reason why you told me all of this. Because you feel guilty. Because you've known all this time that the girls are in danger—you even suspect that they could be dead—and you've done nothing. Even for your own daughter."

"Watch yourself," Castor growled.

"I don't know if I'll be able to do anything." Larken squared her shoulders. "But I'm going to try. And I can't do it without you. So, please, Castor. Help me. And know that you're helping those girls, too. I'm going to find out what happens to the Chosen girls—to Brigid and Imogen—and I'm going to try and bring them home."

Castor stared at her for several uncomfortable moments, and then something shifted in his eyes. "Even if I wanted to, girl, I'm being watched. You might have made it past the Guard, but I won't."

"I know a way out," Larken insisted. She and Brigid had used it many times during their adventures. "This tavern used to be a brothel before the rise of the Order in the North. The cellar has a tunnel that empties a half-block from here so patrons could come and go discreetly. The Guard didn't see me come through the back, so even if they see me now, they won't suspect anything. I'll find you a horse, and I'll meet you there." Larken held her breath, waiting for his reply.

Castor scrubbed his jaw. His hand fell to the chain around his neck, and he rubbed at the gold ring. "Fine. I'm not saying it isn't a fool's errand, but I'm not going to be responsible for you and your family's punishment at the hands of the Guard. So, I'll help you." He stood. "You only have seven days until the bridge seals, and then you'll be trapped there for another year, if you even live that long. Best hurry, now."

Larken's heart picked up a frantic rhythm. Was she truly doing this? She had no supplies and hadn't even left a note for Mama and Papa. She had no other family, no friends—her parents were all she had.

Please forgive me. She would be back, she had to come back. Hopefully with Brigid, Imogen, and the butcher's girl in tow—as well as any of the other previous Chosen girls who wished to return home.

Larken pictured Brigid's face, the tiny splattering of freckles across her nose. Her blue eyes, always filled with such kindness. She had been there for Larken through every hardship, every triumph. They had both said things they regretted, but Larken would make it right.

"Let's go."

She and Castor stood hidden in the tree line on Snowfoot and Helen's brown mare. Larken was glad she wouldn't have to see the tavern owner's reaction when she discovered that Larken had borrowed her horse.

Larken had arrived at their meeting spot before Castor, half afraid that he wouldn't show up. But he had.

Before them stretched a grassy plain, and beyond, the chasm. Countless stories from Ballamor centered on this place: the deep divide that separated the human and faery lands, and the bridge that joined them. Fog billowed from the chasm like smoke from the mouth of a firedrake. Moonlight shimmered through the mist, turning the very air to silver.

They had left the safety of their village. The pastures, trees, and everything else familiar were all behind her. Had Brigid felt this way, one year before? Had she been afraid to leave behind all she had ever known, as Larken was now?

Ahead, swirling in mist, stood the bridge.

Jutting from the Elleverian side of the chasm and spanning all the way to the faery lands, it rose in a graceful arc like a half moon, the stones strong and sturdy despite their age.

The villagers all knew it, either from stories or from seeing it personally. She and Brigid had received countless dares from other children to go see the bridge for themselves. They had, of course, stealing glimpses of it before the Black Guard chased the nosey children away. Still, it had been years ago now since she'd last seen it. She could barely remember it. She wished she did, for it might have made this moment less terrifying.

Scattered across the grassy plain and near the bridge itself stood members of the Guard. Their black capes fluttered gently in the wind, their bodies obscured by the fog. Only two stood by the bridge itself, with three others spread out on either side along the chasm's edge. So few... Larken swallowed. They were highly trained. They didn't need numbers.

Castor shifted next to her on Helen's mare. Only a small stretch of grass and trees separated them from the ancient stones. Whatever this plan was, they had to time it just right if it was to succeed.

"As I said, the faery lord's palace is to the northwest. Once you're across, keep heading in that direction. Always remember, fey magic will try and deceive you. Keep your mind focused on the task ahead, especially when you experience the magic near the bridge."

Larken nodded, hiding her shaking fingers in Snowfoot's mane. What if she wasn't strong enough to pass through the magic? What if she went mad like the members of the Guard?

"Now, get ready," Castor muttered.

"For what?" Larken hissed back.

"Just ride, girl, and don't look back. Good luck. You'll need it." With that, he jammed his heels into the mare's sides and took off across the field.

"I've waited long enough!" Castor screamed.

The Guard's figures in the mist stirred.

"The fey are murdering our girls"—Castor jabbed a finger across the bridge—"and you're letting them. The Popes aren't our rightful rulers, they're *tyrants*." Castor wheeled his horse around as shouts rose from the Guard. "They let the fey give them magical gifts in exchange for girls from our village. Money and power in exchange for human lives," he snarled.

Larken tightened her grip on the reins.

The Guard swung onto their horses.

"I won't stay silent any longer. You won't be able to pass me off as the village drunk—or madman. I'm going to tell everyone the truth, and I won't stop until all of Ballamor—no, until all of Ellevere—knows!" Castor whooped, circling once more before the Guard, then he took off toward the woods. The Guard tore after him.

Now. She had to act now.

She kicked Snowfoot into a gallop. Dirt flew beneath his hooves as he streaked across the open plain. Shouts rang out. Faster, Snowfoot had to go faster. Before the Guard realized their mistake.

The chasm loomed before them, the rocks dropping away into sheer nothingness. Larken yanked the reins, and Snowfoot slid to a stop. Wind whipped around her, tugging Snowfoot's mane toward the chasm, sucking him in. The thought of the drop alone was enough to turn

Larken's mouth sour with fear. If something spooked her mount, they would plunge over the side together.

Larken clung to the saddle, her muscles nearly paralyzed with terror. This was wrong. Only Chosen girls crossed the bridge. She was nothing, no one....

She clenched her teeth and dug her heels in. Snowfoot's hooves clattered upon the stones. More shouts from behind her, but they sounded far away. Castor had done his job well. Fear enveloped her as she thought about what they would do to him, but no, she couldn't think about that now. He'd made his choice as she'd made hers.

She coaxed Snowfoot slowly across the bridge, worried that anything faster would get them killed. Nothing but air kept them from tumbling into the abyss. Unable to help herself, she glanced past Snowfoot's shoulder and into the chasm below. Vertigo hit her, and she jerked her gaze up, making sure to keep it focused on the end of the bridge beyond.

Black nothingness. That was what was beneath the stones of the bridge. Barely a foot on either side separated Snowfoot from the drop, and had Larken been on a larger mount, it would have been much less than that. Larken heard no sounds of rushing water beneath them. Somehow the thought of nothing below was even more terrifying. The idea that there was no beginning or end to the abyss. That it cut straight to the center of the world, or straight to the Twins' Hell.

She glanced behind her, but only mist greeted her. The Guard's shouts faded away into silence, sucked into the chasm below.

At the end of the bridge, Larken pulled Snowfoot to a stop. One more step and she would enter the land of the fey. A steady beat pulsed in her ears, a string tugging her toward the entrance. Her fear churned inside her, a living, breathing beast with claws. Home had never felt so far away. But she had made it. Made it all the way here, and she would make it a little farther. She would find Brigid.

Breathing in, she urged Snowfoot on.

PART II
BONDS AND BLOOD

CHAPTER FOUR

The caress of an entirely different world brushed against her skin. Like a shift in the breeze, the slippery, equivocal feeling disappeared as quickly as it had come.

The faery realm. A place supposedly a thousand times more vibrant and beautiful than her human one. The stories claimed that instead of grass there would be a carpet of wildflowers, and the rocks would be jewels instead of stones. The landscape before her did not quite live up to those legends—the stones were still stones, but they somehow felt older than the ones back home. Like they had stood in their positions for thousands of years, watching and listening to what occurred around them. No, the faery realm was not quite the legend she had imagined, but it was beautiful all the same.

The moon spilled silver light onto her path. While Ballamor was on the very cusp of winter, here the land was in high autumn. The tall grass whispered on the breeze. Crickets chirped. The leaves hanging from the trees were nothing like the brittle, dead things of Ellevere. Here, they were awash with color—dipped in ruby reds, fox oranges, and buttercup yellows. If Larken hadn't known better, she would have mistaken them for precious gems, strung up in the trees like dew clinging to blades of grass in the early morning.

41

The human world had never experienced autumn, not truly. This was how autumn was meant to be seen.

Still, she needed to be careful. She tensed, waiting for the magic Castor had spoken of to overpower her. Would she become the next Laila? An ordinary girl who had followed the Chosen One into the land of the fey, only to return under an enchantment?

Stay focused, she told herself.

Larken guided Snowfoot northwest, and he walked on, his furry ears alert.

A breeze caressed Larken's skin, blowing strands of hair across her face. The wind was cool, but not unpleasantly so. They passed under the branches of a tree, and an intoxicating smell drifted toward her. It was exquisite, a mix of crushed leaves and crisp night air.

Snowfoot relaxed. Larken's limbs grew warm and heavy. Something pulled at the back of her mind, something she needed to remember, something about time running out. But as soon as the anxious thoughts entered her mind, a soothing calm washed over her like warm honey, carrying them away with it. This world was too beautiful to be treacherous. What ill could befall her here? She had been wrong—the fey weren't conspirators or murderers, they were benevolent beings, just as all the villagers had thought.

They traveled deeper into the forest. A smile played about her lips. Her mind slowly drifted from one thought to the next. The girls would be happy here in this lovely place, and she was sure Brigid and the butcher's daughter were safe. Why had she come here again? She should turn around now. It felt as though some string was tugging her back toward Ballamor. Her hand working of its own accord, she began to pull Snowfoot back the way they'd come.

Snowfoot stopped abruptly and Larken lurched forward. Cursing, she righted herself. Snowfoot's ears flattened down his neck. The pony took a step back.

Larken leaned on his neck, patting him. "It's all right Snow, nothing to be afraid of here." Her words slurred.

His nostrils flared, his eyes trained on the dark forest beyond. The crickets fell silent. Larken frowned. There was something she needed to remember, something about magic…

Dark clouds drifted across the moon, plunging her into near darkness. A flash of white flitted past in the gloom.

A huge, scuttling thing lunged out of the edge of her vision and Snowfoot reared. He let out a terrified equine scream, throaty and wild. Larken lost her grip on the reins and grabbed desperately for Snowfoot's mane, her hands clutching empty air.

He reared again, haunches bucking wildly toward the side, sending Larken sprawling from her seat and halfway down his shoulder. Her world tilted, everything working in slow motion as Snowfoot bucked once more, and Larken fell, hands outstretched but not quite quick enough to stop her head from smacking into a tree branch. Her vision spun, but she could still see Snowfoot galloping off through the trees, leaving her far behind.

Larken cursed, clutching her head while scrambling to her feet. Though the pain nearly blinded her, her thoughts were clear. She had nearly succumbed to the spell Castor had mentioned. It was as though her mind could no longer be addled by the magic as it was now consumed with pain. The flower crown from the Choosing Ceremony dug into her scalp, and she ripped it off, tossing it aside. The bridge, the trees… some *thing* crawling through the forest, and Snowfoot…

Her mount was gone.

"Stupid pony," she growled, hot tears of frustration welling in her eyes. If only she had clung to the saddle just a little bit tighter, then maybe she could have calmed him down. The thing she had seen… it had to have been one of the monsters Castor mentioned. A part of her wanted to turn back, this time of her own volition. She couldn't face a creature like that.

But the butcher's daughter was in real danger, too. And Brigid, who had lived for a whole year in this place. Larken swallowed. She had to keep going. But her head was pounding so loudly she didn't know which way was up or down, let alone how to find her way again.

Whenever she and Brigid had played in the forest near Ballamor, Larken had always been able to guide them out no matter how deep in they got. Larken wasn't sure if it was from years of drawing maps or some innate skill, but she could always tell where she was going and where she had come from.

She closed her eyes, and doubt swept in. What if her senses didn't work here? What if her skills had depended on Brigid's constant encouragement and faith in her? Gritting her teeth, Larken pushed those thoughts away.

You're here to make sure Brigid is all right, she reminded herself firmly. *And to find the other Chosen girls. Castor sacrificed himself so you could know the truth.*

Sadness welled inside her as she thought of Castor. Had he escaped the Guard? A stab of fear pierced her heart. Seven days. She had seven days to find Brigid and the butcher's daughter. To get back to the bridge before the gate sealed, trapping her here.

You can't think about that now. Larken took a deep breath, letting her mind settle. She brought up an image of the forest surrounding her. The trees came first, then the bushes. However different this place might be, north, south, east, and west were still the four points of a compass. She angled her body north, letting her senses guide her.

Opening her eyes, she scanned the terrain again. Though there were no distinguishable markers, she knew she had angled herself northwest —toward the faery lord, the butcher's girl, and eventually the palace. Larken's lips lifted in a smile.

She would follow the path until she found them. She would keep herself hidden and gather as much information as she possibly could. They would lead her straight to Brigid, and then she would figure out what was keeping the girls there and how to free them. Then she would use her senses to guide her back to the bridge.

She could do this.

Feeling exposed without Snowfoot, Larken hurried on. Every snap of a branch made her flinch, and she quickened her step with each jolting noise.

She reached a small copse of trees and stopped, the back of her neck prickling. Twigs snapped. Branches scraped and shifted against a hide. Some great, creeping thing was making its way through the forest toward her. The noises were accompanied by a deep susurration of breath that certainly was not human or equine. Larken darted toward a clump of bushes on the outskirts of the clearing. She stayed low, peeking through the underbrush.

The thing that crawled from the trees was a nightmare given flesh. It was completely hairless, with pale, wrinkly skin that sagged off its body. Spines lined its head, back, and shoulders. Its hands—if one could even call them hands—sported talons as long and sharp as any knife. Its chest was so bony that she could count the creature's ribs, and its sternum and collarbone jutted out at sharp angles. Tiny black eyes the shape and size of coins sank back into the creature's head, glaring about with a greedy intent.

Yet the most terrifying thing of all was its huge, gaping beak of bone, nearly as long as her arm. Larken swallowed at the sheer mass of it. The creature began to open and close its maw, creating a clacking sound that made every hair on Larken's body rise. It opened its beak, revealing a red mouth. Then it screamed. The rasping, guttural cry grew higher in pitch until Larken was forced to clamp her hands over her ears.

Within moments, more cries reverberated through the forest.

Larken bit her lip so hard she tasted blood.

The creature slowly closed its beak.

Bloooood. Human blood.

No sound came from its mouth besides the horrid clicks, but Larken could hear it as clearly as if it were speaking before her.

More clicks responded, moving closer through the trees.

Master promised us the girl. Now, we feast!

She pressed her lips together, the coppery tang of iron spilling into her mouth. She closed her eyes, certain that the monster would soon be bearing down upon her, but then the creature began sniffing around the bushes on the other side of the clearing. It fell into a sort of frenzy, slashing its claws in the air and emitting more clacking sounds. Shredding the leaves, it let out another cry, then scuttled off into the trees. Its movements were jerky and unnatural—like a corpse brought back to life.

Larken waited until she could no longer hear any trace of the creature, then crawled out of her hiding place. The woods seemed too quiet, like the trees were holding their breath. Larken crossed the clearing to examine the place where the creature had been. Splattered on the leaves were drops of blood.

If the creature had not been searching for her, then which human had it been referring to?

The butcher's daughter. Larken wanted to smack herself. The butcher's daughter would have been here recently. The blood had to be hers. The creature would be headed straight toward the lord and the girl.

Forcing her legs to move, Larken followed the creature deeper into the woods.

The monster did not travel gracefully. The crushed sticks and leaves of the beautiful faery realm littered the beast's path, along with deep gouges in the earth. A pang of sadness struck her at the destruction the creature wrought.

She slowed as the sky's blue-black melded into a feathery gray. Dawn approached. She had lost a whole day of the bridge being open already. A breeze billowed through the trees, lifting the sticky strands from the back of her neck. Larken sucked in a deep breath, willing herself to still, listening to the sounds of the forest.

No, not just sounds. Voices. And not the rasping hiss that had penetrated her mind or the guttering clicks of the monster, but human voices. No, too melodic for that. *Fey* voices. More than one.

A small hill blocked her view. Crouching, Larken pushed through a tangle of bushes on the top of the mound. Stretched before her was a small ravine. The gray light was gone, replaced with hues of orange, pinks, and blues amongst the rocks and trees, and below…

She'd found them. By some astonishing stroke of luck, she had found them.

46

CHAPTER FIVE

The sunlight glanced off the faery lord's hair as he stood scanning the trees opposite of where Larken crouched. The butcher's daughter was with him, as were three other fey. Her eyes widened—she had never seen another faery aside from the lord.

The faery closest to the lord was tall, the tallest of his companions, with rich brown skin and a mass of shoulder-length black curls. His entire body rippled with muscle, and he hovered behind the lord, his gaze watchful. Dark stubble lined his jaw. His eyes, luminous in the morning sun, were a rich, golden honey.

Plates of metal armor covered the faery's shoulders, ending above his pectorals, and the rest of his torso was covered by a brown jerkin. He mirrored every movement the lord made, like he was an extension of his lord's own body.

The butcher's daughter sat on a moss-covered boulder, and at her side was another faery. He was slim, with short, straight black hair. He had a wide, flat nose and a rounded chin, and eyes so brown they were almost black.

The faery rolled up his sleeves, revealing tawny brown skin. He inspected a cut on the girl's hand. The wound did not appear to be deep. If the monster had attacked already, the wound would surely be far worse. Larken's eyes darted around the ravine, but there was no sign of the creature. She frowned; there was no way she could have beat it here. Had the monsters simply passed them by? She remembered the crazed frenzy the creature had gone into upon smelling human blood, and she dismissed the idea immediately. It was coming. And judging by the cries that had reverberated through the forest, there was more than one.

The final member of the group stood nearby, another red-haired faery like the lord, though this one had pale skin and freckles. His hair was lighter than the lord's deep auburn, more akin to the orange hues from a flame. He stood over the girl, watching as his friend tended her hand. A lump of packs lay next to them.

Larken's gaze darted around to each of the fey as she tried to memorize their features. They were not what she expected. In Elleverian paintings, the fey all towered over the humans, their ethereal bodies as slender as tree saplings. The fey before her were undeniably beautiful, but their bodies were more muscular, and they all varied in height. Even the lord, who she had seen several times before, appeared different under her scrutiny. Artistic renditions of him stripped him of his powerful body, which Larken now found unfair. His natural beauty was unparalleled—the artists should have depicted him as he was.

Larken moved closer, trying to hear what they were saying.

"If Dahey hadn't been so bloody stupid with his sword," the black-haired faery snapped, "we wouldn't be stopping at all."

The faery with the freckles, Dahey, smiled sheepishly. "Apologies. Just showing off for the lady." He grinned at the butcher's daughter. The girl gave him a tentative smile in return.

The black-haired faery murmured something to the girl, wrapping a bandage around her hand. She seemed hesitant, but not frightened or angry. Despite her outburst at the Ceremony, the butcher's daughter looked content in her new role as the Chosen girl.

Dahey glanced at the girl's hand, then flicked a piece of dirt from his lapel. While the lord dressed plainly, this faery clearly had a taste for finery. A silky, black coat with gold stitching covered a dark linen shirt and pants. His boots were broken in but shiny as though just polished. A

48

sword, intricately wrought with a pattern of steel leaves, lay sheathed at his side.

The armored faery prowled from his spot by the lord's side and made his way toward his other two companions. He inspected the bandage on the girl's hand, praising his friend's handiwork with lifted brows. The black-haired faery snapped something to the effect of "stop looking so surprised."

Pay attention, Larken chided them.

Scanning the ravine once more, a flash of movement caught her eye. There, creeping down from the trees opposite her. Flashes of white skin, glimpses of that monstrous beak. Larken clenched her teeth. The lord now faced his companions, watching them as they tended to the butcher's daughter. Larken's gaze darted between the group of fey and the thing shuffling toward them, panic rising in her throat. The creature was almost directly behind them now. It slunk in the shadows, its white, saggy skin camouflaged amongst the stones. From any other vantage point, she might not have even noticed it.

Movement caught her eye. To her left, another creature descended into the ravine. It stalked its prey silently despite the destruction it had left in the forest. The monster's talons hooked into the grooves and crevices, and it kept its beak low to the ground.

They were here. They would kill the fey, the girl, and then they would kill Larken as well. She had to do something. *Now.*

The first creature was almost upon the faery lord. She bit her tongue, hesitating. Castor's words rang through her head. *Murderer.* What if the faery lord before her was exactly that? Did he not deserve to die at the hands of the monster, if he himself was one?

Then Larken pictured the knife-sharp talons and what damage they had inflicted on the mere earth. She could only imagine what the beast would do to flesh. The suffering it would render.

She might not know the truth, not yet, but she knew one thing: the faery in front of her, no matter his sins, did not deserve to die like that.

The creature reached out a long, spindly talon toward the lord's back.

"Behind you!" Larken screamed.

The faery jerked, glancing in her direction before he turned, ripping his sword from its sheath in the same movement. The creature let out its horrible scream and launched itself at him, slashing viciously with its talons.

Claws grappled with steel. The lord swung his sword, the light from the rising sun blinding as it lit the metal. The sword appeared weightless in his hand, his movements effortless. The creature scuttled forward, quick, but not graceful. It attacked sharply, jabbing out with its beak, but the lord flowed around it like water. He cried out a warning to his companions, but they already had their weapons drawn facing the second monster. The armored faery shifted toward his lord, poised to give aid, but the lord stopped him.

"Protect her!" he shouted. He hit the first creature on the beak, but his sword rebounded against the bone maw. The creature lunged again, screeching horribly. The butcher's daughter whimpered, clinging to the black-haired faery. The faery lord sliced a deep gash into the monster's shoulder. Black blood sprayed, coating him in gore. The creature's arm was now attached to its body by only a few bloody ligaments, and it screamed in agony and fury.

The black-haired faery hauled the butcher's daughter to the cluster of boulders and left her tucked between the stones. He pulled out two knives before launching into the fray.

Larken's eyes flashed back to where the faery lord battled with the first creature. Despite only having one arm, the creature didn't slow. The lord ducked, lunged, ducked again, then brought the sword up through the creature's sternum. It let out a blood-curdling shriek, beak snapping, then slumped further onto the lord's blade, finally still.

Breathing hard, the faery kicked the dead creature off his sword. It landed in the dirt with a thud.

The other monster battled fiercely but seemed to be slowing down. The armored faery fired bolt after bolt from his crossbow into the creature, but it still staggered forward. The black-haired faery with the knives avoided each bolt faster than should have been possible, slicing at the creature's hide. The creature lunged just as Dahey appeared in a blur of fiery hair, thrusting his sword under the beast's jaw and through

50

its skull before whipping out of the way. The beast made no sound, just collapsed to the ground in a heap, taking the dark-haired faery with it. Shouts rang through the ravine.

"Madden!" the lord cried hoarsely, sinking to his knees before the creature. The fey heaved the monster off their companion.

The dark-haired faery sat up, his skin and olive-green jerkin splattered with gore. He grinned fiercely.

"Thought you could be rid of me that easily, did you?" He turned and spat, the liquid black with the monster's blood. The lord briefly clasped arms with his friend, then rose to his feet. Madden wiped the black blood from his hands on Dahey's coat, making him snarl.

Larken leaned forward, and a twig snapped beneath her. The faery lord's head turned toward her. Impossible—he couldn't have heard her. But he had heard her cry out, so he must suspect she was there. Surely, he would punish her for following them, even turn her over to the Black Guard. They could burn out her eyes, hurt her family—

A high-pitched scream tore through the air.

Across the clearing stood the butcher's daughter—three grisly talons pierced through her stomach. A third creature emerged from the shadows. Larken cried out, tearing down the rocky slope into the ravine before she could think. As she ran, Madden pulled two knives from his baldric and hurled them at the creature. They both struck home, striking the monster in its eye and above its jutting collarbone. It hissed, yanking its talons out of the girl. She choked and fell forward into the dirt.

Madden launched another knife, hitting the creature directly between the eyes in a silvery flash. It sagged to the ground. Larken fell to her knees beside the butcher's daughter, tearing her eyes away from the gaping wounds below and focusing on the girl's face. Larken should have been watching, she should have known there was another creature, but she had been too captivated by the fey battling before her.

The girl's eyelids fluttered, tears leaking down her cheeks. Larken took her hand and clutched it tightly.

"Y—you," the girl said, blood trickling from her mouth. She heaved a wet cough.

Larken nodded, stroking the girl's dark hair. Warmth seeped into Larken's dress as the girl's blood pooled beneath her. The girl grew paler by the second as her lifeblood left her.

The faery lord sank to his knees beside them. Larken wanted to snap at him and tell him to get away—after all, it was he who had brought her here—but the sorrow in his eyes stopped her.

He passed his hands over the girl's wounds, his brow furrowed. His hands hovered over her torn stomach, then lowered.

"If we take her to a stronger vein, we could—" the armored faery began, but the lord gave a tiny shake of his head. Slowly, he pulled the girl into his lap. She moaned, tears still leaking from her eyes, but didn't tell him to stop. He held her, gently stroking her hair and murmuring to her. The three other fey surrounded them, eyes somber. The girl still clutched Larken's hand, her fingers cold and hard.

"It hurts," she gasped, holding her stomach with her other hand. She moved her glassy gaze to the faery lord's stricken face. "Oh, Twins, Finder, it hurts."

Larken stole a glance at the faery lord. *Finder.*

"I know, love," he murmured.

She pressed his hand into her torn stomach. "Can you... can you save the baby?"

Finder's eyes widened and Larken's mouth fell open.

"What did she say?" Madden breathed.

"He's so little," she whispered. "I wasn't even showing. Roger and I were going to be wed today. No one would know..." There was blood everywhere, soaking the ground, coating Larken's hands, running from the girl's mouth. "I was so scared, but I thought—I thought me and the baby could make a life here. Be happy here."

Madden dropped onto his knees, his eyes wide with horror. He pressed his hand into the girl's torn stomach, trying to staunch the flow of blood. She whimpered.

"We have to do something," he said hoarsely. "Finder, *do something.* You have to save the baby, you have to—"

"Madden," Finder said, holding his companion's gaze. "You're scaring her."

The armored faery pulled Madden back by the shoulder. "She's not Senna," the faery murmured. Larken was too preoccupied with the butcher's girl to try to figure out what he meant.

"Everything is going to be all right, Rosin. You and the baby are going to be just fine." Finder tucked a strand of Rosin's hair behind her ear. Tears ran down Larken's cheeks now, but she didn't bother to wipe them away. She finally knew the girl's name.

Rosin turned toward Larken, reaching bloody fingertips to touch her cheek. Warm wetness greeted her, but Larken didn't pull away.

"You..." Rosin whispered. "Tell my Roger...tell my family..." Her voice was fading fast now, and Larken leaned close to her, holding her hand again. Rosin's brown eyes started to darken and cloud over.

"Tell them I know it's a boy. That we're all right," she breathed. "Don't let them worry, please..." Her lips parted and she coughed, spraying Larken's face with blood. Rosin shivered, convulsing slightly.

"We've got you," Finder said, and with gentle fingers he wiped the blood away from her mouth. "Let go now, love." He stroked her cheek once more. "All the pain will go away. I've got you." He held her, and her ragged breathing faded. She took one last hitching breath, then her hand went limp in Larken's. Larken held it tighter, refusing to believe she was gone. But all the light had left Rosin's eyes, and Larken knew she was far from this world.

CHAPTER SIX

The tears dried on Larken's cheeks. She felt empty, completely worn thin.

With careful fingers, Finder closed Rosin's eyes and lifted her into his arms. Larken released the dead girl's hand. He carried her toward the outcropping of stones near the edge of the ravine.

"Did you know?" Larken asked softly. She lifted her head, meeting his green eyes. Larken remembered how captivated she had been by those eyes during the Choosing Ceremony. Such trivial thoughts seemed so far away now. "Did you know she was pregnant? Is that why you chose her?"

"I swear to you, I didn't," Finder said. A strange pulse beat in the air, accompanying his words. Larken studied his face and found that she believed him. She had seen the look on his face when Rosin had asked him to save her baby, and she saw it now. His eyes were haunted.

"What now?" Dahey hissed. Larken regarded him warily. He paced, running a hand through his short hair.

Finder didn't respond. He set Rosin on the ground, cradling her head. He turned toward Larken. "How do you care for the bodies of your dead?" he asked.

"We bury them," she replied, surprised to hear her own voice so steady. He nodded and began moving smaller stones around Rosin's body. Madden and the armored faery moved to help him. Dahey followed them with his eyes but made no move to help.

Larken couldn't move; she just continued to kneel there in the dirt. The moment she allowed herself to move, it would become real. The world would turn again, and she would have to face it.

You still have to find Brigid. You still have to find the other Chosen girls. That thought alone was the only thing keeping her from falling apart.

She forced herself to her feet and began collecting small stones of her own and placing them on Rosin's tomb. Already the stones were piled up high around her.

"Dahey, please," Finder said. Dahey sighed but moved to help his companions.

A rush of gratitude toward the lord filled her. He could have left Rosin's body to rot for some other beast to find and feast on, but he didn't.

Stop thinking like that. If it wasn't for him, Rosin wouldn't even be here in the first place. Her heart hardened once more, her gratitude replaced with resentment.

Finally, it was done. No trace of Rosin remained, aside from the blood-stained ground; her body was now safely encased in the stone tomb. Larken knelt and placed one of her hands on the stones.

The moment I return to Ballamor, I will tell Roger what you asked of me. Rest, now.

Finder approached, kneeling down beside her. "You saved my life," he murmured in a lilting, rich voice. "Will you tell me your name?"

"Larken," she said.

"I remember you, Larken," Finder said. His companions exchanged glances. Her heart fluttered unexpectedly at his words. He truly remembered her?

"My name is Finder, and these are my companions. My cousin, Dahey." He gestured to the other red-haired faery, who said nothing. "Madden"—the black-haired faery dipped his head to her—"and Saja." Finder gestured to the armored faery last, who gave a small bow.

"Was she a friend of yours?" Finder asked. "You stood next to her when I chose her." It took Larken a moment to realize he was talking about Rosin, not Brigid.

"Yes," she replied, unsure of why she said it. Truly, she didn't know Rosin. Until a few moments ago she hadn't even known her name. But after holding Rosin's hand, stroking her hair, and watching her die... It was hard to call her anything but a friend.

"I'm so sorry, love," Finder said, and to Larken's surprise, he looked it.

"Don't call me love," she snapped. What right had he to grieve for Rosin? He'd taken her from her home and into his world—a world that had instantly gotten her and her baby killed.

Her stomach hollowed out. He needed Rosin for the special task. Now that she was gone, who would take her place?

A sudden cold hit her core. What if they used her instead?

"I'm sorry, Larken," Finder amended.

"I hate to interrupt..." Dahey started, his fingers drumming at his sides.

Finder's gaze flicked away from Larken to look at Dahey. Some of their facial features bore a strong enough resemblance that she could tell they were related. Broad foreheads, high cheekbones, and thin, straight noses. Yet from there, they drew apart. Finder's jaw was strong and square, while Dahey's was more pointed. And while Finder's eyes were the green of spring leaves, Dahey's were of the earth, as dark brown and cold as soil before a winter freeze.

Dahey's eyes studied her now. "I thought the humans had taken certain precautions to prevent this sort of thing from happening. How did she get here? And what exactly are we planning on doing with her?"

Larken froze. Dahey was referring to the Black Guard. "Don't hand me over to the Guard," she blurted. "Please."

"You saved my life. I'm not planning on relinquishing you to the Guard in exchange." Finder rose gracefully and extended a hand to Larken. She ignored him, pushing herself to her feet.

Dahey jammed his hands in the pockets of his coat. "We could—"

Larken cleared her throat, cutting Dahey off. He lifted his brows, affronted, as if no one had dared interrupt him before. Madden hid a small smile behind Dahey's back.

"I know I'm not supposed to be here, but I came to—I came to make sure my friend was all right." She glanced toward Rosin's tomb. "Not Rosin," Larken said. "But I have another friend, one you took during the last Choosing Ceremony. Her name was—is—Brigid."

If she could just hear them say it, say that she was all right...if she could just see her, then maybe she could believe Castor had been wrong. But watching those monsters kill Rosin had done nothing to convince her that Brigid was safe.

Finder studied her for a moment. Larken couldn't decipher his expression. "I remember her."

"Please—my lord, Brigid is my dearest friend. We...we had a fight. I need to make things right with her. I wanted to be chosen, but you took Rosin instead, and then all of this happened, and..." *Stop blabbering.* "Please. Is she all right? Is she safe?" Larken tried to subdue her rising panic. "If I could just see her—"

"I'm afraid that is not possible." Finder avoided her gaze.

Sweat began to slick her palms. "Why not?"

"You cannot see her," he repeated firmly.

"Please," she whispered. She'd come all this way. Snowfoot was gone, Rosin was dead... She squared her shoulders. "What about the special task? What will happen now that Rosin is dead?"

Finder bit his lip. It made him look incredibly human. "Now that she is dead, I will not be able to complete it."

Not complete the task? Larken's mind reeled. Wouldn't that anger the gods and the Popes? "And you won't use me instead?" she asked, unable to stop the tremble in her voice.

She couldn't believe that the task simply wouldn't take place. Larken had never heard of this situation happening before. Of course, the humans never saw the Chosen girls again, so there was no way to be certain, but surely the Popes would find out if the task wasn't completed. Undoubtedly, there would be a punishment for both fey and humans alike if the task didn't occur.

"I cannot use you instead. Even if I wanted to."

"You're absolutely certain?" Dahey asked, addressing Finder.

"Dahey," Finder murmured. "She saved my life."

Dahey's shoulders slumped, but Larken could swear she saw a hint of relief there.

Larken gritted her teeth. "Can you at least tell me if she's all right?"

"She's all right," Finder said. Their gazes locked. Out of the corner of her eye, she saw Saja and Madden exchange a glance Larken couldn't read.

She narrowed her eyes. "All the same, I would like to see her for myself. I know you planned to take Rosin to your palace. If I could just accompany you—"

"How do you know that?" Dahey interrupted. "How do you know where we take them?"

"Well, I'm not *supposed* to know," Larken admitted. "But the Guard knows. And one of them told me."

"Castor," Finder surmised. "The Guard has kept me updated on him ever since he attacked me after I chose Imogen. I heard he's been sowing the seeds of dissent. And it seems that someone has taken up his plow."

Larken opened her mouth, but Finder held up a hand.

"If we could let you see your friend, we would, but we simply cannot," Finder said, his voice kind but his green eyes as unreadable as glass. "We are grateful for your service to us, however, and thankful that you stumbled into our midst."

No, no, that couldn't be it. She was glad to hear him say that Brigid was safe, but that is what she had been told about the Chosen girls for her entire life. It wasn't enough. She wouldn't rest until she'd seen them with her own eyes.

"I need to see her," Larken pushed. "You take girls year after year, and we never get to see them again. Castor believes that the girls are in danger. That they're dying." Now a girl *had* died. "If I could just talk to Brigid, then I could return home and reassure everyone that the girls are safe. Maybe some of the previous Chosen girls could even come with me as proof if they wanted—"

"*No*," Finder's voice deepened. "No. You cannot see them. The Chosen girls must remain here forever."

Larken jerked back, stung.

"Fine," Larken bit out. She hadn't expected getting answers to be easy, but what else could she do? She had already given herself away; there would be no element of surprise. The faery lord claimed the task wouldn't happen at all, which meant she couldn't see it for herself even if she did manage to sneak away and then follow them to the palace.

Her shoulders curled inwards. Images of the monster's claws tearing into Rosin's stomach flashed through her mind again and again. It was easy for the people of Ballamor to slip into the illusion that the fey and their lands were just a myth. Even though the fey visited every year, the humans knew so little about them. When so few had actually seen the faery realm for themselves, they created a fantasy to fill in the gaps.

Larken had done the same. She had set Castor's warnings of magic and ancient beings aside, intent on finding the girls, though she had no definite plan on how to do so.

But now the monsters were real. A girl—a pregnant girl—had died before Larken's very eyes. The fey surrounding her were honed for killing, and even they had been unable to save Rosin. Larken hugged herself. She wanted to find Brigid and the other girls. But a girl like her would hardly be of any help in a world like this.

"Well, I'm glad to know that Brigid—that she's safe." Larken almost choked on the words but forced them out. Castor was right; she shouldn't have gone sticking her nose where it didn't belong. It had only brought pain. She had failed. Utterly and completely. "I'm going home, then."

She sucked in a breath. The lord had shown her some kindness by refusing to hand her over to the Guard, but she would have to find a way to sneak past them again, if that was even possible a second time.

She forced her fear down. Anywhere was better than here. She wanted to forget about her failure to find Brigid and the other Chosen girls as soon as possible, pretend it had never happened. An ache spread in the back of her throat. She would just have to live with the fact that she would never be able to make her peace with Brigid.

"I'm afraid that is not possible, either," Finder said.

"I'm afraid I wasn't asking for your permission," she snapped, shocked by her own words. Exhaustion and grief had made her bold, even in front of the storied fey. But why should the lord be the one to give her orders? He wouldn't let her stay and see the Chosen girls, and he wouldn't let her leave. So, what did he want from her?

"It's not my permission you need." Finder smiled tightly. "If it were up to me, I would return you to Ballamor immediately, along with— well." He looked away. "I'd see you home if I could," he finished.

"You are certain that the bond is in place?" A low rumble—Saja's— came from behind him. Finder gave a sharp nod.

"What bond?" Larken growled.

"By calling out to warn me about the Fomari beasts, you saved my life," Finder said, looking as if each word were being forcibly pulled from him. "The laws of Airodion demand that I repay you for that debt. The bond is known as a life debt. Both of us will be tied to one another until the debt is paid."

Larken's jaw fell open. A small part of her mind registered that she now had a name for the faery realm: Airodion. It was beautiful, and it swirled perfectly with the lilt of Finder's voice. The sound of a life debt to a faery lord was far less appealing. "Wouldn't crossing over the bridge force the bond to break?"

Finder shook his head. "The bridge will not allow your crossing, now. It will seal itself against you. The debt must be paid."

Larken frowned. Surely that problem could be easily rectified. She had nearly died more than once since entering Airodion; it wouldn't be that difficult to save her. "Well, if you have to save my life, why doesn't he"—she gestured toward Madden—"just throw a knife at me? Then you can block it."

A twitch of a smile crossed Finder's lips. "Unfortunately, that won't work. You saved my life with no thought of your own safety or self-interest. You owed me nothing and gained nothing in return. You did it simply because you believed it was the right thing to do."

Larken blinked. It was true.

"In return, I cannot gain anything by saving your life; it has to be a true selfless act, as yours was. If I blocked Madden's knife, it would be with the goal of breaking the bond in mind. Therefore, the bond would stay in place."

Larken glared at Finder. What if they were just trying to keep her here? They could be lying about not being able to use her for the special task—or they might want to use her for something worse, especially because she wasn't the Chosen girl. They weren't allowing her to see the other girls and refused to tell her about the task, but they were awfully chatty about this supposed life debt.

"I—I don't believe you," she said, almost tripping over herself as she backed away. She had no proof that she couldn't just go home, that she couldn't just return to safety across the bridge.

"I swear to you it is true," Finder said.

A ripple seemed to pass through the air, adding weight to his words. Still, Larken resisted the urge to laugh. Why should she take him for his word? "Prove it," she blurted. "Prove that you aren't just trying to keep me here for some reason you won't say."

Finder didn't hesitate. "Madden, your knife, if you please." Finder held out a hand. Madden glanced at Finder in alarm, but still handed him the knife.

"Any harm done to you will also be done to me." Finder held the blade to his palm. "I cannot hurt you, nor can my companions, without hurting me as well. Our bodies as well as our souls are tied—bonded."

Her gaze fell on the knife, realizing his intentions. If what he was saying was true, then any mark on his skin would also appear on hers. It was so unfair—she had already saved his life. Why should the hurt have to go both ways? It was impossible, something out of a bedtime story meant to scare children. Not something that happened to a baker's girl stupid enough to go into the woods.

She stuck out her chin. "Do it."

Finder nodded, then put the knife to his skin. The moment the blade parted his flesh, Larken gasped, more from shock than pain. It was a shallow cut, and the same wound was mirrored on her own palm.

She ran her fingers over it, smearing the blood. It was real. All of this was real. They weren't lying—at least not about this. A wave of nausea rolled through her.

Finder hesitated, then added, "I'm afraid we are tied so completely that if either of us dies before the debt is repaid...the other dies as well."

Black spots dotted her vision and she pitched sideways.

"Easy." Finder reached a hand toward her. She lifted her own hand to ward him off, steadying herself by bringing her hands to her knees. All of this was too much. She forced herself to remain upright.

"It's simply something we will have to maneuver around," Finder said.

"*Maneuver* around?" Larken's wheeze turned into a snarl. "Are you joking? Twins, how can you not be angry about this?"

Larken felt herself spinning out of control. There had been too much fear and sadness since she'd crossed the bridge. Anger felt much better.

"If I die, *you* die. You understand that it would be really rutting easy for me to die in a place like this, right? I'd say your days are dwindling, *my lord*." Her hands started to shake along with her rising hysteria. She wanted to cry. She wanted to break something.

Saja opened his mouth, no doubt in order to reprimand her, but Finder gave a tiny shake of his head. Somehow it only made her angrier. Why was it impossible to get a rise out of him? She wanted him—all of them, to feel what she was feeling. Helpless. Cornered. Wronged.

Larken whirled on Saja. "Don't you see? You have to protect a vulnerable human now. Which, by the way, you already failed at." Her eyes darted toward Rosin's tomb. "And now his life"—she pointed at Finder—"depends on me staying alive. You couldn't even protect him from those monsters without my help."

Saja paled.

"Larken." Finder spoke to her as if she were a spooked horse. "We're not going to hurt you. Saja will protect you like he protects me, as will Madden and Dahey. The life debt is temporary. We'll find a way to end the debt before we end up hurting each other."

She wanted to lash out at him, but she hesitated. Her cheeks heated with shame. She had never yelled at strangers before. It wasn't like her. The anger had been a blissful reprieve from her fear, but now all she felt was exhaustion.

"No one can know," Saja said, his voice low. "No one but those in this circle can know about the life debt between you. If they did, if our enemies in the other courts found out, they would target her immediately—send assassins, torture her, even kill her...all to get to Finder."

Larken paled. All this talk of courts and assassins, she couldn't be involved in that. It wasn't her world. She knew how to frost a cake and that Brigid was her dearest friend and that all she wanted to do was draw maps of faraway places. She was not some tool to be used against Finder and his people.

"No one will know but us," Finder said. He raised his hands in what she assumed was meant to be a placating gesture, but his hands were still covered in Rosin's blood. Larken's hands were as well. Even her gown was wet with blood. Larken lifted a hand to her mouth, feeling sick again.

"Ah, and perhaps clean clothes will help," Finder said, lowering his hands.

Larken didn't complain. She didn't want to look at Rosin's blood any longer, or the blood of her... Larken squeezed her eyes shut.

"Already tried," Dahey grunted. "Nothing to draw upon here."

"There's no need to point out something we all *know*, Dahey, you aren't the only one who can use magic," Madden scoffed with a roll of his eyes.

Magic. Castor had talked about how the fey could control the earth itself and even move objects with their minds. Though it terrified her, a part of her wanted to see it.

"We'll do it the old-fashioned way, then," Finder said. "Luckily for us, we summoned our packs before the ravine."

Without ceremony or shame, they all pulled off their shirts, exchanging them for clean ones from their packs. Wetting cloths from their waterskins, they wiped their bodies clean, removing the worst of the monsters' black blood. Finder took extra care to scrub away Rosin's blood from his hands. Larken averted her gaze, unable to stop the blush creeping up her cheeks as they switched their pants as well. Did the fey have no modesty?

When she finally judged it safe to turn around, the fey were rolling up their dirty clothing and stowing it back in their packs.

Finder handed her one of the wet rags. She took it gratefully, wiping Rosin's blood from her hands and face. She didn't have any extra garments, so she just had to wipe the blood off her gown as best she could.

"What did you mean when you said there wasn't any magic to draw upon here?" Larken asked, shifting her gaze to Madden and Dahey. She didn't want to speak with them, but she couldn't resist. She wanted to learn as much as she possibly could about magic.

For your own protection, she told herself.

Dahey raised his eyebrows, as though shocked that she had been paying attention. "Usually, we prefer to clean our garments with magic. However, in this particular valley, there are no veins from which to draw upon."

She frowned. "Veins? Like in the body?"

"Yes. Like blood or water, magic runs through this world in streams beneath the land. The wider the channel, the easier it is to call the magic to us. We tried to use it earlier to fight the Fomari, but then realized there were no veins here. Unusual, to say the least."

Larken tossed the rag back to Finder, who caught it with unnatural speed. He smiled. She looked away.

"We need to leave," Finder said, shouldering his pack. "Another Fomari pack could be drawn by the blood."

Dread pooled in Larken's stomach. "Where are we going? To the palace?"

Though her fear had almost overtaken her, and she had wanted to return home, she couldn't forget her true reason for coming here. She couldn't allow herself to give up, even with the life debt in play. The fey had the answers she needed. She had to focus on the Chosen girls, on getting the fey to take her to the palace.

"We cannot return to court and risk someone discovering the life debt," Finder replied. "Though it is my home, I still have enemies there. I need time to think. Home is as barred to me as it is to you, but we cannot remain here."

His companions shouldered their packs as well and made no move to question their lord.

Oh, excellent. So, they would wander around the faery realm until Finder saw fit to include them in his decision making.

She had to focus on convincing him to return to the palace or court, as he had called it. And if she couldn't convince them, well, then she would have to slip away from them and try to find it on her own, life debt or no.

She believed Finder that the life debt would hurt both of them, but he had so many other secrets. He could have simply lied about the bridge being closed. If the life debt still wasn't broken by the time she found the Chosen girls, she would just have to take her chances and pray that the bridge would break the spell. She couldn't consider the alternative.

Madden lifted two fingers to his lips and released a clear, shrill whistle.

The pounding of hoofbeats rippled through the air, and a moment later the most stunning creatures Larken had ever seen trotted gracefully into the ravine. They maneuvered between the rocks with ease, coming to a prancing halt in front of them.

Larken sucked in a breath, then scowled.

Even the damn fey horses are prettier than me. There was one for each of the four fey, and they each sought out a particular rider. They bore no saddles or bridles, and Larken had a feeling that they never had, and never would.

A massive, dappled grey approached Finder, snorting and nickering. He smiled, patting the beast hard on the neck. The horse nuzzled his chest, nipping at his white shirt.

"Rhylla has been at my side through many adventures," Finder said, his eyes gleaming. Larken narrowed her own. She could see what he was doing—trying to include her, talk to her, but she wanted no part of it. Befriending the fey was out of the question. She had to stay focused, clearheaded.

After watching Finder tear Rosin away from Roger, Larken didn't know how Rosin could have been able to be so friendly toward the fey. But Rosin had wanted a better life for her baby; perhaps she simply had been trying to make the best of her situation, be as affable to the inhabitants of her new world as she could.

Larken turned her shoulder to Finder but couldn't resist taking one last peek at the beautiful horse. Her silken, white mane fell in long, braided strands.

Madden jumped onto the back of a stunning bay stallion, the beast just as tall and massive as Rhylla. The stallion snorted and tossed his head.

Dahey grasped his white mare at the base of her mane and swung himself expertly onto her back. Jealousy sparked as she watched the ease at which the fey interacted with their horses. She had always felt so awkward on Snowfoot. A small jolt of pain stabbed her at the thought of her pony. She hoped he had found his way home and wasn't lost somewhere deep in Airodion.

Saja rode a night-black stallion. The horse lowered his head, the long, curling mane rippling gently. Fluffy hair covered his hooves, which were pawing the dirt in anticipation. Saja towered above her, head and shoulders blocking the sun behind him. Larken barely reached his horse's chest.

"My lady," Saja rumbled in his deep, smooth voice. His horse extended his nose and brushed it against her forehead, huffing a gust of hot air across her face.

Saja smiled. "He will allow you to ride."

The thought of being even more reliant on the fey made her gut churn. But she saw no other alternative. Her chances of ending the life debt were higher if she stayed with Finder—and she could work on convincing them to take her to their court so she wouldn't have to sneak away. She shuddered at the thought of coming face-to-face with the Fomari again on her own.

If she had to accompany the fey, at least she didn't have to ride with Finder. She wasn't ready to be so near to him. Ever. And if the most distance she could put between herself and the faery lord to whom she was now bound was atop the backs of different horses, then so be it.

But how am I supposed to get on the stupid thing? Larken approached Saja's giant beast awkwardly from the side.

"Let me help you, love," came Finder's voice from behind her. She scowled at his outstretched hands.

"I'm fine," she snapped. Arrogant faery. "And I told you not to call me love."

Still, she couldn't help the wave of relief that washed over her when Saja lowered a hand to help her up. Larken worried for a moment that he would not be able to hoist up her weight, but in one smooth motion he lifted her effortlessly into the air and in front of him.

She shifted, unsure of where to put her hands and if she should lean back or not. The horse was slippery beneath her, the stallion's breath gusting in and out like a pair of bellows. She pitched sideways, sure she would slide off despite Saja's arms on either side of her. Yet after a moment she settled, her legs hugging the horse's sides in a familiar clench. She marveled at how much more balanced she felt on the stallion's back than on Snowfoot's. Saja's scent washed over her, a mix of mulled spices and woodfire smoke.

"What's his name?" she asked, nervously patting the horse's neck. Twins, did horses really get this big? Her legs were very, very high off the ground. She swallowed.

Saja chuckled. "Arobhinn," he rumbled. Arobhinn swiveled a huge ear toward the sound of his name. Larken jerked, the name pulling at a memory inside her. Mama, singing nursery rhymes to her. *A-roving, a-roving, a-roving we will go. Across the hills, across the dales, a-roving we will go.* The sound of Mama's voice practically echoed through the trees, making Larken's heart compress.

"Arobhinn," Larken repeated. She tentatively clutched the stallion's mane as Saja pressed against her back. The contact seemed too intimate for two strangers. His breath ruffled by her ear, and she thought she heard a slight wheeze shudder through his exhale. Larken's brows rose before she quickly schooled her face back into neutrality. Could the fey get illnesses? Impossible. The fey were perfect. Perfect bodies, deadly sharp minds, and immortal. No illness could touch them, surely.

Without any word from Saja, Arobhinn began to move forward. His gait was smooth and surefooted, but Larken still felt off balance. Saja tightened his arms around her, feeling her slide.

They followed single file behind Finder and the rest of the group up a small, rocky path leading out of the ravine. Despite the uneven shale and upturned roots, their mounts did not stumble once.

Larken reminded herself that she needed to keep track of where they were headed so she could find her way back to the bridge when the time came. But there were no roads here, only an endless span of trees and leaf-scattered underbrush.

"Are there no paths to follow in Airodion?" Larken asked.

Finder chuckled. "There are many paths in Airodion, though not all are clearly marked. I follow the same route every year to retrieve the Chosen girl, though it remains unmarked. Larger roads lead to the citadel, though they are far from here." He tilted his head at her. "You must have extraordinary tracking skills to have found us. Airodion is no easy place to navigate."

Her cheeks warmed at the compliment.

"But worry not. Dark as the forest may be, you have us to guide you now."

Though the words were meant to be reassuring, they did nothing to comfort her. She didn't like relying on others while traveling. Knowing where she was going and how to get back was essential if she wanted to return with the Chosen girls. She needed to stay vigilant.

But her body could take no more. Her eyelids drooped. She fell back against Saja's chest, trying not to focus on the slight rattle in his breath.

Her exhaustion did nothing to help quiet her mind. It was as if she were putting together a puzzle blind, groping around at the pieces and trying to force them to fit together. The fey. The Popes. The Chosen girls. Brigid. They all fit together, but as soon as Larken thought she had it figured out, one of the pieces slipped from her hand.

Time was running out. If she didn't find the Chosen girls soon, they would all be trapped here for another year. And while the fey seemed kind enough, they weren't telling her everything.

And she was terrified to know what would happen to her when she found out what they were hiding.

CHAPTER SEVEN

A sharp stone digging into Larken's back woke her. She shifted into a more comfortable position, then bolted upright.

Panic gripped her. How could she have fallen asleep? She had only six days to find Brigid and the other Chosen girls, break the ridiculous life debt with Finder, and return home.

The sun was still high in the sky, and her heart rate slowed. She hadn't been asleep that long. Glancing around, Larken found she was in a small clearing surrounded by saplings. The horses grazed nearby, tails flicking back and forth. The four fey lounged in the grass a few feet away, talking quietly. All but one of the packs had disappeared.

Finder, upon noticing she was awake, waved her over.

"You fell asleep during our ride," Saja explained. "We didn't want to wake you when we stopped."

Saja had even been able to move her from Arobhinn's back without waking her, so she must have truly been exhausted. Still, Larken resisted the urge to scowl. Of course, they didn't want to wake her; then they could talk without fear of her overhearing. What was she in their eyes but a simpleminded human, not even fit to discuss what they might do next.

Her stomach growled. Loudly. Her hand flew to her belly, heat

69

rushing to her cheeks. The fey all turned to stare at her, making the very tips of her ears burn.

"Here, take this," Finder said as he pulled an apple from his pack.

Larken shook her head. She was far from the day when she would break bread with him.

"It's not as if I can poison you." Finder gave her a small smile. Madden coughed. Larken scowled, then snatched the apple from Finder's outstretched hand. Fine, she would eat, if only because it would do her no good to faint from hunger. If only Castor had let her pack her own food.

She bit into the fruit, juice flooding her mouth. She almost gasped. It was unlike any apple she had ever tasted before, perfectly ripe and crisp.

"Good?" Finder asked as Madden suppressed a grin.

"Amazing," she admitted. "I haven't had an apple this good since our tavern owner Helen made roast mutton and apples last Feast of Asphalion." The Feast of Asphalion was Ballamor's winter holiday, celebrating the male Twin and the ruler of the winter months. It was one of Ballamor's only holidays aside from the Choosing Ceremony.

Dahey scoffed.

"What?" Larken asked, frowning. "Do you not celebrate—?"

"We do not eat the flesh of other living creatures," Dahey said, his words laced with judgement.

They don't eat meat? A small part of her couldn't believe it. The fey were so much *more* than humans—she only expected that they would be expert hunters, trained and skilled in a way that humans were not.

"We have no need to eat the flesh of animals," Finder explained. "Airodion provides us with all the food we require. A faery could go out into the forest and never starve, for the land would give them the nourishment they need. Animals exist in this world for their own reasons, and it is not our right to take them and bend them to our will. We use no part of them in our food or clothing."

Larken crossed her arms. "We only kill animals because we have to. It's not as though we enjoy it." They must think humans to be some race of savage barbarians who relished killing other creatures.

"Not all are as lucky as we," Saja acknowledged.

"Well, I suppose I can understand if all the food in this realm is this good," Larken admitted, gesturing to the apple. She resisted the urge to add *but I'll die before I give up mutton*.

"Apples have been my and Finder's favorite food since we were children." Dahey grinned. "Remember that summer when we swore we would eat nothing else? The cooks at Shadeshelm began a competition to see who could come up with the most creative dish."

"Ah, so that's how those competitions got started," Madden said, chewing idly on a stalk of grass. He turned to Larken. "The court is always throwing some kind of baking competition. At one of Finder's birthday banquets, Saja made desserts that *flew*. Truly flew—each pastry had wings woven from tiny threads of sugar." Madden's eyes sparkled, and Larken's own eyes grew wide at the thought of flying pastries, and at the thought of Saja making them.

"You're a baker?" She lifted her brows at Saja. He dipped his head.

"Only in my spare time."

"And a damned good one, too. Luckily, we have him along on these adventures, or else I would never leave Shadeshelm." Dahey rubbed his stomach idly, as if imagining all the food he could stuff inside.

"Oh, please." Madden rolled his eyes. "We all know you'd never leave Shadeshelm if Finder didn't make you."

"Shadeshelm?" Larken frowned.

"The main city of the Autumn Court," Finder said. "Where I, as well as my companions, reside. The fey that are close to me—or those who want to get close to me—live there, as well. My loyal subjects." His lip curled on the word *loyal*.

"You can barely stand to be in Shadeshelm since she died, Finder. Your court would be loyal to you if you would only—"

"Enough, Dahey."

"They want you to come home. To stay there—"

"Dahey," Saja rumbled.

Dahey fell silent. Finder stared into the grass, refusing to look at anyone, even when Saja tried to catch his eye.

Madden cleared his throat. "Ah, since I doubt no one's formally introduced you, welcome to the Autumn Court, Larken. You already knew about Shadeshelm in a way, though you called it a palace. We usually escort the Chosen girls to Shadeshelm for a time but—" Madden caught himself. "Erm, things are different this year."

Larken tucked this information away in the back of her mind.

Shadeshelm. I need to get to Shadeshelm.

But Madden had said they take the girls there for a time... did that mean they eventually left? The girls had gone there at some point—it was a start. But the fey had also mentioned other courts. What if the girls went to one of the other ones—or were still there? She couldn't afford to waste time going to the wrong one. "You mentioned before that there are other such courts in Airodion as well? Courts that, if they found out about the life debt..." She trailed off, unable to finish her sentence. *Would use me to get to you.*

Finder nodded. "Yes. There are four: Summer, Autumn, Winter, and Spring."

She had a sinking suspicion that she already knew the answer, but she asked anyway. "You also mentioned having subjects. So that makes you a—ruler?" she asked Finder, her throat growing dry.

Finder nodded, his curls dipping down across his forehead.

"A prince," Dahey corrected.

Larken swallowed again. She had thought him a powerful faery lord, but a prince?

"And they"—Larken gestured to Dahey, Madden, and Saja—"are members of your court?"

"We are more than that," Dahey said. "We are a part of Finder's *dornán*. We are bound to his soul. We protect him with our lives, and we never leave his side unless commanded to do so."

So, they were in a kind of life debt too, though they had entered it willingly. But were their lives so tangled together that if Finder died, they did as well? She doubted it, judging by their concern for her and Finder's life debt.

The injustice of it all made anger flare to life inside her. Of course, the fey had a choice to enter a bond with Finder, but when she had saved his life, she had no choice in the matter.

She lifted her head. "And what need could a faery prince possibly have for human girls from my village?"

The temperature in the clearing plummeted. None of the fey, save Finder, would look her in the eye.

"I cannot tell you."

"What you mean to say is you won't tell me."

"Telling you could put more than just your life at stake. We are all spokes in a wheel, and if one breaks, if one falters, we will all suffer for it." The fear in his eyes reminded her of the panic she had seen cross his face during the Choosing Ceremony.

"You owe me, Finder," she growled. "I'm stuck here, bound to you, with no way of getting home. You take girls from my village and tell me they're safe, but you won't let me see them. The task isn't just to honor the gods—that much I can tell. Castor told me that ancient creatures walk this earth, and there's a being strong enough to rule over them all. I deserve to know what happens to the Chosen girls. I'm a part of this now, just as much as you. Another spoke on the wheel, you said so yourself."

The fey gawked at her, and a glimmer of satisfaction went through her. They hadn't expected her to know about any of this, but thankfully Castor had prepared her as best he could.

"We could go back—say we need another girl," Madden murmured. His gaze flicked to Larken's and then darted away.

Finder shook his head. "The bridge will not allow Larken or me to cross. And even if we could, what would we tell them? That we require another girl because the one we chose was slaughtered by the Fomari?"

Larken flinched, and Finder's voice lowered. "It could place our relations with the humans at risk."

"If they find out the truth, it could destabilize everything for their leaders," Saja agreed.

"They already know too much," Dahey hissed. "She mentioned the ancient ones. Think of what could happen if other humans found out."

"Can you *please* stop talking like I'm not here," Larken snapped.

The fey all looked at her in surprise, as though they had indeed forgotten that she was there.

"Just tell her, Finder," Madden murmured. "You won't be able to keep it from her much longer, especially with the two of you bound in a life debt."

"All right!" Finder pressed his palms into his knees. "All right," he said again, and he sounded tired. He kept his head bowed, but his eyes lifted to hers.

"We fey are ruled by a king known as the Starveling. But do not mistake us for his subjects. We are his slaves. He has checks on all of the court rulers' powers—ensuring we will never have the strength to rise against him." Finder clenched his fists. "He siphons off a part of each of my powers. It is like there are great chains on me, preventing me from ever moving fully. It is maddening." He released his hands slowly. "And that is not the worst of it.

"Though the Starveling is the ruler of Airodion, he has power over the human world as well. He wants to ensure that neither humans nor fey ever challenge his rule. The court rulers have to swear fealty to him. And every year, he demands a sacrifice from us, his *obedient subjects*." Finder spat out the last words. "Every year the rulers of the courts must cross the bridge and select a mortal. We offer them up to him as tithes."

Larken's blood iced over in her veins. *No. They said Brigid was safe. They said she was fine—*

"We travel to the Stone Circle, and I lay her down on the altar," Finder continued, swallowing thickly. "And I carve out her heart as she lives."

Larken barely heard him.

Brigid was—Brigid was—she couldn't think. She couldn't breathe. She fisted her palms, bringing up handfuls of grass. Memories poured over her, unwanted. The two of them talking long into the night about their plans for the future. Running through the woods together with bare feet and wild hair. Brigid defending Larken against any who teased her. Their fight. Brigid, dead.

Brigid. *Dead*.

Larken couldn't open her eyes, couldn't look at Finder. Her people trusted him. They trusted him with their girls, certain they were moving on to a better life. They cheered when a girl was chosen, as she was led away. A scream rose in her throat, but she couldn't draw in any breath—

"I take her heart in my hands and present it to the Starveling. He feasts on it while we watch."

Larken opened her eyes and forced herself to meet Finder's gaze. His own eyes were so pained, so haunted—but it didn't matter. He had been murdering girls from her village for centuries. She thought about all the girls who had been taken from Ballamor and died on that altar. How Brigid had died there.

How *she* likely would have died there in Rosin's place if she hadn't been tied to Finder in the life debt.

Nausea swept through her. She moaned a horrible, wailing sound.

"Larken—" Finder was beside her, his hand reaching for her.

"Don't touch me!" Larken snarled.

Finder withdrew his hand, the agony in his eyes cooling into a blank stare of nothingness.

"I don't believe you. She can't be dead. She can't be." Larken's lower lip trembled. Her mind could not accept a world that her friend was no longer in.

"I swear to you—"

"Forgive me if I don't take you for your word," she snapped.

"Faery oaths are not like human ones," Finder explained. "Once we give you our word, we cannot lie. Larken, I give you my word that all of what I have told you is true. The Chosen girls are dead. The Starveling will come for Ballamor." A strange beat pulsed through the air. Something snapped in place in Larken's mind, every time one of the fey swore an oath, she could feel the magic in the air.

But that hadn't stopped him from lying to her before he'd given her his oath.

"We trusted you. And you lied about *everything*." Larken's fury burned so bright in her chest that she could barely get the words out. "You said she was fine, you—!"

Suspecting that the girls might succumb to terrible fates and actually realizing it was true were two very different things. No part of her had been truly ready to believe Brigid was dead. She hated herself for

75

believing the girls were taken away to a better life, hated herself for believing she would ever see Brigid again.

Hated herself for saving a faery's life.

"You should have told me. You should have told me *before*," she snarled.

"I know," Finder said. "And I would have—but I worried that you would refuse to go with us. I could not risk it, not with the life debt, not with the Fomari—"

She stopped listening. Hatred and shame and grief warred within her, tearing at her mind. She could believe that Finder didn't want to do it, did not want to sacrifice the girls to this beast king called the Starveling, but it did not change the fact that he had. He had carved out Brigid's heart, carved it out even as she breathed—

Larken buried the heels of her hands into her eyes. Not just Brigid. All of the Chosen girls. Imogen, too.

"Larken, please—I know you never wish to be near me again, and I would not make you, but I fear that when the Starveling realizes Autumn has no tithe, he will take his wrath out upon my court. While I do not always love being at Shadeshelm, I will not let my subjects die. And I fear that your people will suffer as well. The Starveling's power extends beyond the bridge, and nothing will contain his fury."

Her previous goal of visiting Shadeshelm in hopes of finding Brigid crumpled within her. She had nothing now. No choice but to be chained to the faery before her.

Her friend's murderer was still indebted to her. She still only had six days to break the curse and return home. She had nowhere to go, no choice but to rely on the fey. And unless something was done, the Starveling would keep sending his subjects across the bridge to take her people.

And now Larken knew the truth. One even Castor didn't fully know. She had to tell the people of Ballamor. But then what? Would the Popes come after them—would the fey? Would they be punished by them, or worse, by the Starveling?

"We could go to the Starveling," Dahey said. "Tell him the human died. Tell him about the life-debt. Beg him for mercy."

Finder's face darkened. "Beg him for mercy? Does he seem like a being who would offer clemency, Dahey? All he would see is that we have no tithe, and he would punish us all the same."

Dahey's eyes hardened.

"One of the girls had to have died before," Saja said gently. "Airodion is a dangerous place for humans."

"You know very well that part of the test is protecting the girl, making her trust you. Making sure she is happy and calm before she goes before him," Finder choked.

Larken thought she might vomit. No wonder the fey had been so nice to her. It was instinct. It was what they had done to all the other Chosen girls—to Rosin, to Brigid, even Imogen, all those years ago. They plied them with kindness, and then tore out their hearts.

"And a girl *has* died before," Finder added.

Madden nodded. "A tithe from the Summer Court. The Starveling demanded that the lives of the entire human town be forfeit in payment for the transgression."

Larken stilled. Madden's words tugged at her memory. Long ago, a town to the east that performed the Choosing Ceremony had been completely wiped from the map of Ellevere. After one of the Choosing Ceremonies, everyone in the town had disappeared. An entirely new town had to be selected to perform the Ceremony the following year.

Rumors had spread that the town had been infected with ghosts, that the townspeople had offended the fey and had been taken across the bridge as slaves, that the Popes had punished them for some unspeakable sin and burned them all to ash in the night. But it was because the Chosen girl had died. Because the Starveling had killed them all.

Cold sweat trickled down Larken's neck. Ballamor could be next.

"How could the Popes allow that to happen? Why do they allow the fey to take the girls at all?" she rasped.

"The Popes wish to keep the Starveling satisfied as much as the fey do," Finder replied. "They fear his wrath should they refuse."

Larken's mind struggled to digest all she had heard. She and Finder were both out of options: backed into a corner with no way out. Without a tithe, the Starveling would hurt her village. Mama and Papa,

Brigid's family—all of them were at risk. She did not have to trust the fey before her, or forgive them, but she had to work with them. They had a common enemy now.

"That can't happen," Larken whispered. "He can't have Ballamor."

Can you really stay with the person who murdered your friend? Be bound to him like this? She wiped her mouth with the back of her hand. It sounded sick even to her own ears.

"He won't," Finder said. "Because we're going to stop him. We're going to end the tithe. Forever."

CHAPTER EIGHT

The reactions were instantaneous.

"You would endanger your court so recklessly? Your own subjects?" Dahey shouted.

Simultaneously, Saja said, "Finder, you cannot do this."

Madden was silent for once, though he clutched the baldric of knives strapped across his chest.

Dahey jabbed a finger at Finder. "I knew you would do this. I knew you would jump at a chance to get at the Starveling, no matter the cost. But there are other lives at stake here, other lives than yours. Than *ours*," he spat.

"Don't you dare," Finder snarled, "don't you dare try to pin that on me. Ever since that night the Starveling has been waiting to retaliate. To dispose of me for good. He wants someone more easily controlled on the throne. I wouldn't be surprised if he set this whole thing up, sent the Fomari to kill Rosin, just so he would have an excuse to finish me."

Dahey now looked uncomfortable. Saja fingered the quiver of crossbow bolts at his side.

"What about our allies in other courts? Spring is completely devoted to him, but what about Summer or Winter?" Madden asked.

Finder shook his head. "I have asked for their aid in the past, and they refused. They do not think it justifies the chaos that could ensue if the Starveling falls."

"Maybe it doesn't," Saja murmured.

"How can you say that?" Finder's voice broke. "You see what the tithe does to me. What it does to all of us. Rosin was *pregnant*. I will never bring another girl to his altar. Never."

Saja looked stricken. "I know, Finder. And you know I would follow you anywhere. I just don't want you to be rash."

"We have suffered beneath him for too long," Finder said. "And I will do what is right, with or without you. But I ask you now, will you follow me?"

"If you hadn't suggested this, I would have fought the Starveling myself after what happened to Rosin and her child," Madden said. "I'm with you, brother."

"As am I," Saja said after a moment's tense silence.

The three of them looked at Dahey.

He nodded tightly. "Our court deserves better than a false king."

"And you, Larken?" Finder tilted his head. "I know that it is cruel to even ask, but whether we will it or not, you're bound to us and our plights now. Are you with us in this?"

Surely Finder made it sound easier to overthrow a king than it actually was. After all, the Starveling was powerful enough that he had controlled the rulers of the courts for centuries.

She was just one human girl. One girl, with no fighting experience, no worldly knowledge at all. She had absolutely nothing to offer them. In fact, she would slow them down, and they had to protect her in order to keep their prince alive. Larken's hands fisted in her dress. Bitterness coated the back of her throat. What help would she even be against the Starveling? Let them overthrow their monster of a king if they wanted to, she would have no part in it. Finder could do it for her, for both their people. He owed her that much, at least.

And when they returned to Ballamor, she would force him to reveal the truth. Force him to admit his sins. It would be hard for the families of the Chosen girls at first—they were likely happier at the thought of their girls being well taken care of in the faery realm. But the truth of it all was better than a lie—no matter how beautiful.

"I'll stay with you long enough for us to break the life debt. Then I'm returning to Ballamor to tell everyone the truth. My people deserve to know." She was surprised at the steadiness in her voice.

Finder didn't seem particularly taken aback by her answer. Good. At least he wasn't dim-witted enough to believe that she would willingly help her friend's murderer.

She closed her eyes briefly, praying to the Twins that this life debt between her and Finder would end before he attempted to take down the Starveling. Hoped that she would be back on her side of the bridge whenever Finder made his move against the king. Maybe that made her selfish, but she didn't care. She could only hope that they would break the life debt before he fought the Starveling so if he died, she wouldn't die, too. And that was only if they didn't kill each other first.

Nervousness pinched at her gut. She still had to think about what she would tell her people. About what it meant that the Popes and the Starveling clearly had some sort of dark bargain between them, paid in the blood of innocent girls.

Finder nodded his thanks, trying to offer her a smile. She stared him down coldly.

"Let us get one thing clear," she said, trying to ignore her shaking hands. "I don't trust you. I don't like you. I will *never* forget you murdered one of the only people who mattered to me. That you murdered hundreds of girls from my village. When this is all over, if you even survive the Starveling, you're going to pay for those sins."

"I wish for nothing more than repentance. But I fear it is far too late for that." Finder turned away, his emotionless mask slipping into place once more.

CHAPTER NINE

Larken tapped her fingers on her leg as the sun slipped lower in the sky. She had remained silent as the fey argued about how to defeat the Starveling. Saja and Madden were on the side of brute force; of trying to catch the Starveling unawares and then overpowering him. Dahey and Finder wanted to gather information first, but from different sources.

"If we return to Shadeshelm, I could consult the library—" Finder began, but Dahey cut him off.

"Oh *now* you want to go to Shadeshelm? For the last time, the city is the opposite direction of where we need to go," he growled. "Need I remind you that we only have six days to kill the Starveling and break the life debt?"

Larken's insides churned. Who knew what horrors awaited her if they failed to break the life debt and she was trapped here for another year?

"The Dark Priestesses can help us, I just need you to trust me," Dahey said.

Ah yes. Then there were the Dark Priestesses, another source of debate amongst the *dornán*. According to Dahey, the Priestesses were a race of ancient fey, collectors of whispers and rumors, truth and secrets. They'd weathered an untold number of seasons hidden away in the forest, listening, remembering. They only asked a small price in return for their services.

Larken remained seated, her arms wrapped around her knees as the fey paced before her. Any bargain struck with a being from this realm seemed like a terrible idea.

I would know, she thought tartly. *And I didn't have a choice about mine.*

"No," Finder said. "We can't risk it. Such ancient beings cannot be trusted, especially after their part in the first war." He paused, turning to Dahey. "And how is it you know so much about them? I only know they settled in the Autumn Court after the battle."

"As your general of diplomatic relations, it is my duty to document the creatures that live in the Autumn Court. I learned several interesting pieces of information about them when I conducted one of my censuses. They regret their part in the first war, but they have atoned, and now—" Dahey scowled. "Why must I explain this all again? Maybe if you'd bother to *read* the reports I made—"

"What is their price?" Saja interrupted.

"Occasionally a favor. An exchange of whispers. It varies."

Finder ran a hand through his curls. "The price could be too high. They could harm Larken."

Larken resisted the urge to roll her eyes. Kind of him to be interested in her well-being, when he had murdered all of those other girls from Ballamor.

"They won't be interested in her—they will only be interested in us. In you, Finder."

"He is a prince," Saja said, brows furrowing. "They could ask of him something that would put our court in danger."

"More danger than trying to overthrow the Starveling?" Dahey threw up his hands in exasperation. "If we do this, we have to do it right. If we fail..." His fists clenched.

"We don't know what we'll be up against," Madden added, unconvinced. "I can't believe we're even entertaining the idea of the Priestesses at all."

"You have to trust me. They could be the only source of information on how to defeat the Starveling. Need I remind you of the stakes? If the

Starveling gets even a whiff of what we're up to, he will purge the Autumn Court of its traitors. Guilty—or innocent. If we don't find out if the Starveling can be killed, he'll go after them all. Families, *children*. No one we know will be safe. I know Rosin's death reminded you of Senna's. If we fail, think of how many others like her will perish. Fey and human alike."

Madden's shoulders slowly curled inwards. Saja and Finder exchanged worried glances.

Dahey turned to Finder. "The Priestesses will have the answers we seek. We will deal with the price when it comes to it. Who knows, we might not even be alive by the night of the tithe, and then we would have worried for nothing," Dahey said bitterly. "Madden, tell these two what we risk if we fail."

"Dahey, enough," Finder hissed.

"We can't do this," Madden muttered.

"It's all right, Madden," Finder said.

"We'll fail," Madden whispered. "Do you really believe it will be that easy to defeat him?"

The hair on the back of Larken's neck lifted. A pulsing filled the air, a deep hum steadily growing in intensity. The forest began to twist around her, the trees blackening.

Magic. Larken's eyes widened.

Finder gave a short flick of his wrist toward Larken. Dahey nodded, and slowly slid toward her. Madden crouched, hands fisted in his inky hair, breathing hard. The pulsing beat quickened, the hum growing louder in Larken's ears until it blossomed into a roar. Madden was breaking down, and the magic was coming, powerful and alive.

Dahey reached her, placing his body before hers. A small wave of relief rushed through her; though she had no love for any of the fey at the moment, she knew Dahey was here to protect her. And at the sight of Madden before her and the magic writhing all around them, she knew she would need it. What was happening to him?

"It's not real," Dahey muttered to her. "No matter what you see or hear, it's not real."

Larken's stomach coiled. Castor had said that the fey had the magic of deception, but this felt real. All around her the trees began to change. They sunk into the ground and spread like oil across the dirt, black tendrils reaching for her. Larken gaped, not wanting to believe her eyes. One of the tendrils wrapped around her leg, cold as ice. She cried out, trying to shake free.

"What's happening?" she cried, desperately trying to free her leg. The tendrils latched onto her hands, slimy and cold.

"Look at Finder," Dahey commanded. She did, training her eyes on the prince. Her gaze clung to every detail, the curved bow of his lip, the way his auburn brows drew together in concentration. Slowly, the icy feeling in her hands and legs faded. Larken looked down, but as soon as she laid eyes on the tendril, the cold returned.

"Look at Finder. Focus on the bond between you. Let it tether you."

"I can't," she gasped. The tendrils grew, tying her down. Creatures slunk from the trees, surrounding them. Their white eyes bulged, and they smiled, their mouths filled with jagged teeth.

Dahey gripped her arms, shaking her.

"Look at Finder. Look nowhere else."

Look nowhere else, Larken commanded herself, locking her eyes on the prince. She imagined the bond between them like a chain—no, like a golden thread. A thread that grew thicker the more she focused on it.

Dahey released her but still stood by her side, tapping her whenever he caught her looking away from Finder. Every time she looked at the creatures, at the dark trees, they grew stronger. Finder and Madden knelt, their muscles stiff as they faced each other. Madden was causing this nightmare to happen. Whatever magic he possessed had somehow called this darkness.

"Madden," Finder's voice rang out. "Breathe, *a chara*."

"You can't fight back. You can't fight him. You know what he does to traitors, you know what he does to those who oppose him." Madden's voice was low and husky, so unlike the airy tone Larken had started to associate him with. Tears poured down his face and sobs racked his body. "I've lost everything to him. It was her—I know it was Etain who really did it. But she is loyal to him. Without him keeping her in check, she'll come for us," he gasped.

Larken hadn't the slightest inkling who he was talking about, who this Etain was, but Madden's magic frightened her more than anything else at the moment.

"I won't let that happen," Finder said. His voice was so gentle, but the malevolent pulse of magic did not stop. The creatures twisted and smiled, necks bending at impossible angles.

"You can't think—" Madden choked again, body shuddering. "You can't think I want him as King. After what he's done to us all these years."

Finder had eyes only for him. "I know, Madden."

"But we can't fight. We can't fight. Not after what happened to my— my—not after she killed them. You know what it is like to lose someone," he said, voice edging from pain to fury. "You know Embryn would tell you not to do this. Not after last time."

Last time? So, they had tried to rise up against the Starveling before. And had lost.

"I know what it's like to lose family," Finder replied softly.

"She took them out of their beds. She tortured them. She killed them. Because of me." Madden's voice sounded so dead, so unfeeling that Larken shuddered.

"And she will pay for that, Madden. I swear she will. But we can't live like this. Once we rid ourselves of the Starveling, we can rid ourselves of her, too. We can finally avenge them."

Finder edged toward Madden, hands outstretched. The black fog curled around them, hiding the fey from view until she could only see flashes of them through the mist. But the golden thread tying her to Finder remained.

"We can't bring back the dead. But we can fight *him*. For our lost ones," Finder said.

Larken blinked. Madden and Finder had lost loved ones to the Starveling, just as she had.

"We cannot live like this anymore. Help me fight," Finder pleaded.

Madden let out a strangled cry. The fog consumed her, rendering her completely blind. The cord between her and Finder vanished. The tendrils wrapped around her like black snakes, forcing their way into her mouth, choking her. She screamed, clawing at her throat. The fog moaned, throbbing like a deranged black heart.

Two hands grabbed her, and she squirmed away, but it was Dahey's voice that stopped her. "Damn it, hold still."

"Help me," she cried, tears running down her face, her tongue heavy with acrid smoke. She was dying. She was dying and choking, and the darkness would rip her apart.

"I've got you," he said. She couldn't see—but he had her. She wasn't alone. She gripped his hand, allowing it to ground her. "Focus on my hand. What it feels like in yours. There you go."

She squeezed Dahey's hand tightly, feeling the bones and tendons beneath. He was here with her. Slowly, the tendrils released her. He was here. Dahey was here.

"How long will it last?" she moaned.

"Until Finder can pull him out."

As if on cue, the shadows pulled away from her and Dahey. Over stone and root, the black tendrils and creatures now raced toward Madden. Madden drew the darkness to him, and within a few moments, it enveloped him completely, a rippling, writhing mass.

Then it exploded from him, the dark mass screaming and roaring through the trees before winking out of existence completely.

CHAPTER TEN

Light flooded Larken's vision and she let out a tiny sob of relief. She threw herself at Dahey, hugging him tightly. He froze, dumbfounded, then folded her in a hug. He'd helped her. She released him, giving him a wobbly smile in thanks.

Finder knelt by Madden, gripping his friend's shoulder. He whispered something unintelligible, then helped Madden to his feet. Madden's eyes had glazed over. He looked like a corpse.

"What was that?" Larken asked.

"Glamour." Dahey scrubbed a hand over his face. "The fey can use it to create illusions. Convince the body to see, hear, touch, smell, or taste things that are not truly there."

"I could have died." Larken hugged herself tightly.

Dahey shook his head. "Madden didn't mean to hurt you, Larken. And every illusion has a hole—you have to latch onto it and pull through it until the illusion shatters. I hoped that your bond with Finder would help ground you, as would something physical, like my hand. To see what was real and what was imagined."

Larken wasn't convinced. The tendrils had choked her. They had almost killed her. Maybe Madden wouldn't have let it get that far, but maybe it was out of his control when he was in that state. A shiver ran down her spine. She would ask Dahey later how to combat the illusions better, once she had recovered. For now, the thought of enduring another experience like that, even for practice, made her knees tremble.

Finder whistled, and the fey horses came cantering out of the trees. They whinnied and pranced nervously. Their fear was contagious.

Madden's stallion knelt on the ground before his rider, and Finder helped his friend onto the horse's back. He slumped forward immediately, his eyes still glassy. Larken felt a twist of sympathy. Still, she could not stop the distrust that spread through her—Madden had caused that illusion. He had hurt her. The bay stallion rose to his feet. Madden wound his fingers in his black mane.

Finder turned to Dahey. "Do not push him just to get your way." His voice was deathly quiet.

"I know," Dahey said tightly. "I never meant him harm, I only wanted him to—"

"Leave it alone, Dahey." Saja was behind her, already mounted on Arobhinn. He extended a hand to her.

"No," Finder cut in, pulling himself onto Rhylla. "She rides with me."

Panic kicked in Larken's chest. "No, thanks—I'll ride with Saja." She turned away from the prince.

"Please, I know it is difficult to be so near to me. But I would feel safer if you rode with me. My ability to draw on the veins of magic is stronger, and it will be easier to protect you."

"He's right," Saja replied, and she reluctantly nodded. It wasn't as if the day could possibly get any worse. Rhylla bent her graceful head toward Larken, sniffing curiously. Then she brushed her velvety nose across Larken's forehead, giving her permission to ride. She tentatively stroked the horse's nose. Then she grasped Finder's outstretched hand.

Rhylla wasn't as tall or wide as Arobhinn, and it took Larken a moment to adjust. Finder's scent washed over her. How could he possibly smell so good after days of riding, trekking through the woods and fighting the Fomari? She scowled.

Oh, Twins. She had been so caught up in everything that she hadn't thought about how *she* smelled. Rosin's blood still stained her clothes, as well as stains she could not and did not want to identify.

"I would not go to them for answers if we had another choice," Finder said. "But you are right, Dahey. We are out of options." His green eyes rested heavily on his cousin. "Show us the way to these Dark Priestesses."

CHAPTER ELEVEN

The scenery morphed around them as they rode. Tree trunks widened, their long branches stretching into the sky like giants. Foliage adorned in ornate orange-and-gold latticework waved gently as they passed. Even with their large hooves, the horses made little more than a rustle as they ambled steadily through the forest.

Larken found she was sore, but keeping her balance bareback was easier. She tried leaning as far away from Finder as possible, but eventually, she gave up and settled against him.

Dark thoughts nipped at her mind until she thought she would scream. She rubbed at her temples, where an ache began to spread. All of the answers to her questions just led to more questions, and her companions didn't always offer to explain unless she asked them to. And even then, they refused to tell her everything. Annoyance prickled through her. It wasn't as if she was some ignorant human, too simple to understand the complexities of their world.

Had they talked to Brigid, as they led her to her death? Grief tore through Larken anew, painful and swift.

Had Madden talked to Brigid, as he did to her? Did he make her laugh before the end? He had been the kindest toward Larken out of all of the fey, and yet Larken could not bring herself to look at him. Not

91

that there was much to look at, as he hadn't moved from his position sprawled on Bresel's back. Finder had tried to speak for him, telling her that Madden hadn't meant for his glamour to get out of hand, but she'd stopped listening. She felt betrayed by Madden, somehow. Shocked that he had made something as terrifying as those dark tendrils manifest. According to Dahey, Castor had been right about the fey having the magic of deception—or glamour, as they called it. Castor had been right about so many things. She had to make it back to him and tell him he had been right about everything. Even Imogen.

Larken felt lost, like she was floating in a lake so surrounded by mist that she could not see the shore. Deep enough where her feet could not touch the bottom and she had to wave her limbs constantly to keep her head above the dark water.

She had no purpose now. Her mission to find the girls and discover the true meaning of the special task was over. Thoughts about her fight with Brigid consumed her. Worse still, she was chained to the fey now, being dragged behind them wherever they decided to go. Powerless against the life debt, she had no choice but to wait on fate or chance to break her and Finder's bond. And while she wanted to protect Ballamor, she knew she was no match for the Starveling and had no real way to help the fey destroy him. They had made the decision to go to the Dark Priestesses, and she had no choice but to follow.

Stop feeling sorry for yourself and think. She could find a new purpose here. All the people of Ballamor deserved to know what was happening in Airodion. All of the humans needed to know. She had to find out as much information about the fey as possible so when she returned to Ellevere she could spread the word, as Castor had. It would be dangerous, of course, but she wouldn't rest until all the humans knew. There were tyrants everywhere she turned—in this world and in Ellevere. But the Chosen girls deserved to have their stories told. Their deaths known and mourned. Larken was the only human to know the truth about the dark contract between the fey and the Popes. It was her burden to carry now.

Cold wind bit through her clothes, making her shiver despite Finder's warmth behind her.

"Here," he said, unfastening his cloak. He made to drape it over her shoulders, but she shifted away.

"I'm fine."

Finder sighed. "No, you're not. And I doubt hating me is doing much to keep you warm, so you might as well take it."

Frowning, she snatched the cloak from him, wrapping it around herself. It was a deep forest green, and delightfully warm.

Why does he have to smell so good?

"The color suits you," he said.

"Right."

"I mean it. Goes with the gold of your hair."

"Flattery isn't going to make me forgive you," she snapped.

He was quiet for a moment. "Well, everyone enjoys flattery, at least."

"Not me."

That made him smile. She could feel it against her cheek. She scowled back, but at least she was warm. Between the cloak and Rhylla, the chill had disappeared.

Still, she couldn't stop the flush that crept up her neck at the feeling of Finder's legs pressed against the back of her thighs. Even the tiniest flex of his muscles did not escape her notice.

The fey horses never stumbled, and they kept a steady pace without tiring. Despite the lack of reins, saddle, or commands, Rhylla went exactly where Finder wanted.

"How does she know where to go?" Larken asked, offering up the question as a slight peace offering.

Finder gave a low laugh and patted Rhylla on her neck.

"Rhylla has been my companion for many years," he replied. "She does not understand our language or communicate as you and I do, but she understands a great deal. Our mounts are as precious to us as gold or jewels. Even more so. They are our family, and each horse will only carry one rider for their entire life. Should a child be chosen by a foal, they will train together until they are more one being than two. Arobhinn and Rhylla gave you their blessing to ride them, and they do not give that blessing to everyone."

Rhylla flicked an ear back toward Finder, and Larken felt a subtle shift in his body that she guessed meant he was smiling.

"Our mounts are immortal, but can be felled in battle, similar to us. If Rhylla were to fall, I would take no other mount. I would rather walk until blisters marred my feet than ride on another back than hers."

"How old is she?" Larken ran cautious fingers through Rhylla's mane.

"As old as I am."

Now Larken could hear the smile in Finder's voice. She turned back to look at him and found him grinning at her.

"And how old are you?" Her eyes narrowed. He didn't look much older than she was.

"One hundred and fifty."

Larken choked.

"Oh," she said once she'd regained her composure. Finder, Saja, and Dahey chuckled. "And how old are the rest of you?"

"I am one hundred and sixty-three," Saja rumbled, "and Madden is one hundred and sixty-two." He gestured to Dahey. "And Dahey is only one hundred and forty-seven."

Only one hundred and forty-seven. The humans knew the fey were immortal—after all, for as long as she had been attending Choosing Ceremonies, Finder had looked the same. But it was hard for her to wrap her mind around such long lifetimes. "Is it your magic that keeps you from aging?" she asked Finder.

Finder frowned. "I'm not sure. I assume they are tied in some way, but—" He ran a hand through his curls. "Forgive me. Magic is difficult to explain, especially to someone who has never felt it. Magic is a living, breathing thing that courses through this world. It is something that touches you, and only you, while uniting us all. I call it and it obeys me, but not because it has to. Because it wants to, because it has chosen me." Finder dipped his head, hiding a dark flash in his gaze. "It is the most beautiful thing in the world and the highest honor. But also, the greatest shackle."

A small tremor went through her. Though it shamed her to admit—

scared her, even—she wanted to see them use more magic. Even after seeing Madden's glamour.

Slowly, Dahey and Saja's conversation behind them fell away. Larken was so absorbed in her own thoughts that she barely noticed when Saja inhaled sharply.

Then he began to choke.

"Saja!" Dahey cried, and Larken and Finder twisted in time to see Saja fall from Arobhinn's back. Arobhinn whinnied, but the horse didn't move his legs as Saja lay close to his hooves.

Finder was off Rhylla's back in a heartbeat, pulling his friend from beneath Arobhinn. Dahey dropped down beside them, hand grasping Saja's shoulder.

"How long?" Finder asked.

Dahey ran frantic fingers through his hair, face growing paler. "I—I didn't notice anything. It's been so long. He stopped talking, and I thought he was breathing a little faster but—"

"Why didn't you tell him to stop?" Finder growled.

Saja struggled to pull air into his lungs. A horrible hacking cough tore from his throat, and his breathing grew shallower still. His eyelids drooped.

A voice nudged at the back of Larken's mind. Mama, talking about her life as a healer before she married Papa. Mama, helping the baby at the Choosing Ceremony with a persistent cough...giving them...

"Yellow thorn!" Larken cried. She slid off Rhylla, eyes scanning the nearby underbrush.

"What?" Dahey muttered distractedly.

Larken grabbed his arm and he turned to face her. "Yellow thorn. It helps with coughing fits and people who have trouble breathing."

Dahey didn't question her. "What does it look like?"

They scoured the surrounding woods, the sound of Saja's weak coughing leaking through the trees. *Tall stem, spiked yellow leaves.* Larken sent a quick prayer to the Twins that Airodion even *had* yellow thorn.

"Found it!" Dahey shouted from a few yards away.

They rushed back to their companions, Larken's heart leapt into her throat at the sight of Saja. His eyes had rolled back in their sockets, his mouth gasping like a fish.

"Through your nose," Finder murmured. "Breathe deeply through your nose."

Larken ripped off one of the leaves with her teeth, chewing it hastily. Her eyes watered as the bitter taste filled her mouth, the flavor similar to peppermint but much sharper. She spat the pulp onto her palm. "Lift his shirt," she ordered.

Dahey pulled up his companion's shirt, exposing his muscled torso. Larken chewed another leaf and knelt, rubbing the pungent liquid onto his chest.

Saja's coughing didn't stop, but Larken was relentless. She chewed every leaf on the plant and then made Dahey get more.

Relief pulsed through her when Saja's breathing finally evened out after the third application. His eyes closed in exhaustion. Dahey released fisted hands from his hair and sighed in relief.

Once he was sure Saja could breathe again, Finder stood, turning to her.

"Thank you," he breathed. She nodded, a tiny bloom of pride opening in her chest. She had helped. She, an ordinary mortal girl, had helped a faery.

Oh Twins, this better not lead to another life debt... But her companions had known about these breathing attacks. Saja had clearly had them before, and terrifying as they were, they hadn't killed him. She had only helped him—not saved his life.

"How did you know that the plant would help?" Dahey asked.

"My mother used to work as a healer before she married my father," Larken replied. She wished Mama had been there to see how she had helped Saja. "Do the fey not use herbal remedies? Or couldn't you use magic to heal him?"

"My position as a court ruler affords me healing magic, but some illnesses, like Saja's, cannot be healed or alleviated by magic," Finder said. "We knew of no plants that could aid him. And some wounds, like Rosin's, are too great for even me to heal," Finder said. "All fey have accelerated healing and do not fall prey to the illnesses and diseases humans do. Yet sometimes they are born with an illness." His eyes flickered toward Saja. His voice lowered. "Usually when he has an attack, we just wait for it to pass. Now we know to use yellow thorn, thanks to you, Larken." His eyes hardened as he turned to Dahey. "You should have been watching him."

"I was!" Dahey cried. "I was listening for his breathing, I was, but—"

"But what?" Finder snarled.

Larken flinched. She had never seen him this angry.

"But I'm not his nursemaid, all right?" Dahey spat. "Nor does he want me to be."

"It's not up to him what he wants!" Finder roared. Dahey stepped back jerkily. "We need always be watching so he doesn't overwork himself and push himself into an attack."

"He was fine a moment ago!" Dahey shouted back, throwing up his arms in frustration. "It's not always something we can prevent, and it's not your job to baby him."

"Stop it," Saja wheezed. He struggled into a seated position, then tried to stand. Finder, dropping his threatening stance, fell to his side.

"No." Saja pushed Finder away. Hurt flashed across Finder's lovely face. "You know I am grateful for your help. I know I need it, however much it destroys me to admit it," Saja said, finally making it to his feet. Dahey watched the two other fey silently.

"Saja," Finder began.

"No. You have no idea what I endure. You have no idea what it's like for you to need me, for my court to need me, and yet I can do nothing. At any moment, I could be sprawled on the ground, choking on my own fluids," he said, voice quiet as death.

Finder and Dahey wisely stayed silent.

"Everyone wants to contribute to their court. To fight for them, to do something with their lives. But what happens when you can no longer contribute? What happens when you are *worthless* to your prince and your court?" Saja spat, voice growing louder. "Do you know how it feels to know that everyone else in the *dornán* has to pick up my slack? It's humiliating." Saja's voice shook, his cheeks burning with anger and shame.

Sympathy trickled through her. She knew what it was like to feel worthless. But she had already seen Saja play an essential role in the *dornán* as a protector and peacemaker—he was far from useless.

"Saja," Finder tried again, but Saja held up a hand, breathing heavily, though it looked more from anger than anything to do with his condition.

"You've said enough." Saja swung himself onto Arobhinn's back, a little less gracefully than usual. He looked down at Larken. "Thank you for helping me," he said, eyes softening. Then he cantered ahead through the trees without another word or backwards glance. Larken had a feeling he wouldn't go far. Even though he was angry, he would never stray far from his prince.

"What I would give to have you all fight like that over me," Madden bemoaned, propping himself up on Bresel's neck. Larken gaped at him. Dahey just rolled his eyes. "Hope Saja left to get ahead on the cooking. I'm starved." Madden stretched, then urged Bresel on, and the horse trotted into the darkness.

CHAPTER TWELVE

Finder and Dahey exchanged a few rude comments about Madden before Dahey followed his companions into the trees. Their fight was over, but Larken could tell their conversation was strained.

"Are you ready?" Finder asked. She nodded and forced herself toward the faery prince and his mount. "I'm sorry you had to see that." Finder rubbed the back of his neck. "Our relationship has been... strained, as of late, but I love him like a brother, and I know he feels the same."

Though she hadn't been with the group of fey very long, she could feel the tension rising between Finder and Dahey like an oncoming storm.

"Dahey seemed angry that you spend so little time at Shadeshelm," Larken said carefully. "Why?"

Dahey might have pushed all of them to go to the Dark Priestesses instead of Shadeshelm for answers, but it was still clear that he believed that Finder had abandoned his court. But why would a prince abandon his subjects? He was fighting the Starveling himself to save them.

Finder untied one of Rhylla's braids, combing his fingers through her mane. He re-braided the strands with deft fingers.

"The one thing you must understand about Dahey is his fierce love for his court," Finder said. "Dahey's father was the prince before me, and though he gave his son little else, he did instill in Dahey a love for the Autumn Court. And when his father wouldn't show him love, Dahey leaned on his court instead.

"My relationship with Dahey changed the moment I created my *dornán*, and it has only grown more strained since. Dahey's first loyalty has always been to his court. But when he joined my *dornán*, his first loyalty changed to me. He believed that my first priority would be to my court as well, but he was mistaken. My loyalty will always lay with my family—my *dornán*."

"But that still doesn't explain why you don't like being at Shadeshelm." A thought struck her then. "Does this have anything to do with what happened the first time you attacked the Starveling? With Embryn?" Larken remembered that name—though she still didn't know who she was.

"It has everything to do with Embryn," Finder murmured.

Larken waited for him to continue, but he remained silent. "Who was she?"

"She was my friend," Finder answered slowly. "A very dear friend. We met while I trained for combat at the Autumn Court's military academy."

"Was she part of your *dornán*?"

"No, she never wished to be a part of it. Although I tried very hard to convince her." He didn't stumble over the words, but Larken heard a shift—a small one, but there nonetheless—in his voice.

"We faced many evils together, she and I. And yet, there was one evil too great for either of us to face.

"Embryn was by my side for many tithes. She knew it was wrong —*told* me it was wrong from the very beginning. She said that we needed to fight back, that what we were doing was tearing us apart. Eventually, she couldn't take it anymore. She said that whether I joined her or not, she was going to kill the Starveling herself or die trying."

Respect and even gratitude flickered through Larken toward the female faery. Embryn had been willing to face the Starveling alone to save Finder and her people from the king. Doing so would have bene-fitted the humans, whether she had intended to or not.

Finder gave a low laugh. "With an ultimatum like that, who could say no to her? I agreed to help her, as did Dahey, Saja, and Madden. By then they were members of my *dornán*, but we had all been close companions at the academy.

"Embryn convinced one of her friends, Toma, to help us, as well. We crafted a plan and swore to keep every part of it a secret. We tried to catch the Starveling unawares while he lay dormant. In the years since the war, he has become more reclusive, tending to stay burrowed away in his domain, waiting for the tithe.

"We almost had him. Almost." Finder's breath billowed out. "We all fought as hard as we ever had. But it was not enough. He was too much for us, as we should have known. As I think we did know, deep inside, but felt that we had to keep trying all the same. We had gone through so much." Finder's eyes turned distant. Was he there now, playing over the battle in his mind?

Larken tried to ignore the dread seeping through her as the story progressed. If Finder and his companions had fought the Starveling before and failed, then what made them so sure that this time it would be different?

"Saja told me the moment the Starveling's blade pierced Embryn's stomach I made a sound he had never heard before in this world." Finder blinked and the distant look was gone, replaced with cold emptiness.

"He sliced her clean open, the smile on his lips matching the one baring her insides. He tied her to the back of his mount and rode, drag-ging her in the dirt behind him. He mangled Toma's leg beyond repair, and even my magic could not heal it. The only thing I could do to save her was to cut it off." He braced his forearms on Rhylla's back. "It was completely my fault that she lost her leg. After that, Toma dedicated her life to healing others." He shook his head. "That was eight years ago, now. I've told myself every day since that I would never be that foolish again. That I would never endanger the lives of my friends. But my anger never lessens with time. It only grows. I can't let him live. Not after all he's done. And I knew that if the time came, if there was another chance to bring him down, that I would take it. That I would not hesitate."

The way Finder spoke about Embryn was the same way she talked about Brigid. Finder had lost one of his dearest companions as well, and now struggled to live a life without her in it. Larken knew better than anyone how that felt. Though she had just learned that Brigid was dead, Larken had been grieving her loss for a whole year. The thought of grappling with her guilt for eight years... Larken tried not to shudder.

But Finder clearly hadn't let go of Embryn. His hatred for the Starveling and his need for vengeance had only grown. Larken's gaze travelled over the prince, lingering on the dark circles that marred the skin under his eyes. Did she want revenge for what he had done to Brigid? Larken frowned as she tried to sort through the emotions roiling within her. Her hatred toward him lingered, but the thought of enacting vengeance on him herself felt wrong. Perhaps it was just their bond softening her feelings toward him. She wanted him to pay for what he had done, to confess to the people of Ballamor, but did she want him to die after they broke their life debt? Would his life pay the price for Brigid's death? She wasn't sure.

"Being at Shadeshelm only reminds me of her—of what I've lost. Since she died, I have only returned to stay with the tithe girls or for other important events, but then I take to the woods or outlying cities. Dahey thinks it is wrong of me to blame my court—but I don't blame them. I just hate that I must be a part of something that causes so much pain."

"If he's so unhappy, couldn't Dahey just leave your *dornán*?" Larken furrowed her brow. She remembered Dahey explaining the *dornán* bond and how they were bound to Finder's soul. But perhaps he could leave if he no longer wanted to be a part of it.

Finder shook his head. "He cannot. Once he swore his oath to me, he gave his life to me forever. My *dornán* and I are bonded so deeply that we can feel when one of the members of our party are badly wounded or in great emotional distress—or if one of us dies. I could choose to release them, but to do so would be a great dishonor, one that Dahey would never forgive me for."

A sudden thought came to her, making her suck in a breath. "Can they feel me through the bond, since you and I are tied in a life debt?"

"No. The bond you and I share is much stronger. While my *dornán* and I can feel each other's pain, we cannot die from it."

"What is it with the fey and their oath swearing," Larken muttered.

Finder gave a tight smile. "A faery oath is its own form of magic. We cannot lie, and whatever we swear to do we are forced to obey. To resist is agony."

Larken wondered what it was like to have magic bind you in word and deed. A sudden gratitude for her free will filled her. She didn't have to keep her promises, and that somehow made them more meaningful.

Finder seemed to read her thoughts, for he said, "Fey do not enter such contracts lightly. Many refuse to make oaths at all, and others only do so under great duress. Others only swear oaths to show loyalty—like my *dornán.*"

"And like you did to the Starveling," Larken murmured. Finder had said the Starveling forced the court rulers to swear fealty to him.

"Yes. The court rulers swore to obey the Starveling's tithe," Finder said. "When the time comes, I only have a few moments to resist before I am compelled to obey."

Larken's heart climbed into her throat. "Does that mean you'll be forced to attack me? Even though I'm not your tithe?" She didn't know what she would do if it came to that.

Finder met her gaze. "I don't know. I'm not sure if the magic will sense you are not the tithe, or if whoever touches the altar must be sacrificed."

"Oi—you two." Madden appeared, lounging against a tree. Larken nearly jumped out of her skin. "My stomach is trying to eat itself. Save all the dismal chatting for later."

CHAPTER THIRTEEN

Saja had indeed begun cooking dinner for them, though he looked particularly disgruntled about it. He monitored their meal, still refusing to look at or speak to Finder as he scanned the darkened trees for any potential threats.

He worked with a full set of pots, pans, and cooking utensils—though Larken hadn't seen any of the fey carrying them. But Castor had said that the fey could move objects with their minds. Larken stared at the pans, waiting for them to fly through the air, but they remained motionless. Potato pancakes sizzled on one, and stew bubbled in another. Larken's mouth watered at the scent of the cooking vegetables and spices. Saja must truly have been as talented as the others claimed to have been able to produce all this on the road. He tossed her a piece of bread—warm and fresh from the fire. It had a similar taste to Papa's legendary brown bread, but Saja's was lighter and sweeter. The dark brown loaf was moist with a velvety fine crumb. She tried not to cram the entire piece in her mouth.

"Castor told me that the fey could move objects with their minds," Larken said around a mouthful of bread. "Is that true?"

In response, Dahey flicked his hand at her. She gasped as all the dirt, blood, and sweat from her travels sloughed off her in a great coagulum,

104

falling to the forest floor with a smack. "You have no idea how long I've been wanting to do that," Dahey sighed.

"How did you do that?" She fisted her hands in the fabric of her newly cleaned gown. It still smelled a few days too ripe, but at least it was clean.

"The fey call it summoning," Finder said. He held out his hand, and a silver spoon winked into existence on his palm. "We summon everything from Shadeshelm and return it whenever we desire." He twitched his fingers again and the spoon disappeared.

"Why bother cooking all this food then? Why not just summon it?"

"Food is difficult to summon," Saja explained. "It likes to turn cold and stale in the process. I summon ingredients from the palace when needed, though I prefer to make everything fresh." Saja held out his hand, and a waterskin appeared in his palm. "Things get even more complex when summoning elements such as water or earth. While we can summon waterskins, if I were to try to summon water itself, it would merely splash upon the ground. Same with the dirt and blood Dahey removed from your clothes. He could summon it, but not manipulate it further. Only the court rulers have the power to manipulate the elements."

Larken's stomach dropped to her toes. Castor had said the fey had power over the earth itself. Castor was seen as the village drunk—and yet his information was true about so many things regarding Airodion. Larken feared for his life should the Guard or the Popes ever find out how much he truly knew. She hoped he had escaped the Guard so when she returned to Ballamor she could tell him that his research hadn't been in vain.

"You can control all of the elements?" Larken swallowed, looking at Finder.

The faery prince laughed. "No, not all of them. Each court ruler has power over one of the elements. The Spring Court's element is earth. Winter's is water. The Summer Court's is air. And the Autumn Court's is fire."

He held a hand out at the fire, and the flames roared in response, leaping toward his touch like eager hounds greeting their master. The fire pulled at Làrken, urging her to come closer, to reach out and touch it. She leaned forward, her fingers slowly inching toward the flame.

Finder jerked. The flames sank back down, returning to normal. She shook herself as the strange urge to touch the flames ebbed away.

"Why didn't you tell me about this before?" Larken asked.

"I wasn't intentionally trying to keep it from you," Finder replied. "I have a difficult relationship with my powers. I can never use them at full strength—the Starveling prevents me from doing so. But I have lost control before, and I will never allow myself to reach that point again. That's why I keep them locked away, where they can't hurt anyone but me." He stared at the flames with lowered brows. The flames waved at him gently, but when he looked away from them, they drooped.

Larken didn't know what to think. How it would feel for Finder to know that a part of him belonged to the Starveling. That his magic was tied to such a horrible king.

Saja tossed Finder the waterskin and he drank deeply. The texture of the material caught her eye. Her gaze flew to the packs—seemingly made from the same leather as their waterskins, as were their greaves, tunics, and boots. Larken frowned. "I thought you said you all didn't eat animals or use any part of them."

Finder tilted his head. "We do not."

Larken's frown deepened, and she pointed to his leather boots and then to their packs.

Finder gave her a sly grin. "That is no animal hide. That is firedrake skin."

Larken gaped at him. He couldn't be serious. Firedrakes were a myth, something so shrouded in lore that even children knew them not to be real.

Finder tossed her his waterskin. She barely caught it, fumbling before clutching it to her chest.

Though she had expected the texture of leather, the skin was much tougher and had the rippling feel of overlapping scales. It was as though she were holding a legend made flesh, a childhood dream come to life. She looked up at Finder, who watched her with something indescribable in his eyes.

"What?" she asked suspiciously.

"We have lived on this earth for centuries." Finder gestured to himself and his *dornán*. "We have seen monsters and magic beyond belief. It is difficult for us to be surprised, or awed, by anything in this world. But everything in Airodion is new to you. Everything you discover is met with such wonder, and it—" Finder paused, struggling to find the right words. "It is a sight to behold." He gazed at her again with such intensity that her cheeks warmed and she looked away.

"You don't just see me as some ignorant human?" Larken huffed.

"No," he rumbled, and Larken believed him.

You hate him, remember? A cold voice in the back of her mind hissed.

"The fey have a trading system set up with the firedrakes," Saja added. "Drakes are hoarders, and they love anything gold or glittery, especially when it has magic. We give them these objects in exchange for their shed skin, which is tougher and more durable than leather and requires no loss of life."

Madden tossed a stick into the flames. "The drakes aren't picky about what kind of magical object they receive, either. It could be something like, say, a whistle enchanted to attract birds, and they would find it enormously satisfying. The lands of Airodion are infused with magic from the rivers that run beneath it. Many plants and minerals have taken on magical properties." Madden smiled tentatively at her, and she gave him a small smile back. He'd been mostly quiet since his recovery from the glamour but was slowly coming back to them.

Larken swallowed, her mind flickering to the only reason why humans came into contact with magical objects. "Are they similar to the ones you give the families of the Chosen girls?"

Her heart squeezed tightly in her chest. All the families of the Chosen girls had been compensated with riches. As if any amount of gold or jewels could amount to their daughters' lives.

Finder nodded. "I know it will never be enough to recompense them for their daughters' sacrifice. But I hope it ensures that they never go hungry and allows them to live in comfort for the rest of their lives."

The gifts Finder offered the families of the Chosen girls would never be enough, but he was right—it could keep them comfortable. Larken had to admit it was kind of him to think about the villagers' wellbeing when he and his *dornán* were nobility, the elites of Airodion. They had never known what it was like to be hungry or to be cold. Larken thanked the Twins she hadn't either, but she had come close.

The fey before her had no idea what it was like to know one's own mortality. What need did they have to think of starvation in a land such as this? What need did they have to think of death, when centuries stretched out before them? Larken wondered what they even lived for. How could they live—*truly* live, when every day was just another part of eternity? Especially when such a dark cloud hung over their heads in the form of the Starveling and his tithe.

Though Larken would never be so bold as to say she did not fear death, she was suddenly reassured about the idea of her very mortal life. She understood Finder's fascination with her discovery of everything new in Airodion. For what did he have to enjoy, to savor, when he lived forever?

Larken curled her arms around her knees, watching as the fey before her fell into an easy chatter. Saja began whittling a spare piece of bark, saying something that made Dahey chuckle. Finder fashioned a tiny shadow-lion out of the smoke from the fire, and it pranced about, leaping in and out of the flames. The lion lifted onto its hind legs, twirling into a dance. Madden came and sat beside her, settling his legs before him.

"I wanted to apologize for earlier."

Larken didn't reply, keeping her eyes trained on the flames.

"Glamour is a fickle thing, especially the illusions it calls forth. I wasn't thinking. Dahey, Finder, and Saja can all see through them so clearly, and I forgot that you couldn't. I lost control." There was no scorn in his words, only deep regret. Larken peeked at him out of the corner of her eye. Madden scrubbed at his face with one hand.

"I used to make illusions for my daughter. Create a new dream world for her to explore every week. My glamour is powerful, more powerful than most. I could create something that felt so real that I wondered if I held it for too long if I might slip away into what I'd created, never to return. But for her, it was worth it. To see her delight in every new creature I made, every new paradise I conjured, and know it was just for her."

Larken stayed silent, allowing him to finish his story. Though the change in his tone made her tense—she didn't think his story had a happy ending.

"When she died, my glamour became an agony to use. I created illusions of her, pretending she was still alive. But she was...wrong, somehow, and something evil spread from her. I created dark creatures from the mist, and something dark began to grow inside me as well. I could never bring myself to create something that would bring joy again.

"I didn't mean to scare you. I'm sorry for hurting you. If you have any idea how much I hate myself for what I've done—" He fisted his hands in his hair, taking a shuddering breath before continuing. "When fey experience strong emotions, their powers can lash out as well. To protect them. For humans, your heart races and your muscles flood with blood, preparing you to either fight or flee. My glamour sensed my panic, and rushed to save me, hoping the illusion would distract my attackers. When the only one doing the attacking was me."

He turned to her, his shoulders hunched. "I can't promise it will never happen again. But I will do better. I promise I will do better."

Heat caressed her face like two warm hands holding her, lifting her face to the glow. Madden's words settled into her. The sweet smoke from the fire blew toward her, the burning logs still crackling, exploding with embers. Slowly, she scooted closer to Madden until their arms were touching.

"I forgive you."

They sat like that for a time, saying nothing, gazing at the fire. Eventually Madden began to sing, a song that sounded like a rippling stream. His voice leapt and bounded over the notes, the rest of the *dornán* accompanying him with a dance of their smoke and shadow creatures, whirling long into the night.

CHAPTER FOURTEEN

"So how far until we reach these Dark Priestesses?" Larken asked as they packed up the next morning. She rubbed her eyes. Sleep hadn't come easily for her. She kept imagining Brigid using the same bedroll the fey had given her.

She picked at the pink wound on her palm. The cut she shared with Finder had healed quicker than should have been possible. She vaguely remembered her hand itching something fierce in the night, but by morning it felt like a distant dream. She shivered. The dawn rose cold and misty, and Larken ached to be back on the warm horses.

Dahey finished tying the knot on his bedroll. "Hopefully by tomorrow."

Larken's stomach sank. *That long?* she wanted to ask, but she held her tongue. "And these Priestesses," Larken continued, "do they worship the Twins?"

"They serve no gods but themselves." Dahey wrapped a hand around his sword, knuckles white. "They once worshipped the Masters, but no longer."

"The Masters?" Larken's brows knitted. Finder helped her onto Rhylla's back as her companions mounted up. A flick of Finder's hand and the pots, pans, bedrolls, and tents disappeared into thin air. She

110

wondered if she would ever get used to the fey using magic around her.

"You do not know faery lore?" Saja tilted his head at her. "I only assumed because humans play such a vital part in it, they would know their origins. Your holy ones don't teach you these things?"

"Vital part? How is that possible?" Larken wrinkled her brow. "Humans and fey have always been separated—at least until Asphalion allowed humans to cross." But that wasn't true, it hadn't been the male god at all—it had been the Starveling who allowed girls to cross. "Or until the Starveling began the tithe," she amended.

"Separated?" Madden gaped at her. "Humans and fey used to live together in this world for over a thousand years."

Larken shook her head. "That's impossible. When the Twins made the world, they separated it into two realms—one for the fey and one for the humans."

"The Masters—" Finder began, but Dahey cut him off with a groan. "Let someone else tell her, Finder, we don't have all day."

Finder threw up his hands in exasperation as he settled onto Rhylla's back behind her.

"There's little Finder loves more than history, and sometimes we have to cut him off when he gets started on a tangent...or twelve," Madden smirked.

Dahey took the lead out of the clearing, and Madden guided Bresel alongside Rhylla. A breeze rustled through the trees, shaking free a few of the leaves. They fluttered through the air like strange, golden insects.

"Oh, fine. Madden, you tell it," Finder said.

Madden cleared his throat theatrically. "Long ago, the gods looked upon the earth and decided that they would bring life into it. From the stars, they created a tree. And from the tree's bark, they made four creatures. Soon, the creatures begged the gods to make them something of their own to protect and sustain. So, from the tree, the gods created the fey."

"You mean the Twin gods?" Larken interrupted.

Madden cocked his head. "I suppose we have no way of knowing. There are few written records stating what those beings were, however, it is the fey's belief that the Twins were created by the Popes, and they were based upon whatever gods the fey and humans both worshipped during their time together."

Larken's breath caught. Though she was not a firm believer in the Twins, it was still astonishing to be told that her gods were only a figment of the Order, created during the crusades four hundred years ago instead of at the beginning of time.

"But these creatures wanted to rule, as the gods did above. Though they had never had a name for themselves before, they began to call themselves the Masters."

The horses stepped over tree roots as big around as Larken's thigh, their hooves crunching softly through the leaves. By the position of the rising sun, Larken sensed they were still headed northwest, though they were now headed toward the Dark Priestesses, not Shadeshelm. She couldn't make out the clouds through the latticework of branches, something that might have unnerved her once, but she felt protected here, cradled beneath the towering boughs.

"For a time, they were content. But as the fey's numbers grew, the four Masters began to worry. Though they were much more powerful than the fey, they worried that their hold would slip. And so, they separated the world into four areas for each of the Masters to rule. They named these lands after the four seasons of the first tree: Summer, Autumn, Winter, and Spring.

"Growing bored of dealing with the petty problems of their underlings, the Masters selected four fey to rule the courts in their stead, bestowing them with special magical abilities."

Finder rubbed his jaw, adding, "The Masters only gave the court rulers more power than the average faery. But none had as much power as the Masters themselves."

"Quiet, you," Madden admonished.

"Well, you aren't giving her all the details," Finder retorted.

Madden ignored him. "The Masters and the fey lived in harmony for nearly two thousand years. But then things began to change. Three of the Masters began to think they were too lenient with their fey subjects and began to enslave them, forcing them to do terrible things."

"But why?" Larken asked. "Didn't they beg the gods to create the fey?"

Madden shrugged. "Who knows? Perhaps they were bored, burdened with their great power and nothing to do with it but face the yawning maw of eternity. Immortality can breed cruelty.

"But one of the Masters did not agree with the others. He traveled to the first tree and decided to create another life, one that would help free the fey from slavery. A life that would have no magic itself, but who would be shielded from the Master's magic. The gods aided him, and, cutting the bark from the tree with his knife, the Master formed the first human.

"Upon discovering that one of their kin had betrayed them, the other three Masters killed the fourth. The fey and the humans fought back against the remaining Masters. The war lasted for hundreds of years. Side by side, the humans and the fey fought until there was only one Master left.

"The land was devastated. Fey and humans alike had suffered terrible losses, as had the Master, for he was the last of his kind. Though some of the fey fought on behalf of the Master, he knew he was losing. He feared death above all else and fled deep into Airodion. The four fey who ruled the courts took command. For many years, the humans and their faery companions lived in peace."

Larken still couldn't wrap her mind around the idea of humans and fey living together. "That isn't the creation story humans are told. The Popes told us that the humans and fey have always been separated, but when the fey became powerful, Aleea—our female god, joined with the dark forces of the world to take some of the magic for the humans. Asphalion and his sister fought, and because of their turmoil, the humans and fey began wars of their own in their separate realms."

"The Popes took the parts of the truth that served them well and used them," Finder said. "Though I do not understand why they wouldn't want the humans to know that the fey and humans used to live together."

Surprise flared within her. She expected Finder to know everything about the Popes and what they told the humans. But he had questions as well.

"But the story isn't over yet," Madden carried on. "Darkness flooded into Airodion. Creatures, monsters in numbers that should not have been possible, terrorized the fey and the humans."

"The creatures that had fought for the Master?" she interjected.

Finder shook his head. "They thought that too, but no. None were of the likes they had ever seen before in Airodion. It was as if they had been conjured—or made." Finder frowned. "Made by..." He trailed off, his gaze turning hazy.

"Made by who?" Larken pressed.

Finder shook his head. "I'm sorry, where did we leave off?"

"You said it was as if the creatures were made," Larken said, puzzled by Finder's confusion. When she glanced around to see if his companions noticed something was amiss, their attention seemed to have drifted elsewhere.

Madden shook his head as though clearing it from a fog. "Made? No. That sort of magic is impossible. Maybe with glamour, but to create another being entirely is not possible. Even the Master who created the humans needed help from the gods, and the gods had by now turned their backs on their creations, ashamed of what they had become.

"Another war had begun," Madden continued. "These strange creatures were overwhelming Airodion. Both fey and humans alike knew they needed help, so they sought out the last Master.

"He agreed to help, asking only two favors in exchange. He wanted the title of King, and he demanded that a portion of the courts be collected as a tithe for his aid. He claimed he would reside in the most remote, desolate part of Airodion, returning only once a year to collect his tithe. Usually, the fey and the humans would never bargain with him, but they were desperate. So, they swore an oath to obey the treaty. Together, the humans, fey, and Master fought off the dark creatures, and imprisoned the monsters' leader, though his name has been lost to the winds of time."

Though some part of her suspected, she finally knew now: the last Master was the Starveling. Sweat trickled down her back. How could they possibly hope to defeat a creature like that? The amount of history the Starveling had lived through was staggering. The story she was now a part of had been unfolding since before she was born. Before humans even existed. All of this had been happening before she had ever set foot in Airodion or become bound to Finder. It was a relief, somehow, to know that she hadn't set everything into motion, even though it still felt that way.

"With help from the Dark Priestesses, the Master was able to twist his magic and sap power from the court rulers, reducing them to mere husks of what they once were."

Larken clenched her teeth at the mention of the Dark Priestesses. Dahey had said they regretted their part in the first war—but they had still helped the Starveling take the court rulers' powers. How could they be certain that the Priestesses weren't still loyal to him?

"Drawing from the powers of his allies, the Starveling was able to banish the dark creatures from our realm, but in order to ensure the humans and fey never rose up against him, he also separated Airodion into two lands: one for the humans, and one for the fey. He closed the border between the two realms with an endless chasm, with only four bridges connecting the two worlds. The humans were rounded up by the Master's servants and forced into their new realm. The bridges were then sealed, cutting the humans off from the fey forever—or so they thought."

A horrible thought came to her. "But if the Starveling created the chasm, will killing him end the magic that separates our realms?"

Her stomach churned. If the magic sealing the bridges or the chasm itself ceased to exist, then the fey could enter Ellevere at will.

Madden shook his head. "The Starveling created the chasm and the bridges to withstand even his death."

Larken breathed a sigh of relief.

"Humans and fey alike were devastated by the separation," Finder murmured. "Imagine fighting together for decades, dying together, only to see it all torn away."

Madden nodded, his eyes downcast. "And the Master was not finished yet. The treaty demanded a tithe, and the fey had sworn to obey it, whatever the cost. He gathered the rulers of the courts and told them the enchantment on the bridge had been lifted. He demanded that they each bring a human to him so they could discuss the tithe. So, the four fey rulers crossed the bridges and joyously reunited with their human friends." Madden trailed off, looking toward Finder.

Finder took a breath. "At first, neither the fey nor the humans saw what was coming. The humans had fought with the Master and knew his magic couldn't harm them."

She had almost forgotten that humans were protected from the Starveling's magic.

Well, that's one less thing you have to worry about.

"The fey laid their human companions on the stone altars. And then the Master commanded the fey to bring him their hearts."

Larken's chest tightened. *Of course.* The Starveling couldn't harm the humans, but the fey could.

"He had named his tithe. The humans were bound to the stones, unable to escape, and the fey had no choice but to obey. The deep magic commanded them to. And so they did, their own screams mingling with the humans on the stones. The Master made sure every one of the rulers watched as he devoured the still-warm hearts. The fey had chosen their closest human companions, as the Starveling knew they would. He knew that the human hearts would be filled with all the emotions he coveted, happiness, love, and in the end... fear. He became obsessed with the tithe, and only fed from the sacrificial hearts. He became withered, bone-thin with horrifying, sharpened teeth. He came to be known by a new name.

"The fey thought they had won the war, ended slavery and tyranny in Airodion. But it was only the beginning. The pain of the separation, watching the trust in their human companions' eyes even as they plunged the knife into their chests, the hate that grew in the humans' hearts, all of it was agony to bear. Some of the rulers went mad. Others slit their own throats. Some pushed that pain deep inside them until only darkness remained."

Finder's arms tightened around her.

"That's not what the humans were led to believe at all," Larken's voice came out a rasp. Her mind whirled, trying to absorb all the information the fey had told her. "We were told that the Popes rose to power while Aleea and Asphalion were fighting. The Popes convinced Aleea to beg for her brother's forgiveness, and as a sign of Asphalion's good will, he allowed four girls to enter the faery realm each year to experience the magic for themselves and to help the fey with a special task. I know about the Starveling now, and the true reason the girls are chosen, but is nothing the humans were told the truth?" Another thought struck her. "And you said nothing about the Starveling only choosing girls—you said the first tithe was just the humans who were closest to the fey rulers."

She had been so overwhelmed by the sheer amount of information over the past few days that the question had almost slipped from her mind: why were only girls offered up for the tithe?

Another question lingered in the back of her mind, one she was not quite ready to ask. About why Finder and the other court rulers chose the girls they did. Finder had mentioned the strong emotions humans felt and how the Starveling fed upon those, but Larken knew if she asked him, if she asked why he had chosen Brigid, she would have to think about her friend's final moments on the altar, of the Starveling eating her heart. The precious memories she had of her friend would be spoiled by thoughts of her death. And those memories were already tarnished enough by their fight, by the last words they had spoken to each other. Larken recoiled from those thoughts, shoving them back into a dark corner of her mind. Later. She would deal with them later.

"I believe that the humans are offered a half-truth by the Popes," Finder said. "Your creation story is filled with war and greed, the jealousy of ancient beings and the dark forces they used to bring themselves power. And in the end, our two realms were split—after which the human world turned to chaos and a theocracy was born. To your Popes, the splitting of our world *was* the beginning of Ellevere—as they named it, for that is when the Order began."

His arm brushed against hers as he rubbed his chin. "And you are right—the tithe does not specify that we must only select girls. Though we communicate with your Popes, they do not tell us everything. They told us that they would comply with the Starveling's demand—as long as they were compensated with money and magical gifts to bolster their growing empire. Another one of their conditions was that only young girls between the ages of twelve and eighteen would be chosen. I'm glad you told us fully what the Popes told you—otherwise I never would have known. I've never spoken our true history to the Chosen girls, for fear of scaring them."

Again, Brigid appeared in Larken's mind. She hadn't known what was coming. Larken couldn't decide if that was better or worse.

"The Popes wanted to link the tithe to their religion to solidify the Order of the Twins," Larken realized. "Believing that the tithe was good kept the humans complacent and happy, which made things easier for both the Popes and the Starveling."

"Yes," Finder agreed sadly. "Both the Starveling and the Popes believed it was better for the girls to feel happy until the very end. The Starveling is a beast of old, and he thrives off of fear and torment, but from humans, the most desirable emotion they can feel is happiness, for he can feel none. Humans are so fleeting, a mere flash of light in the dark stretch of eternity, but their passions burn bright. When he feasts on their hearts, he feasts on that, too."

So, it was completely the Popes' idea to offer up girls for the tithe. Larken's very being stung at the betrayal—how was it fair that men were bypassed the pain of the Choosing Ceremony? Even though the girls believed they would live a better life in the land of the fey, Larken knew now that the girls who were chosen were more apprehensive than they let on. Rosin proved that. They were still frightened at the thought of having to leave their homes and families behind.

Larken hadn't thought much about the exclusion of men from the Choosing Ceremony. According to the Popes, it was Aleea's jealous nature as a woman that caused the fight in the first place—which is why Asphalion made the requirement that it be young girls, before they reached womanhood, that could enter his realm. And the true puppet master, the Starveling, had no reason to refuse.

But why did the Popes tell their subjects that girls got to enter the faery realm as a sign of Asphalion's forgiveness?

Control. The answer sank into Larken's mind. They wanted to control the women. If Aleea was known to be prone to jealousy, even violence, then why would human girls not be the same? Being forced to participate in the ceremonies, allowing families to enter their daughters in exchange for coin—it was all to subdue them. To show women that they were never in control, that everything a woman achieved was just because of a man—just like Aleea was only forgiven after her brother deemed her worthy.

The Popes' betrayal struck her deeply. Women in Ellevere didn't have many opportunities for jobs or education; their main purpose in the eyes of the Order was to reproduce and create more members of the faith. The Black Guard allowed women to join, but only if they were barren.

Larken had always known she would have a difficult time studying cartography. People from Ballamor looked down on her for pursuing what they saw as such a strange career, and the Order only saw her as a useful member of society if she could bear children. Unless a woman showed signs of an undeniable talent in some profession, she could do little else besides aiding her husband in his job. The Choosing Ceremony was one of the only good things they were offered, and even that had been a lie.

"It's a punishment," Larken whispered. "The Popes are punishing us for being women—and offer us up to the Starveling under the guise of it being a great honor." Her companions looked at her silently, unable to offer her any words of comfort. "But how did they convince people that the tithe was good in the first place? After the humans and fey were separated, it wasn't as if the humans simply forgot the wars and the time they spent with the fey."

Finder shifted. "I could guess at some of the methods they used. Lies. Fear. As I said, when the Popes rose to power it was a time of chaos, and in chaos people cling to stability, wherever that stability lies. The Popes saw the fear in their people's eyes and turned it into something good— an elaborate ceremony and a promise of a better life."

"People believe what is easiest to believe," Madden added softly. "And sanctuary is easier to believe than death."

Larken's stomach twisted. "The humans have a story from one of the first tithes, that the sister of a Chosen girl, Laila, followed her kin into the faery realm and saw that she was safe." Swallowing her bile, she said, "Was that a lie, too? Or a deception—a glamour of some sort?"

Finder looked as though he was unable to continue, so it was Saja who supplied: "The Popes made a deal with the fey that another human should be allowed to enter Airodion besides the Chosen girl—and she should be glamoured with an illusion to believe that what the fey were doing was good."

"Then she could be used as an example and to prevent others from going after the girls," Larken surmised. "That explains how strange I felt around the bridge—and why the members of the guard went mad when they returned. The fey placed glamour around the bridge, right? To ward off any humans who entered and convince them to return home?"

"Clever girl," Dahey murmured, his first words during this entire exchange. "How did you even overcome the spell? It's nearly impossible without proper training."

Larken frowned as the image of Snowfoot galloping off through the trees after her fall came back to her. "I'm not sure. My mount spooked at something." Her eyes widened as she put it together. "He spooked at the Fomari. And then I fell and hit my head. I remember it hurt so badly I could think of nothing else but the pain."

Dahey smiled. "That's how you broke through the illusion. Physical pain or sensations that are not intended to be part of the glamour can bring someone out."

Larken remembered how holding Dahey's hand had helped to ground her during Madden's episode. "Would I have been stuck in there forever?" she asked. A few members of the Guard had made it out, but Larken wasn't convinced that she would have escaped, especially after seeing Madden's powerful glamour.

"No. The intention of the illusion was to make any humans who made it into Airodion return home. If you resisted for too long, it might have muddled your brain—glamour does have a stronger effect on humans, especially since they have no training. But that glamour was only in a certain area surrounding the bridge, eventually it would have convinced you to return home, or if you kept traveling, you might have been able to make it through. Albeit with a bit of a scrambled brain."

"I want you to train me," she blurted. Dahey's brows lifted. "I don't want to be caught unawares by glamour ever again. I want to know how to fight it—to see through it."

"Don't ask for something you can't handle," Dahey said, flashing her a devilish grin. Larken couldn't help her blush.

"Dahey is a ruthless teacher," Finder warned. "Better for me or Saja to teach you."

Larken didn't miss how he hadn't mentioned Madden. "No," she stated. "I want him. He can be as ruthless as he wants. I need to be tougher, in a world like this."

"It seems I may have underestimated you, my lady." Dahey bowed his head to her, but he never broke eye contact. She finally had to look away from his brown gaze.

"I can't believe the Black Guard doesn't know more about glamour," Larken murmured. "How can they hope to prevent the fey from crossing if they don't know the full extent of their powers?"

"Prevent the fey from crossing?" Finder shook his head. "Only the court rulers are permitted to cross the bridges."

"Then why allow any human to cross?" Larken frowned.

Finder shrugged. "An unavoidable flaw in the Master's magic, I assume. While he could specify that only court rulers were allowed to cross, he did not know which human they would pick, and therefore had to open the gateway for all of them."

Another lie the Popes had told the humans. An endless stream of them, and for what? All of it for power. Heat rose beneath her skin, so hot she felt feverish with rage. The Starveling manipulated the fey. The Popes manipulated the humans. All of them were connected but torn apart—forced into the darkness where the only light were tyrants masquerading as a theocracy and a king.

The humans had been deceived so many times, from the first tithe all the way to Rosin. And yet, the fey had suffered, too. Was it worse to be hated by the humans as they laid them on the altar, or loved by them?

She wanted to hate the fey—she *had* to hate them after what they'd done. Finder had murdered her friend. But he had suffered for it. Suffered for years. Did that matter? She didn't know anymore.

But something about she and her companions sharing their history had shifted something inside her. Though she had known about the Starveling before, she had always seen Finder as manipulative as any other person in power in her world. She saw him as deceiving the humans with his powers and offering them to the Starveling while bemoaning the fact that he had no other choice. But now she saw something within him—within all of them, that showed her that they were all pawns. Finder was just a piece being moved around in this game. As influenced by the secrets hiding in the past as she was.

"I know why the Popes didn't tell us about the fey and humans living together," Larken said. "The Starveling didn't want the fey and humans to rise up against him, and neither do the Popes. They don't want us to believe we could have allies in another realm, that we could ever rise up against them. They want us to feel alone."

Finder was quiet for a beat. "Well, you are not alone anymore, Larken. We have just shared our entire history with you—and you have done the same for us. Think of all we have learned, and how we will share it. Neither of our worlds will ever be the same."

And there was the weight of all of it, the weight of knowing she was the only human alive who knew these histories fully, who had talked with the fey themselves. She was more determined than ever to get home, to share this story with others, and to make the Popes reveal their secrets to their subjects. Four centuries worth of secrets.

If she and her companions killed the Starveling, then there would no longer be a reason to conduct Choosing Ceremonies. The Popes would have no choice but to explain themselves.

"I think... I think we are very alike, Finder," Larken said. "More so than I ever could have imagined. I'm not the leader of my people, but I care for them. I want them to be free of the Popes—of all the beings who oppress them. And I know you want the same, to free your people from the Starveling. But I'm seeing now they are tied so completely that if we destroy one..."

"We destroy the other," Finder finished.

"Yes," Larken said, "I should not have been so quick to leave this burden for all of you to deal with." She glanced around at each of her companions. "But now I understand just how intertwined the Starveling and the Popes are. I understand now why you want so desperately for your subjects to be free. So, I'm going to help you in whatever way I can. I'm going to fight with you however I am able. Because we have to end this together."

Finder dipped his head, his lips grazing her ear as he said, "It is an honor to have you by my side. An honor to be bound to your soul." Heat bloomed inside her, though this one had nothing to do with rage.

"Oh yes." Madden grinned. "I'm with her. Let's spill some beast king blood!" He whooped.

Dahey and Saja exchanged grins, copying their friend's raucous cries.

Finder whooped as well, jostling her. He steadied her in a heartbeat, and when she turned, his cheeks were pink with embarrassment. But she only laughed and let out a wild cry of her own.

It felt good—like finally getting to exhale after holding her breath. She was terrified, horrified by the lies the humans believed. But she knew the truth now. The thought of the Popes and the Starveling being enraged by what she and the fey knew, about how they planned to tell the world and expose their poisonous leaders, made her unbelievably happy.

Larken and her companions' cries soared through the air, so disruptive that the very birds took to the skies to escape it.

CHAPTER FIFTEEN

The group's joyous mood clung to them, and Madden started up a song, accompanying it by beating his hand against his thigh. The way the fey sang was personal, deeper and more intimate than the way humans did, and yet it was light with mirth at the same time.

As they rode on, the songs turned more frivolous and dirty. So much so that Larken's face burned red.

"Another round, lads?" Madden crowed to a collective groan from everyone in the party. Truthfully, Larken could have listened to the song a hundred times without tiring of it. All of them had voices beautiful enough to put any human minstrel out of business, but Dahey was particularly gifted. His voice wasn't the deep, husky tenor she so often heard in human men. Instead, it was light and airy, still reaching the low notes but without the gruffness. She wished they would pick a song where he could sing more than just the chorus.

"How about a song about a—"

"Or," Finder interrupted, "we could ride in silence." He gave Madden a pointed look.

Larken's heart sank with disappointment. She had never been that interested in singing, but hearing the fey sing was something else entirely. Knowing that so few humans had ever heard faery songs was humbling.

"Nonsense," Madden scoffed. "We'll just change the tone a bit, eh? I tire of all these songs about female lovers. Where's one about a nice, long—"

This time, Finder cut him off with a pointed cough, but when she turned around to look at him there was amusement in his eyes. Larken hid her smile.

"Well, if Larken hasn't gathered that you prefer males by now, Madden..." Dahey rolled his eyes. *Males.* Not men. Larken still hadn't gotten used to the word. Here, the fey were not men or women—not human. Fey.

Larken frowned at Madden. "I thought you said you had a daughter?" But how could he, if he preferred males?

"Not that I couldn't have a family with a male," Madden corrected gently, "but yes, I did have a daughter with a female." He gave a small grimace of pain, but it quickly disappeared. He shot a look at Dahey. "Because I don't *prefer* males. In fact, I appreciate both males and females quite equally. And I would say they appreciate me equally in return." He winked at her.

Larken blinked at his honesty. "And are...male and male," she paused, "or female and female...pairings...allowed? In Airodion?"

The Popes strictly forbid such relationships, mainly under the guise that such pairings could produce no children that could be brought into the Order of the Twins. They cared nothing about bastard children—they encouraged them, even, as long as they were taught the ways of the Order.

Madden chuckled. "Of course. The courts would never presume to tell their subjects who they are allowed to love."

Larken felt Finder nod his head behind her.

Madden's face hardened. "Though I take it Ellevere does not share this idea?"

"No," she answered. "It does not." For all the savageries that took place in Airodion, it seemed as though Ellevere had just as many, though different in name.

They stopped for the night only when the sun slipped entirely from the sky. Larken sat down heavily, massaging her aching calves. She suspected that the fey had no issue with riding for days on end and stopped only for her sake.

Finder and Dahey chatted as they rubbed their horses down. Saja and Madden sparred with two long sticks, their footfalls dancer-like across the forest floor. Saja whacked Madden lightly upside the head with his stick, making him release an overly dramatic wail. A smile tugged at her lips, but a pang of loneliness shot through her chest, too. She wished she had friendships like the ones between the members of the *dornán*.

You did. But she's gone now.

She felt closer to all of the fey now, but it couldn't compare to the friendship she and Brigid had shared. Larken tried to imagine how Brigid would have interacted with the fey. At this exact time a year ago, Brigid had been with them, though surely, they would have reached Shadeshelm by now. Had Brigid asked about the other Chosen girls, about the special task and the life she would get to lead? A smile quivered at Larken's lips. Of course, Brigid would have. She loved to bombard people with questions, and probably would have pestered them with more questions than Larken had. Whenever she and Brigid had been together, Brigid had dominated the conversations. Brigid knew Larken so well she often talked for her when they were with other people. Perhaps Larken had only seen herself as quiet because she had always had Brigid by her side to do the talking for her.

A hard lump climbed up her throat. She wanted to ask the fey about Brigid, but at the same time she didn't want to hear them talk about her. They had all led Brigid to her death, and Finder had killed her. The thought lingered in her mind like a bruise, the ache spreading whenever she touched it.

In her mind, her memories of Brigid were untainted. She could visit them whenever she wanted, turning back the clock to exact moments she wanted to relive. It killed her to know that Finder had been there in Brigid's final moments, that he had his own memories of her. If Larken spoke to him, if she heard about his time with Brigid, his memory of Brigid and her death would only ruin Larken's own memories of her. It would bleed into her mind like an ink stain, destroying everything beneath it.

Her friendship with Brigid hadn't been perfect—she knew that. Their fight was proof enough of that. But in her memories it was, and now that Brigid was gone, all Larken could remember was the good. She was too afraid to give that up. Too afraid to unpack the final things they had said to each other. So, she chose to only remember the good.

She was struck with the desire to spend a moment alone, so she murmured something about relieving herself and disappeared into the bushes. A sigh of relief escaped her as the pressure on her bladder ebbed away. She had long since abandoned her embarrassment at asking the group to stop in order for her to tend to her needs. Still, she made sure never to wander more than a few feet from them in case some beast decided to attack her as she squatted.

Finder had similar ideas of an ambush, and it took more than a few tries to convince him not to hover protectively around her while she relieved herself. The first time she excused herself to the woods and hiked up her skirts, she had turned to find the green-eyed faery anxiously watching her—terrified that the thought of her leaving the group without an escort. "Mortified" didn't even begin to cover it, nor did howling at him seem to make matters better. At her shrieks to cover his eyes, Finder had closed them and spun around, careening into a low hanging tree branch. It was the first graceless move she'd seen him make. Lured by the sound of Finder's loud cursing, the rest of the dornán had arrived, all of them wisely hiding their smiles and laughter until they were out of earshot. Mostly.

They'd all come to an agreement not to disturb Larken when she took to the woods, as long as she stayed within her sight of the group. Words like "modesty" and "privacy" were lost on her faery companions, but they respected her wishes on the subject, nonetheless.

Larken pushed her way through the bushes back into the clearing. She walked over to the horses, patting Rhylla as she grazed. Finder, Dahey and Madden now lounged around a cookfire nearby, but Saja stood nearby, talking quietly with Arobhinn. She went and greeted the big horse next; she had developed a bit of a soft spot for him.

She patted his neck, laughing as he lipped at her hair. His nose was as soft as the finest velvet, though his whiskers tickled her fiercely. The tender moment from the beast made her throat close.

Saja noticed her expression. "Are you all right?"

"I just don't feel like I belong here," Larken admitted. "With any of you on this journey. I want to help, I want to fight the Starveling. I just feel so useless."

Saja turned to look at her, brows knitting together. "There is no one else I would rather go on such a journey with."

Larken stared at him, waiting for him to tell her it was some kind of joke. But he just gazed back at her, dark eyes serious.

"You saved Finder's life. You saved it because you didn't believe he deserved to die. You helped me when I was at my weakest simply because it was the right thing to do. That *means* something. It doesn't matter what skills you have—skills can be learned. It doesn't matter what you look like—that's all chance. But your heart, your sense of justice and respect for life...that cannot be taught."

Larken blinked, shocked at how precisely Saja had picked up on her insecurities. But he had chosen the perfect words to bring her comfort. Arobhinn huffed, blowing strands of hair across her face. She smiled.

"Arobhinn agrees."

Larken laughed, patting the big horse as he lowered his head to graze.

"He likes you," Saja chuckled.

The statement made her smile again. "I like him, too."

"I have not seen him take to anyone this quickly since my lover, Kahal," Saja said. A flash of pain lit his eyes, but just as quickly it was gone. "I was convinced Arobhinn loved him more than me."

"I haven't heard you speak of him—this Kahal," Larken said.

"Ah." Saja fingered Arobhinn's curly mane. "That is because we are no longer together." He smiled grimly. "The problem with being immortal is that you have to deal with past relationships for an eternity."

Larken shuddered in sympathy.

Saja smiled. "Yet there are worse things, I think."

"Oi, Saja, hurry up, we're hungry!" Madden shouted.

The three other fey sat expectantly around the small fire.

"Insufferable," Saja muttered.

After they'd eaten, Finder and Dahey sparred around the fire. While Saja and Madden's sparring had a playful air, Finder and Dahey were vicious, holding nothing back. They fought with their own swords, the steel glinting in the moonlight. Dahey wielded an exquisite blade with gilded autumn leaves forming a guard around the pommel. Tiny gems glinted in the leaves—rubies, amber, and carnelian. Finder's was a plain, two-handed sword with a single green stone set in the pommel. Both fey were whip-quick, gliding through the grass like snakes before lashing out at each other. Larken caught herself holding her breath, sure the two males would tear each other to pieces.

"Dahey is the Autumn Court's prize sword master," Madden said from where he lounged beside her. "The courts host competitions from time to time, and Dahey is undefeated."

Larken could see why. Dahey's muscles clenched and relaxed, each movement seeming more effortless than the last. He touched Finder again and again with his sword, each time feather-light, but in places that could kill should he use more force. Though Finder had several pounds of muscle on Dahey as well as a few inches in height, he was no match for his cousin.

"Finder is the only one who poses even a bit of a challenge for him," Madden continued. Finder landed a mark occasionally, but nowhere near as many as his kin.

"Dahey loves swordplay, but he only began competing to gain attention from his parents. Pricks, the both of them." Madden shook his head, lowering his voice. "He can occasionally earn their pride, but never their love."

Larken's heart gave a painful tug. She knew what it was like to have a passion, to have something that pulled at the strings of one's very soul. But what she could not imagine was having parents who did not support and love her no matter what.

When her gaze returned to Dahey, her vision was stained with pity.

But then another thought came to her. "Finder said Dahey's father was Prince before him. But how is that possible? Why isn't Dahey the prince?"

Dahey's eyes flew to hers, but before she could say anything else he launched himself at Finder, forcing his cousin to step back.

"The position of court ruler is not passed from one member of a ruling family to another. Each time a prince or princess dies or becomes unfit to rule, that court's magic chooses another ruler. It's rare for it to remain in the same family—which is why it was such a shock when it chose Finder. Though they grew up in court royalty, Dahey and Finder never expected the magic to pass to either of them."

Larken studied Dahey. Was he jealous that his father's magic had passed to Finder and not him? He loved his court, and there was clear tension between him and Finder because of it.

"Did Finder want to become Prince? Even though it was unlikely?"

"No." Madden's gaze turned toward Finder. "He never wanted it. That is the risk that comes with magic choosing the next ruler. It might stop a family from monopolizing power in the court, but there is always the chance that the magic will choose an unwilling host. It has happened before, and it will happen again. But Finder has handled the burden well."

Madden's eyes glowed with pride for his prince.

"Everyone says he has all this power," Larken said carefully, "but I rarely see him use it. Is it because he didn't want to become Prince?" The memory of Finder pushing away the flames came to her mind.

"The transition of power can be difficult for a new ruler," Madden explained. "Finder was completely overwhelmed when it chose him. He lashed out, and there was a terrible accident. He's never forgiven himself."

Finder often looked like he was in pain whenever he used his powers. The accident had to be the reason why. "What happened?"

"That is Finder's secret to tell," Madden said, his voice gentle.

Larken swallowed her disappointment.

"Yield," Finder said, baring his teeth at his cousin in a fierce grin. Dahey swept his sword in a flourish and bowed.

The two males collapsed by the fire, both of them now panting and shining with sweat.

"Larken, teach us a song from Ballamor," Madden said. He tossed a small carved figure back and forth in his hands, the object flying through the air too quickly for Larken to get a good look.

Larken laughed, certain he was joking, but Madden just looked at her expectantly.

She shook her head. "I can't sing. I'll sound pathetic compared to you."

Finally, Madden was able to bully it out of her.

"A-roving, a-roving, a-roving we will go. Across the hills, across the dales, a-roving we will go," she sang. She winced as her voice cracked—her voice was too low for the soprano required of the song. She sounded like a child, and embarrassment would have stopped her mid-song were it not for the sight of Finder and Dahey exchanging grins, beginning to tap out the beat on their thighs. The fey caught on quickly to the melody; it was a nursery rhyme, no less. After a few rounds, Larken couldn't keep the smile from her face. Saja added a hum and Dahey accompanied her until they had formed a merry little troupe.

"A-roving, a-roving, a-roving we will go. Through the woods, down the trails, a-roving we will go."

The horses, grazing nearby, twitched their ears at the sound of the singing. Arobhinn bobbed his head up and down, sending them all into fits of laughter.

"He thinks the song is for him!" Madden gasped, wiping a tear from his eye.

"Arobhinn, Arobhinn, Arobhinn he does know. How to buck, and how to kick, land Saja on his nose," Madden added the last chorus, and Arobhinn's accompanying whinny echoed with their laughter through the trees.

CHAPTER SIXTEEN

The ring laying in Dahey's palm glinted in the morning light.

Larken squinted, studying every aspect of the ring, searching for any flaw or blemish that would alert her that it was glamour. She found nothing.

"Summoned," she decided.

Finder, Saja, and Madden gave a collective groan. She knew it wasn't directed at her—but at the huge boost to Dahey's ego he received every time she failed another one of his tests. Dahey grinned. The ring melted into a silver pool, then disappeared. She had failed to see through the glamour yet again.

Glamour or Summoned was a game her faery companions had all played as children. It was simple enough—one of the fey would either summon an object or create one from glamour, and it was Larken's job to guess which it was. She had yet to get one right.

Larken gritted her teeth. "I don't understand how you all see through it so easily."

"Again," Dahey commanded. He held out his palm, revealing a smooth stone streaked with black.

She studied the rock, trying to find any holes in the illusion that she

133

could grab on to. The rock was a strange color, perhaps that was part of the magic that stuck out to her.

"Glamour," Larken said, more certain this time.

Dahey tossed the rock into the air and it disappeared. "Summoned."

"You'll get it eventually," Finder reassured her. "It's a difficult skill to master."

"No, she just isn't trying that hard," Dahey quipped. "Your life could depend on you figuring out if something is glamour or not, never forget that."

"He's right," Larken said glumly. "Give me another."

Dahey nodded in approval. He held out his hand again, and a book appeared in his grasp. The spine read *The Beings and Beasts of Airodion*.

"Summoned," Finder breathed in her ear. She scowled, swatting him hard on the arm.

"Good girl," Dahey said. "Don't trust his help. I've fooled him before."

"Prat," Finder muttered, rubbing his arm.

Larken ignored him, focusing on the book. Her gut reaction told her it was summoned; why would Dahey bother creating an entire book from glamour? And Finder had said so as well, she should trust his judgement.

Something made her hesitate. A corner of the book's cover was bent backwards. But the very edges of the corner appeared to be blurry. She narrowed her eyes, refusing to look away from the blurred corner. A real book couldn't be blurry. Immediately, the whole book flickered.

"Glamour!" she shrieked, pointing a finger. "It's glamour!"

Dahey smiled. The book crumpled into ash, then disappeared.

Madden and Saja clapped.

"What gave it away?" Dahey asked.

"The corner was bent strangely, and then, it's hard to describe." Larken narrowed her eyes. "But the whole book became blurry, and then it seemed to flicker out of existence for a moment."

Dahey nodded in approval. "You found a flaw, and once you latched on to it, it became impossible for the illusion to hold. Excellent work."

Larken beamed.

She played a few more rounds of Glamour or Summoned with Dahey and then Finder, and she grew better each time. Still, it was difficult, and she soon became tired from the mental strain.

The precision to which the fey could create illusions was astounding and frightening. It disturbed her that she might not be able to distinguish with true certainty when her senses were her own and when they were deceiving her.

They rode on, the horses' hoofbeats and breathing the loudest sounds in the chill air. The trees shed their bright colors and turned into a murky brown. The horses began to trip over sharp stones and gnarled shrubs as the underbrush became thicker and harder to navigate. A few times, Larken saw a parallel path that looked easier to maneuver. At first, she bit down her suggestion, certain that the fey would know the woods better than she did. But when Rhylla's hoof caught for the third time she could take no more.

"There's an easier path there," Larken said, pointing to where the underbrush thinned slightly.

"You have a keen eye, Larken," Finder said, steering Rhylla onto the new path. The terrain was still rough, but not as bad as before. A small glimmer of pride sparked within her.

The brown trunks faded to black and emitted a rotten stench. Larken shivered whenever a passing branch skimmed her face or arms. Trees were living, growing things, and yet here they were not alive. The branches were as cold as ice, and the sensation that they were still touching her lingered long after they had passed.

Larken wondered if they had somehow entered a gateway into the Twins' Hell. The air was both cold and hot, terribly uncomfortable and ever shifting. Even her faery companions seemed similarly affected. Their brows glistened with sweat.

On they rode, the ground squelching as the dirt turned into mud. The faintly sweet scent of decay crept toward her on every stale breeze.

The horses struggled, ignoring the sharp bushes that racked their sides with relentless claws. Countless scrapes covered their elegant faces, some of them dripping with blood.

Finder dismounted, drawing his sword and hacking through a bramble patch that ensnared Rhylla. Once he had cleared a path, he turned toward the horse and placed his hands on her bloody face.

"The Priestesses corrupt this land like a tumor." He frowned. "You should have told me about this, Dahey."

"It was in the report," Dahey replied cooly.

Finder dipped his head, turning back to Rhylla. He gently brushed his fingers across her head, and every cut he crossed over closed up, completely healed. Rhylla stiffened, her nostrils flaring.

Larken bit her lip. "You're hurting her."

"I'm healing her." Finder lifted his hands from Rhylla's face, and she relaxed.

Of course. Finder had mentioned having healing powers.

"I have the power to heal, but I cannot take away the pain that accompanies it. Speeding up the healing process only magnifies the pain. If I heal a severe wound too quickly, the pain could kill them."

Finder helped Larken off Rhylla's back. She winced as the mud swallowed her up to her shins. Dahey, Madden, and Saja waited as Finder healed the cuts on their horses' faces, their muscles loosening once their mounts were cared for.

Finder and Dahey cut a path with their swords, stopping only when they reached a small glen. Black mushrooms with speckled grey caps clung to the roots of the trees like festering sores.

"We're here," Dahey said, nodding at the center of the glen.

A dark hole, barely wide enough for a grown man to squeeze through, gaped in the ground. An utterly rancid odor rose from it. Blood roared in Larken's ears.

"A tunnel leads to their den below ground. One way in—one way out. No one leaves without the Priestesses' permission."

"I don't like this," Saja stated. His hand hovered above the quiver of bolts at his side.

"The Priestesses are only dangerous if we don't give them what they want," Dahey said. "If we uphold our end of the bargain, they will uphold theirs. They are as bound to their oaths as any faery."

Finder looked at Larken, waiting for her to choose. She didn't have to follow. She didn't have to do this. But she was a part of this now. And the more she learned about the ancient, dangerous beings of Airodion, the more she could warn the humans back home. Dahey had visited the Priestesses before. He would know how to handle them. She gave a jerky nod of her head.

"Let's go," she said.

The darkness of the forest was nothing compared to the immediate pitch black they were thrown into. Larken felt too big for the tunnel, and the way her sides brushed the walls made her skin crawl.

They crept deeper, Dahey leading the way. Her hands passed over stringy lumps in the dirt as she felt her way along. The tunnel was at a decline, so she and her companions often slid into each other. Her hand caught on a stone, fingers sinking into two deep holes. She shook her hand free, trying to ignore the feeling of slimy moss giving way beneath her fingers.

The tunnel seemed to stretch on forever. One thing was clear: once they were in, they would not be leaving with any haste.

"Almost there," Dahey whispered.

Larken could practically feel Madden and Saja stiffen behind her, aching to draw their weapons but unable to do so in the cramped space.

Up ahead, Larken could make out a faint glow. They crawled on, her need to get out of the tunnel almost blinding her. She would do anything if she could just get out, if the darkness and stench would end.

Finder gave a startled cry, and Larken yelped as she began sliding down a steep slope. She tried to find a grip, but there was nothing for her to hold. She grabbed a root, but it snapped, falling along with her. She tumbled out of the tunnel and sprawled onto the floor. Larken looked down at the root clutched in her hand.

Not a root—a rib bone, bits of flesh still clinging to it. She shrieked, flinging the bone from her grasp.

It bounced twice before coming to a rest at the feet of the three cloaked figures standing before them.

CHAPTER SEVENTEEN

Larken's wild glance around the room told her two things:

One, the den was kept from collapsing by thousands of bones plastered into the mud.

Two, the Dark Priestesses were creatures who belonged deep within the bowels of the Twin's Hell.

They had grotesque, misshapen faces, with bulbous noses, short foreheads, and heavily sunken cheeks. Their grey skin stretched thinly over their bones. Strings of greasy black hair hung from their heads. And most unnerving of all, where eyes should have been there were only deep slits.

Just when Larken thought they could not possibly become any more terrifying, they opened their mouths and began to speak.

"We meet again, Dahey of Autumn." They spoke all at once, their voices low and guttural. "What brings you here?" Their teeth flashed—long and thin like a rat's.

"We have come to ask you something, wise ones." Dahey's voice was steady, though the white knuckles clenched on his sword betrayed his fear.

"The price," they replied, "will be steep." They smiled one by one.

Finder stepped forward. "I am willing to pay the price. What would you ask of me?"

"Three questions we shall ask, and three answers you shall return. Then, you may ask the same of us."

"Swear it," Finder said.

The Dark Priestesses tilted their heads. "We swear to uphold our end of the bargain."

Finder nodded in consent. "And I swear to uphold mine, so long as it does not endanger my companions or the Autumn Court."

"Agreed."

A tingle went through Larken. She could feel the weight of the words upon her skin.

"Let us begin," the Priestesses said. "Which one of your *dornán* is the weakest?"

A muscle twitched in Finder's jaw. Larken's heart thundered in her chest, the silence stretching as Finder still did not answer.

"I can't—"

"You can, and you will," they said, a smile playing at all of their lips. How could he answer a question like that?

"Saja," Finder murmured at last. Larken did not turn, did not dare to look and see Saja's reaction, but she swore she could hear his shoulders cave under the blow Finder had dealt him. His own leader, his prince, had said such a thing.

How could Finder say that?

But how could he not?

The Priestesses slowly turned, their gaze fixating upon Larken.

"Leave her out of this," Finder warned. "Your bargain was with me."

The Dark Priestesses smiled as one. "On the contrary, Prince, it was with all of you. Any of you. Whomever we choose."

Larken bit her lip. What could they ask of her that would be of any interest? Still, perhaps it was better this way. Finder was an immortal faery prince with an entire court to protect as well as powerful magic at his disposal. They could ask him for something that would cause irreparable damage to Airodion. She, on the other hand, was just a mortal girl.

The Priestesses examined her with those gaping slits. Larken resisted the urge to fidget.

"You were not the one he chose," they said finally. "A mortal girl, untouched by fate, who took those strings and tangled herself all the same."

Sounds about right, Larken admitted, though *strangled* might have been a better word than *tangled.* She didn't dare ask how they knew. A cold sweat dampened her neck. What if they asked about the life debt? That kind of knowledge, in their hands…they could sell it to the highest bidder. Other courts, creatures Larken couldn't imagine…

"Please," Finder ground out, losing his careful calm, "do not bring her into this."

"She brought herself into this. And she will answer what we ask of her." They smiled wickedly. "If you could only see one of them again, who would you choose: Brigid, or your family?"

Larken's mind seemed to speed up and slow down all at once. Could the Priestesses have some kind of power that could allow her to see Brigid again?

Brigid is dead, she reminded herself. But how many impossible things had she seen in Airodion by now? Could she say for certain that some kind of magic couldn't bring Brigid back to her? She hadn't considered it, not when Finder had reiterated so firmly that Brigid was gone.

He swore she was dead. But she had no idea what powers the Priestesses possessed. They had helped the Starveling in the war; they had to possess magic she couldn't even begin to comprehend. She couldn't say for certain that these creatures would not be able to allow her to see her friend again.

This could mean that she had a chance to make things right with Brigid.

But what if this was the Priestesses' way of telling her that her family was in danger? That they would fail, and the Starveling would come and destroy Ballamor? What if she got to see Brigid again… but at the cost of her family's lives?

She swallowed. It was too quiet. Everyone was looking at her. She couldn't answer something like that. Not when she had no idea what the consequences were.

Larken was locked deep inside herself, drowning in her memories. Papa, bandaging her up after every scrape, Mama, always offering her steady advice and a shoulder to cry on. But Larken had followed Brigid into the faery realm all that time ago—or had it been only days?—and she had left Mama and Papa behind. She had known in her heart that leaving them would not be as hard as never seeing Brigid again. Larken's throat burned. How could she think that? What kind of daughter chose her friend over her family?

But if she didn't take this chance, she worried that her guilt over Brigid would swallow her whole.

She couldn't lie. Well, she could. But if the Priestesses somehow sensed her lie, she could endanger her companions. Finder had answered the impossible, and she had to as well. Whatever it cost her.

"Brigid," she whispered. "I would choose to see Brigid again."

She waited for something to happen. Despite her doubt, she still held her breath, waiting for Brigid to appear.

Nothing.

Her heart sank, and she cursed herself for being naive enough to believe that they could bring her friend back from the dead. The Dark Priestesses licked their lips, like they could taste her disappointment.

The horrible beings looked to Dahey next, then Madden. Finally, they landed upon Saja.

"Do you swear to answer our question truthfully?" they asked him.

Saja nodded. "I swear it, so long as it does not endanger my prince or my court."

"Which other member of the *dornán* would you sacrifice, if it meant saving your prince's life?"

Saja paled. These questions the Dark Priestesses asked, they could ruin the *dornán*. They were designed to wreak as much emotional havoc as possible—not a price paid in flesh or bone, but in broken hearts and shattered fellowship.

Dahey had come here for a mere report? To collect information on the creatures that inhabited his prince's land? Dahey stood calmly before the Priestesses, his shoulders squared, but sweat dampened his brow, betraying his nervousness. Larken shuddered. He must truly love his court, and Finder, if he was willing to come here again.

"D—Dahey," Saja stuttered after a long pause. Dahey looked at Saja with an unreadable expression, saying nothing. She couldn't imagine how any of them were feeling, except that she could. A part of her felt cracked, twisted by answering their question, and she knew Finder and Saja felt the same. Still, she only had to answer for herself, while the Priestesses had pitted Finder and his *dornán* against each other.

She could only hope that it wouldn't destroy them.

"Enough." Finder pressed his lips together. "Three questions, asked and answered. Now, you must keep your promise."

The Priestesses bowed their heads.

"Can the Starveling be killed?" Finder asked.

Confusion prickled through her. They knew the Masters could be killed. Three of them had been killed during the first war. But Larken didn't know what power the Starveling could have amassed in the years since. Perhaps he *was* too powerful to be killed, now. Her stomach filled with dread.

The Priestesses paused, then replied, "Yes."

Finder's shoulders slumped in relief, as did Larken's. Their quest so far had not been for nothing. The Starveling could be destroyed. At least the answers she and her companions had surrendered had not been in vain. The Priestesses turned toward Larken, and panic flooded her again. What if she asked the wrong question? What if she—

"No, Dark Ones. I shall be asking the questions, as it was not specified who would do the questioning in return," Finder said. The Priestesses raised their lips in a snarl but said nothing.

"What power must we possess to destroy him?"

"Not power," they replied, baring their teeth. "A weapon."

"Where can we find such a weapon?"

The Priestesses considered this last question, the two on the outside turning slowly to face the one in the middle, who bowed her head, as if in...what? Sorrow? Resignation? Larken couldn't say.

"Givrain, do not speak," one of them hissed. It was the first time one of them had spoken on their own. Finder casually positioned himself in front of Larken, sensing the growing malice in the air.

"We have helped others before, why not them?" Givrain asked.

"Those who have come before did not ask how to bring down our king. They sought power only for themselves."

"He is not my king!" Givrain shrieked.

The three Priestesses fell into a fit of hisses and squawks, their words turning unintelligible.

"Time to leave." Saja placed his hand on Finder's arm.

"No," Finder growled. "We paid the price. They will give us the answer we are owed." He pulled away from Saja. "Where can we find this weapon?" he demanded.

Givrain shrank back, subdued by her siblings. The two remaining Priestesses turned on Finder.

"We knew arrogant fey would come asking questions." The Priestesses shuffled closer to Finder, and he raised his sword. "Our beneficent lord—the King of Kings, the Undying One—will not stand for it. And neither will we."

Larken's skin went cold.

"No. *No*," Dahey growled. "That wasn't the deal!"

"We don't want to fight," Finder warned. "Tell us what we wish to know and let us leave."

The two Priestesses smiled and shook their heads.

"You will die," they said. Then they lunged.

Finder shoved her behind him as Dahey lifted his sword. Givrain shrank back into the darkness as her sisters pulled blades of what looked like black glass from their robes and hurled themselves into battle. Madden and Saja battled one, Dahey and Finder the other. The two Priestesses were both wickedly fast despite their hobbled appearance, slicing with their knives and baring their teeth.

Saja leveled his crossbow, but the Priestesses were too quick. Madden lashed out at her scuttling body with his knives, but he couldn't land a blow.

Finder stumbled backwards as the other Priestess's knife sliced into his bicep—and into Larken's. Then the Priestess lunged at her, sinking rat-sharp teeth into her flesh. Larken screamed as pain lanced up her arm. Finder howled, feeling her injury as his own, and swung at the Priestess's unprotected back. She let go of Larken, her teeth stained with blood. Larken wailed as Finder cut at the Priestess again, but she continued to evade him. She launched herself at Dahey, who forced her away from Larken.

Larken clutched her arm with her right hand, cradling it as best she could as she dragged herself backwards. Tears of pain rolled down her cheeks and streams of fire shot up her arm.

*Get out of the way...I have to hide...*she thought.

Saja and Madden had managed to kill their Priestess who laid in a heap of rags and blood on the floor. Whatever Larken looked like must have alarmed them, for they came running toward her.

"Larken!" Madden crouched beside her, grabbing her by the shoulders. She hissed as he touched her arm and he released her immediately, but the pain did not stop. Oh, Twins, she was *on fire.*

Larken moaned. Dahey and Finder still battled the other Priestess, trying to keep her back. Finder grimaced in pain, his teeth clenched. She wanted to close her eyes—just for a moment.

"Go—*go!*" Madden told Saja. "I'll look after her."

Larken curled herself into a ball. She didn't remember sinking to the floor.

"Let me see it." Madden tried to pry her hand away from the bite. Larken shook her head. How was Finder still standing?

Madden forced her hand away, exposing a mess of linen and blood where the Priestess had bit her. He gently touched her arm below the bite, and Larken could not hold back her scream. He swore and released her.

"We need to get you out of here," he muttered. "Both of you." He lifted her into his arms. She moaned as the world spun out of focus. Shouts and clangs rang out as Finder and his *dornán* fought the Priestess.

"Finder!" Madden shouted. Finder turned to meet him, his eyes glassy with pain. "We need to leave. *Now.*"

"Wait, wait—" Givrain emerged from where she hid in the darkness.

Saja leveled his crossbow. Her sister still battled fiercely with Dahey. Givrain lifted her hands.

"Saja, help Dahey," Finder commanded. Saja immediately complied.

Givrain lowered her voice. "Deep within the Wyld, there lives a Guardian," she said. "A circle of mushrooms marks his prison." She pulled a bundle out of her robes and pressed it into Finder's hands. "A knife of great power," she hissed. "Alone, it will not be enough to defeat the Starveling. Bring it to the Guardian and he shall make it whole."

She pressed the sharp nail of her finger into Finder's temple. He staggered, his lips twisting into a silent cry. Givrain released him, and before any of them could blink, she scuttled up into the hole and disappeared.

Larken struggled to focus on Finder. She curled against Madden, her vision turning hazy.

"Finder, now!" Madden cried.

Finder swept his gaze over Larken and gave Madden a sharp nod. Then he turned, lifted a hand, and a white cylinder of flame blasted directly through the wall.

CHAPTER EIGHTEEN

When Finder lifted his hand and the flames roared to life, something tugged inside Larken, drawing her toward the fire. She lifted her hand to touch the flames, but they had already disappeared.

The remaining Priestess hissed, tearing toward the hole where Givrain had made her escape.

Saja fell to one knee and fired, the crossbow bolt hitting the Priestess in the back of her dark robes. Her arms flew wide and a cry tore from her throat before she fell to the floor, dead.

On the other side of the den lay a new tunnel directly to the surface. The mud had hardened and there were steps carved deep into its surface. Ash littered the stairs.

Saja lurched toward the tunnel where the last Priestess had disappeared, but Dahey grabbed his arm.

"She helped us," Dahey said. "Let her go."

"She could warn the Starveling," Saja growled.

"She just told us how to kill him," Dahey snapped.

Finder stumbled and Dahey caught him, his face paling.

"You're hurt, you bloody fool." Dahey pressed his fingers into Finder's arm and the muscles of the prince's neck bulged as he tried to withhold a scream. Larken's mouth fell open as the pain tore through her as well.

Dahey and Saja helped Finder up the stairs, Madden carrying Larken close behind them.

"She helped us," Finder gasped once they were out. "I don't know how, but when she touched me, she showed me where we must go. And she gave me this." Finder fell to his knees, pulling out the bundle that the Dark Priestess had given him.

Dahey unsheathed his sword and flipped the corners of the fabric back, revealing the weapon beneath.

The knife was simple yet stunning, made of some smooth material that Larken had no name for. It was opaque and transparent, shimmering and dull, opposites and equals all in one. An ornate hand guard swept around the hilt. Larken had never seen anything like it.

"She just… gave it to you?" Saja said, disbelief coloring his voice.

"You said she showed you where this Guardian was." Madden frowned. "How?"

"I don't know." Finder shook his head. "She touched me, and it was as though I was seeing the path from her eyes. I've never experienced anything like it."

"We have to trust her," Dahey said. "She gave us the knife. She wants to help us defeat the Starveling."

Madden and Saja frowned, clearly unconvinced.

"Dahey's… right," Larken gasped. "If she wanted us dead… she would have… attacked us, too. She wants… to help."

Twins, forming words had never been so difficult.

Stomach heaving, she twisted in Madden's arms and vomited, narrowly missing his boots. Madden cursed.

"Give her to me," Finder ordered, leaving the knife in the dirt. Dahey wrapped it up and tucked it away in his jerkin.

Madden hesitated. "You can't—"

Finder placed his shaking hands on her collarbone. His hands were cool. She flinched, but he murmured to her, trying to soothe her. She was far away, trapped in an abyss of her own pain. Every nerve in her body burned. She clutched at Madden's tunic, fear tingeing the edges of her agony. She was going to die. Oh, Twins, she didn't want to die, but the pain was so much.

Finder dropped his hands. They trembled slightly. "I can't pull the poison out. It is everywhere inside her."

He didn't have to add *and in me*.

"Hurts," she gasped.

"I know, love, I know." His breath came in short gasps. She wasn't alone. He felt it, too.

Finder tilted to the side. Saja caught him, sliding him to the ground. The prince leaned against Saja's legs, his eyes closing. Saja looked to Madden and Dahey, eyes wide with panic.

"They're in no state to travel," Madden said. "We'll take them to Shadeshelm, get a healer—"

"Don't be a fool," Dahey snapped. "Might I remind you that the tithe will be called at midnight only two days from now. Even with the horses, we'll barely make it to the Wyld and back to the Stone Circle."

"We know no healers in the Wyld."

"Perhaps the Guardian could heal them? Whoever he is?"

"Oh, yes, that's a fine plan, that is."

"I'm only saying—"

Finder lifted his head. "Remira and Toma can help us."

Larken remembered Finder talking about Toma and Embryn, but Remira was new to her.

Madden bit his lip. "Bad idea."

Dahey and Saja nodded their heads in agreement.

Finder gritted his teeth. "Toma is as good a healer as any in Shadeshelm. And from what the Dark Priestess showed me, the Guardian is not far from Remira's domain. Perhaps she knows about him and can help us prepare."

His *dornán* clearly wasn't convinced, but he continued: "I can create a portal there—we'll have enough time to heal and find the Guardian."

"You're too weak, Finder," Madden protested. "Creating the portal could drain you of the power you have left."

Saja tilted his head. "Can you be sure that they will even offer to help us, after what happened with the Starveling?"

149

Larken's stomach roiled with nausea and she vomited again, this time covering herself and Madden. Finder squeezed his eyes shut, swallowing hard. Larken found it terribly unfair that he was exempt from the vomiting.

"We don't have a choice." He reached an arm out to Saja, letting the faery haul him into a standing position. Larken coughed and began to shake.

Finder lifted his hand and fire exploded in the air. He moved his palm and the flames followed, forming a crackling, burning circle.

"Finder," Saja warned, eyeing the prince's feet. Beneath Finder's boots, blades of grass withered and died. The patch of earth surrounding him turned grey and pale as smoke.

"Finder."

Finder ignored Saja, his hand still lifted. The circle was only halfway complete. Madden stepped back, his grip on Larken tightening as the dying patch of earth spread to his boots.

The ends of the circle connected. Hot air gusted back, lifting strands of their hair. A shimmering substance filled the inside of the circle. Through the silvery waves, Larken could make out the shape of huge, dark trees.

Finder dropped his hand. The dead land seeping toward them ceased.

"It's done." Finder wiped his mouth with the back of his hand. Madden held Larken tightly to his chest as one by one, the fey stepped through the portal.

One moment she was looking up at the circle of flames, then Madden stepped through it, passing under the silvery substance. It felt like passing under a thin sheet of warm water.

Once they all reached the other side, Finder lifted his hand once more. The flames sizzled out of existence, taking the silvery substance with them. Finder stumbled, but Saja caught him.

Saja let his prince lay heavily upon him. "You took too much."

The fey told her their magic came from the earth, pulled up through the veins that ran beneath the land. It looked as though Finder had sucked the life out of the surrounding flora in order to have enough energy to finish the portal.

"I did what had to be done," Finder replied, though his head fell, his face burning with shame and exhaustion.

His *dornán* pressed in close, keen on protecting their wounded prince. Dahey drew his sword, and Saja loaded his crossbow. While the Autumn Court had been filled with oranges and yellows, here the forest was olive green. The trees loomed before them, massive and dark, but they didn't reek of rot like the ones surrounding the Priestesses' den had. Magic curled around them. The undergrowth reached for them, tangled and untamed. A new smell lingered on the breeze, a heady musk that dominated her senses.

The Wyld. Well named, and dangerous, if the *dornán's* tense muscles told her anything.

"Remira, I need your help," Finder rasped.

One moment, nothing. The next, it was there, flying out of the heaps of briar and branches. All speed and strength and muscles, snapping teeth and bristling fur.

A wolf, bigger than Larken had ever seen—bigger than a pony—with its jaws clamped around Finder's throat.

CHAPTER NINETEEN

Saja lifted his crossbow, training it on the beast.

"Saja, stop!" Finder cried. Saja hesitated, but his finger didn't leave the trigger. Madden crushed Larken to his chest. If the wolf closed its jaws, she and Finder would die instantly.

Still, it was a beautiful creature. White fur with tufts of gold. In her delirium, Larken wanted to touch it. Amber eyes flashed as the wolf looked at them. The beast planted a firm paw on Finder's chest before releasing him from its jaws.

"Finder of Autumn, back in my realm at last," the wolf said. "Why?"

Larken's mouth gaped open. The beast had just talked. A she-wolf, too, by the timbre of her voice.

"They've been poisoned by the Priestesses," Madden murmured. "Please, Rem. They'll die."

Remira jerked back as though stung. She swung her head toward Larken. Her huge nose twitched.

So, this was the Remira they were referring to. A wolf.

"I haven't forgiven you for what you did," Remira said to Finder. Her lips pulled back to reveal yellow teeth. "But I will honor the friendship you have with my mate. Toma and my sisters will heal you."

"Thank you. I will not forget this," Finder said.

Larken's vision blurred. Darkness leaked into the edges of her vision, and then she knew no more.

Fragments of memory flashed behind her eyelids as she rolled in and out of the fields of consciousness. Two wolves flanking a massive cave opening. A cavern with a large center dome, tunnels and alcoves streaming from it. Larken smiled at the thought of a giant taking a finger and poking holes in the stones. A huge hand scooping out the caves. She couldn't remember where she was.

"I can't—" Finder's strained voice pulled her fully awake.

"No use trying to use magic here," Remira said. "We know that your kind tends to gather around arteries of magic. We keep ourselves away, knowing that we would not be wanted there."

Finder made a noise of pain or protest, but Remira simply waved her tail like she would wave a hand. "We are tied to magic differently. Our healing, our powers—they are different than yours, but no less in strength. You and your kind would do well to remember it."

Larken drifted again, but she was glad Finder was there. They were tied, he and she, both in this world and the next. She was bound to him, body to body, soul to soul, as he was to her. One could not leave without the other, and the thought comforted her now, whereas mere days ago it had frightened and frustrated her. Whatever happened, they would never face it alone.

Larken jerked as she was placed on a bed of soft furs. She blinked away the film coating her eyes and reached for Finder, wherever he was.

"It's all right," came Madden's voice. Finder lay in the small bed across from her. Dahey and Saja were nowhere to be seen.

A small female hobbled into the chamber. She leaned heavily on a wooden crutch, for her right leg stopped above her knee. Strangely enough there was no scarring—the stump of her leg was perfectly healed.

Toma.

The healer's dark hair was pulled into a tight braid, accentuating her lovely face. An apron covered her body. Larken couldn't help but notice the bloodstains.

"Both are gravely ill," Remira said. "Poisoned by the Dark Priestesses."

"There's a life debt between them, as well," Madden added.

Larken's fists clenched at his words. He shouldn't have revealed their secret.

"Leave us," Toma commanded. She tottered over to the cabinets and began pulling out an array of bottles and bowls. She placed them all on a wooden tray. Clean rags came next, then knives.

Larken turned away, blinking back tears. The thought of more pain terrified her. She wouldn't be able to bear it. Finder extended his hand and she grasped it tightly.

"I'm not leaving them," Madden growled.

The healer didn't bat an eye. "I won't ask again. They need to focus on healing, and I won't have you here as a distraction."

Larken's heart pounded. She wanted Mama.

Finder groaned in pain. Madden clenched his jaw. Finally, he nodded, following Remira out of the chamber.

Drool dribbled out of her mouth. Toma appeared by her side, wiping it away with a cloth. Shame burned in Larken. She stank of sweat and urine and vomit. When had she pissed herself? She wanted to cry.

Larken flinched when the healer laid her hands on either side of Larken's face.

"It's all right, child," she said. Her voice was soft and soothing. Her tawny brown face was so beautiful.

Larken didn't remember anything after that.

Larken awoke slowly. Wisps of half-remembered dreams stretched behind her eyelids like spiderwebs, and she clung to them, knowing as soon as she opened her eyes they would disappear forever.

She moved her toes first, then her fingers, and found them both embedded in soft furs. For a split second, she thought she was in her loft, tucked in her own bed, but then her mind righted itself. She was in the caves Remira had led them to, but her pain had disappeared. The healer had done it—she had ridded them of the Priestess's poison.

"You're awake," came Madden's relieved voice.

He leaned forward from his place on a fur-draped armchair beside her. Dark circles lingered beneath his eyes. He rubbed a small wooden figure between his fingers. Larken wondered how long Madden had been there, waiting to see if she'd survive the poison.

She knew he wasn't dead, but she still couldn't resist asking, "Is Finder—?"

"He's fine." Madden moved to help her out of bed. "Toma said she barely had to touch you. As soon as she pulled the poison from Finder, you were cured."

Of course. Recognition settled over Larken like a mass of stones. The healer had tended to Finder first. All of it was for him. They hadn't even healed her for her.

It pained her to know that. She had helped them, saved Finder's life, helped Saja with his breathing illness and guided them through the woods they called home. Even though Finder was a prince, even though it made sense that his *dornán* would put him first, she and Finder were tied. They were equals, as much as a human and faery could be.

But the *dornán* would never see her as Finder's equal. It frightened her that so much of their protection relied on the life debt. For the first time she was afraid what would happen if she and Finder ended their life debt before they reached the Starveling and her companions decided that her life wasn't worth theirs.

They would never do that, she told herself. But how well did she truly know these fey? She'd only been with them for a few days, while they had likely known each other for over a century. How could she blame them for choosing their prince, their family, over her?

Larken shooed Madden out of the room, craving a few moments of privacy. She wore an unfamiliar white shift, and her ceremony dress had disappeared. She pulled on the more practical pants and linen shirt that had been laid out for her. A pang of sadness hit her as she tugged on the accompanying leather boots. She wanted to finish this journey in the same dress she'd started in. It would have made things feel like this was still temporary. Like there was no doubt she was going to get home.

She wasn't so sure, now.

CHAPTER TWENTY

Females of all ages filled the seats of the wooden banquet tables in the hall. They chatted and laughed, enjoying their evening meal. They lacked the pointed ears of the fey, but after Madden's story about the war and the separation, Larken knew they couldn't be human.

"Who are these females?" she asked. "Do they keep the wolves as pets?"

"Not exactly," Madden replied. "Remira is their leader."

Their leader was a wolf? Things in Airodion just kept getting stranger.

"And before you ask," Madden said, herding her toward a table that was mostly free of occupants, "you were only asleep for a few hours."

She let out a sigh of relief. At least they hadn't wasted any more time than that. Still, guilt tinged her mood. If she had just stayed out of the way during the fight with the Dark Priestesses, they could have been on their way to the Guardian by now.

The smell of spices, roasting meat, and a tinge of something sugary wafted toward her, pulling her attention away from her dark thoughts. The underlying scent of wet stone and cold air remained, but it wasn't unpleasant. In fact, the whole place was rather homey. The wooden bench beneath her was worn smooth, and she ran her fingers across it, savoring the texture.

The females filling the benches around her interacted like a large family. Some of the females were strikingly beautiful, some not. The youngest ones couldn't have been older than seven, and there were old crones amongst them as well. All different skin colors, all different sizes, yet all so familiar—no, *comfortable*—with each other. A sudden pang of loneliness struck Larken as she sat there at the edge of the group, not knowing how to interact with these new strangers. She had finally begun to feel like a true member of Finder's company, but the realization that they hadn't tried to heal her first, even when she was the one who had been bitten by the Priestess, made her feel isolated again.

Madden returned, slamming down heaping platters of food on the table. He also produced two plates, a napkin, and two sets of forks and knives. Larken had no idea how he'd carried it all or where he'd been stowing the silverware.

And, Twins bless him, he had brought her a fair share of meat. Before them sat an entire roasted duck drowning in honey-butter glaze. Surrounding the fowl was a variety of roasted greens and carrots. The next platter held a mutton stew. Potatoes roasted in garlic and parsley covered the next. Mushrooms the size of Larken's fist stuffed with wild rice and spices sent steam into the air. Disregarding the greens and assorted vegetables entirely, she stabbed the roasted duck with her fork and dragged it onto her plate.

Madden had already crammed two of the stuffed mushrooms into his mouth and was groaning with pleasure. Larken bit into the duck slowly, eyes fluttering as flavor flooded her mouth. The meat was so tender it almost melted on her tongue, and the honey added just enough sweetness to balance the spices. Larken abandoned her fork and grabbed the duck with both hands, ignoring the juices that ran down her chin. She couldn't remember the last time she had eaten food as good as this.

Madden was already on his fourth stuffed mushroom and was eyeing a fifth. Larken grabbed one, eager to try it before they disappeared into Madden's bottomless stomach. He growled at her and she grinned, his presence and the food lifting her spirits considerably. Everything she tried was better than the last, and she found she had eaten four helpings of the garlic potatoes before she even realized what she was doing.

Madden had conquered his sixth mushroom, and Larken was beginning to think him unstoppable when a voice behind them commented, "You do realize it would be incredibly rude if we ate *all* of our hosts' food."

Larken and Madden whirled to find Finder standing there, staring at them with an arched eyebrow and amusement lighting his eyes. Madden, his seventh mushroom suspended in midair, crammed it hastily in his mouth before further chastisement and possible mushroom confiscation could ensue. He looked like a chipmunk with his cheeks distended and his eyes wide. Larken laughed so hard she choked on her bite of potatoes. Madden leaned across the table and pounded her on the back until she hacked up the morsel on the table. Finder stood and watched the entire ordeal unfold before him, muttering something about not being able to leave children alone for five minutes.

Finder sat with them, helping them eat the rest of the massive spread of food. He opened a bottle of blackberry mead and filled all their glasses. Larken had never had much of a liking for alcohol, but the mead was exquisite. It was as sweet as nectar, cool on her tongue but warm on her throat.

"Madden, how did you come to join Finder's *dornán*?" Larken asked, the mead making her voluble.

Madden drank deeply before replying. "Bit of a sad story, really. Are you sure you'd like to hear it?" At her nod he continued. "It began when I met Senna."

Larken remembered that name—Saja had mentioned it when Rosin had died and Madden had been distraught over her baby.

"The fey are different from humans and the other creatures of Airodion." Madden twirled a fork through his fingers. "We do not have wives, husbands, or partners. We do not have mates, nor do we imprint. No, the fey have something special, something unique to us. When two fey love each other, truly, deeply, despite any faults, a bond is formed. The fey call it *laithnam*."

A warm tingle went down Larken's spine. It was a beautiful word, and she rolled it around silently on her tongue, savoring the feel of it.

"For the fey, the *laithnam* bond is sacred. Coveted. It is impossible to describe what your *laithnam* means to you. It is like seeing your heart walk outside your body in the form of another being. Not everyone finds it in their lives." Madden shook his head, struggling to find words. "The bond two *laithnam* feel is beautiful—and terrible. The *laithnam* bond is magic and can be fickle. It can bring great pain and sadness to someone's life, just as easily as it can bring joy."

Finder's green eyes met Madden's from over the rim of his glass. Had Finder ever experienced this *laithnam* bond before? With Embryn?

"For instance, sometimes two lovers may find the *laithnam* bond, but then have it fade, or even break, over time. The two fey could each find new lovers and share the bond with them. Or, they might never find it again. And the pain one feels if their *laithnam* dies is indescribable. Some go mad with grief. Some seek death if only to see their hearts again."

That doesn't sound so different from humans, Larken thought. She wanted to hear more about the magic involved in the bond, however.

Madden smiled softly. "When I first met Senna, I was young and stupid. I was used to getting what I wanted. Males, females... Not arrogance, but I enjoyed sex. I reveled in it. I had many lovers, but none lasted long."

A flush crept up Larken's neck. She had never laid with anyone. Her fingers had found their way between her thighs more than once and she had enjoyed it, but she knew sex would be different. And in truth, she *wanted* it. More than she cared to admit. And Madden's casual talk of sex had her thinking about it, and worse, thinking about doing it with a faery. With centuries of experience, their lovemaking must be exquisite.

"But Senna evaded me," Madden continued, jerking Larken out of her thoughts. "She didn't just want sex, she wanted to find love. She wanted to find her *laithnam*."

Madden ran a hand through his hair, the strands falling through his fingers like silk. "I fell for her. And eventually, she fell for me, too. And when I realized she was my *laithnam*, and I was hers, I cried from sheer joy. It was the first time I had ever cried from something other than sadness. That kind of love—it was true happiness," Madden said. "That was, of course, until we had Ainsley."

Larken sucked in a breath, remembering how he'd said he'd had a daughter. *Had.*

"When Senna got pregnant, I thought I couldn't get any happier. I was wrong. The moment Ainsley was born was the happiest moment in my existence. I know I will never feel that happiness again, nor do I want to." His eyes were far away now. "She was perfect. She was fat—so fat." He smiled, shaking his head.

"Beautiful," Finder murmured. "She was beautiful."

Madden gave his prince a nod. "The three of us lived in a stone cottage. I can still see it perfectly in my mind. Sometimes I think I could still go there."

Larken thought back to when Madden had mentioned he had tried to form Ainsley out of glamour and had created some dark version of her. It must pain him to know he had such extraordinary powers over glamour, but he could never use it to see his family again—not without darkness tainting it.

Madden picked at the edge of the wood table with a fingernail. "We were happy. Ainsley grew, though she was still a baby by fey standards. Then came the battle."

"The war with the Starveling?" Larken asked. But that couldn't be right. Madden and her companions hadn't been alive during the first war with the Masters or the second war with the Starveling. The separation between humans and fey had occurred four hundred years ago, and her companions were only a century and a half old. Still, she hadn't heard them mention any other battles—except for when Finder and the others had attacked the Starveling and Embryn had died.

"No, that was long before our time. This battle was much more recent, only ninety years ago. The courts occasionally have skirmishes on the borders, but this one was more serious. Our border with the Spring Court has always been troublesome. Etain, Princess of the Spring Court, is ruthless, to say the least."

Finder stiffened. Another memory flickered back to her: Madden had mentioned that name during his dark illusion in the woods.

"Etain is bored with immortality, and it has made her cruel," Finder said. "She has been content to play the villain for centuries."

Madden had echoed those words, once. That immortality bred cruelty. She wondered then how her faery companions could be so kind and good, or if they had simply not lived long enough to fall.

"Etain and Finder have a troubled past," Madden added. "She has tried to seduce members of our court in an attempt to turn them into spies. She uses her subjects as political whores. At one meeting, an Autumn Court female laid with one of Etain's knights. The Autumn Court female, convinced that she and the knight were in love, begged Etain to let her be with her lover. Etain ended the girl before Finder could free her. In retaliation, Finder took the knight prisoner. Etain sent soldiers across the border to burn a few Autumn Court fields in the hopes of antagonizing Finder further." Madden swallowed heavily, then continued. "They did much more than that, whether Etain ordered it or not. They pillaged the nearest towns."

Finder's jaw clenched.

"I was one of Finder's generals at the time. What the Spring Court did was inexcusable, and though we would never destroy their towns in return, something had to be done. Finder ordered me and Saja, another one of his generals, to the Spring Court border to meet with Etain's ambassadors. Waiting for us was a legion of Spring Court soldiers led by Etain's most bloodthirsty general: Bavvard. Saja and I had only ten soldiers with us.

"Bavvard, the bastard, disappeared once the fighting got thick. After Saja got hit with two arrows, I ordered him to fall back and bring reinforcements. It was up to my soldiers and me to hold the line, or the Spring Court army would have had free reign on the nearby towns. And my family's cottage."

Larken's heart flew up her throat.

"My soldiers and I held the line. And when they fell, I held it. Finally, Saja returned with aid, and we pushed Etain's forces back. I decided to stay at Shadeshelm that night to discuss what the Autumn Court should do next. Finder woke me the next morning with news of another attack. Bavvard had told Etain about the massacre of her soldiers and about the Autumn Court general who'd held the line against all odds. He wanted revenge, and Etain gave her consent."

Larken knew how the story had to end, and she didn't want to hear any more of it. But she had to if he wanted to tell it. For Madden's sake.

"I do not think Bresel and Rhylla could have carried us any swifter than they did that day. But it was not enough. My *laithnam* and my daughter were gone. A note saying only 'We have them' pinned to our door."

Larken's throat closed. *Oh, Madden...*

"I destroyed the house. With my fists and my magic. All I knew was my *laithnam* had brought down six soldiers who'd tried to take her and my daughter. *Six.* She had fighting experience, yes, but to take down six soldiers is no easy feat." Pride suffused his words.

Larken stayed silent, too overwhelmed to say anything.

"Finder sent word to Etain, begging her to let them live." Madden shook his head, black hair sweeping down across his brow. "They dumped the bodies across the border that night. They had tortured them. Ainsley was only a child," Madden whispered. "She was innocent.

"I tore the clothes from my own back to cover them. I dug their graves with my hands. I raged, and I raged, and I raged. I should have died on that battlefield. If I had died, Bavvard wouldn't have taken them. I was in a dark place for a very long time. I crossed the Spring Court border and killed anyone I came across until Finder had to imprison me. I tried to kill him for it.

"Finder saved me," Madden continued. "He didn't have to, but he did. He brought me back from the edge of oblivion more than once. He still does. He asked me to join his *dornán,* and I agreed. I've been with him ever since."

Finder smiled at Madden, and the two fey clasped forearms. They had all been through such pain, such loss, yet they still loved. They went on living.

Finder went off in search of more mead, giving her a moment alone with Madden. Larken wiped a hand under her eyes.

She missed Brigid. Sometimes Larken nearly forgot her friend was gone, with everything happening in Airodion, but occasionally the grief would strike her, threatening to drown her in her own memories. She would never see Brigid again. She would never hug her, or laugh with her, or see the way the lines crinkled around her blue eyes. How long would she even remember her friend's face?

If only she could go back to the moment they had fought. She should have known better than to leave things like that before the Choosing Ceremony. She should have apologized and hugged Brigid tight. Instead, Brigid had left without so much as a goodbye. The thought that Brigid had died thinking Larken was upset with her—or worse, if Brigid herself had hated Larken at the very end—nearly tore Larken's heart in two.

This is your fault. You deserve for her to hate you.

Madden took her hand and squeezed it.

"I'm sorry," Larken whispered, wiping more tears from her eyes. "It's stupid, I know. You lost your family, and I only lost my friend."

"It's not stupid," Madden said, using his thumb to brush away her tears. "Others' grief often reminds us of our own."

"I know I should just move on, but I can't," Larken said. She didn't want to. She didn't know how to live without her.

"Grief isn't something you move on from," Madden said. "Your life with Brigid—the love you had for her isn't just a collection of moments that you can forget and leave behind. Nor should you want to. Your time with her made you the person that you are, and even though she is gone, you don't have to move on from her. Grief marks us as much as joy. And once it touches you, you understand." He gave her a sad smile.

Larken wiped away her tears. "I wish I could have met them. Ainsley and Senna."

"I wish you could have, too, *a cara.*"

CHAPTER TWENTY-ONE

Torches lined the walls of the tunnels, illuminating the dozens of fur pelts hanging upon the stones. Some of them were dyed and braided, while others were patterned with string and beads. Others were matted with age, worn down to the frayed skin. They reminded Larken of the fur pelts she and her family kept to warn off the cold northern winters. They reminded her of home.

When Finder had returned with more mead, he told her and Madden that he had spoken with Remira about the Guardian. The wolf had invited them to hold council with her to discuss their plan.

Finder came to a halt in front of a massive wooden door. Snarling wolf heads wrought from metal studded the wood, their teeth filed into tiny points. Finder pulled the iron handle and beckoned them inside.

Larken took in the stone antechamber, a colossal room with domed ceilings. The smell of cool water and stone greeted her. A massive oak table dominated the center of the room, a few high-backed chairs scattered around it. She itched to spread paper upon the wood and map out all she had seen of Airodion so far. She'd had a good sense of which direction they were traveling at first, even after she had fallen asleep, for the fey continuously pushed northwest. But after Finder had made the portal, she had no idea where they were in relation to the bridge and Ballamor.

Larken clenched her fists, feeling suddenly adrift. Was Ballamor north or south of here? How could she get home if she didn't know where she was?

A growl from Remira snapped Larken's attention to the wolf. She stood at the head of the table, her muzzle and shoulders easily extending above the worn surface. Saja and Dahey were there as well, standing on either side of the massive creature.

"You dare to ask for my help against the Starveling? After what happened last time?" Remira's lips curled, revealing her teeth. "Toma saved your life that day, and now you're trying this foolish venture again. You're going to get yourself killed," Remira spat. "And this time, Toma won't be there to help you."

"I don't have a tithe, and Larken and I are bound through a life debt," Finder said, his voice flat. "In this, we have no choice. The Priestess told us we must find the Guardian. Only he can help us end the Starveling's reign for good."

"You should have gone to him and begged his forgiveness," Remira said, though her voice betrayed her doubts.

"I told him that," Dahey muttered, as if wanting to remind everyone that he had done the rational thing.

"You know I would never do that," Finder growled. "You know he would have killed me, punished my court and the humans—"

"No, what I do know is you'll jump at any opportunity to overthrow him after what happened to Embryn," Remira said.

"I told him that, too," Dahey said.

Finder ignored him. "Just tell us what you know about the Guardian and we'll leave. Please, Rem. I don't want to lead my friends into a trap. Not again."

Larken's heart stirred at the word friend. Was she included in that word, now?

The wolf stared at him for a moment, then lowered her amber gaze. "I do not know of the Guardian you seek."

"Don't lie to me," Finder warned.

Remira snarled. "Do not accuse me of lying just to save you, Prince."

"You clearly wish to sabotage this venture just to claim your revenge—"

"You think me so selfish as to—"

"Selfish and shortsighted, yes! And what's more, you—"

"Both of you, stop it!" Larken shouted. Both Finder and Remira turned to look at her, their faces wide with shock.

"I'm tired of all this fighting between everyone." She tried not to look at Dahey when she said it. "I know what happened last time you all tried to take down the Starveling, and I know Toma lost her leg. But it wasn't all Finder's fault, was it? He said it was the Starveling who mangled her and that he was just trying to save her life. Don't you want revenge on the Starveling more than you want to punish Finder? Clearly you care for each other. Finder, you trust Remira enough to come here and tell her of our journey, and Remira, you saved us from the Priestesses' poison." She took a breath, then kept going. "He's taken from all of us. We have to bring him down, but we need help. So, please, if you have any information about the Guardian, please tell us. Not for Finder, but so we can bring down the beast that hurt Toma and so many others."

After an excruciating pause, Remira gave her a slow nod of approval. Dahey's lips quirked up, a glimmer of respect lighting his eyes. Saja and Madden stood completely dumbfounded, and Finder gave her a small smile. Pride burned inside her.

"I'm sorry, Larken," Finder said. "And apologies to you, too, Remira. My fear and frustration have made me rude. Is there anything you know of this Guardian, even the smallest detail, that could help us?"

Remira's eyes narrowed. Then, like a puppet with cut strings, she slumped. "The name stirs something in my mind, like something terrible that I have forgotten. I have not heard of a Guardian living in the Wyld. This frightens me. The Wyld is my home. It is dangerous, but rarely for me or my sisters. We have prowled this forest for a thousand years, and for any creature to escape our notice—fey or otherwise—is no simple feat. I worry this Guardian may be more than you bargained for, or a trap laid by the Priestesses."

Finder pressed his hands into the table. "Could he have concealed himself from notice somehow?"

"Well, we wouldn't know if he had, would we?" Madden pointed out.

"A memory curse is possible," Remira mused, "but Madden is right—we would have no way of knowing."

"Memory curse?" Larken furrowed her brow.

"They have the ability to make someone forget. Extremely powerful curses can wipe the memories of an entire population, but even the Starveling doesn't have that kind of power. Not alone, anyway," Remira supplied.

Finder ran a hand through his hair. "Regardless, we must find him. More lives will be forfeit if we fail to bring the knife to him. The Priestesses may have tried to kill us, but we made a bargain—they couldn't lie. If they said the weapon is the only way to kill the Starveling, then it's worth the risk."

"Why don't you just use the knife against the Starveling as it is?" Remira asked.

Finder shook his head. "The Priestess said that the knife has no power on its own. We must go to the Guardian to make it whole, but she did not say what that entails."

Remira said nothing and tried to look away, but Finder pinned her with his gaze.

"You know me, Rem," Finder said softly. "You see what the tithe does to me, to all of us. This can't go on. I will take no more girls to his altar. There has been enough death. You know that, and so did Embryn."

Remira let her silence stretch out between them.

"I'm sorry," Finder whispered. "I'm sorry about what happened to Toma and Embryn, and I will never forgive myself for my part in it. But there only needs to be one more death. It can all end when the Starveling dies. We'll be ready this time. We have a chance to end it."

Remira looked at him for a moment, neither of them speaking. Finally, she rose and padded over to the shelves of scrolls lining the wall. She pulled one free with her mouth, then trotted back to the table.

"I have heard whispers in the forest," Remira said. "Of a glen where creatures do not dare to tread, even the fearsome ones. I have sent sentries to investigate, but they all return muddled and confused, unsure of what they had seen. Show me where the Priestess claimed the Guardian would be," Remira said.

Finder spread the scroll across the table.

Larken nearly gasped. It was a map of Airodion—rendered in such exquisite, precise detail that the ink seemed to lift from the paper and appear before her eyes.

She had been right—she and her faery companions had been pressing northwest since leaving Ballamor. She could see the rest of Ellevere to the south, and although Ballamor wasn't labeled, she knew exactly where her village was on the flatlands north of a narrow mountain range. Tracing with her eyes, she followed the path she had taken into Airodion; across the bridge, through the ravine where Rosin was killed, and northwest to the Dark Priestesses' den. Now they were much further north at the top of the map, in a forested area labeled THE WYLD.

The precise detail of the chart comforted her. Larken seared the lines and images into her mind, storing them away so when it was time to return home, she would know how to get back.

But something caught her eye, a cross-shaped territory, situated right between the Autumn and Spring Court lands. It was the strange shape that caught her eye—as it reminded her so much of the sigil of the Black Guard and the Order.

"That's where we're going, isn't it," she asked, pointing to the shape. After learning how intertwined the Order was with the Starveling, she knew the similar shapes couldn't be a coincidence.

"Yes," Finder replied. "That is the Starveling's domain, and where the tithe takes place."

Silence fell over the room. Some part of her hadn't seen the Starveling's domain as a tangible space in Airodion. Though she had always known it would be their final destination, she had pictured it as some kind of underworld, not a true space.

But seeing that little mark upon the map made everything feel real. That is where their final battle would take place, where everything would come to an end. They had all been so focused on the next step of their journey, gathering information from the Priestesses, surviving the poison, and now finding the Guardian and the weapon he kept—that they hadn't stopped to truly plan how they would kill the Starveling. Taking him totally by surprise wasn't an option—Finder and his companions had already tried that. But how could they focus on future battles when they had to face life-or-death situations at every turn?

"I cannot describe it." Finder's voice shook her from her thoughts. He brushed his fingertips across the map. "But the Priestesses showed me where the Guardian dwells. I can see it clearly in my mind." He tapped a small glen near the Warga cave.

Recognition flashed in Remira's gaze. Along with something akin to fear.

"Is this where your sentries have gone?" Finder murmured.

"Yes," Remira said. A chill trickled down Larken's spine. "One thing they can remember is a circle of grey cap mushrooms."

Larken and her companions exchanged glances. *A circle of mushrooms guards his prison*, the Priestess had said.

"What if it's a trap? The Priestesses attacked you—would they not try to lead you astray?" Remira said.

"She has a point," Saja said. "Why would the Priestesses tell us of the Guardian if he was no threat to us?"

"Two of the Priestesses didn't want to tell us. Their sister betrayed them," Larken reminded them.

Dahey braced his knuckles on the table, deep creases lining his mouth. Finder looked at him, his hands splayed wide on the map.

"Cousin, I trust your council. You have always looked out for me and our court. Is this the right path?"

All eyes fell on Dahey. Larken was shocked by his appearance. Deep shadows hung beneath his eyes, and his clothes were wrinkled and unkempt. He looked afraid.

"We can't turn back now," he whispered. "It's too late. We must go on."

Larken felt an unexpected jolt of sympathy for Dahey. Out of the *dornán*, she had connected with Dahey the least. He was always the first to argue, the first to challenge Finder, and the first to offer some snide remark. Looking at him now, she felt as though she were seeing him for the first time. He was afraid. And while Madden and Saja's loyalty would compel them to follow Finder anywhere, Dahey would do that and more—he would also question him, push him for the good of their *dornán* and their court.

Remira peered at the fey before her. "You would really let your prince go into this danger?"

"To not try would be even more dangerous," Saja replied.

"Time is running out," Dahey added. "The Guardian is our only chance."

Finder looked at her.

"Dahey is right," Larken said. "Without the Guardian completing the weapon—we have nothing."

And they couldn't even be sure that the Guardian *would* help them. Yet if they gave up now, or tried a different path, time could run out.

"As you wish." Remira turned and walked toward the table. Mid-step, the wolf launched herself onto two feet. Larken gasped as Remira transformed. Her limbs shortened, her fur and lupine face morphed into hair and skin. In a matter of seconds, it was done. Larken gaped at the human that now stood before them. Remira had been beautiful as a wolf... but now she was stunning. Her skin was a rich umber, and her hair fell in tight ringlets. Her lips were full and red. Her glowing amber eyes were the only thing that still tied her to her wolf form. And she was completely naked.

"You're—" Larken choked.

Remira raised an eyebrow. "Breathtakingly beautiful, intelligent, and immortal?" She grinned devilishly, tucking her hair behind a round ear.

Finder rolled his eyes at Remira. "Yes, Larken. Remira is a Warga. A wolf shifter."

CHAPTER TWENTY-TWO

Larken found it difficult to hold a conversation with someone in the nude. She tried to study the wall just behind Remira's head, but her traitorous eyes kept darting to Remira's breasts or catching glimpses of the dark mound of hair between her legs. She could tell that her faery companions were trying not to stare, as well. Remira's body was flawless, strongly muscled yet curvy. A pang of jealousy shot through Larken. She wondered if men would ever look at her like that, wanting to drink in the sight of her.

But being poisoned by the Priestesses and nearly dying had caused something to shift inside her. It still stung that the fey had only been interested in saving Finder, but she was still alive. She had almost died on too many occasions over the past few days, but somehow it only made her feel more determined to keep going, to eventually get home and tell her story. She was still alive—despite everything—and was still fighting. She had helped the fey, too. She was finally beginning to feel like part of the group, like she could use her skills to contribute. The past few days had taught her she was capable of more than she thought —and that had nothing to do with the way her body looked.

Finder shot a glare at Dahey, who hadn't torn his eyes away from

Remira. "She has a mate, Dahey," Finder reminded him under his breath. Remira just laughed, twisting a curl around her finger.

"Oh, don't be a spoilsport, Finder, he can look. He'll find that, desirable as I am, I have absolutely no interest in what he keeps in his pants." She winked playfully at Larken, and a smile pulled at her lips. She had never met anyone with as much confidence as the female before her.

Dahey reluctantly looked away and Finder laughed. The prince unfastened his cloak and wrapped it around Remira's shoulders, making her huff in mock protest.

"Come now, we all know Toma is a very lucky female. No need to taunt us with what we can't have," Finder said with a wink.

"Toma is your mate?" Larken asked. "Is she—is she a Warga, too?"

"Yes, Toma is my mate. Explains why I'm so protective of her," Remira chuckled. "And, yes, to your second question, as well. All of the females here are Warga—and I am the leader of the Darktree Clan." Remira took a seat at the head of the table. Clutching the cloak Finder had given her, she beckoned for Larken to come and sit next to her.

Encouraged by the gesture, Larken joined Remira at the table. She sat up straighter. She had earned her place here. She had earned the right to make decisions with the group.

Remira leaned forward. "Once you feel up to it, I can give you a proper tour of the caverns and you can meet everyone. They're dying to meet you."

Larken's brow rose. "They want to meet *me?*" A flicker of warmth bloomed in her chest.

"Of course." Remira beamed. "As soon as they sensed a human was here, and a female at that, they got all riled up. You should have seen them when I made the announcement. Some of the ones in their wolf form were yapping like puppies. You see, all Warga are female, and we are fiercely protective of other females. It's just our nature, I suppose," Remira shrugged.

That explained all the curious stares she had gotten. "All female?" After traveling for so long with males, she could scarcely remember how to interact with other females.

Males, females. How soon she had grown accustomed to the wording, putting the human realm further and further behind her.

"We have our pups by mating with males, of course. Male fey, or really, male anything..." Remira trailed off, her face growing grave. "Well, I would hope not *anything*, as there are some foul beings that lurk in the forest, but in theory... Oh, Mother, I haven't even thought about it—"

"Remira," Finder cut in, raising a sardonic eyebrow.

"Right, right. Anyway, we have our pups with males, which makes them useful for *something*, at least." She bared her teeth playfully at Dahey, who retained his look of vague discomfort. He stuffed his hands in his pockets and found something particularly interesting to gaze at on the wall.

"If the offspring is female, she is now a Warga pup. The female offspring of any Warga has the Warga gift. If the offspring is male..." Remira shrugged. "The father will take him. Or kill him. Or possibly eat him. But the father will usually take him and raise him as his own."

Larken grimaced. "That's a little—"

"Barbaric?" Remira cut in, smiling tightly. "I agree. I do not think the male offspring should be abandoned in the forest to the will of the father, with only the female offspring taken into the Clan, but it is our way."

Finder cleared his throat.

"I know I'm getting off topic. Don't piss yourself."

"Remira, your breast," Finder said calmly. Her eyes widened. Larken wasn't sure how he was able to keep a straight face. One of Remira's breasts had slipped out of the cloak. Dahey's eyes practically bulged out of his head. Madden too couldn't seem to keep his gaze occupied with anything else for long.

"Oh, for Mother's sake, it's just a *breast*." Remira rolled her eyes as she stuffed it back under the cloak just as one would tuck a stray lock of hair behind an ear. Larken snorted. She wanted to be friends with this female. "You'd think they've never seen one before, honestly," Remira muttered to Larken.

"Now," Remira continued, straightening her cloak. "On to important business. I know time is a pressing issue, but you and Larken need to rest."

"We are well enough to travel," Finder said. "We need to leave in the morning. We only have two more days to reach the Starveling."

Annoyance buzzed through Larken at Finder's dismissive tone. She understood his urgency to continue their journey, Larken felt the clock ticking away as much as anyone. But both of them had nearly died only hours before. They would all need their strength once they reached the Guardian and then the Starveling.

Larken's stomach dropped at the thought of leaving. She felt safe here. There was good food and a warm bed. Even more than that, she could see herself making friends here. She didn't want to leave.

Brigid had been her only friend her entire life. Larken had spent the past year alone, with no one to share her secrets about the village boys or her hopes for the future. But the way Remira had spoken to her, as if they were already friends, comforted Larken in a way she could not describe. She didn't want to leave, to give up on the potential of more friendships akin to what she had had with Brigid.

Remira turned to Larken. "The offer remains for you to stay. You would be safer, here. The prince and his companions could return to you after they complete their task."

For a moment, Larken was tempted by her offer. Madden opened his mouth, but Finder held up a hand. He was letting her decide.

"Thank you," Larken replied, hoping she sounded as sincere as she felt. "But I can't. I want to, truly, but I have to go with them. I'm a part of this quest—journey, whatever it is. And I'm not giving up now."

She was frightened of what the future held—there was no denying it. But she no longer wanted to sit to the side, allowing fate to take her where it willed. She was here to help her people, to return to Ballamor and enact as much change in her world as she could. And she would not leave it to Finder and his companions to do that for her. They had some care for the humans, yes, but not as much as she did. She would not be left behind. She would contribute what she could, as she had already proven she was capable of doing. Of helping Finder and his company. And though she could see the potential for a friendship with Remira and perhaps even other Warga, she was beginning to think that she already had friends, here.

Remira bowed her head.

"As you wish, Larken."

CHAPTER TWENTY-THREE

Sleep evaded her. The smell of the animal furs reminded her too much of home, and thoughts of what lay ahead chased all ideas of rest from her mind.

Grabbing a candle, she shuffled away from the warm bed. She stepped out into the hallway and winced as the door creaked shut behind her.

"Couldn't sleep?"

She whirled, almost bumping into Finder. He had changed into a new white shirt and simple brown pants—no weapons in sight. Larken wondered how often he was comfortable enough to go unarmed.

"No," she admitted, tucking her hands into her shift. Finder nodded, his dark copper hair gleaming even in the dim light of her candle.

"I found sleep difficult, as well."

Larken shifted her feet.

"Care to join me?" she asked, waving her hand awkwardly. Her face burned. Why had she said that? Join her where, exactly? But Finder's shoulders relaxed, and he nodded.

They walked side by side, Larken holding the candle aloft between them. Their footfalls echoing against the walls were the only sound for a time. Doors lined the hallway, likely leading to other guest rooms.

She had never felt as much conflict as she did with Finder. She couldn't deny the favorable feelings she was beginning to have toward him. But every good thought that crossed her mind about Finder made her feel like she was betraying Brigid.

But one thought dug into the back of her mind like a thorn, constantly digging into her with no way to escape it. She hugged herself, unable to say the words lingering on the tip of her tongue, afraid of the pain that could accompany it. Her heart pounded. Sweat coated her palms, a slight tremor shaking her fingers.

Finder noticed her expression. "I know how hard this has been for you. You have been forced to travel and ally yourself with someone who has disrupted your entire world. And even more than that, your life is tied with that of your friend's murderer. If there were any way—"

"Stop." Larken took a deep breath. She wanted to move on, but she needed closure. And there was one question she still had to ask. One that had weighed so heavily upon her. "Why did you choose Brigid?"

Finder was silent for a moment. "You remember I told you that the Starveling craves human emotions. The one he desires most is happiness. That is what he demands we bring to him."

Finder gave a small smile, but his eyes held a vast, unending sadness. "Brigid burned with the light of a star. Her happiness was as bright a flame as I have ever known."

Larken's eyes filled with tears. But this time, they came from anger. That was how she always wanted to remember her friend. Bursting with happiness. But she couldn't. Because Brigid hadn't died happy. No, she had died scared and alone, with the being who had lied to her about her true reason for being there. She had died after fighting with her only friend in the world.

"Rosin, too," Finder said. "She loved Ballamor. She adored her family. I was drawn to her—but when I took her, her light almost went out." Finder stopped, looked down at the cool ground.

"Then why did you take them?" she growled. "Why did you choose the person who had that much joy, knowing you would ruin that happiness? That it was exactly what the Starveling wanted? Knowing that everyone that knew and loved her would lose that in their lives?"

Larken's hands shook with rage. "You act as though the tithe destroys you. You act as though you have no choice in any of it. But you do. You could choose someone with a different emotion. You could resist the Starveling in other ways. But you don't. And you destroy just as many lives as he does."

Anger tore across Finder's face, distorting his features. "You think I don't know that?" he snarled. "You think I just sit idly by and do whatever he commands? We don't have a choice—we must bring him whichever emotion he desires. Part of the tithe magic allows us to sense the girls' emotions, so we can bring him exactly what he wants. We cannot disobey our oath to serve him." His eyes turned cold. "And you have no idea what I've done to end the tithe. When I first became Prince, I fought my oath. I spent ten minutes in agony so intense I can barely describe it to resist killing the *child* I had chosen. She had to watch as every other girl was killed and eaten. Her name was Corrigan. I remember all of their names. Every single one.

"I realized I would much rather lie to them to keep them happy and only have them experience a moment of fear at the end. Do you think it was easy to lie to them for six days? To convince them that they would live in happiness? I do that for them, not for me." He was shouting now, trembling with rage.

"The year after that I woke the Starveling from his slumber before the tithe and begged him to end it, if there was anything else he would accept as a tithe. He tortured me for so many days I lost count. And then when he freed me, he went back to sleep, as if I was so insignificant to him, he couldn't even be bothered to stay awake.

"I've tried to rally other courts. I planned the attack with Embryn. I did everything I could, but with each failure, I became more and more defeated. I have lost my friends, I have lost my family, I have lost myself because of this tithe. You do not get to say I haven't suffered."

Larken had never seen Finder so agitated, even during his spats with Dahey.

"I'm trying, Larken," he whispered. "I'm trying. And I keep trying, and failing, and that makes me a failure as a prince because it's my job to protect people. I didn't ask to be Prince. I didn't want it. But I tried to

179

accept it—tried to make the world a better place. But I failed at that, too."

Larken clenched her fists. "*Enough* with the pity! You think I don't feel like a failure too?" Larken cried. "I came here to help the Chosen girls, and they're all dead. And I saved the life of the being who killed them!"

"Oh, you're regretting that choice, are you? Are you starting to think you should have just let me die? Maybe you should have. Maybe that would have taken care of all of this, and neither of us would have to feel the way that we do. You should have let me die, Larken," Finder growled.

"Oh, you bloody, stubborn, pig-headed male!"

Finder's eyes widened.

She waved her hands at him. "Of course, I don't regret it. That's why I'm so bloody angry at myself! I should have wanted you to die, especially when I found out what you did to those girls. I should want revenge—I should want you to suffer. But I don't. I never have. And if you're one-hundred and fifty years old and can't see why you deserve to live a life free from suffering, then I'm sure in the Twins' Hell not going to be able to convince you. And if one more self-deprecating, melodramatic word comes out of your mouth I swear on the Twins that I'll slap you."

She stood there, fists shaking, absolutely fuming at the faery prince before her.

All he did was smile. It was slight—but there. "I've been waiting for you to ask about her," he said. It was the last thing Larken expected him to say. "I remember you two standing together. I remember when I took her, she was glowing with happiness. But when she turned around and looked at you one last time, when she knew she would have to leave you behind, a small piece of that light went out. I was curious to know why she reacted in such a way—what made you so special. Now I know."

Tears ran down her cheeks, hot and slow. "We had a fight," Larken whispered. "We had a fight the night before you chose her. I said things I shouldn't have, but she hurt me, said things about my life and my body that I couldn't bear to hear, not from her." Larken's voice broke. "I was so angry with her that I didn't even say goodbye."

Finder looked at her from beneath his lowered lashes. "She spoke of you, Larken. Often. My *dornán* and I knew who you were the moment you told us your name; we just weren't sure when you would be ready to talk about her. She told us that as soon as she completed the task for me, she would return to Ballamor, even if she had to wait an entire year for the bridge to open again. But she never told us about any fight. She only ever spoke about you with love and kindness," he finished gently.

Larken's bottom lip trembled. Brigid hadn't spent her final days angry at Larken. Brigid had wanted to return to her after the task. Larken had spent the past year agonizing over their fight, about how she would make things right with her friend. Larken would never know how the fight had affected Brigid, but she did know that her friend hadn't held it against her.

"I'm scared to let her go," Larken whispered. "I relied on Brigid for everything. Without her, I don't even feel like a complete person."

Finder had his regrets. She did, too. But they couldn't allow that to hold them back.

Larken took a deep breath. "We all have to live with the choices we make. We have to keep fighting, not just for them, but for ourselves, too. For that better world. I haven't given up, so neither can you. We can't do it alone. But neither of us are alone anymore, are we?"

"No, we are not alone," Finder murmured. He took a step closer to her, waiting for her to pull away, but she didn't. He wrapped his arms around her, crushing her to him. She stood there for a moment, completely still, then wrapped her arms around him.

"I'm sorry for all of it," Finder whispered. "For all the pain I have caused for you and your village. I'm not asking for forgiveness—I just needed you to hear it."

Something broke inside of Larken then. Some great structure she had built with walls of denial and desperation to keep the flood of feeling at bay. She hadn't forgiven him for Brigid, nor did she know if she ever would. But something happened between them in that moment, something she couldn't explain.

Your life with Brigid—the love you had for her isn't just a collection of moments that you can forget and leave behind. Nor should you want to. Your time with her made you the person that you are, and even though she is gone, you don't have to move on from her. Grief marks us as much as joy.

Madden's words echoed through her head. *They chose joy.* The part of her that had clung so desperately to Brigid loosened its hold. She would never forget her friend, but for the first time, she felt like she could let her go.

"The only Airodion I have ever known is this dark one," Finder continued. "We long for the past—a past where humans and fey lived side by side—but I also long for a better future. And now I must work to make it happen." His voice tightened. "We can do it—together."

She had come this far, and she would keep going. For herself, for Mama and Papa, and for the fey that she had come to care for more than she dared admit. They would end the reign of the Starveling, and then she would return to Ballamor and begin the fight for a better world there, as well.

"A better world," she said. "For both of us."

Finder brushed a hand along her jaw, a smile on his lips.

CHAPTER TWENTY-FOUR

Four of Remira's sentinels accompanied them the next morning, all in their wolf forms. Larken had the unbearable urge to run her fingers through their thick fur, but she resisted. Barely. Two of the wolves had bracken-colored fur, gorgeous as molten tree bark. The other two were opposites, one with white fur and the other with black.

Remira shifted back into her wolf form for the journey, as well. Before she transformed, she had given Larken a hug. It had been a bit awkward as she was still naked, but Larken was grateful for it all the same. Remira told her that if she ever had a chance to come back, the Darktree Clan would welcome her. Larken appreciated Remira's words more than the Warga could have ever known.

The moment felt like ages ago. The sun brightened, the rays of light battling the tapestry of branches above. Ahead, Dahey and Madden played a game of riddles with the sentinels while Finder and Remira exchanged stories from their time apart. Saja padded beside her, and she found herself grateful for the big warrior's company.

Remira's sentinels bounded in between the trees, their long, lithe bodies carrying them swiftly up ahead. The forest seemed to watch them, but it didn't seem threatening. How many years had these trees stood, silently keeping watch over the life below? They had seen countless successes and failures, lives and deaths, but none of it mattered to the trees.

Madden eventually became bored of the riddles and came to join her and Saja instead.

Larken studied Finder as he talked and laughed with Remira. He seemed so happy now—so different from how he had acted the night before.

"The accident you spoke of when Finder became Prince," Larken said, "what happened?"

Madden and Saja looked at each other, a silent conversation clearly passing between them in the space of a second.

"If you ask him," Madden said, "he'll tell you."

Saja nodded. "It is Finder's story to tell."

Larken swallowed her disappointment. She had asked Madden about it before, but she hoped one of them would crack now and tell her. "Oh, all right. I'll talk to him."

It wasn't as though she was scared to talk to him. She didn't want to bring it up because she didn't want to cause him any more pain.

Madden and Saja both chuckled. Larken glared at them.

"You sound as if you'd rather lick the bottom of Bresel's hoof," Madden snorted, and a smile crept across her face despite herself.

"I do not! I just—it's a difficult topic to broach, that's all." She tried not to think about last night, of how easy things had been between them.

"Finder?" Madden scoffed. "A puppy is more intimidating. Well, unless you beat him at King and Court. Honestly, he is the *worst* sore loser. Won't talk to you for a week, the prick."

"I lose on purpose to make him feel better," Saja admitted, and Madden laughed again.

The confusion must have shown on her face, as Madden gawked at her.

"Don't tell me you don't know what King and Court is…?" His eyes widened when Larken shook her head.

"Humans." Madden heaved a dramatic sigh. "So deprived of life's simple pleasures."

Larken lifted a brow. "Are you going to tell me about this game or not?"

"Each player has an army, and every member of the army is represented by a different piece. The game is played on a circular board equipped with different castles. The point is to seize the other player's castle with your army. Your 'king' leads your army, and your 'court' stays in the castle. If another player kills your king or invades your castle, you lose. But the game gets harder as you play, because more levels can be added to the board. Your army then has to navigate the spirals, making them more prone to ambush. It teaches battle tactics—and in Finder's case, how to hold a decades-long grudge." He grinned at her. "But, as I said, the fact that he's about as intimidating as a puppy doesn't do him any favors."

"He is too intimidating," Larken snapped. "He's..." Her face heated as she trailed off.

"Beautiful as sin?" Madden smiled wickedly at her. The heat spread all the way to the tips of her ears. The words had come so easily between her and Finder the night before, but here in the daylight it was different.

"Yes," she finally admitted, giving Madden a playful shove. "Also, I saved his life, and if I die, which is very likely, then he dies, too. And it doesn't help that I can't talk to males who—" she broke off, "who look like he does."

"Excuse me." Madden pointed to himself. "*I'm* extremely handsome, and you talk to me all the time."

"Larken didn't speak to me for longer, so I must be handsomer than you," Saja said, face grave and eyes not betraying a hint of humor.

"Well, that's hardly *her* fault, you never talk to anyone you've known for less than a decade!"

The three of them burst out laughing, the sound rippling through the forest, bouncing off the ancient trees. Larken was comfortable there, between her faery companions. Friends. They were her friends. She couldn't hold back her smile.

After their laughter died down, Madden looked at her.

"Truly, Larken, just talk to Finder. He wants to talk to you, he really does, but he's afraid. Finder gets attached to things very easily, and they have a tendency to be taken from him."

Larken blinked. Was Madden implying that Finder had become attached to her?

And do you feel the same about him? She wasn't sure if she was ready to face that answer.

"Taken from him in very brutal ways," Saja added darkly. "It was Dahey who convinced Finder to form his *dornán* in the first place, and that took years."

"Finder has a true heart. You'd think that by now, after everything, after all that's been taken from him, that he'd just keep to himself. But he isn't like that. He'll give his all to you, if you earn it." Madden's expression as he spoke was so fierce, so protective.

Well, Madden would know all about loss, she thought with a twinge in her chest.

"Quiet!" Remira's voice echoed through the trees.

Larken and her companions stopped short. Remira lifted her nose to the air. One of her sentinels growled. The wolves' hackles raised as one, their muzzles wrinkling.

"Stay very still," Remira hissed.

Larken glanced around warily. The *dornán* reached for their weapons as the sentinel gave another low growl.

"They're all around us," Remira whispered, taking a step back.

A rustle from between the trees was all the warning Larken had before a black shape lunged at her, and one of the wolves leapt to meet it, tackling it to the forest floor.

CHAPTER TWENTY-FIVE

The creature was a grotesque combination of a dog and a snake. Jet black and corded with muscle, it was smaller than the Warga and slender, but whip-quick and vicious. A long neck swung from its scaly body, slender legs ending in clawed feet. Its mouth opened wide in a roar, exposing rows upon rows of sharp teeth. It snapped at the wolf until the Warga ripped out its throat.

"Basiogs!" Finder cried, unsheathing his sword.

As if his voice were a summoning, more of the creatures poured from the trees.

Madden launched himself in front of her, two long knives drawn from the sheaths on his back. Saja leveled his crossbow, shooting one of the monsters straight through the jaw.

Remira gave a blood-curdling howl. It was a mix of a shriek and a scream, one long note that tore out of her throat like a beacon. It filled Larken with such terror that she forgot for a moment which side the Warga were on.

Finder whirled, slicing the sword into the skull of the Basiogs leaping toward him. The creature darted away, jaws opened wide. The black wolf bounded past Larken and launched herself onto the Basiog's back. The creature gave a chilling scream as the Warga tore viciously into its shoulder. Chunks of flesh flew under the wolf's jaws, her maw covered in stinking blood.

Everything around her was a blur of motion, though Larken stood still. Madden shielded her with his body as Saja and Dahey fanned out to help the Warga.

Larken hissed as scratches opened on her arms from Finder's injuries.

Another Basiog slithered down from the trees, but the white wolf was ready, teeth gleaming as she lunged for the creature's face. The monster swung a clawed foot, catching the wolf in the flank. She howled in pain, blood staining her white fur. Then Dahey was there, plunging his sword into the Basiog's chest.

Finder drove his sword into another Basiog's stomach. Larken stepped back, and Madden took the opportunity to shove her, sending her careening into the trees. He followed, unstrapping a knife from the baldric on his chest.

"Take this," he hissed as he pressed it into her hand.

And just like that, he was gone, back into the thick of the battle. Larken stared down at the dagger in her palm. She tightened her fist around it.

Her head snapped up as a high-pitched yelp spilled through the trees. A Basiog had one of the brown wolves pinned, its snout dripping with the Warga's blood. The creature reared its head to strike, biting the wolf again and again. The wolf yelped pitifully. The other brown wolf leapt at the Basiog, but the creature held firm. Larken glanced around desperately, hoping aid was coming.

But the creatures were everywhere, swarming them. The black and white Warga battled three at once, while Madden and Dahey fought two more. Dahey used his glamour to distract the beings when he could. Remira and Finder were surrounded. No one was there to help the two brown wolves.

Think. She had no experience with knives or fighting of any kind. What could she possibly do?

The pinned wolf was not long for this world. Her companion

desperately tried to drag the Basiog's attention away to free her, but it had its prey firmly in its claws. It would not let go.

Larken took a deep breath, steeling herself. *I am not helpless. And I will not hide in the shadows while my friends die.*

Larken hurled the knife straight at the Basiog's chest.

Larken's breath caught as she watched the knife fly through the air. It tumbled blade over hilt and connected with the beast's brow—hilt side. The knife fell uselessly to the ground. The beast looked up, releasing its jaws from the Warga, and Larken could swear a sneer passed over its features.

Larken tried to swallow, but there was no saliva left in her mouth. One of the wolves dragged her injured sister away by the scruff as the Basiog stalked closer to Larken, each muscle coiled to strike.

Larken stumbled back.

Well, this will be a death written about in songs. Girl throws a knife at a monster and it rutting bounces off.

The beast opened its mouth unnaturally wide, a hissing roar blowing the hair back from her face. It tensed, ready to leap at her, when the two brown wolves lunged at it from either side. One latched on to the Basiog's hind leg while the other went straight for the throat. Although blood flowed freely from the injured wolf's wounds, she attacked the Basiog with renewed vigor. Larken crawled backwards.

Claws, fur, and the tearing of flesh spun through her vision until finally one of the Warga clamped down on the Basiog's neck. Larken coughed as blood sprayed her. She spat violently onto the ground.

The Basiog stilled, a final hiss escaping its mouth. The two wolves growled at the corpse, hackles raised.

Fire exploded around them. Larken lifted her hand to shield herself from the heat, but excitement stirred within her, pulling her toward the flames. The flames snapped at the Basiogs, pushing them back. With a few more shrieks, the remaining Basiogs fled into the trees.

"Don't let them get away, kill them!" Remira cried.

"No," Finder said, sheathing his sword. "I will not use my powers for killing. Not anymore. It is too easy to lose control, and I will never lose control again." His face twisted.

"Your powers are a part of you, Finder," Remira said. "To deny them is to deny a part of yourself."

"That is a part of myself I will never accept," Finder spat.

The glen went quiet. Was Finder referring to the accident that had occurred when he had become Prince? Was that what he meant when he said he had lost control? Had he killed someone?

Larken wanted to ask but didn't want to do so in front of the Warga. She wanted time alone with Finder to talk—just as they had the night before.

Remira lowered her head. "I am also to blame. I had no idea the Basiogs had formed a nest here. If I had known, I never would have led us this way."

Finder's face softened. "It's all right, Rem." Finder glanced around, checking that his *dornán* was safe. "Where's Larken?" he barked.

"Here," she cried hoarsely. The two Warga turned as Finder and Madden rushed through the trees. Finder knelt before her, taking her face in his hands.

"Are you all right?"

She nodded slowly. She stared wide-eyed at the wolves, who regarded her with light brown eyes.

"You saved me," Larken breathed numbly.

One of the brown Warga, the one who had been pinned, replied simply, "You saved me." The huge wolf dipped her head, dropping back on one knee into a bow. Her nose touched the forest floor. Larken, Finder, and Madden all gaped at her.

"You saved my sister," the other wolf said. "Thank you." She copied the bow and touched her nose to the forest floor. Then they shook out their fur and bounded off to meet Remira.

"Is everyone all right?" Larken asked.

"You actually *used* the knife I gave you?" Madden cut in. He stared at her like he had never seen her before.

"No, well…" Larken began, wondering how to tell them that the knife had hit the monster with the hilt and instead continued, "It, um, served as a distraction. The two Warga are the ones who really brought the creature down."

"You attacked the Basiog even though you have no training, and you still managed to save that Warga's life?" Finder stared at her with the same incredulous look that Madden wore.

"Well, yes, but—"

"You foolish girl," Finder said, but his voice wasn't harsh. "You brave, brave girl." He gripped her face with both hands, huffing out a breath that was almost a laugh.

The intoxicating smell of him was so strong she could barely think. But then Finder stood, helping her to her feet, and the moment was gone. He squeezed her hands once, then turned to check on the rest of the group.

"Right then." Madden scrubbed a hand through his hair. "He can be a little intense, but I think that means he's proud of you, Lark."

Larken smiled, happiness blooming within her. Then a terrifying thought struck her. "Saving that Warga's life doesn't mean I'm tangled up in another life debt, does it?"

"No. Life debts only occur between humans and fey."

"Oh, thank the rutting gods," she sighed, and Madden snorted at the relief in her tone. There were only so many life debts she could handle.

Despite a few scrapes and bruises, Larken and her companions had all made it out relatively unscathed. Finder healed her wounds first. Warmth bloomed through her at the gesture, though the wounds stung fiercely as they healed.

Some of the Warga's wounds were more serious, but Remira assured them that Toma would patch them up and told Finder not to use his strength.

"This is where I leave you," Remira said. "Be careful."

"Thank you, Remira," Finder rumbled.

All of them echoed his thanks, and Remira nodded.

They turned to leave and Larken made to follow, but Remira stopped her.

"Thank you for saving the life of my sentinel," Remira said in a low voice. Pride burst to light inside her. While her knife throw hadn't gone as planned, she had still intervened to save the wolf's life. And had succeeded.

Remira studied her. "My offer remains open to you, Larken. You are always welcome in the Darktree Clan."

Larken nodded in thanks, unable to find words. The edges of Rem's lips pulled up into a lupine smile, and she cocked her head.

"You would make an excellent Warga," Remira said, then she turned and bounded through the trees, leaving nothing but swirls of dust behind.

CHAPTER TWENTY-SIX

Larken missed the comforting presence of the Warga. Finder walked slightly ahead, Saja and Dahey flanking him. Madden never strayed far from Larken's side, nor did his hands ever leave the hilts of his knives.

The deeper they ventured into the woods, the thicker and taller the trees became. Every so often the wind would sigh, sending the leaves stirring. Larken looked up to the sky. She could still see slivers of light, though they were faint. Not evening—just dark from the sheer bulk of the trees.

Spiderwebs of glistening silver draped from tree to tree. One of them hung directly before her, strung up between two slender twigs. But what pulled her up short was what was depicted in the web.

It was a portrait of a gorgeous female faery, spun delicately out of the fibers. The strings swept over high cheekbones and huge, silvery eyes. The whole web blew gently in the breeze, making the faery look as though she was half submerged in water. Rays of sunlight caught on the dewdrops lining the web like glittering diamonds.

"Cynyadas," Finder said from behind her. He lifted a hand to touch the web, then stopped, his fingers hovering less than an inch away. "Deeply magical beings. They love making art in their webs."

Cynyada webs surrounded them, filled with portraits, landscapes, and swirling, abstract designs, all made from the silver threads.

"Horribly vain creatures, too." Finder smiled. "They adore compliments. Just think of your compliment, then blow."

Finder drew in close, still not quite touching the web, and blew gently on the strands. A ripple went through them. Then, to Larken's astonishment, a spider the size of her fist scuttled onto the middle of the web. Larken stepped back, having to firmly remind herself that it was not a spider from her world. It was not a spider at all. Though it still had eight legs and eyes, it was covered in shaggy blue fur.

"Thank you, milord," the Cynyada squeaked in a high female voice. Finder smiled at Larken, and she beamed back at him, delighted. The Cynyada looked at Larken with eight huge eyes, waiting. Her front two legs fiddled with each other.

"Oh... Oh!" Larken said.

It's beautiful, she thought, leaning forward to blow gently on the web. The Cynyada shivered.

"Thank you, milady!" she squeaked, and then the little creature scuttled off.

Larken turned back to Finder. "I want one," she said seriously. Finder laughed and Larken smiled at the sound.

"Oh, now look what you've done," Madden groaned. "You've made the other ones jealous."

Larken and Finder turned to see the trees in a flurry of motion. Cynyadas of all different colors were dropping from the branches, frantically spinning new masterpieces in hopes of pleasing them.

Within minutes, all of their faces were plastered around the grove. Some of the paintings showed the fey fighting valiantly in battle, and others showed them performing valiantly in... other feats.

Larken blushed at a depiction of Dahey, completely naked, surrounded by six gorgeous females.

"Yes. This one. This one is a masterpiece." Dahey pointed at it and blew his compliment. Madden rolled his eyes.

Larken busied herself with examining a portrait of her own face. Surprise rippled through her. She had assumed that the Cynyada would have made her stunningly beautiful in order to please her. Instead, the Cynyada had depicted her exactly as she was. Her round, plump cheeks. Her wild, curly hair. Freckles splattered across her nose. It was beautiful. Tears pricked her eyes as she blew her thanks onto the web. A red Cynyada peeked out from behind a leaf and waved a tiny foot in her direction. Larken gave a little wave back.

"No, no, no, they've got this one all wrong." Dahey stood across the clearing, looking at a massive portrait of Finder, also depicted completely naked.

Larken tried not to gape. She forced her gaze away from the web.

"There's no way it's that big," Dahey said, shaking his head sadly. "Absolutely not. They're just fishing for compliments with embellishments."

Finder grinned and slung his arm playfully across his cousin's shoulders.

"Ah, Dahey, don't be upset. They've already told us who's come in first there, and it wasn't either of us."

He pointed to another tree which showed all of Larken's faery companions. Larken found she couldn't tear her eyes away from this one.

"What?" Dahey growled, pointing at the painting. "Why is mine the smallest? *Why do they think I have the smallest?*"

All of them burst into laughter.

"Sorry, mate." Saja grinned at him, clasping him on the shoulder. "Someone has to come in last."

"Well, of course, *you* can bloody say that." Dahey's voice climbed in pitch the angrier he got.

"The Cynyadas are known for their universal truths," Saja said with a sage nod.

"Oh, piss off," Dahey huffed, sending them all into another fit of laughter.

After paying their compliments to all the webs, they continued on their way, winding deeper into the Wyld. Dahey, still irritated, was not speaking to any of them.

She glanced at Finder, wondering why he'd taken the time to show her the Cynyada webs. But some part of her knew why. It was because he cared. He'd stopped to compliment the Cynyadas because he believed in their importance despite—or perhaps even because of—their desire for praise, and so she could see something precious in Airodion.

An eerie trance fell upon the group as they drew closer to the Guardian. Madden and Saja would try to pull them all back, sensing some kind of danger. Larken found herself taking steps backwards instead of forwards with no inkling of what she was doing. Finder herded them all along, constantly reminding them where they were going. Yet the closer they got, the more panicked the group became. Larken trembled, filled with inexplicable terror. She needed to turn back. They all needed to turn back *now*.

"Almost there," Finder urged. "The wards are powerful here, but we must keep going. When the Priestess showed me the path, she must have given me some kind of protection against the glamour." He pushed Saja away as he attempted to wrestle him away from the path.

After a few more unbearable steps, Finder came to an abrupt halt.

Before them lay a ring of mushrooms.

Black as night with grey specks dotting their caps, they formed a wide arc that led deeper into the forest. Larken blinked. She had seen this kind of mushroom before—dotting the grove around the Dark Priestesses' den. Her heart beat so loudly that it was the only sound she could hear.

"We're here," Finder said.

CHAPTER TWENTY-SEVEN

Every bone in her body told her *not* to enter the mushroom circle. Her terror nearly blinded her. It was wrong here—she needed to leave, to run away and never return. She now understood why the Warga hadn't gone near this place.

She sucked in a breath as Finder stepped into the circle. Nothing. No sprung trap, no monsters tearing out of the trees. She followed the rest of the *dornán* inside the ring. Instantly, the fog in her mind lifted.

Though it couldn't have been close to night, they were thrown into pitch darkness as soon as they stepped into the circle.

Glamour, not true darkness, she reminded herself.

She moved to Finder's side, mirroring his movements as he crept through the undergrowth. Even in the darkness she could tell that all the plants, shrubs and trees surrounding her were dead—a sickening echo of the forest around the Priestesses' den.

She crept on, treading lightly. Despite her nerves, she felt protected by the fey around her. A pang of sadness jabbed at her as she considered that one day soon she would have to leave them. Perhaps when this was all over, when the Starveling was dead and all the fey were free, Finder could still come visit her every year—he just wouldn't have to collect a tithe. He could make amends with Ballamor and alleviate the burden that weighed so heavily on his soul. It wasn't as if they would never see each other again. Or maybe she could come visit, too. With no life debt tying her and no Starveling to worry about, she might even like it. She couldn't imagine never laughing again with Madden or having quiet conversations with Saja. Even Dahey—she would miss him, too. He might be all sharp edges, but she could see that there was good in him.

Something had changed during her time with Finder. His body was honed for killing—for strength, power, and magic—and yet he still kept goodness in his heart. And while she didn't blame herself for her anger toward him, she was grateful that their relationship had changed. That it now resembled something akin to friendship. She could not imagine a world without him in it. They would see each other again, when it was all over.

Thick, inky darkness surrounded them now, and a scent lingered in the air, sharp and acrid. A strange pulse of energy beat at the back of her neck, like the feeling of being watched. Hunted.

Larken shifted her feet, unnerved by how fast her vision had gone out. She could make out blurry shapes in the darkness, but other than that, she was completely blind. One blurry shape approached from her left, nothing more than a shadow. It sidestepped a little behind her, and she was about to tell Madden to not bump into her when Finder spoke again.

"Stay close," he instructed. Larken wished he would light a fire, but perhaps he didn't want to attract the Guardian's attention too soon.

"Want me to hold your hand?" Madden asked from Finder's left. Finder's firm "no" echoed through the silence. Larken almost laughed, then squinted her eyes. No, that couldn't be... Madden was just behind her. And Dahey was already by Finder, she had heard his voice before. And Saja was to the right.

But then who was behind her?

Terror poured over Larken the same moment that a gravelly voice cooed in her ear:

"Hello."

Larken did not scream. She just stood there, frozen.

A cylinder of fire exploded in the air. Whoever was standing behind her hissed, and Larken used the distraction to shove the being away. Sharp bones jutted into her palms, making her recoil.

Saja pulled her close to his side, backing away from the figure. He ran his hands lightly down her arms, simultaneously comforting her and asking her silently if she was all right. She nodded, not daring to speak.

Saja gave a nod to Finder, who turned back to the cloaked figure. The low hood concealed all his features. Finder, his face illuminated by his still-sparking hand, wore a look of pure fury.

All of them had drawn their weapons. Larken drew Madden's knife.

"Who has ventured into my domain on this fine night? Might they be a welcome sight?" The hooded figure tilted his head.

"Are you the Guardian?" Finder asked, knuckles white on his sword hilt.

The figure made a sort of snuffling, grunting sound, and Larken wondered if he was having some kind of fit. "A Guardian yes, a Guardian no, that all depends on friend or foe."

To his credit, Finder did not let his exasperation show. "We were told that a Guardian was imprisoned here, and that he can help us wield a weapon of great power."

"Told by whom? Did they seek a ruler's doom?" The hood tilted to the other side, and Larken could hear the smile in his voice.

"Does it matter?" Dahey growled.

"Few know the reason why I lie imprisoned beneath a darkened sky."

"It was the Dark Priestesses," Finder said. "They gave us a weapon—a knife—and told us of a Guardian who can make it whole," he continued firmly, trying to steer the conversation back on path. "And yes, we do want to destroy a great enemy of ours. The Starveling, King of the Fey."

"Finder, Prince of the Autumn days seeks the king of old to raze," the Guardian mused.

How could he know Finder, but Finder not know him? Larken desperately wanted to see his face. Something told her that there was something unnatural under that hood, and though she dreaded finding out what it was, curiosity still itched under her skin. She should just reach out and pull it back...

The Guardian hunched over, turning away from them. He muttered to himself, hissing and spitting on occasion. It was though he was conferring with someone who wasn't there—and Larken wondered if perhaps insanity had taken hold of him.

Finally, the Guardian turned back to them. "Show me the knife you believe will end your strife."

Finder jerked his head at Dahey, who pulled out the knife. He stiffly handed it to the Guardian. The creature unwrapped the bundle as carefully as a mother removed the swaddle from her babe. When he laid eyes on the knife, he hissed in pleasure.

"Will you make it whole?" Finder asked, unable to keep the anxiety from his voice.

"I shall complete this weapon, so deadly quick and deftly hewn," he said. "But you must give the Guardian something in return for this great boon."

"Name it."

The Guardian inhaled suddenly, as though catching a scent. Larken stiffened, pressing closer to Saja.

"When you plunge the weapon into the Starveling's breast, say these words, and so end your quest."

He took a breath, and at first Larken thought he was going to tell them what words he wanted spoken, but all he did was beckon a gnarled finger at Finder. Larken's stomach turned. The flesh was pulled taught over the tendons, the bones standing out in stark relief.

Finder moved closer. The Guardian rested his hand on Finder's forehead. Finder's eyes rolled back in his head and Dahey lunged forward, hand on his sword, but in a moment it was over. Dahey hauled Finder away.

"Once I speak the words the weapon shall be whole?" Finder asked. The Guardian bowed his head. Finder made to reach for the knife, but the Guardian pulled back.

"Do not touch the blade or speak the words until the moment you face your foe. It is crucial that you heed me, lest the magic bring you only woe."

Finder nodded. He wrapped up the knife carefully, tucking it away at his belt.

"And the meaning of the words?"

"They will bring me peace, in time, in time. I cannot leave my grove —the mushroom ring is my boundary-line." The Guardian gave a hair-raising laugh. "The words will find their way back to me to tell me when the Starveling breathes his last. Let us say that we are enemies of old, the king and I, and that our days of kinship are long past. Though I cannot be there to witness his demise, I shall know when he is gone, and the end of his reign shall be my prize."

"Swear to me," Finder said. "Swear to me that this weapon can defeat the Starveling."

The Guardian tilted his head. "Fear not, little prince of the autumn bower. I swear to you that the weapon can overcome the Starveling's power."

Larken sighed in relief as she sensed the magic.

"Promise me you will speak the words," the Guardian hissed.

"I swear I shall speak the words." Finder bowed his head.

Larken shifted, her skin feeling as though it were covered in rough wool. Something still felt wrong. They had the knife now in all its power, so surely it was a victory. So why didn't it feel like one?

The Guardian waved that horrid hand and spoke again. "Leave now and bring my evil foe to his knees. Drive that knife straight through his rotting heart and bring freedom for you and me.".

"Thank you," Finder said. "What you have done for us, for Airodion... We are grateful beyond words."

The Guardian hissed a laugh, then stepped backwards into the lengthening shadows.

They picked their way silently through the undergrowth, Finder lighting another orb of fire to ease their way. They all stayed within an arm's length of each other, none of them speaking, all lost in their own thoughts.

When they stepped out of the mushroom ring, the darkness remained. Larken's breath quickened. They had spent longer in the Guardian's grove than she thought, though it had only felt like a few moments. She shook her head, her mind muddled. That meant that Starveling would call his tithe the following night.

"Finder," she murmured. "The deal you made, the whole exchange, it just felt—"

"Too easy?" he finished for her. She nodded. Finder smiled darkly. "Whoever this Guardian is, whatever he wants, he is not our friend. He placed the words in my mind, just as the Priestess did with images of this grove. The words have great power. I can feel it. Magic is not bound by words, but I fear something else is at play here. I recognized the language as if from a dream…" His gaze turned distant, and he shook his head. "I'm hesitant to speak them, but I gave him my word."

Larken touched his arm briefly. She wanted to tell him that he wasn't alone, that they would face the Starveling together, but the words stuck to her tongue.

"Yes, it was far too simple," he murmured. "No doubt once the Guardian is free from his ring in the forest—if indeed that was what he meant would happen if we kill the Starveling—we will see him again. And when that day comes, I fear whatever he has in store for us."

CHAPTER TWENTY-EIGHT

Finder whistled to summon the horses.

"How did they know where to find us? And how did they make it here so quickly?" Larken asked.

"Our bond with them allows them to sense where we are. They were already on their way to find us," Finder explained. "Fey horses can outpace a human mount, and they do not need to eat or rest for long stretches of time. Portalling is still the fastest way to travel, but it takes a vast amount of my power. I use it only in dire need." Finder pulled Larken up onto Rhylla and settled her in front of him.

In truth, Larken was relieved, if not overjoyed, to see the horses again. She had grown fond of them. She had forgotten how much easier it was to ride than to walk, and she liked that she could spend time talking alone with Finder.

Finder conjured orbs of fire to light their way. The flames basked her face, comforting her as it drove away some of the darkness. Larken sighed as heat touched her face, letting her eyelids close. They comforted her. Rhylla swayed rhythmically beneath her and Finder's arms encircled her in a secure embrace.

Larken leaned back into his chest, despite her muscles seizing up with nervousness. When he didn't shift away, she allowed herself to relax, settling back against him. She could swear he leaned closer, moved his arm into her side a fraction. He hummed a tune behind her. She could feel the vibrations strumming through his chest and neck from the sheer closeness of him.

"Finder," she said.

"Hmm?" he replied, the tune still infused in his voice.

"Why don't you like using your powers? Madden spoke of an accident when you became Prince—is that why?"

Finder sighed. "Accident makes it sound much too harmless. I was fifty years old when I became Prince, which is incredibly young by fey standards. My uncle was Prince before me, so I never imagined that the magic would choose me or someone in my family. It was possible, but unheard of."

Madden, Saja, and Dahey subtlety moved further ahead, though she knew their fey ears would hear every word.

"But I was still a part of the royal family. Dahey and I went away to combat training at the military academy I spoke of where we met Saja, Madden, and Embryn. We were constantly sent out as units to simulate battles with other courts. In one such scenario, the five of us were sent to a small farming village in the Autumn Court. We were told to form a perimeter and monitor for threats. After we were finished, I wanted to do one last sweep, just to make sure I didn't miss anything in town that our general had laid as a test. I sent Dahey, Madden, Saja, and Embryn back to camp.

"It was then that the magic chose me. I had no control over my body. I couldn't move, but the magic exploded inside me. It was euphoric. I felt like a god," he murmured. "But when I finally came to, every single faery in the village was dead. Their houses, shops, and fields burned to ash. If my companions had been there, they would have died as well."

Larken's stomach dropped. It was easy to forget what Finder was capable of. But she understood now, why he hesitated to use his powers when that was the first experience he had with them.

"I began my reign of Prince by killing my own people," Finder said. "And I will never forgive myself for it."

"The powers were new, you weren't expecting them," Larken said. "It isn't your fault that you lost control."

He buried his head into the crook of her shoulder, making her breath hitch.

"My powers terrify me. So much so that I keep them locked away. It's why I try so hard to keep my emotions in check, should it trigger some response from my magic. I have to stay in control."

"No one is in control of themselves all the time," Larken murmured.

"I have to be," Finder said dully, pulling his head away. "Or it could happen again. And when I killed those fey, that wasn't even at the full strength of my powers, not with the Starveling sapping their strength. And what terrifies me most about killing him is that there will be no one holding me back."

"You just have to trust yourself and believe that you have more control now," Larken said. "It's been a hundred years—you have to believe that it won't happen again—even when the Starveling falls. You have to forgive yourself," she finished gently.

Of course, what Finder did was terrible. Of course, it terrified her. But it didn't help any of them on this journey if Finder tortured himself and refused to use his powers.

"You see the good in everyone," Finder said. "Embryn was like that."

Wind whispered through the trees, accompanied by the steady beat of the horses' hooves.

"Was she your *laithnam*?"

Finder hesitated for a moment. Larken bit her lip, wondering if she had gone too far. "No," he said finally. "No, we loved each other, but not in that way. As friends. As warriors. But never as lovers."

Rhylla stopped, arching her neck to bump Finder's boot with her nose.

"Great brute," Finder chuckled, patting her shoulder. "She wants to comfort me but doesn't know how to reach me while I'm riding her."

Something about the moment made Larken's throat close. She took Finder's hand in her own, and he squeezed it gently.

"Not you, too," he breathed in her ear, and her lips turned up into a smile.

"You don't have to tell me anymore." Larken turned to face him and blushed when her nose grazed across his cheek.

"I want to," he said. "It's a relief to talk about her. She wanted to help the humans so badly. In the years leading up to her death she was working on a way to warn the humans about the Starveling, but I made her swear that she wouldn't endanger her court. But she was always there to comfort the tithe girls during our journey, and she always took some keepsake of theirs to burn. To honor them."

Larken gasped as the realization struck her. "Do you remember what she took from Imogen?"

"She took her ring," Finder replied, confusion coloring his voice. "But why—"

"It was her!" Larken nearly shouted the words, elated by her discovery. "It had to be. Castor told me that a female faery visited him while he guarded the bridge. She told him the girls were in danger and gave him Imogen's ring. Without her, Castor never would have started his research. He never would have warned me about the dangers of Airodion. I likely wouldn't have come here at all." The thought struck her hard in the chest. "I wouldn't have been there to save your life."

Finder sighed, a small release of pain. "It would have brought her great peace to know that she helped the humans in some way. But know this, though she might have set things in motion by talking to Castor, it wasn't Embryn's actions that saved my life that day. It was yours."

He brushed his thumb across Larken's knuckles, making her shiver. He pulled away. "She would hate me for it, all the grieving. She would tell me that it was taking me away from my court—that the sadness is too much of a distraction."

"I don't think that anyone gets to tell someone else how to grieve, no matter how much they love them," Larken remarked.

Was Brigid judging her, somewhere in the afterlife, for holding onto her memory long after she was gone from the world? It didn't matter. Grief was the living's journey, and not a matter for the dead to decide.

They paused before a clearing, which Larken could still make out fairly well thanks to Finder's fire and the silver light of the moon.

The forest came alive in a breathtaking meadow, full of gently rolling hills, wildflowers, and green grass. Several floppy-eared rabbits nibbled at dandelions or dozed in the moonlight. A family of spotted deer with graceful legs grazed nearby, the buck lifting his head to peer at them. Trees burst with fluffy pink buds, and everywhere she looked there was a different kind of flower. Foxglove, peonies, wild roses, and sunflowers shot from the ground in bursts of color. The air no longer reeked of decay and fear, but rather a cool breeze tickled her face and senses, bringing with it the smell of lilac and rain. Larken desperately wished it was morning so she could see it all bathed in the sunlight.

"The Spring Court border," Finder said.

The Spring Court. Madden, explaining how his *laithnam* and daughter had been brutally murdered by members of the Spring Court. By their princess, Etain.

Each of her companions wore expressions of weariness, dread, distaste, or, in Madden's case, rage. A muscle ticked in his jaw, and he had his fists wound so tightly in his mount's mane that Larken worried he would pull clumps of Bresel's hair out. Why had they come so close to the border, when Madden had such terrible history here?

But the image of the map of Airodion she had seen when they had met with Remira slowly came to life in her mind. The way the boarders of the Autumn and Spring Court aligned formed a strange swath of land where the Spring Court cut into the Autumn Court. She knew what Finder would say before he even said it.

"If we cut through the Spring Court, we will reach the Stone Circle by tomorrow evening," Finder said. "If we don't..."

His *dornán* exchanged uneasy glances. Larken traced the image of the map in her mind. If they cut through the Spring Court, it would be a straight shot to the Starveling's land.

"We can't risk an encounter with Etain," Dahey said.

"She'll be on her way to the Stone Circle by now," Finder countered. "Etain likes to spend the night before the tithe in her estate in the south."

"Couldn't you create another portal to take us directly to the Stone Circle?" Larken asked.

Finder shook his head. "We would arrive with my powers too drained to face the Starveling."

"It would be unwise—" Saja began, but Dahey interrupted him.

"No, Finder, this wasn't part of the plan," Dahey growled. "We can't veer off course."

"Do you want to take the risk of going around?" Finder said. "What happens if we run into trouble?"

If Remira's map had been to scale, as she assumed it was, she agreed with Finder that it was too far to go around. "If we went around, we would lose all the ground we gained by portalling here," Larken said. "I might not know everything about Airodion, but I do know everything about reading a map. I think a shortcut might be worth the risk."

"You're sure Etain has left?" Saja rubbed his jaw.

Finder nodded. "I'm sure of it. Nor do I think she would risk a fight this close to the tithe. She wants to keep her tithe girl safe and happy." Finder turned to address Madden. "You do not have to come," Finder said.

Madden shook his head, jaw still tight. Wisps of black hair blew across his face, but he stood resolute. Ready to follow his prince wherever he went.

Finder tipped his head in what might have been a bow, or a thank you. He looked at the rest of his *dornán* in turn, making sure they agreed with the decision. But they clearly didn't agree, and Finder had still dug his heels in. Of course, it did not look as though they truly had another choice, but would Finder even let them choose?

She wondered if it grated on them that Finder made all the decisions. Dahey disagreed; that much was plain. Madden would do it—for Finder, but it was clear he was uncomfortable. Saja also seemed to have his doubts.

All bowed their heads.

Larken knew they wouldn't let any harm come to her. But the shard of icy fear that had wedged itself in her gut when she'd realized where they were just got sharper.

"What about the labyrinth?" Dahey asked.

Larken's stomach sank. "Labyrinth?"

"A magical labyrinth guards this area of the Spring Court as we are so close to Laurelith, the main citadel," Finder replied.

"We have never entered the labyrinth before," Dahey said. "What if it costs us more time than if we skirt the border? And what if we get trapped within?"

"I can get us through it." Larken squared her shoulders. "You all have your own skills. This is mine. All I've done since I was a child is make maps. In my head, on paper, in my dreams—and if there's anything I do know, it's where I've been and where I'm headed. I can lead us through the maze."

Finder and his *dornán* looked at her.

"You've asked me to trust all of you. Now it's time for you to trust me."

Larken looked back to the meadow. It seemed innocent enough, though her time in Airodion had taught her that her mortal eyes could deceive her. She would have to rely fully on her skills when they reached the maze; all of their lives depended on it. But this was the one thing she was good at. The one thing she knew she could do—and had proved to herself that she was capable of.

"I can do this," she said.

"We trust you, Larken," Finder said.

"At least she's had *some* glamour training from me," Dahey said, rubbing the back of his neck. "That should be of some help."

"She's helped us find an easier path before," Madden acknowledged. "I trust her."

"I trust you, Larken," Saja rumbled.

Her friends' words lifted her heart.

They were all in agreement: they would take the shortcut. The horses walked side by side toward the meadow. A shimmer hung in the air before them. When they passed through it, Larken's eyes widened in disbelief.

There, spread out before them as far as the eye could see, was the labyrinth.

CHAPTER TWENTY-NINE

A massive gate rose before them, patterned with intricate gold designs. They swirled and twisted, almost seeming to move of their own accord, like dozens of huge snakes. Dark hedges loomed on either side, the foliage dense and unyielding. Thorns glinted alongside blooms of roses, and strange sounds echoed from within. The gates swung open on silent hinges, beckoning to the horses and riders. The path disappeared into darkness, the maze drinking in the light from Finder's orbs. The horses dropped their heads and pressed their ears against their necks.

"We'll leave the horses here. Their speed and stamina won't help us in the maze—not with the labyrinth's shifting nature. And I don't want them attracting unwanted attention. We can summon them when we reemerge," Finder said.

The horses tossed their heads and stamped their great hooves, clearly upset by the thought of leaving their riders in such a place. They finally relented after some firm words from the fey, and they trotted off back into the Wyld.

Larken's heart sank as the horses disappeared completely into the darkness, and she and her companions entered the labyrinth.

Larken led the way, Finder at her side with his sword held aloft. The steel glided through the fog. She wiped her palms on her pants. The fey were putting so much faith in her skills—what if she let them down? After all, she had never been in the maze before. Not to mention, Finder had made it clear that it would not act like a normal maze.

Just focus, you can do this, Larken reassured herself. She had helped the fey before, proven that she was a useful member of the group. A maze was just its own kind of map, one she had to solve. She could do this.

The path widened until Larken could no longer see the opposite wall of the maze. A silvery mist concealed the dark sky above them and the path ahead of them. Larken could see through it enough to spot the faint outline of Finder beside her, but not much else. Yet that didn't stop her from catching glimpses of *things* moving through the mist.

The first time she saw one of the creatures, she had gasped. Instantly, Finder's hand covered her mouth. He shook his head and pressed a finger to his lips. Larken had gotten the message well enough. If the creatures weren't bothering them, they shouldn't bring attention to themselves, lest they change their minds. Finder didn't light the way with his flames—making sure not to attract the creatures.

Though she knew not to acknowledge the things in the fog, it didn't make her any more used to them. And the mist partly obscured the creatures well. Sometimes their only warning was a quick motion from Finder to press themselves against the wall of thorns. Some were big hulking things that lumbered past, illuminated only by flashes of moonlight. Others were tall and skinny with sharp fingers and long noses like rats. Their heads peeked out from the mist, and Larken knew she would have nightmares for months. Or years.

She used Dahey's methods for seeing through glamour—and sometimes she could tell that the creatures weren't real, but others she couldn't tell. A mix of real and unreal was somehow worse, for she could never fully know.

Though they passed many creatures, none of them made any move to attack or engage the group in any way. Larken found this both comforting and unsettling. Why didn't they strike? It wasn't as though the creatures couldn't see them. They made eye contact often enough, eyes glinting, nostrils and mouths opening to breathe in their scent.

Her mind turned and turned, mirroring her feet as she led her companions around the endless curves and twists of the maze. She kept track of the path they had taken and created a mental image to trace, predicting where the dead ends would be. She hadn't led them to one, yet.

She couldn't stop thinking about the things in the mist. The more she thought about it, the more nervous she became. It was as though the creatures were waiting for something. Or maybe they had orders to leave them alone. Was Etain the one giving those orders? Was she planning something? What if it wasn't Etain at all? Could the Starveling be a part of the labyrinth? Larken's mind ran from her, unravelling bit by bit.

The thorny walls showed no signs of acting appropriately, either. Sometimes the path became wide enough for five horses to ride abreast, and sometimes the huge hedges knitted so closely together that Larken and her companions had to drag themselves through. Her face burned from the scratches. Her clothing was in shreds.

It didn't seem to matter how much distance she put between herself and the wall of thorns; she always got cut.

She led them around another right turn.

"I can't make sense of this place—it muddles my senses. But clearly yours are working fine. It's a good thing we have you to keep us on the path," Finder murmured.

Larken smiled at his praise.

They walked for minutes, or hours—there was no way to tell time within the maze—not encountering a single thing. Then shapes would appear again in the mist, calling to her, beckoning with misty fingers. Mama and Papa. Villagers from home she thought she'd never miss but did. Rosin, clutching her bloody stomach.

She dug her nails into her palms, determined to ignore them.

She wondered who her companions saw. Some figures she could vaguely make out—a male called to Saja, a female to Finder. While the figures she knew from her own life were near-perfect copies, the ones of her companions were grey and foggy, with blurred edges that she couldn't quite make out.

Dahey lunged toward one of the figures, letting out a strangled gasp. Larken could faintly make out the name on his lips: *father*.

Finder hauled Dahey in by the back of his shirt. A tiny figure beckoned to Madden, its little fingers straining to touch him. Madden turned away, jaw clenched so tight Larken thought his teeth must be grinding to dust.

She forced her mind to focus on Dahey's training. The figures couldn't be real. While she had been startled when the figures first revealed themselves, they now only gave her a deep sense of sadness. She knew Mama and Papa weren't here, nor was anyone from Ballamor. And she knew that the dead were gone.

As she thought this, the figures slowly faded into the mist, disappearing. A small victory, at least.

She knew the feeling wouldn't last.

CHAPTER THIRTY

As they rounded yet another long curve in the labyrinth's winding corridors, Finder grabbed her arm, pulling her to a stop. He peered warily ahead. Larken didn't see anything. The pathway had narrowed somewhat, forming a hallway of thorns. Madden and Saja shifted behind her, and Dahey stared silently ahead.

Finder lifted his sword, his *dornán* leveling their weapons, as well. He stepped forward.

As if springing a hunter's trap, the maze launched its next attack. Hands reached from the thorns, straining toward them.

Saja had an arm around her in an instant, hoisting her back from the uncurling fingers. Dozens of arms appeared through the thorns. The fingers twisted, desperately clutching at her, reaching, reaching...

"Don't touch them," came Finder's calm voice. He kept his sword aloft, but stepped back, trying to escape. More hands came through the thorns behind them, sealing off the way they'd come. They had no choice but to press forward.

"Don't touch them, and don't try to see what they're attached to," Finder continued, cautiously walking forward again. Larken swallowed, her throat dry. She tried not to look at the hands. The fingers quivered like they wanted nothing more in this world than to touch her.

They walked, inch by inch, narrowly avoiding the grasping fingers on all sides. They could barely move without their boots skimming against flesh.

The walls turned into a tunnel. A tunnel with arms, with hands that grabbed at her, threatening to pull her beneath the thorns.

On they went, each step an eternity. Some of the hands had nails bitten down to the quick; others had claws; some had the arms of burly men; others had scales... all reaching for her.

She didn't see it happen. One moment, Finder and Dahey were upright, the next, Dahey was stumbling, tripping into Finder.

An accident. A harmless trip.

If not for the hands that reached out to grab them both.

Saja moved. He lunged for Finder, pushing his prince out of the way.

Pushing Dahey straight into their grasp.

Finder cried out as Dahey fell back into the thorns, the hands immediately dragging his cousin to the ground. Dahey strained, panic filling his eyes at the strength the limbs possessed. He pulled back, but he was in range of the other hands now, and they latched onto his clothing, his boots, his hair—anything they could reach.

Madden and Finder seized Dahey's arms. Saja stood frozen in place, his face deathly pale.

Madden drew one of his knives and sawed through one of the hands holding his friend. Blood spewed, and the stump retreated back into the thorns. More of its brethren rose in its place.

Larken fell to her knees at Dahey's side, drawing her knife. She went to work on the hands latched to his clothing, trying not to flinch when the fingers fell to the grass in soft thumps.

Finder had one hand at Dahey's shirt collar, hauling him back, and the other held his sword. The mist of the maze swirled around them.

Dahey jerked, his legs already completely pulled under. Larken could hear every beat of her heart. She heard Finder yelling. The mist swirled thicker around them.

The hands pulled.

"Don't let go," Dahey cried, both of his arms wrapped around Finder. His eyes were so filled with terror Larken thought she would drown in it. She sliced at two of the hands holding him. Blood spewed anew, and the hands slowly retracted. But more hands were already emerging, their fingers bent into claws, wrapping in Dahey's hair and jerking his head back. He gasped in pain.

"No!" Finder snarled. Spit flew as he yelled with effort, hoisting Dahey back with all his strength. He had nothing to brace his feet on, and they toiled uselessly in the dirt. Larken cut again and again with her knife, but it did nothing to stem the tide.

"There's too many of them!" she cried.

Finder howled, flames leaping from his hands. Shrieks and cries rose from the thorns, making the hair on Larken's neck rise. Some of the hands retreated, blistered from the flames, but more rose in their place. Sweat beaded on Dahey's brow, though none of the flames touched him.

Saja hacked at the limbs with manic rage, his golden eyes filled with fury. Madden whirled his dagger, severing any hand that came near it. Blood sprayed through the air, coating the fey and the thorns.

Dahey's arms slackened around Finder, sliding down as the hands dragged him into the thorns.

"Don't you dare," Finder snarled. "Don't you dare give up!"

"It wasn't supposed to be like this. This wasn't supposed to happen," Dahey whispered, looking up at his cousin's face. He had been dragged up to his chest now, and the thorns scratched Larken's arms as she tried to pull him away. She grunted, her muscles straining with effort. She would not give up.

The fire blazed around them, burning away the mist, blackening the thorns, and filling the air with the scent of charred flesh.

Saja fell to his knees, wrapping his hands under Dahey's shoulders, pulling them as much as he dared. Dahey screamed and Larken heard a sickening pop.

"I'm sorry." Tears fell down Saja's cheeks. "I'm so sorry."

Finder gritted his teeth, pulling Dahey as hard as he could. Blood poured from his mouth from a bitten cheek.

"I'm sorry," Dahey whispered. Hands circled his head, yanking him backwards until the thorns swallowed him from view.

Finder turned into a madman.

"I can feel that he's still alive, I can *feel* it," he snarled.

Of course—the *dornán* bond.

Finder threw himself at the thorns. They cut into him—and into her, making her scream.

Finder pulled back at the sound of her cries, falling to his knees before her. "I'm sorry," he whispered. "I'm so sorry, Larken. I forgot..." He ran his hands over her scrapes, healing her. They burned so badly, she clenched her teeth.

Saja berated the thorns with his fists.

Larken stood next to Madden in a daze. Saja began to wheeze.

"Stop," Finder said. But Saja kept fighting, kept tearing at the thorns, trying to find the lost member of the *dornán*.

"I said stop," Finder growled. Saja ignored him, pressing on even as hacking coughs tore from his throat.

"Damn it, Saja, enough. You're too weak!" Finder shouted. "You're too weak to save him."

Saja flinched. Larken knew that Finder's words had cut him deeply.

Finder sighed. "I'm sorry, Saja—I didn't mean it that way—"

"It was my fault," Saja rasped. "I pushed you out of the way. I chose him."

"We all would have done the same," Madden said, digging the tip of his knife into the dirt. "Finder is our prince. His life comes first."

Finder said nothing, though cold resentment lit his eyes. He might be their prince, but he wished for them to be equals. But his *dornán* would never see him as such—he would always be their prince.

"We'll—we'll find a way to get to Dahey. We won't leave him. But we won't do him any good here. We have to move," Finder said.

Larken looked at him through blurry tears.

"Get up," Finder told them. "We have to keep going. Get up."

Larken hoisted herself to her feet and led the way once more.

CHAPTER THIRTY-ONE

The table was an ornate, gorgeous thing made of glass and marble, delicately wrought with gold. Finder had seen it first; the small table blocking their path deeper into the maze. Curiously enough, the fog didn't come near the table, but roiled a few feet away.

The four of them had approached the table warily. Atop the surface was a white porcelain plate edged in golden leaf-work. On the plate itself rested four bite-sized cakes. Flawlessly frosted with white buttercream, a delicate script adorned the center of each cake:

Eat Me.

Larken frowned at the cakes. None of them were ignorant enough to actually eat something the maze produced, especially when it had "eat me" written on the top.

"Let's try to go around it," Larken said. They skirted around the edge of the table, all keeping their eyes on the cakes. *A band of seasoned warriors afraid of some pastries*—an absurdity she would have found funny had they not been in the labyrinth.

A few steps later they found themselves face to face with the same table they had passed a moment ago. The plate of cakes remained.

Eat Me.

Dread washed over her.

"We have to eat them," Saja said, his voice hollow.

"We have no idea what they'll do to us!" Madden protested. He speared one of the cakes with his knife and flung it into the thorns. The cake vanished.

Another cake appeared on the plate in the exact same position it had been before.

Eat Me.

"What if only one of us eats them, so then only one of us suffers the effects?" Larken suggested. As if in response, three more cakes appeared on the plate.

"If you eat four," Finder said, eyes dark, "another three will appear, for the rest of us still have to eat one." He kicked the entire table over. It landed without a sound and disappeared.

"Go," he said. But as he turned to charge ahead, he rammed his left knee into the table. A marble table, laden with four cakes with perfect frosting.

"*Move,*" he snarled, and Larken wasn't sure if he was talking to them or the table. Finder made it two steps before the table materialized again.

"*Eat Me.*"

The hairs on the back of her neck rose when the voice spoke the words. Just a faint whisper echoing in the mist.

"Finder."

He paid her no heed.

They tried everything. They each put a cake in their pocket, trying to convince the table that they had eaten them. But as soon as they tried to leave, the cakes would vanish and reappear on the table before them. They smashed the cakes with their fists, cut them with knives, even cleaved the table in two. Each time, the table returned. Each time, four cakes stood stacked atop it.

And every time the table reappeared another voice added itself to the rising clamor.

"*Eat Me. Eat Me. Eat Me.*"

She clapped her hands over her ears, but she couldn't block the sound.

"EAT ME. EAT ME. EAT ME."

The voices rose to shrieks and screams, and her head almost split in two.

"Finder," she moaned, clutching her head.

"What if we eat them one at a time? So we can see what it does?" Larken suggested, near shouting over the din.

"EAT ME. EAT ME. EAT ME!"

Saja reached for a cake, intending to be the first one to try. Finder snarled at him to stop, yet as soon as Saja's hand closed over the cake, it refused to move. He pulled, but the cake had turned to stone, welded to the plate beneath it.

Finder clenched his jaw. "They must be eaten together."

"EAT ME. EAT ME. EAT ME!"

"Together, then," Larken said.

"EAT ME. EAT ME. EAT ME!"

As one, they each took a cake. Larken's lifted easily in her hand, the texture suggesting a delightfully moist crumb. But the thought of putting it in her mouth made her nauseous. Steeling herself, she looked at her companions.

"Cheers, you lot," Madden said.

"EAT ME. EAT ME. EAT ME!"

"One," said Finder.

"EAT ME. EAT ME. EAT ME!"

"Two," said Saja.

"EAT ME. EAT ME. EAT ME!"

"Three," breathed Larken.

"EAT ME! EAT ME! EAT ME! EAT—"

She took a bite.

CHAPTER THIRTY-TWO

Larken stared into the face of her dearest friend as she said the words that would tear Larken apart.

"Because I can't make a life out of a hobby! And neither can you." Brigid clenched her fists. "Can't you understand that? There's nothing keeping me here."

Larken flinched. "If you truly think that, then you aren't the person I thought you were. You're just like every other girl stupid enough to dream about being chosen."

Brigid's blue eyes turned to ice. "You know very well that it's been impossible for Da to work or train my brother after his accident."

Larken pushed away her sympathy for Brigid's father. He had shoed horses thousands of times, but a young mare had spooked and kicked him in the face. Most days he didn't even recognize his own family.

"They could use the coin, Larken. And I would gladly leave them behind if I knew it meant they never had to work a day in their lives again."

Brigid's older brother could have taken over the smithy in a few years if his father had been well enough to continue training him. And Brigid's younger brother was barely out of diapers. Larken felt for them, she truly did, but she couldn't stop the hurt and betrayal that roiled within her that Brigid would leave her family behind for the faery lord but not for Larken.

Brigid's face softened. "I can't go away to school. Not when that would only cost them money."

Tears welled in Larken's eyes. "When were you going to tell me all of this?" She'd known things had been bad for Brigid's family since the accident, but not once in her life had Larken ever heard Brigid mention that she wanted to be chosen. That she would even consider it in dire circumstances.

"I knew you'd be upset. But we all have to grow up sometime. We can't chase silly dreams forever." She turned away from Larken to look out the window, her back stiff.

Anger bubbled inside Larken at Brigid's dismissive tone. How dare Brigid call her cartography a silly dream when Brigid herself wished to be swept away by a faery lord? Larken would have to work for her dream, claw and toil for any ounce of respect at the schools in the South. She would have to fight to make a name for herself, a living for herself. But Brigid wanted someone else to solve her problems for her. She would rely on her looks to elevate herself, while Larken had never had that chance.

"Why can't you admit that the true reason you don't want to move south is because you're scared that your art is too inadequate to make you any coin, so you have to whore out your body to the faery lord instead," Larken seethed.

Brigid's face crumpled.

Larken's eyes widened, and she reached for her friend, wishing more than anything in the world that she could take back the words she had just said.

But Brigid had already run out the door.

❧

Larken's eyes flew open, her heart pounding as though her fight with Brigid had just happened. Shame flooded her as the wounds from her fight with Brigid scraped open once more. She glanced around, half expecting that Brigid would reappear and she would be doomed to relive those moments with her forever. But Larken was still surrounded by the thorny walls of the labyrinth.

It was just a dream, Larken told herself. Larken groaned, pushing herself up. The cake was still in her hand, a perfect bite-sized chunk missing from the side. It read:

AT ME

Larken glared at it. The cake, unsurprisingly, did nothing. She tossed it aside. She didn't feel any different. In fact, it had just tasted like a regular cake.

Her companions were gone.

Oh, Twins, she moaned inwardly, scrambling to her feet.

The labyrinth looked no different than it had before, except for the fact that she was completely alone. Her heart punched into her throat, the memory of her fight with Brigid disappearing from her mind. Where was Finder? Where had her companions gone? The top of the maze was still shrouded in a thick fog. She reached a hand toward one hedge, making sure it wasn't an illusion of some kind. But something about her hand pulled her up short.

Her fingers were longer. She frowned, flexing her hand. It was barely noticeable, but still there. The soft flesh had been whisked away, making the bones and tendons more pronounced.

Strange. She dropped her hands to her sides, unsettled by the sight of them. The movement brought her attention to another change in her body.

Her sides, previously padded and curved, were now lithe and taught. Larken's eyes widened as she ran her now-slender hands over her belly. The soft stomach she'd always known was gone.

Her legs had slimmed, too. Her thighs had all but disappeared, replaced with long, slender things. Larken lifted careful fingers up to her face, terrified at what she might find there. She had lost the fat around her neck, and her jawline had grown sharp. Her lips were fuller, her nose was a perfect slope, and her lashes were so long they grazed her brows when she blinked.

Though she already knew what she would find there, Larken reached for her ears, trembling fingers stretching up, up...

To find delicate points.

"Holy Twins," Larken breathed, "I'm fey."

As if the labyrinth heard her unspoken plea, a mirror appeared out of the mist, lying face-up in the grass. Larken shifted, now uncomfortably aware of her body.

The maze had given her something she'd always wanted but had never quite been able to speak aloud. An unattainable dream that Ellevere pushed upon its female subjects. The maze had made her beautiful. No, beyond that—it had made her *perfect*. Because the fey were perfection.

Details of the maze sharpened, her heightened sight able to pick up on images her human eyes never could. Upturned leaves and single blades of grass popped out at her. Tiny branches within the walls of the maze came into sharp focus. She rubbed her temples, wondering how her companions never grew tired of all this *seeing*. Her sense of smell had sharpened, as well. It wasn't just damp earth she smelled, but lilacs and roses, sweet rain and honey.

Larken wiggled her toes in the grass, watching as they moved. They were her feet, though she felt detached, as though she were watching someone else make the same movements. An itching sensation covered her body and she shuddered. It felt wrong, somehow, being in this body. Like she was sleeping in a bed that wasn't hers.

This had to be an illusion. Yet some part of her hesitated to use Dahey's training because some part of her wanted it to be real.

Nervously, she knelt down, placing her hands on either side of the mirror's golden rim, and paused. Her fingers curled in the lush grass, a sweet floral scent wafting by on the breeze. The fog that concealed the top of the maze had also lowered to the grassy labyrinth floor, caressing her hands and legs as she knelt there, braced against the mirror.

She took a breath, then looked down.

It was her, but it was not her. Larken gaped at her reflection, and the girl in the mirror did the same. Seeing the sloped nose, long lashes, and pointed ears with her own eyes was more shocking than just feeling them with her fingers. The color of her hair was different, too—a shining, ash-white instead of dirty gold. It fell in a silvery sheet to the bottom of her ribcage. Her eyes had even turned into a light chocolate brown, illuminated by the faint light.

It was everything she wanted to be. Larken cupped her own cheek, marveling at the smoothness. Gone were the angry red spots that plagued her, gone was any plainness. She was beautiful now, and her heart swelled from some unknown emotion. Was it happiness? She pushed away the itch crawling across her skin. The feeling that tugged at the back of her mind.

Not only that, but she was *fey*. Would Finder see her differently? She couldn't control the thrill that ran through her at the thought. She wanted him to see her. She wanted all of the *dornán* to see her. No longer was she a drab mortal girl, awkward and useless in this magical faery realm. She ignored how shallow she was being. If she was a faery, all of her human problems would fade away.

"Larken?"

Larken froze, hands clutched on the rim of the mirror. She turned, not wanting to believe, not daring to hope...

Brigid stood before her.

Her friend was exactly how she remembered. Willowy and tall, with long black curls. Eyes as clear blue as a summer sky. Hundreds of freckles spread across her face, visible even from Larken's place a few feet away. She looked the same as the day she'd been chosen.

Her dearest friend.

"Brigid," Larken breathed. Suddenly they were in each other's arms, laughing, crying, touching each other's faces.

"You're so beautiful now!" Brigid exclaimed.

Larken blinked. Brigid would never have said—

"And look—I have them, too." Brigid brushed back her hair, revealing her pointed ears.

"How—how is this possible?" Larken asked, memories of Finder and the Choosing Ceremony crashing into her. Brigid couldn't be here. "Finder, he—" Larken paused, unable to make herself finish the sentence. "He killed you," she murmured finally.

Brigid smiled. "He didn't kill me, silly." She took Larken's hand in her own. "He lied, that's all. I completed the special task for him, and now I'm here."

A seed of doubt sprouted in Larken's mind. Brigid's face twisted into a spasm, but it quickly disappeared, making Larken wonder if she had seen it at all. "That can't be," Larken said, squeezing Brigid's hand. She felt real. Alive. But that couldn't be right. "There is no special task. The fey use girls as tithes to the—"

"They don't," Brigid snapped. "Finder lied to you. We complete the special task, and then we get turned into fey." Her friend took her hand. "I know you were jealous of me when I left. The Twins blessed me to look like the fey even when I was human, and I know that was hard for you to bear. But look how perfect you are now."

Brigid would never say something like that. Or would she?

My body's changed since we were girls. I have a real chance now. The words Brigid had spoken during their fight tore into her.

"Don't you want to be a faery and be with me? Forever?" Brigid pressed Larken's hand to her cheek. "I'm *real*, Larken. Can't you feel me?"

She did feel real. Her skin was soft and smooth, her hand so warm.

"We can live forever," Brigid whispered. "We can have everything we've ever wanted."

"I can't stay here, Brigid. I have to get back to Ellevere, to warn the humans about what's happening here. I have to get back to my family," Larken said, her voice breaking.

"But you said," Brigid pouted. "You said if you could only see one of us again that you would choose me."

Larken's breath whooshed out of her. How could Brigid have known that? She had only ever admitted it to the Dark Priestesses. Larken's blood went cold. "But the Starveling—"

"Forget about him." Brigid waved her hand. "Think of what we could accomplish, here. You never would have gone away to school in the South without me. You couldn't do anything without me, could you?" Brigid gave her a pitying look. "But we can be together, now. I can help you with your maps again. You obviously need it."

Larken curled inwards, shrinking away from Brigid's words.

Brigid would never say that. But Larken had said those very things to herself hundreds of times—that she couldn't accomplish anything without Brigid by her side.

Larken clenched her fists. No. Venturing through Airodion had only proved that Larken was capable of living without Brigid. She had learned that her mapmaking and directional skills weren't dependent on Brigid at all.

Brigid would never have said such things. Brigid would never focus so intently on Larken's appearance or try to make Larken leave her loved ones behind. This wasn't real. None of it was real.

They had fought. But Brigid hadn't wanted to be chosen for some vain reason. She had only wanted to spare her family from hardship. Larken knew that, now. Reliving the fight had only reminded her of it. They had both spoken from fear and anger. Both said things to hurt one another that they didn't truly mean. But Larken had still loved Brigid until the very end. And she knew in her heart that Brigid had forgiven her too, even though they had never spoken those words aloud to each other.

Larken wanted to apologize to the girl who stood before her, but the words died on her tongue. Larken would not be able to get closure, not from this wraith. Because the being that stood before her was not the real Brigid.

Larken backed up a step, but Brigid latched onto her forearm with an iron grip.

"Don't you want to be with me?"

Larken had thought that being reunited with Brigid would put an end to all her pain. She had relied on Brigid since they were children; for confidence, for support, for everything. True friendship required balance. Larken wished she could have experienced that with Brigid, but her friend was gone now. And Larken had to let her go.

When Larken looked up, Brigid had vanished. The mirror remained, set upon the ground like a silver pool. Larken knelt down beside it.

"Don't you want to be beautiful?" the mirror seemed to say.

And Larken was beautiful. The kind of beautiful that men died for, that songs were sung about. But it was not really her in the mirror.

Larken thought about her life. How she had fought to accept herself the way she was. That kind words, gentle actions—those were worth so much more than looks. And her companions in Airodion had helped her realize it, too. That she could make herself beautiful by being a good person—a good *human*.

She thought of all the pain and torment Finder and his *dornán* had gone through in their long lives, and she didn't want that. She didn't want to be fey. She didn't want to be immortal. She wanted someone who would love and accept her for who she was. Someone she could grow old with. Someone who could go on adventures, understand what it meant to be mortal.

If she truly became the beautiful fey princess she saw gazing back at her, it would destroy the human inside her. And she wouldn't accept that.

She would never trade her own body, the one that had gotten her through so much, for some stranger's. She had crossed the bridge to find her friend. She had saved Finder's life. She had eased Rosin's passing. She had helped save one of the Warga from the Basiogs. She was guiding her friends through the maze. All of this—*herself*. No one else. And she had done it all in this body. A body she had hated, and, somewhere along the way, grown to rely on and respect. Larken had fought a war inside herself—and was still fighting it—to accept herself as she was, to see herself as beautiful in her own way, and she would never give that up.

"Don't tell me what I need to look like to love myself."

Larken snarled as she brought both of her fists down on the mirror as hard as she could, shattering it into glinting shards.

CHAPTER THIRTY-THREE

Larken blinked, shielding her eyes from the sun. Her nightmare dreamscape had ended. Her companions lay in a half-circle around her, all alive and awake. Finder breathed a sigh of relief at the sight of her. They had all eaten the cakes, so they had to have experienced their own visions as well. She wondered briefly if her companions knew about what she had seen but dismissed the idea. She sensed that the point of the dreamscape was to face your desires and fears alone. But if they had all woken up, then why did everyone look so afraid?

She followed their gazes and swallowed heavily. Before them stood a cadre of armed knights. Their armor blazed in the light of the rising sun.

"Ah, my old friends, here at last," came a high, chillingly sweet voice.

One of the guards hauled Larken to her feet before she could blink. Finder lunged forward, flames flickering around his hands, but the guard unsheathed his dagger and pressed it against her ribs. Finder stilled.

"Oh, we *will* have fun today."

Showered in flower petals and beautiful as a dream stood the owner of that lovely voice. Her long, white-blonde hair flowed in loose curls down to her ribcage. A dress of pale gossamer silk embroidered with floral designs clung to her frame. Lips red as a cut throat curved into a smile, revealing straight, white teeth.

The Princess of the Spring Court.

Etain.

No, no, no, she isn't supposed to be here! Larken thought desperately.

Etain was the kind of beautiful mere mortals could not even conceive of. Her beauty defied comparison. The only thought Larken could form was that she was as beautiful as death—the kind of death people begged for after suffering. When Etain looked at her and smiled, Larken could swear she saw her own death reflected in the faery's eyes. She was beauty and terror spun into one.

Each of her guards' breastplates bore what Larken assumed was the sigil of the Spring Court. Whorls and intricate designs framed a winged deer taking flight in the center. Freshwater pearls were studded throughout, glimmering softly in the sunlight.

"Here, milady. I found this one wandering about in the maze," one of the guards said, throwing down a battered-looking faery before them.

"Dahey," Larken gasped.

Dahey scrambled away from the soldiers and into Finder's embrace. Finder buried his face in his cousin's neck. Madden sat back, his shoulders slumping in relief. Saja was pale and panting, his face drawn.

Larken closed her eyes as relief flooded her. Dahey was okay. He was safe.

Saja reached out to touch Dahey, as if to make sure he was indeed still with them. "I'm sorry," he whispered, and Dahey clasped his arm.

"It's okay, brother."

One of the guards lifted his visor to peer at Madden. "I know this one, milady." He sneered down at Madden. "I remember how his *laithnam* squirmed on our tables."

"Bavvard," Madden snarled.

Etain gave a laugh that sounded as joyful and innocent as a little girl's, and she clapped her hands merrily. "I think we should return to the gardens, should we not?" She turned on her heel with a flourish, revealing dainty blue shoes.

"Etain," Finder hissed.

"I was so surprised to find *you* in my labyrinth, with the tithe being so close. Whatever were you doing there?" She held up a hand as if to stop him from a reply. "No, don't tell me," she said. "I'm sure you'll be spilling your secrets soon enough." She gave them a smile steeped in falseness. "You almost made it, too. No one survives all my traps, and yet, it seems like you lot have been particularly lucky." She glanced down at her nails. "But you see, no one leaves the maze without my permission. The final safeguard puts you to sleep long enough for me to arrive to investigate. The dreamscapes are rather nasty, though, and if you can't master your own mind, you don't ever wake up."

The guard's arm was wrapped around Larken's chest, but she could still move her hands. Making sure to keep the movement hidden by her shirt's billowy fabric, she slipped Madden's knife from her belt and pushed it up her sleeve. She pulled the sleeve back down and grasped it in her fist to keep the knife in place.

"I was on my way to the Stone Circle already, but when I heard you and your companions were stuck in my labyrinth, I had to return. You know I would never pass up an opportunity to play," Etain purred.

The soldiers crowded in further, spear shafts so close to her face that Larken could make out the engraved leaves and flowers on the steel tips.

"Come now, darlings," Etain called in a singsong voice, waving her hand in the air.

Finder rose, his *dornán* following suit. They weren't foolish enough to reach for their weapons. Madden's dark brown eyes, usually so filled with warmth, were now cold and distant.

Hold on, Madden, she pleaded. She knew he wouldn't use his glamour while she was in the guard's grasp, but what if he lost control like he had in the woods? If the guard cut her, the mark would appear on Finder as well—potentially revealing their life debt. They couldn't allow that to happen.

Ten Spring Court soldiers surrounded them, all heavily armored and laden with weapons. Not only did they each clutch the wickedly sharp spears, but they also had swords strapped to their sides, the pommels each sporting a different spring flower. Their helmets were fitted with low visors, hiding their faces completely from view. The curling deer horns engraved upon the helmets gleamed.

Etain lifted her slender hand, and the thorny hedges split apart to reveal a tunnel and a grassy knoll beyond.

Larken's eyes bulged. They had been so close to the outside world, and they hadn't even known it.

"Come, come."

Larken struggled against her captor, but it did as much good as pounding her fists against a stone wall. She tried to find a gap in the guard's armor to no avail. Despite all the decoration, the breastplate clearly served its purpose well. At her thrashing, he poked the dagger into her side. Anger burned in her throat.

Rage simmered in Finder's gaze as well, and his tense muscles screamed of his want for release.

"My lady, what of the others?" another guard asked, gesturing to Finder's *dornán*. Larken was surprised by the sheer adoration in his voice. He actually *loved* her.

"They will accompany us, and they will behave," Etain said, continuing to stroll through the thorns and into the field beyond.

"They won't risk any harm coming to their human friend. The Starveling must have his tithe, isn't that right, Finder, dear?" Etain continued.

"Speaking of tithes, where is your girl, Etain?" Finder asked coolly.

"Oh, she's back at the palace. No need for her to see what's coming next." She smiled, bending down to touch a late-blooming flower. The flower shivered, then burst into bloom, unfolding at the mere brush of Etain's fingertips. The fey princess rose to her feet as graceful as a deer and continued on her way. Larken almost laughed at the absurdity of it. Etain was a lioness in a faun's skin, gentle as it suited her, vicious when it didn't.

The guards closed ranks around them in unison, lifting their spears away from her companions' backs. With Larken still prisoner in the guard's arms, they had no choice but to behave themselves. She had to escape the knight's grasp. She tried to catch Finder's gaze, but he was facing away from her, walking on through the meadow after Etain. The flowers and grass turned toward their princess as lovingly as they would the sun.

The guard hauled Larken after them, and Finder's *dornán* had no choice but to follow.

❧

Larken shuffled along beside her guard, trying not to get stepped on. It turned out that walking with a knife to the ribs was extremely difficult. Larken tripped over herself multiple times, sucking air through her teeth in annoyance. This was the last time anyone would jab a rutting knife at her.

The Spring Court lands were gorgeous, and it was clear that Etain was their goddess. Every flower, tree, shrub, and blade of grass worshipped her. Larken wondered if this was how Finder felt in the Autumn Court lands, if each tree and leaf sang to him.

What would it feel like to have all that adoration, to be loved by both your people and the very land you walked on? To have magic roar through your veins with every heartbeat, to pull it in with every breath?

Ahead stood the stone walls of Etain's palace. Laurelith, Finder had called it. Light stone made up the exterior, leafy green vines creeping up the surfaces. Larken glanced back, but the labyrinth was gone. Somehow, the idea that the entire labyrinth had disappeared as though it had never existed barely surprised her.

No, the time spilling from the hourglass worried her. The tithe would be called that very night. They had to escape Etain—and she couldn't find out about the life debt or the Guardian's dagger.

Trees sprouted here and there, with flowers scattered across the lush, green carpet of moss and grass. Rabbits of every color hopped through the undergrowth. They nibbled on flower petals, looking up with limpid eyes that drank in their every move.

A brown-and-white speckled rabbit hopped tentatively up to Etain, lifting up on its hind legs to twitch a velvety nose at her. The Princess of Spring knelt down, cooing softly as she lifted the rabbit into her arms.

Larken stiffened, sure that Etain would snap the rabbit's neck, but

234

she didn't. She held the rabbit gently in her arms, stroking and murmuring to it. The rabbit gazed up at her with naked adoration in its eyes. Larken wanted to vomit. This was the female who had ordered Madden's family to be tortured and killed—yet animals adored her. Her court loved her.

The guards herded them around a corner of the garden, stopping in a grassy field surrounded by more thorny walls.

And that love was not tempered by Etain's clear love of violence.

For hanging suspended by thorny vines, soaked in blood, was a human man.

CHAPTER THIRTY-FOUR

He hung, completely naked, limp against one of the vine-covered walls
of the courtyard. Horror engulfed her. The vines were not simply
around him, but *in* him, plunging in and out of his arms, legs, and torso,
pinning him in place. The vines spared no part of him, cutting viciously
into his groin and abdomen. His head hung to the side, and the contin-
uous moan spilling from his lips was the only sign of life.

"But...he's a man," Larken gasped. "How did he get here?"

"A tragic story, really." Etain ran a finger down the man's leg. "I chose
his lover, you see, and he just couldn't live without her. He was a soldier,
too, and he fought his way through the Black Guard to get here. The
injuries they gave him only helped him see through the glamour."

Larken's mouth hung open, shocked at how similar the story was to
Roger and Rosin's.

"He had no intention of bringing her back or disrupting the Chosen
girls' special task; he only wanted to be with his sweetheart. Unfortunately for him, I would never allow that to happen."

Etain still held the rabbit gently in her arms, its ears flopped over,
completely relaxed.

"My heart sings for romantic tragedies," Etain breathed. "My sweet
girl has no idea he's here—but he knows she walks, talks, and breathes

mere yards from his prison, always out of his reach." She lifted the man's chin. His limbs trembled. Every time the man breathed, it dragged his chest up and down the thorny vines that impaled him. Tears leaked from his eyes, and Larken swallowed. The sheer misery radiating off the man broke her heart.

"Just let them see each other, Etain," Finder said, the slight quiver in his voice betraying his horror. "You know her happiness would increase tenfold. Just let them have a last moment together."

Some part of Larken knew that was what Finder would have done if Roger had crossed the bridge instead of her.

"Oh, Finder... You've always been such a human-lover, haven't you? Yes, I've learned that happiness does satiate our king the best. But then I have no one to play with." She pouted. "I'm sure the Starveling wouldn't object to an extra tithe tonight, but I can't resist having a bit of fun."

Larken forced herself to look away from Etain's captive. She couldn't help but think about what would have happened if their roles were switched, if Etain had been Ballamor's court ruler instead of Finder. If Larken had journeyed into the Spring Court instead of the Autumn Court, she would be where that man was now. She shivered.

Finder's jaw clenched. Etain gave him a cruel smile, and the vines slowly began to move, coiling up the man's torso to his neck. The thorns sliced viciously through his skin. The man let out a horrible, gritted scream, chest heaving as the thorns moved across his body, cutting him, torturing him.

Etain looked at Finder during the entire ordeal, daring him to make a move to try to help the human. Finder did not. Larken wanted to attack Etain with her bare hands or watch Madden slice her from gut to grin. She wanted Finder's hands to erupt into flame and to watch his fire consume her. Rage, utter rage, simmered beneath her skin. She had never wanted someone to die, not truly. She wanted Etain to die now. But Larken did not attack her, Madden did not draw his knives, flames did not lick at Finder's palms. They all simply stood there, mute with horror and disgust, as Etain toyed with the human before them.

The man grew even paler. His head fell forward. He was still breathing, but barely, and shallowly. The blood pooling at his feet spread. The puddle was large enough that Larken knew there would be no replacing it, that the life's blood was leaving him and would soon be gone.

Etain set the rabbit down, and its feet grew stained with blood. Etain approached her captive, placing two small hands on either side of his face. Almost immediately, his color returned, and he gave a shaky gasp. A pink flush flooded his neck, chest, and arms, spilling down to his legs. Etain had brought him back from the brink of death when nothing should have been able to save him.

The puzzle pieces of Etain's powers finally snapped into place in Larken's mind. Not only did Etain have power over the earth, but she could bring things back to life, just as spring could bring life back to the earth after a dark winter. Larken looked at the princess with new eyes, horror mixing with awe.

Etain leaned in and kissed him softly on the lips. His eyes fluttered open and he looked at the princess, who smiled at him. Larken could almost hear the strains of a minstrel's song recreating the scene before her—a fair lady rescuing her tortured lover, bringing him back to life and bestowing him with a gentle kiss. It had the makings of storybooks and legends; two lovers caught in eternal spring.

Larken wasn't afraid of dying here anymore. She was afraid of *not* dying. Of being kept here for Etain to play with and torment for as long as she wanted.

"Look at her, poor thing," Etain cooed at Larken. Glaring at the faery, Larken held her ground.

Don't give her what she wants. Don't let her know she frightens you.

Encouraged by her display of boldness, Etain breezed over to Larken. The fey princess shooed the guard away, who released Larken immediately. Finder lurched forward, but Etain reached out and casually wrapped her fingers around Larken's throat. Finder froze, but Etain did not stop touching her. Larken stood, fists clenched, as Etain circled her.

"Oh, darling," Etain purred, stroking Larken's cheek. Larken didn't let herself flinch away from the princess's cool fingertips. "I'm not going to let him *die*. Not yet, at least." She giggled shrilly, shaking her head as though Larken had said something incredibly stupid.

"No, no. You see, I like seeing how far I can go." She wound a finger in Larken's hair, so many shades darker than Etain's pale strands. Larken closed her eyes, breathing in deeply.

"Humans *do* like to try to die on me." Etain's lips pulled down into a pout. "But I always bring them back. Perks of having such a decadent power, right, Finder, dear?" She winked at Finder, who glared at her. "Though, its inflexibility does pain me." She frowned. "But you know what a blessing our powers are."

"Etain." Finder shook his head—a warning.

Etain gave a girlish gasp, sliding behind Larken and pressing hands to either side of her face. Larken met Finder's gaze.

"Oh my," Etain purred, tucking her head into the side of Larken's shoulder. She suppressed a repulsed shudder.

"You haven't told her, have you?" Etain breathed. "Finder, dearie… Have you actually grown attached to this one?"

Etain's hands gently encircled her throat. Finder snarled, actually snarled like an animal, as Etain's hands found her pulse. Larken's hands quivered. What was Etain talking about? She already knew about Finder's power over fire. Was she referring to the accident that had occurred when Finder became Prince?

"Enough," Finder growled at Etain. But Etain had found a new toy, and she wouldn't give it up that easily.

"Show her what you can do, Finder," Etain said, her voice cold. She tightened her grip on Larken's throat, and air rushed out from between Larken's lips.

Finder threw out his hand and flame burst from his palm, leaping up his arm, across his torso, engulfing him in a pillar of flame. Heat poured from him in a wave, basking them all in its glow. The fire burned, then lashed out like a whip. It winked out of existence, a coil of scorch marks left on the cobblestones.

"Yes, yes, we all know your power over flame." Etain waved a hand dismissively, and her guards laughed. "Show us your *other* power." She squeezed harder, and Larken's heartbeat pounded in her ears.

Finder's eyes bulged slightly as he felt the pressure through their bond. Etain clearly knew what Finder's other power was, but Larken knew how badly it pained him to use any of his powers—and though it frustrated her that Finder had kept yet another secret from her, she silently begged him not to give in to Etain's game.

Finder lunged forward, and the guards instantly raised their spears, ready to impale him should he get any closer to their princess.

"The magic you keep so hidden inside you," Etain murmured, continuing on as if unaware that Finder had moved at all. Etain gently stroked the hair back from Larken's face. It was sticky with sweat, and it clung to her cheek and Etain's fingers.

"I can't," Finder growled. "I haven't accessed them since I first became Prince. They are too buried inside me—I couldn't access them even if I wanted to."

Larken's mind reeled. So, it did have something to do with the town he had destroyed.

"See how scared she is?" Etain breathed. Rage boiled within Larken, mixing with her fear, all of it churning inside her. Etain inhaled deeply at Larken's neck. "There's nothing quite like the scent of human fear." The hair on the back of Larken's neck rose.

"Come now, Etain." Finder straightened his shoulders. "She's just an ignorant human, enchanted by our realm. If I show her my powers, it might shatter her fragile human mind." Finder smirked, and his eyes were cold. "You wound me by calling me a human lover. They are mere swine compared to the beauty of the fey—especially those as exquisite as you."

Larken couldn't hold back her flinch. *He's just saying that to discourage Etain.* But she couldn't stand the look in Finder's eyes. And how scared he must be if he was willing to say those things and flatter her.

"Mmm." Etain narrowed her eyes, but Larken's flinch had helped to convince her that there was some truth to Finder's words. She took the bait. "We'll see your powers later, perhaps. For now, I want to know what you were doing in my lands."

Etain couldn't find out about the life debt—or the knife. Something of that immense power in her clutches... Larken did not even allow herself to consider it.

Finder lifted his hands. "We were on our way to the Stone Circle. We needed a shortcut—"

"I don't seem to recall you needing a shortcut across my lands before." Etain tilted her head. "You wouldn't be lying to me, would you?"

"No," Finder growled. "I swear it. We were in the Wyld. We needed to cross through in order to reach the Stone Circle by the night of the tithe."

It was the truth. The feeling of the words in the air signaled it.

"The Wyld? This close to the tithe?" Etain's eyes glittered. Despite his oath, she knew he was keeping something from her. "And what were you doing there?"

"I was trying to show the human girl the wonders of Airodion, trying to bring her as much joy as possible before—"

The faery princess shook her head, her curls spilling across her shoulders. "I don't think you understand how this game works."

Thorny vines shot from the earth and coiled around Saja, Madden, and Dahey. They cried out, first in surprise, then in pain, as the vines dug into their legs, climbing up their chests and arms, dragging them to the earth. They fought, trying to reach for their weapons, but the vines were faster, pinning their arms to their sides and slicing into the flesh of their hands.

Larken thrashed in Etain's grip, but the princess still had her by the throat, and the tiny faery was much stronger than she appeared.

Madden cursed, struggling wildly against his bonds, but the vines just tightened, tearing his shirt and pants and slicing into the flesh beneath. He screamed as the edge of a vine burrowed into his hand, and then *through* it, thorns dragging through the hole. Bavvard laughed as he watched Madden writhe.

"*No*," Finder screamed, throwing himself toward his *dornán*. Etain snapped her fingers and the stone floor surrounding her prisoners dropped away into black nothingness, creating a chasm between Finder and his companions. The newly formed platform rose, lifting her friends a few feet in the air. Dirt, vines, and crumbling stone fell away into the chasm.

The Spring Court guards seized Finder from behind, dragging him down to his knees, forcing him to watch the events unfold. Finder burst into flames, and the guards leapt back, hissing at the heat. Etain clicked her tongue, pulling a knife from the folds of her dress.

It was beautifully wrought, studded with gems, gold as sunshine. Etain slashed the knife and pain flashed at Larken's bicep. She cupped her shoulder, her hand filling with blood. She glanced in horror to Finder's shoulder where a matching cut blossomed. But with the chaos around them, Etain didn't notice.

"Behave," Etain snapped at Finder, pointing the bloody knife at him. "Or next time she loses a limb."

Finder screamed with frustration and agony. "I'll show you my powers! Give me someone to demonstrate on and I will. I swear I will!" he cried.

"Please, let them go," Larken begged. "Please let them go. *Please,*" she sobbed. "He's telling the truth!"

Etain ignored her, pushing her into the arms of the guard next to her. The guard wrapped an armored forearm around her neck, pinning her. She clutched at his grip with both hands, trying to pull it away to no avail. The blood from her arm dripped onto his flawless greaves in a steady patter. Madden's knife slid around in her sleeve, and she stopped struggling to avoid getting cut.

"Tell me what you were doing in the Wyld with your tithe," Etain called to Finder. "Don't give me any nonsense, I know you aren't a complete imbecile. What could possibly be so important that you would risk her life in that forest?"

"We were visiting one of my companions, a Warga," Finder said desperately.

"I seem to recall that the last time you allied yourself with the Warga, you led a coup against our king," Etain purred.

Larken's blood froze. *No, no, no.* She was getting too close to the truth.

Saja had gone completely limp, blood dripping from his mouth as though he had bitten through his tongue. His dark curls hung over his brown forehead, both damp with sweat. Dahey was a bloody, torn-up mess beside him, head lolling forward as he fell unconscious.

"None of that," Etain snapped, flicking her wrist at Dahey. His brown eyes flew open, and he gasped, jerking against his bonds. The vines reared up in response, more bursting from the ground, doubling the ties on his legs and pushing the thorns beneath deeper into his skin. They circled his head, cutting across his eyes. He screamed, and his hand reached for Finder, pleading.

Finder gritted his teeth. "The girl was injured. I needed Remira to heal her, nothing more."

"And I suppose the healers in Shadeshelm were just too far away."

"I'm telling the truth," he bit out, then his anger wilted into desperation once more at the sound of his friends' cries. "Etain, I beg you, I'm telling the truth. It was a mistake," Finder pleaded. "I'll grant you a favor, anything within my power to give."

Larken's eyes widened. Finder couldn't offer her that. She could ask him something unthinkable.

"Mmm." Etain pretended to consider it. "No, I don't think so. I'm having quite a lot of fun."

The vines encircled the *dornán*, dragging them down.

"Finder," Madden gasped. "Remember what you promised me, *a chara*." The emotion and love in his voice was as raw as a wound.

"No, Madden," Finder growled. He turned to Etain, every fiber of his being straining toward her. "Please... I'll do anything, Etain."

Saja lifted his head and groaned in protest at Finder's words. Dahey was motionless on the ground beside him, his eye sockets a bloodied mess.

"Anything," Finder pleaded. "Please. Etain, please, I beg of you."

Etain knelt down and took Finder's face in her own. "All I want is the truth."

Finder closed his eyes. Numbness spread through Larken. If he told Etain the entire truth, everything would be lost. Etain would have the knife and the knowledge of the life debt. She could keep them captive and hand them over to the Starveling or warn him and crush the small element of surprise they had over him. Or she could simply kill them and do the Starveling a favor.

But what choice did Finder have but to tell her? His *dornán*'s lives were hanging in the balance.

"Were you invading my court? Planning to attack us?"

"I swear to you Etain, *no*."

"I will make them suffer beyond imagination," Etain murmured, stroking Finder's cheek.

In response, a vine tore through Saja's throat. The faery screamed, or tried to, as blood gushed down his neck. Larken screamed and thrashed, hot tears spilling down her cheeks, but the guard holding her may as well have been made from stone.

"*Saja!*" Finder bellowed, trying to claw his way to his friend, but the guards held him fast.

Saja collapsed, his face purple. Etain turned to look at him, flicking a finger, and the vine pulled from the faery's neck and his throat healed. Saja gasped, jerking back to life like a puppet on a string.

No matter how close to death they come, Etain will always bring them back.

"Etain, listen to him!" Larken cried. "He's telling the truth—he gave you his word! He was just trying to get us to the Stone Circle in time for the tithe."

Etain paid her no heed. Larken screamed and clawed at the armored arm holding her, not even noticing when her nails broke and bled. Her friends were dying before her eyes, dying and being brought back, again and again.

"It's almost time, Finder." Madden's voice was soft, his eyes gleaming with tears. "You know no matter what happens, she will never let me leave here." Two flickering figures appeared before him, a beautiful female holding the hand of a small girl. The illusions flickered once, then disappeared.

"Finder, dearie, I'm growing bored." Etain picked at her nails. "All I wanted was to see your little powers or at the very least hear the truth."

"I'll show you my powers, I will, just let them go," Finder begged.

"Honestly, you're irking me with all this..." Etain rolled her eyes, waving her hand in a flourish, "*Drama*. So, one of your darling *dornán* is going to pay for it. You are going to decide which one of them dies—but I'm going to make it easier on you. Tick tock, dearie."

She raised a hand and twisted, and thorny vines plunged into the hearts of Finder's *dornán*.

Time slowed as the three bodies collapsed. Larken could barely comprehend what had happened. Barely noticed when her mouth fell open and she *screamed*. Finder tore wildly at his guards.

"Ten seconds, Finder. I will bring two of them back. Two of them can live. Who will it be?" Etain's eyes gleamed with hideous pleasure and blood poured from Finder's mouth—he had bitten through his cheek. Larken screamed for Finder. She screamed for Saja and Madden and Dahey. She screamed and she screamed and she screamed.

"Tick tock, Finder, dear."

Larken was very, very far away from her body. It was as if she were watching the whole horrific scene unfold from above.

"Dahey," Finder rasped. "And…"

Larken was far away. She tilted her head, wondering if what she was seeing was real.

"And Saja."

Etain flicked a hand and the vines pulled out of Dahey and Saja's battered bodies. They inhaled, gasping and choking—but alive.

Madden lay motionless in a pool of his own blood.

Larken's knees gave out. The Spring Court guard hauled her to her feet. Out of the corner of her eye she saw a gap in the male's armor, revealed when he lifted his arms. The dagger dropped into her hands. She jammed the dagger into the vulnerable space. The spring guard dropped her, releasing a howl. Larken kicked away from him, stumbling toward Finder.

Her blurry gaze met Finder's.

And the Spring Court guards erupted into pillars of flame.

CHAPTER THIRTY-FIVE

Etain's half-triumphant smile turned to fury. Larken crawled backwards as her guard screamed, his flesh melting. The other fey guards wailed and thrashed about blindly, unable to escape their prisons of fire. The pearls and metalwork dripped from their armor as they threw themselves to the ground, trying to smother the flames.

Bavvard disappeared into the hedges surrounding the courtyard, leaving his soldiers to die.

Finder turned to face Etain.

"*Bring him back,*" Finder hissed. He hurled a ball of fire into her face. She raised a hand, and an earthen shield sprang up before her, taking the brute impact of the flames. Finder smiled terribly. He hurled another cylinder. And another. And another.

"Bring. Him. Back."

"I can't, you fool, that's not how it works! I—" Etain screamed, but the Autumn Prince was relentless, cascading her in fire.

Larken glanced toward the rest of the *dornán*. They needed to get their weapons, they needed to help Finder...

Her gaze stopped at Madden's listless form. This couldn't be happening. She forced herself to stand, forced herself to run toward her companions. She hurled herself across the chasm and landed on her hands and knees, her fingers tearing into the dirt.

Behind her, Etain howled with fury, raising her hands. A thick vine tore from the earth and shot toward Finder, but he swung his sword, slicing it in half.

"Bring him back," Finder snarled again, and a faint smile touched Etain's lips.

"He's gone."

Finder showed no mercy. The faery she had learned to trust was gone, buried beneath his pain at the loss of his friend. Something inside Finder had been set loose, and the flames came to his call with fury and vengeance. The guards stopped thrashing, dead.

Etain lifted her hands toward Finder, but he was too fast. Vines tore from the ground, ready to drag him to the earth, but they turned to ash. Fear lit Etain's eyes, and she twisted her hand, using a swirling motion while pointing at the ground.

Huge cracks split the surface, the earth answering Etain's command. As the ground crumbled away beneath him, Finder jumped. He tackled Etain and the fire leapt at her like a snarling beast. She paled, trying to conjure another earthen shield, but she was too slow. She turned a mere second before the blast of fire hit her in the face. Too slow to shield herself, it burned her right side from chin to forehead, the flesh blistering.

Etain let out a scream of pure agony, trying to cocoon herself in the earth. Finder answered with his fire.

Larken pulled the vines off of Madden. Saja and Dahey lay motionless beside him, but at least their chests were moving. She stroked Madden's face, smoothed his hair.

"Madden," she whispered, but his eyes were glass, his soul already in another world. She buried her face in his chest. He smelled of spruce and smoke and crisp autumn air. She squeezed her eyes shut, tears staining his green jerkin.

"Goodbye, *a chara*," she whispered. *My friend.* With gentle fingers, she closed his eyes. Glancing down at his hand, she found it was clenched tight around a small object. Prying his fingers open, she found the tiny wooden doll.

Deep scratches rubbed against her palm, and she flipped the doll over.

AINSLEY.

Larken's throat closed. She pocketed the doll.

A moan from her right reminded her that Saja and Dahey still lived, tangled in the thorns. She touched Madden's cheek one final time before stumbling over to Dahey. He was crying tears of blood, moaning and shaking.

"It's me, it's me," Larken said, pulling away the vines. They tore into her skin, but she didn't care, couldn't feel anything but numbness.

"Shh." Her hands worked at the vines and thorns embedded in Dahey's face.

He clung to her. "I can't see, I can't see," he moaned, fingers gripping her. She murmured soothingly at him and pulled the vines away from his face.

The damage was unspeakable. Chunks were missing from his lips and nose where the thorns had cut him as they moved, and his eyes... Larken hissed in a breath. His eyes were a pulpy mess beneath his lids.

"I can't see," Dahey whispered.

"I know, Dahey," she said. "I know. But Finder will help you. He's going to get us out, all right? I need to help Saja, don't move."

Saja breathed heavily beside them, eyes closed. At Larken's touch, they flickered open, landing on his lifeless friend beside him. He let out a cry, but the thorns at his mouth silenced him.

Larken pulled away the vines from his mouth, wincing as they sliced her fingers. Once she freed him, he dragged himself toward Madden, pressing his forehead into his dead friend's chest.

"I can't see," Dahey murmured over and over to himself.

Etain and Finder battled on. Around the fey princess, the grass shriveled and died as it had near the Dark Priestesses' realm when Finder created the portal.

"No," Etain gasped. "Not my land..."

Flowers shriveled and turned black. The soil crumbled to dust.

Finally, Etain could take no more. She was unable to shield herself, and Finder would show her no mercy.

Thin tendrils of fire, so hot they glowed white, slowly wrapped themselves around Etain. She screamed and screamed, but Finder was incessant, his eyes dead.

"I can't bring him back! Finder, please, I can't—"

Finder roared, his hands twisting and the flames heeding his call. Etain writhed.

Larken didn't know what happened when a court ruler killed another, but she didn't want to find out. Not now, anyway. She could hear horns blowing in the distance: more knights rushing to Etain's aid.

"Finder!" Larken screamed. They needed to leave, *now*. Twins knew what would happen after the reinforcements arrived. Death, or most likely worse. They needed to leave while Etain was weak and constrained.

Finder didn't move. Saja still had his forehead pressed into Madden's unmoving chest. She choked back a sob, pulling at his shoulder.

"Saja, we have to go. You have to help me with Dahey." She pulled again and he stood up, stumbling over to where Dahey knelt. He spoke some unintelligible words to his friend, hoisting him to his feet.

Larken hurled herself across the chasm, running toward Finder. She grasped his shoulder, shaking him. He ignored her. Etain screamed, twisting horribly on the ground.

"Finder," Larken begged. "Please. We need to leave."

She stood before him, grabbing either side of his face.

"Your powers don't make you a monster," she whispered. Something deep within Finder's eyes registered her words.

That's right, come back to me.

"We need to leave. Dahey and Saja need help, and more Spring Court soldiers are coming." Larken grabbed Finder's hand, pressing it to her heart.

"I'm alive. I'm still here. Saja and Dahey..." She pointed toward them, and Finder's eyes followed. "They're alive, too. And they need you."

"Yes," Finder said softly. Larken shuddered with relief. She would sort through her troubled feelings toward Finder later. She would deal with her resentment and anger later. She pulled him away from Etain, and Finder let the threads of fire wink out. Etain lay in the dirt, motionless, half of her face still badly burned.

Saja and Dahey jumped the chasm and stumbled, Larken reaching out to steady them. Finder lifted a hand, tears pouring down his cheeks, and set Madden's body alight. It burned with heat so intense Larken shielded her eyes, then it was gone—not even ashes left behind.

"Farewell, brother," Finder rasped, his tears dropping to the soil.

"Wait—wait!"

Larken and her companions turned to the sound of that voice—toward the human man.

"Please," he groaned. Larken didn't know if he pleaded for his lover or his freedom. Saja raised his crossbow and shot him through the heart. Larken turned away, squeezing her eyes shut as tears poured down her cheeks.

"There will be no more suffering today," Saja said.

Finder pulled Dahey under his shoulder, bearing most of his weight, and Larken helped Saja on the other side. Together, they half limped, half ran toward the gate on the opposite side of the courtyard, away from the sounds of the approaching guards.

PART III
ALTAR AND ASH

CHAPTER THIRTY-SIX

They ran as best they could, Dahey draped between Finder and Saja. There was too much open field before them. Horns rang out in the distance.

Larken lifted a hand to her lips, letting out a shrill whistle.

Please come, she begged. If the horses could cover great distances, maybe they could get here in time to save them.

Whoops and shouts sounded behind them, the Spring Court guards closing in. Dahey's feet dragged listlessly in the grass. Larken raced alongside her companions, her breath coming in ragged gasps.

Pounding beats grew louder behind them, matching her racing heart.

She stole a glance behind her.

"Finder!" she gasped. For behind them were not the Spring Court soldiers, but the horses.

Finder let out what could have been a laugh or a sob. He wasted no time throwing Larken upon Arobhinn's back, Saja behind her. Saja leaned into Larken, his breath a choking rasp in her ear. He was strong enough to hold onto her torso, but only just.

Finder hauled Dahey onto Rhylla's back before climbing up himself, holding fast to his cousin. Dahey's mare nosed at her rider's foot.

Beside them, Madden's horse snorted and whinnied, tossing his head.

"He's not coming, Bresel," Finder said tightly. "You must leave him."

Bresel stamped his feet, whinnying.

Calling for his rider.

Larken's heart clenched so tightly she thought it might burst.

"Go, Rhylla." And Rhylla did, all but flying across the plain. Arobhinn took off behind her, Larken holding tight to his mane. Dahey's mare followed close behind, but Bresel continued to whinny inconsolably. He took off back toward the Spring Court, ignoring their calls for him.

They kept a bone-breaking pace as they tore through the woods. Soon they left the eternal beauty of the Spring Court lands and crossed the border back into the Autumn Court. Larken couldn't help but glance back over her shoulder, unable to accept that they had left a member of the *dornán* behind in the realm of Spring.

Larken turned her face forward again, hunching her shoulders and settling into the roll of Arobhinn's gallop. She had to keep her mind focused on the Starveling, on what came next. On the final battle. If she stopped to think, if she stopped to sort through her feelings, she would fall apart.

Once they were a safe distance into the Autumn Court, Finder slowed Rhylla to a stop.

"Will they follow us?" Larken asked. She remembered the map, the two interlocking pieces of the Spring and Autumn Courts. It would save Etain time to cut through Finder's lands, just as he had done with hers.

"I don't know. She usually stays within her lands, but after the battle we just had I don't know if she will feel too pressed for time and cut through after us. Though I doubt she'll start a fight again after what happened—she won't risk the life of her girl this close to the tithe."

Finder turned toward Dahey, gently pushing his cousin to the ground. It frustrated her that he didn't know if Etain would pursue them. Should they even be stopping to rest at all, then? Guilt flooded her at those thoughts—Dahey clearly couldn't continue in his state.

Dahey was still muttering "can't see, can't see," repeatedly under his breath. Finder murmured, tilting his cousin's forehead up to get a better look at his eyes. Or what was left of them.

Larken slid from her place in front of Saja and helped him down into the grass. Collapsing to the ground beside him, she put her head in her hands. She could take a moment. One moment to process everything that had happened.

Her grief rose in her like a tide, threatening to drown her. Finder had let Madden die.

You can't think like that, Larken reminded herself. It had been Etain who had truly killed him. Etain didn't want the truth. She didn't want to see Finder's powers. What she truly wanted was to make them suffer.

But no amount of rationalizing ebbed the resentment that boiled inside her. It had been Finder's idea to cut through the Spring Court. They should have risked going the long way around.

Saja slumped against her legs, his golden eyes far away. His shoulders heaved, and for a moment Larken thought he was crying. She placed a hand on his shoulder, but it wasn't sobs that shook him. He was struggling to breathe.

Larken opened her mouth to call for Finder but Saja's hand shot out, grasping her wrist. His eyes bulged, and he gave a minute shake of his head. It didn't seem like he was having a breathing attack like before, but his lungs were clearly struggling. It pained Saja to ask for help during his attacks, but what if he passed out and they couldn't revive him? Saja squeezed her wrist again and finally she relented.

"Oh, all right," she whispered, "but if it gets any worse, I'm finding more yellow thorn." Saja let go of her, eyes filled with grudging gratitude.

"Al...ready...better," he ground out, and though he was short of breath she heard no sound of the wet, hacking cough and labored breathing that had plagued him during the first attack.

Finder was still at Dahey's side, his hands placed over his cousin's ruined eyes, his own closed.

Then Dahey began to scream. He thrashed as Finder healed his eyes, keeping his hands firmly on his cousin's face. Dahey tried to push Finder away but Finder was stronger, pinning him down. After long, agonizing moments it was finally done, and when Finder lifted his hands, Dahey's eyes were healed.

Dahey blinked at the light, lifted his hands to touch his eyes, and a sob racked his body. Finder pulled him into a hug.

Finder held Dahey for a moment, then turned toward Saja. Finder knelt in front of his friend, passing hands over his lips, throat, and torso where the thorns had cut most viciously. Saja groaned in pain but didn't move as Finder's hands worked over him. The wounds healed under his touch, leaving nothing but a faint redness in their wake.

"Let me heal you," Finder said, kneeling before Larken. She nodded. He touched his fingers to the cut, and she hissed in pain. Needles seemed to dig into her skin—pulling, knitting together—and then it was over. She looked down at her completely healed bicep, the pain turning into an ache, a dull throb, and then nothing.

"Thank you," she murmured.

"Thank you," he said, his eyes still filled with pain, but also gratitude. "For bringing me back."

She bit the inside of her lip, Finder's words echoing in her mind, tormenting her.

Bring him back.

But Etain hadn't. And they would never see Madden again.

"We can rest here for a bit," Finder said, "but then we have to keep going if we hope to make it to the Stone Circle by midnight."

"That's all you have to say?" Larken snapped. "All of us have almost *died*, Madden is gone, and all we have to show for it are a knife and a couple of words against the most powerful being in Airodion."

Finder flinched, and as much as it sickened her, it felt good to make him hurt.

"We shouldn't have taken the shortcut. We never should have started out on the insane quest at all. But you just decided for us. Do we ever have a choice? Or will you always just decide for yourself what's best for us?"

She trusted Finder—with her life, even, but wondered if he wasn't the leader his *dornán* thought he was. With no tithe and their life debt, she and Finder had been backed into a corner, yes, but would a good ruler truly sacrifice his entire court, and possibly his entire world—for just a slim chance of change?

A part of her realized she was being irrational. What was the alternative? That Finder use Larken in Rosin's place and have both of them die on the altar? Then girls from Ellevere still would be offered up as tithes. Even if Larken had not come here at all, Rosin still could have died. And Ballamor would have paid the price for it.

"I thought you understood," Finder said, his eyes brimming with hurt. "Life was better when the fey and humans ruled themselves. The things the Starveling has done since the war, the pain he's inflicted on your people and mine—"

"You weren't even alive!" Larken screamed, his words only enraging her once more. Why couldn't he just take the blame? Why couldn't he admit that he had made a mistake? "You have no idea what things were like before his rule."

"You truly are an ignorant human to defend the Starveling," Finder said, his green eyes cold.

Larken's face heated. Of course, she wasn't defending the Starveling. But she was tired of feeling like they never had a choice. She had said that she would fight alongside the fey. She believed they were doing the right thing, but Madden's death had shaken her—and reminded her that this journey would come at a cost. That any of them could be killed.

"Don't call her ignorant for pointing out your mistakes," Dahey growled, jabbing a finger at Finder.

Larken's eyes went wide, shocked that Dahey would defend her.

"Mistakes? So, you would rather have both of us die on the altar?" Finder threw his hands into the air.

"I'm not saying he was wrong to try and defeat the Starveling," Larken interrupted. "And I'm not defending that beast king, either. I'm saying I wish we had more of a choice in all this!"

"Oh, you want to talk about choices?" Dahey pointed at Saja. "Then

257

let's talk about how Saja said he would *sacrifice* me, and then pushed me into the bloody maze!"

Saja flushed. "You know that was an accident. I was trying to save Finder's life."

"What you said to the Priestesses was hardly an accident," Dahey spat.

"I'm sorry, Dahey, truly I am," Saja's voice turned pleading, but then his eyes shot to Finder. "At least your prince didn't call you the weakest member of the *dornán.*"

"Exactly. How can you be loyal to him after he said that to you?"

Finder froze. "I was only trying to be objective, I didn't mean—"

"Like that makes it any better," Saja growled. "You know how much it pains me to slow the *dornán* down, to not be able to fight like they can, and you threw that back in my face."

"We swore to serve you," Dahey added quietly. "We cannot challenge you when you decide to do something. We warned you about the danger we would be putting ourselves in if we cut through the Spring Court." He turned to Larken. "And I seem to recall *you* encouraging us to take the shortcut as well."

Larken blushed. Dahey was right. She couldn't keep blaming Finder for all of the decisions. Not when she agreed with them, and even pushed the group to agree as well.

"We warned you," Dahey repeated. "And Madden paid the price for it."

"Enough!" Larken cried. "We can't keep doing this. We all agreed to this venture. It isn't fair to blame Finder for all of it. We all had to say horrible things in front of the Priestesses. All of you suffered in the Spring Court. There are no good choices anymore—but we can't give up now. Not when we've all sacrificed so much. The Starveling has to be stopped. We all know that. And we can't go into this final battle divided."

If they faced the Starveling like this, they were going to fail. They were going to fail, and then the Starveling would bring his wrath down upon Ballamor and the Autumn Court, and everything they had done, everything they had endured, would be for nothing.

Finder, Saja and Dahey all looked at each other.

Finally, Finder spoke. "I'm sorry. I'm sorry for what I said with the Priestesses, and I'm truly sorry for what happened in the Spring Court. Of course, I am responsible for what happened. And I will take the blame. I should have listened to your council."

Saja relented. "I know you're sorry. And you can't take all the blame. We all failed to save him."

Larken awoke hours later to a sob ripping through the air. Finder assured them that they had a few hours to rest—to grieve, before they needed to push on to the Stone Circle. Even if Etain was following them, she wouldn't be able to catch up to the horses that quickly. Larken glanced upwards, her heart pounding—had they overslept? But no, the sun was still high in the sky, untroubled by their grief. She pushed herself to her elbows, peering blearily around. The scent of smoke lingered in the air. The scent was warm and pleasant, calling to her. Saja and Dahey still slept, their chests rising and falling in unison.

Her throat grew tight as the memory of their missing group member hit her. The group felt too small. It was as if Madden were a limb that had been severed, yet the phantom memory of him remained. Larken's eyes played with her, trying to convince her that her friend was curled up in the shadow of a tree, merely asleep, not gone from the world entirely.

She scanned the forest for signs of the cries she had heard earlier. Cautiously, she walked into the trees. The day was cool and gentle, yet she could take no pleasure in it.

The sunlight broke through the leaves, revealing a figure kneeling in the grass. Finder's fists were knotted in his shirt and pulled into his mouth to muffle his screams. All around him, the trees were on fire. The leaves turned to ash. The trunks roared from the blaze. But the trees bared his wrath, allowing their prince to take it out upon them.

Larken almost walked toward Finder, but something stopped her. The fire called to her again. She walked toward one of the trees, her hand outstretched. The power radiating from the flames made her heart quicken.

She placed her hand on the burning trunk.

It didn't hurt. She could feel the heat, enough so that sweat broke out upon her brow, but the flames only gave her hands a warm tickle. Her eyes widened.

"Larken!"

The flames winked out.

Finder crashed into her, hauling her away from the trees. He grabbed her hand, flipping it over. Nothing. No blisters, not even a red mark.

"Did you do that?" Larken asked. "Did you make sure the flames wouldn't harm me?"

"No," Finder said, still holding her hand in his own.

"The life debt," Larken breathed. "Do you think it ties more than just our lives? I think... I think I can touch the flames because I'm experiencing some part of your power."

Finder studied her. "Can you control it?"

Larken paused for a moment, searching inside herself, then shook her head. "No. I don't know how to describe it. It's like they're allowing me to feel their presence, but nothing more."

It explained the strange pull she felt toward Finder's flames. She had assumed it had been because of their comforting light and warmth, or because she knew they were a part of Finder, but it made more sense now.

But what about his other powers, the ones Etain had mentioned? The ones Finder had said he hadn't used since he had destroyed the Autumn Court town?

"The powers Etain mentioned," Larken began. "You can tell me about them. I won't be afraid."

"I know. And it scares me that you won't be frightened." He shook his head, his curls falling across his brow. "I want to talk to you about them. I do. But I keep them so locked away that I'm worried that even the act of talking about them will make them appear."

He paused. Larken considered pushing him, demanding answers, telling him that she deserved to know. That he owed her that. But she held her tongue, waiting for him to continue, if he chose to. She wanted him to be willing.

"I've told you that the court rulers are gifted more powers than the average faery. But our main powers stem from Airodion itself. One gift is elemental, and the other is...not." He bit his lip, turning away from her. "I'm sorry—I can't. I can't."

"It's all right, Finder," Larken murmured. It terrified her that Finder had another power that was unknown to her, but any powers that were a part of him were also a part of her, now. She knew Finder would tell her—just not yet.

"I will tell you this: it was not my power over fire that killed everyone in the town."

Larken knelt beside Finder, slowly taking his hands in hers. They shook ever so slightly. He would not look at her.

"Etain was going to kill all of us," Finder whispered. His hair fell into his face. He looked very young.

"Yes," Larken whispered back, not sure what else to say.

"But it was me." Finder's eyes went wide. Larken wondered if he could even see her, or if he was far away, trapped in his own darkness. "I let him die," he rasped.

"Yes," Larken murmured.

Finder dug his fingers into the dirt. "Any members of the *dornán* would die for me, but Madden was different. After Senna died, he agreed to join the *dornán*, but only if I swore to him that one day, if he was wounded badly enough, I would let him die. That I wouldn't try to heal him." Finder's eyes glazed over with agony. "He wanted to see Senna again. And Ainsley. And with fey immortality, he knew he might never see them again. So, I swore it. I promised myself that I would protect him, that it would never come to that. I did not think—" Finder collapsed into sobs again, and tears ran down her cheeks as well.

Oh, Madden.

She hadn't known her faery companions for very long, but what they had endured in Airodion had bonded them together. Madden's death felt like the loss of one of her senses. And Finder...she felt his agony as if it were her own, as though they were not only tied in life but in emotion as well, and every tear in his heart was mirrored inside hers.

"I'm going to ask you something, and I don't want you to swear any oaths. I want you to choose to tell me the truth."

Finder nodded.

"Tell me the true reason why you want to kill the Starveling. Is it only because you wanted to free yourself from the chains he places upon you?"

Finder's brow furrowed. "Of course not. I want to kill the Starveling because I think everything about him is wrong. It pains me that the Starveling restricts my powers, but I resent my powers anyway. If I could give them up, I would in an instant. I would never want to kill the Starveling just to increase my power."

"Did you use Rosin's death and our life debt as an excuse to attack the Starveling? Would you have challenged his rule otherwise?"

"I've challenged the Starveling's rule before," Finder insisted. "I always knew I would do so again because I despise serving a king like him," Finder said. "Would I have done it this year if we had not become bound in a life debt? I don't know. But I would never use you or anyone else as an excuse. To do so would be putting my court and the humans in danger. I took the life debt and Rosin's death as a sign, the will of fate, that we should challenge him this year. But even without those things, I would have challenged him again."

Larken studied him. She had accused him of all of her suspicions, and those his *dornán* had voiced as well. That Finder was only attacking the Starveling again because he wanted revenge for Embryn, or because he thought he didn't have another choice with Rosin dead and the life debt. But Larken knew he spoke the truth, even without his oath. At his core, Finder was opposed to the Starveling's rule. He believed it to be so wrong that he would risk his life, the life of his *dornán*, and the lives of countless other fey and humans in order to destroy him and make a better world. But he also fought the Starveling because he knew his court and Larken's people were already in danger, already in chains.

Larken wanted that better world. And if she wanted to better the lives of the humans, of her people, they had to destroy the Starveling first. Then she could focus on the evils in her world—the Popes and the Order of the Twins itself. She and Finder had been forced to work together, but even with their bodies tied, that relationship had slowly become a choice. The Spring Court had almost torn them all apart, but they couldn't falter. Larken had to help the fey destroy the tyrant in their world before she could destroy the tyrants in hers.

It all came back to what she would do for a better world. What she would sacrifice for a better future, even if she didn't get to see it.

Finder's words would never right all the wrongs that had been done, nor bring back those they had lost. But they were enough. They had to be enough.

"I believe you, Larken whispered. "And we..." She squeezed his hand, blinking rapidly. "We forgive you."

Tears rolled steadily down Finder's cheeks. Then he bowed his head —a true bow of thanks.

"We're in this together," she said firmly. "We all are. None of us can solely take the blame. We have to stick together, now, at the end of it all."

"I'm not alone," he whispered.

"No, you're not alone."

When Finder curled up in the grass, he looked like a boy, small and scared. The young prince against the world.

Larken wrapped her hands around her knees, watching over him, allowing him just a few short hours to rest. They would have to come up with a more definite plan on how they would attack the King of the Fey, but she knew she could give Finder a moment to rest.

Now that she was alone, thoughts of the night to come consumed her. Tonight, they would face the Starveling. Their quest would finally be over. But she had the Autumn Prince and his *dornán* beside her.

She wasn't alone.

All too soon, she bent to wake Finder. His eyes moved behind his lashes, and she knew he was fighting his return to the world of the waking.

Finder opened his eyes, his gaze flicking up to meet her own. She touched his shoulder, hoping it would convey what words could not.

Saja stood waiting for them, awake and on high alert. Dahey sat apart, clenching and unclenching his fists, staring at nothing. Larken looked around for Madden, then caught herself, breath hitching in her throat. She could almost see the grief clinging to Finder and his *dornán* like a second skin, muting the colors of them, dulling their expressions. Sucking every last bit of joy and burning it to dust, letting the wind carry it away into nothing.

Larken flinched as a huge beast crashed through the bushes, but it was only Bresel. The bay stallion whinnied frantically, snorting and pawing at the ground. His eyes rolled back in his head and he reared, a sound horribly akin to a scream ripping from his mouth.

Finder approached, hands raised. "Woah, my friend." Bresel gave another small rear before calming enough to let Finder get closer.

"He's gone," Finder said. He placed his hand on the center of the horse's forehead. "Your ride is over. Go freely until you enter the dark eternity." The horse snorted, huffing into Finder's hand. Then he turned, giving one final, mournful whinny, before cantering off into the forest.

Fey horses only have one rider, Larken remembered Finder saying. *Once that rider dies, they cannot, or will not, take another.*

She patted Rhylla's neck, murmuring, "Thank you for finding us." The thought that Bresel would never have another rider... Rhylla nuzzled her hand, lipping it gently as she sensed Larken's sadness.

Saja and Dahey were strong enough to ride on their own, so Larken rode with Finder. He pressed his calves into Rhylla's ribs as he turned her toward the Stone Circle.

To the Starveling.

They did not stop to eat or rest. The ritual, Finder had informed her, would take place at midnight. Larken shuddered as she imagined what would have happened if they had not made it out of the labyrinth, or the

Spring Court, in time. Or if they had run into trouble taking the long way around.

"I think we should attack right away—before the ceremony even begins," Dahey called. "We cannot risk him consuming a heart and gaining strength from it."

Nausea rose in her throat at his words. At the thought of the human girls that would die that night.

"Will the Starveling be able to sense that Larken is not your tithe?" Saja asked.

Finder's curls brushed against her cheek as he shook his head. "I don't believe so."

"We have to pretend I'm your tithe, then," Larken said. If Finder showed up to the Stone Circle without a girl, it would already arouse suspicion.

"No," Saja said. "It's too dangerous. If you're on the altar and Finder loses control, he could kill you both."

Larken's stomach twisted. Finder wouldn't have long to resist his oath.

"I will have the strength to resist him," Finder said firmly. "I think we should wait until the moment he calls for the hearts. He'll be high off of the emotions pouring into him from the humans, but he won't have gained strength from their hearts. That is his moment of greatest weakness, when he is distracted but in a hunger frenzy. When we first ambushed him, we believed he would be at his weakest before the tithe, when he hadn't fed in so long, but we were mistaken. The Starveling is always powerful; what we need is a distraction. When he begins to feel the emotions from the humans but hasn't fed yet will be the moment to attack."

His *dornán* fell silent, contemplating his words.

"There's no way to save the other Chosen girls?" Larken said. Guilt swept through her. All this time she had been focused on rescuing the Chosen girls, especially those from Ballamor, and when she had learned they were dead, she had all but removed the girls from her mind. But there were other human girls in Airodion at this very moment, about to be sacrificed.

"If the other court rulers helped us the girls might have a chance," Finder admitted. "But they have never challenged the Starveling before. Even if we told them about our plan now, I doubt that they would offer us aid. It's likely that the girls would die either way, and I don't want to reveal our plan and risk one of the other rulers warning the Starveling even a moment before we attack. Time is everything, now. Even a lost second could cost us."

Larken nodded, swallowing her sorrow. They couldn't save the girls this year, but they fought for a future where the tithe would no longer exist.

"If the other rulers attack, Saja and I will hold them off," Dahey said. "Focus on the Starveling, on saying the words." He looked at Larken. "And you focus on staying alive. You two haven't broken the life debt yet, and that puts both of you in more danger."

Larken clutched Madden's dagger. She wouldn't put herself in harm's way unnecessarily, but she wasn't going to stand to the side. This was her fight, too.

They rode on, and Larken was grateful they kept up such a relentless pace. It prevented her mind from straying into thinking about the Starveling. Or Madden. Instead, she was fully occupied with clinging tightly to Rhylla.

Saja remained silent, his eyes downcast. Larken wondered what he was thinking. If he was wondering if any of them would survive the night.

Dahey kept repeating some phrase under his breath, his brow furrowed. He was tense and jumpy, and anytime they tried to speak to him he snapped some irritable reply and went back to his mutterings. Larken couldn't tell what he was saying, but his mood was contagious, and she found her nerves wearing thin as they neared the Stone Circle.

As Finder had explained it, the Starveling's domain, the strange cross-shaped piece of land in the center of Airodion, was not a part of any court lands, and instead served as a neutral meeting point for the tithe. The Stone Circle was the place where the tithe was called, where the stone altars resided. The Starveling lived within the territory, where he remained in a dormant state until the night of the tithe, or if a true disturbance in the land awoke him. According to Finder, extremely old beings, Master, fey, or otherwise, had to spend a period of time completely dormant in order to conserve their life force. Larken couldn't shake the feeling that the closer they rode to the Stone Circle, the quieter they needed to be lest they wake the beast. But she knew he would wake regardless.

They rode until dusk descended upon the Autumn Court lands, the sun turning the leaves to pure gold and orange. It was stunning, but Larken could think of nothing else but the Stone Circle ahead of them. It became harder to distract herself, and fear clung to her. Madden was dead. She did not think she could survive watching another one of her friends die. The thought of losing Saja, Dahey, or Finder ate at her.

She wanted to be brave—wanted to feel that hot courage that had filled her when she'd first entered Airodion, but she just couldn't find it within her. Too much had been taken from her and too much of the unknown lay ahead.

All too soon, darkness fell, and they left the forest of the Autumn Court behind. The Starveling's land was desolate—filled with grey stones and pale, sickly trees.

Finder murmured a quiet "whoa," and Rhylla stopped.

Saja and Dahey trotted up, taking their places at his side.

"We're close enough to walk from here," Finder said. His voice was calm and steady, and Larken let it flood over her like a wave. She pushed all of her previous doubts aside, willing herself to be strong. They had made it. The end was finally here, one way or another, and if courage wouldn't come to her then she would just have to take it.

"We either survive this night and enter a new world," Finder said, his voice taking on the timbre of a true prince, "or we die in the old one. But we will fight for justice."

She placed her hand on top of Finder's, squeezing it gently. "We fight," she said, her voice steady and strong. "We made it this far, and now we fight. For all the girls that came before, for Brigid and Rosin. And for Madden—for all the fey and humans. They deserve to be free. We deserve to be free."

They all gripped their weapons and turned toward the Stone Circle.

CHAPTER THIRTY-SEVEN

They stopped for a final time amongst a clump of trees in the darkest part of the pale forest.

"Thank you, Rhylla." Larken stroked the mare's strong neck, trying not to imagine that it was the last time she would run her fingers through the horse's mane.

Rhylla pressed her velvety nose into Larken's hand, and then, on some silent cue from Finder, she turned and cantered away into the forest beyond. Arobhinn and Dahey's mare followed close behind, the sound of their hoofbeats fading away.

"It's time," Finder said, looking at Larken. His eyes were so filled with sadness and guilt and fierce protectiveness that Larken took a step toward him, almost reaching out to touch him.

"I chose to be here," Larken reminded him. "To fight for my people and your court."

Finder nodded tightly and turned toward Dahey, looking at his cousin like it was the last time he would ever see him. Perhaps it would be. "If I die," Finder said, eyes boring into Dahey's, "you take care of our court. Do whatever you have to do to save them."

"I will," Dahey said tightly, and Finder pulled him into an embrace.

Finder turned to Saja next. "If I die—"

"Don't," Saja growled.

Finder held up a hand. "If we are able to break our life debt but I still die, get Larken home. She deserves that much." Saja bowed his head.

Her stomach dropped. "We're still bound by the life debt." With everything that had happened, she'd almost forgotten. Trapped. She would be trapped here.

Finder placed his hands on her shoulders. "Don't panic," Finder said. "We still have time. The tithe begins at midnight, and we have until the first light of dawn before the gate closes. And the more we try to force it to break, the less likely we will be to succeed."

Larken took a deep breath and nodded. She couldn't worry about that now. They needed to deal with the Starveling first.

"Now, this is the difficult part," he whispered. She gave a tight nod, knowing what was coming, Finder having explained it to her in detail earlier.

"I'm ready," was all she said. She realized, with a little bit of surprise, that it was true. She was ready to face the monster that had tormented her village, ready to fight till her last breath to see him overthrown. She was here for Brigid, too. She would do it for her. There would be no more tithes.

Saja held a white slip of a gauzy dress that would barely cover her figure, with Dahey holding a matching white blindfold. Her heart beat furiously in her chest, and she tried to calm herself with a few steady breaths. Fear would not cripple her.

She could do this.

She changed behind a tree, though as translucent as the dress was, it wouldn't have mattered if they had seen her naked anyway. She tried to hide the furious heat in her face as she rejoined her companions. *Perfect. The first time I'm half naked around a man, and he's about to carve my heart out on a stone altar.*

Saja crossed over to her, holding out the blindfold. She turned her back to him, resisting the urge to cover her backside with her hands.

He tied it firmly around her eyes.

She lifted her arms and shuffled off, sure she would bump into one of the skeleton trees at any moment.

Finder's arms encircled her. She immediately relaxed at his touch. "Are you ready?" Finder asked, brushing his hands lightly down her arm. She shivered, more from the sensation than from fear.

"Yes." She lifted her chin and her sightless eyes to the path ahead.

"What will you do, when you return home?" Finder asked.

If I return home, she thought. She knew he was trying to distract her, but she was grateful for it all the same. She wished she could see his face. "I think—I think I will become a cartographer. It's always been a dream of mine to travel the world and create maps of the places I've been," she admitted shyly. "A life working at my family's bakery just isn't right for me. A life in Ballamor isn't right. I want to see more of the human world after almost dying in this one." She could practically hear Finder's lips pull up in a smile.

"After your demonstration in the maze, I have no doubt that you will be an excellent cartographer," Finder said.

"The problem is, I'm absolutely horrible at drawing," Larken laughed softly. It felt good, combating a bit of her rising trepidation. "I can chart just fine. It's the drawings that get me."

"I'm certain that you can do anything you set your mind to," he murmured in her ear. All too soon, he was stepping away. Saja and Dahey appeared on either side of her, grasping her arms lightly to help her along.

The blindfolds, Finder had explained, were only to lead the sacrifices to the stone altar. Once they were there, the blindfolds would be removed, so the court ruler could look their victim in the eye.

Saja and Dahey were excellent guides, and she did not fall or stumble once. She wondered how many other times they had helped lead the tithes to their deaths.

Brigid.

She wished her friend were with her now. But she knew she didn't *need* Brigid here. Not like she had before.

A few moments later, Larken heard the voices. Fey voices. They must be entering the Stone Circle.

Saja and Dahey's hands disappeared from her arms only to be replaced by Finder's. He led her a few more paces, then stopped. Larken's knees brushed up against something solid.

The altar.

"I'm going to lift you now, love," Finder murmured in her ear. Larken blinked. He hadn't called her love since... it felt like ages ago. A small smile touched her lips. She no longer felt like slapping him when he said the word. He swept her into his arms. He laid her down on the altar as gently as a lover. Cold sweat started to dampen her brow and palms.

With careful fingers, Finder slipped the blindfold from her eyes. He looked down at her, green eyes calm. She wondered how he could do it, wrestle his emotions down so thoroughly.

She tried to reach for Finder's hand, to seek some kind of comfort, but she couldn't. She couldn't move. Straining against the invisible bonds, she tried to subdue her panic. Finder had warned her that the altar kept the victims bound to the stone, but she hadn't envisioned not being able to move even her head.

She was completely helpless. It was a feeling she thought she'd gotten used to in Airodion, but this was different. Worse. This was how Brigid had felt during her last moments.

"Don't fight it," Finder murmured, quieter than a breath. "Just breathe." She breathed in and out slowly, trying to master her emotions.

It had to be close to midnight. The darkness pressed in around them, heavy and palpable. She could hear the voices of the other court rulers.

And one voice she hated above all others.

Etain.

The name snarled through her mind. A floral breeze wafted toward her, and then Etain stood above her. No scars lingered on her face from Finder's burns, leaving her as prim and lovely as ever.

"Ready for the show, darling?" Etain said, gripping Finder's arm. He ignored her, as though even the slightest glance at her might set him off.

She gave Larken a falsely sweet smile. "I *do* hope she pisses herself."

She trailed a finger down Larken's arm, and if she were able to move, Larken would have tried to bite her fingers off. Etain giggled and breezed away.

Out of the very corner of her eye, Larken could see Etain's human, a pretty young girl with brown hair. The girl smiled at Etain when the princess returned to her side. Etain smiled down at her and stroked her hair. Larken looked away, unable to stomach seeing any more. If only the girl knew that Etain had tortured her lover for days, and that he had died mere hours ago.

A hush fell over the Stone Circle. It was not an instant thing, but rather a slow, creeping kind of silence. The kind of silence that screamed of monsters in the dark and horrid, evil things that nothing can protect you from. Larken's blood turned to icy sludge in her veins.

The Starveling was here.

One by one, a small torch lit around each of the altars. Finder's doing—but by choice or force Larken didn't know.

Then came the voice of the invisible puppet-master behind the curtain of Ballamor's deception. The voice of the being who had taken over the fey, tormented them, subjugated them, and turned them against their human allies.

"Welcome, my children," the Starveling rasped. "What tithe have you brought me on this tremulous night?"

CHAPTER THIRTY-EIGHT

Larken wished that she had never heard the Starveling speak. She wished that she never had to hear him speak again. His voice was old, ancient as death itself, and raspy. It was not the voice of a human, or a faery, or even one of the Fomari beasts. No—this was the voice of a god, a god who had ruled long enough for its thirst for power to turn to madness.

"I smell," he ground out, and Larken could hear it, actually *hear* this monster running its tongue along its teeth. "Human flesh," he finished, breathing in deeply.

Larken could only see the Starveling out of the corner of her eye, but what she could see was enough to turn her stomach. He was massive, so tall and grossly thin that she couldn't believe his bones could support him. He walked upright and was strangely graceful, providing him with the dignity of a ruler. Huge horns jutted from his head, sweeping upwards, almost touching in a circle. A crown of bone. Even with the layers of cloth draped over him, she could still see his bulging ribcage and collarbone straining against his flesh. Ashen skin drew taught over his skull, and his face revealed wrinkled lips and a tiny, slitted nose. A skeleton. Something that should not be alive. The tattered black cloak trailed on the ground, spilling whispers in its wake.

"I think it is time that we begin."

Finder moved from her side to above her, and she tracked him with her eyes. Saja and Dahey must have moved off into the shadows, for she couldn't see them, but knew they wouldn't go far. Finder drew a knife from his belt—not the Guardian's dagger, but his own knife.

Her heart roared inside her.

The Starveling hissed in pleasure and anticipation, and Larken closed her eyes for a moment, trying to block out the sound. His voice was woven from nightmares.

"You all know why we are here." He was so huge that his head and shoulders were lost to the darkness above her. Larken's heart beat faster and faster, trying to claw its way from her chest.

"You tried to rise against me, and now you shall pay. This day, and for eternity," he purred, almost kindly. Larken shivered. "The humans trusted you, and now you will rip their flesh open on the altar. You shall watch the light slip from their eyes, feel their lifeblood flow from their veins. And you shall do so all in supplication to me."

Cries rose from the girls surrounding her as they realized what was happening.

Look at Finder. Look nowhere else.

Larken's eyes flew to Finder's, upside down above her. She could read nothing in his expression. She thought she saw fear, but perhaps that was just her own gaze reflected in his. What if he couldn't resist the Starveling's call, the oath he'd made to him?

Look nowhere else. Do not look anywhere else.

"Do you trust me?" Finder murmured, softly so only she could hear, as he raised the knife above her. All she could see were his eyes, his blade.

Look nowhere else.

"Yes," Larken breathed.

"Bring me their hearts!" the Starveling howled, and Finder brought the knife down.

CHAPTER THIRTY-NINE

Finder sliced the knife down in an arc, severing the tie that held the Guardian's knife in place at his belt. The knife slid from the leather, and Finder caught it in an explosion of light.

A brilliant flash went off behind her lids, and she tried to ignore the sickening sounds of knives connecting with flesh as the other fey sunk their blades into their sacrifices. She opened her eyes and was met with screams and chaos.

Finder was bathed in white, shining light, as though a star had exploded on him, *in* him. The knife in his hand shone brightly, too. Magic and power thrummed in the air, and the Starveling screeched, covering the opening of his hood with a hand.

"Bring me your tithe, Finder of the Autumn Court!" the Starveling shrieked.

Finder trembled, his very bones shaking with the effort to resist the oath. How long would he last?

"You do not know what you are doing, whelp," the Starveling hissed. "You do not remember. You play with magic you do not understand, and you will pay for it."

Finder screamed, his anger sudden and terrifying. Even his eyes shone white, and Larken did not recognize him. She wanted to get away, and she strained against the altar.

"Finder!" she screamed, but he didn't seem to hear her. He just stood there, motionless, looking like a young god himself.

"Give me the knife, Prince of Autumn." The Starveling held out a grey-fleshed hand. "Give me the knife, and all will be forgiven. The human can go free. Your court shall not be punished. Just give me the knife." His voice rolled over her and had it been melodic, it might have even been soothing. But the constant rasp was horrible despite the great creature's tone, rubbing against the insides of her ears like sandpaper.

Finder's eyes darted to the Starveling, torn.

"Don't, Finder!" she cried.

The other court rulers stood motionless, afraid to intervene. They watched with morbid fascination as the scene unfolded before them, the blood of their sacrifices dripping into the soil below their altars.

Finder shook his head. "No. This ends tonight. I will fight until you are dead or my vow ends me." His eyes glowed even brighter, and his grip tightened on the knife's hilt.

"You want to play with magic, boy?" the Starveling growled, and from thin air he drew a war-scythe and a double-chained flail. The spiked balls at the end of the double chains hanging from the flail were covered in sharpened points, made for ripping out flesh. Both weapons gleamed in the moonlight as the Starveling brandished them. "So be it."

Finder jumped onto the altar, shielding her from the Starveling's wrath. With a snarl, the Starveling swung the flail, the two spiked balls flying toward Finder's chest. Finder hurled himself into the air, jumping over the chains and kicked the Starveling in the chest. The Starveling was so large that Finder's weight didn't even sway him; he simply stabbed at the red-haired prince with his scythe.

A blur to her right and Saja was there, raising his crossbow.

"Stay back, Saja," Finder commanded. "I am the only one with enough power to stop him."

Finder clutched his sword in one hand and the guardian's knife in the other, bearing both before him as he lowered into a fighting stance. She had worried that his vow would overcome him within a few moments, forcing him to obey the tithe, but the knife's powers must have somehow given him enough strength to resist. Larken's gaze flew around desperately. She needed to get off this altar.

The Starveling swept the air with his scythe. Finder blocked with the knife, lunging out lightning-quick, but the Starveling was quicker. He twisted the war-scythe, locking the Guardian's knife in place. The Starveling flung out his other hand, blasting Finder with a gust of raw magic strong enough to splinter a tree trunk. Larken gasped, waiting for the burst of pain, but it never came.

His magic can't hurt me, she remembered, *so it can't hurt Finder, either*. Finder glanced down at his body and smiled. The Starveling's brow raised in surprise, and he barely had time to block as Finder twisted, pulling the dagger free and stabbing the now-flaming sword at the Starveling with his other hand.

Hands grabbed her and she cried out, so engrossed with the fight before her that she hadn't heard anyone approach.

"It's me," hissed a familiar voice at her ear. Saja. He grabbed her again and pulled, dragging her off the altar. She was finally able to move again once no part of her was left touching the stone.

Saja pulled her around the altar where Dahey stood waiting. Saja threw his cloak around her shoulders. He stood before her, crossbow leveled. Protecting her.

"You have to help him," she said, unable to look away from the vicious fight between Finder and the Starveling. Seeing the destruction the Starveling and Finder wrought was terrifying. She had seen beauty in magic, yes, but this was indescribable. This was unnatural.

"Protecting you is just as important," Saja argued. "With the life debt—"

"I can take care of myself," Larken insisted. "He needs you more than I do."

Saja looked at her, golden eyes luminous in the torchlight. He exchanged a look with Dahey, then the two of them launched themselves into the fray. Etain hissed from her place by her altar and threw herself at Saja, intent on serving her Master. She drew a beautifully wrought sword, slender yet wickedly sharp. Saja fired once at the

Starveling, narrowly missed, and then Etain struck, nearly impaling him through the ribs. Saja dodged, dropping his crossbow and drawing his sword. He swung at Etain, and their swords met, the ring of steel-on-steel singing through the night.

Saja summoned knives and hurled them at her, but he used glamoured ones as well to further confuse the Spring Court Princess. Etain wasn't fooled. She blocked again and again with her sword.

A faint clicking sound echoed on the breeze, growing steadily louder. Larken froze. She knew that sound. She crawled around to the other side of the altar, concealing herself as best she could.

Eight Fomari appeared between the trees. They didn't attack; they just shuffled back and forth, pecking at each other when they got too close. Beady eyes trained on the Starveling and Finder, they didn't pay her a second glance.

Feast. Feast on them all! one of their screeching voices tore through her head. The fey around her tilted their heads in pain, and Larken could only assume they heard the Fomari, too.

Master promised us human flesh, but not yet. Not yet, chattered another.

In one fluid movement, Saja dodged Etain's downward stroke and rolled, picking up his crossbow and firing. His bolt sank directly into her chest, right above her collarbone. Etain howled, then Bavvard and two of her other soldiers were there at her side, dragging her away into the trees. Larken prayed she wouldn't recover.

Larken hissed as the Starveling landed a blow on Finder, causing a rip in her own thigh. But Finder was still holding his own against the king.

The other court rulers, Winter and Summer, watched the battle between Finder and the Starveling warily. The blood from their humans went up to their elbows, the hearts growing cold on the altars. The Winter Court ruler was female. Her snow-white hair glinted in the moonlight. What were they thinking? Did they want Finder to triumph, or the Starveling?

Dahey stood before them, making sure they did not come to the Starveling's aid. He kept his sword lifted, daring one of them to challenge him.

Saja stumbled toward the altar, and Larken reached out to steady him.

"Are you hurt?" she cried. Saja shook his head, pressing his palm to his chest. She screamed as pain bloomed in her arm. The Starveling had landed another blow.

"You can't breathe," she gasped through her own pain, pushing Saja to the ground. "No more fighting until you catch your breath."

Saja took a shuddering breath and nodded. He had forced Etain to retreat, at least.

Both Finder and the Starveling were bloody, and flames ran up and down Finder's arms and legs. The Starveling clutched a bloody arm to his chest, but he still held his scythe. He bellowed and charged at Finder, but Finder was ready, and instead of trying to block, he sidestepped and whirled, cutting into the Starveling's side with his sword.

The Starveling howled in fury. Larken had assumed Finder's flaming sword would cauterize the wounds it dealt instantly, but no, the sword could either cut or burn. The Starveling was covered in burns and singes, and blood leaked from him.

Finder's arm dripped with blood from the scythe, as well, but aside from that he was mainly unscathed. He still reeked of power, his flames glowing brighter than anything Larken had ever seen. The magic from the Guardian's dagger was consuming him.

A beautiful, black-skinned faery, the ruler of the Winter Court, took a step forward, but Larken did not know if he sought to help Finder or his king.

Dahey stalked forward, sword raised. "Do not interfere," he warned.

"We cannot do nothing," the prince said sadly, beckoning to the princess beside him who brandished an ax made of ice. The two of them lunged at Dahey.

The Winter Court Princess shot chips of ice at Dahey, who had to swipe them from the air with his sword. She tried to freeze him in place, but Dahey was too quick, constantly moving and slashing with his sword. The Summer Court Prince blew gusts of air at Dahey, pushing him backwards, but Dahey always regained his balance and resumed fighting once more. Larken narrowed her eyes. They had to be going

HANNAH PARKER

easy on him. With their heightened powers, Dahey shouldn't have even been a threat to them. It seemed as though the two rulers were trying to help Finder as best they could without interfering directly. Larken felt a rush of gratitude toward them all the same.

"You will die tonight, old one," Finder said. His voice was chilling, not the warm tenor she had grown so fond of.

"I don't think so." The Starveling tilted his head. "After all, you cannot even bring yourself to use your true powers, can you? You have the ability to harness indescribable power, yet you deny yourself because you fear history will repeat itself."

Finder bared his teeth, his eyes filled with rage. But his muscles locked in place. Whatever thoughts raced through his head paralyzed him. The Starveling grinned, creeping toward his opponent. Dahey still held off the other court rulers, fighting them with his sword and his glamour.

She drew Madden's knife.

"Larken," Saja wheezed, grabbing her arm. "You can't fight."

"I can distract him, if nothing else." She knew her own strength. But she had provided a distraction for the Warga sentinel, giving her a chance against the Basiog. If she could distract the Starveling, even for a moment, then she could give Finder a clear window to end him.

Holding the dagger tightly, Larken turned to face the Starveling. He was almost upon Finder now, having goaded him into a place of despair. Cold fury filled Larken's gut.

"Leave him be!" she snarled, raising her knife. The Starveling whirled, facing her with that horrible head of his. He blinked at her, then waved a hand, dismissing her.

"Be gone, girl," he snapped, turning back to Finder. "I will feast upon your heart when this is finished."

Finder's eyes were still blindingly white, but Larken could sense the pain in them.

"It's all your fault, princeling," the Starveling cooed, sauntering closer to Finder. "You brought this upon yourself, on your dearest friends, on your court. You make the wrong choices again and again, and you do it

280

for no other reason than your selfish desire for a world you would ruin without me to guide you."

Finder didn't move, but his shoulders crumpled.

No, no, no. The Starveling could tell he had met his match, and now he would try to tear Finder down with words until he could land the killing blow. Larken couldn't let that happen.

She thought of all the horrible beings she had encountered in her life. She thought of the Black Guard and the Popes, who had lied to her; she thought of the Fomari and Etain. Of every monster she'd ever known. Of every tyrant. She was done being hurt by them. No longer.

Brigid had been her protector once, but she was gone now. Larken had thought she would never make another friend—didn't deserve to— but Finder and his *dornán* had proved her wrong. She thought she knew what she wanted. She thought that being with Brigid again would solve everything, that making new friends would make her happy. That being beautiful, being fey, even, would give her the confidence she so desperately craved. But she didn't need any of that.

It was up to her. It had always been up to her. She had proved herself time after time, and she would be damned if she would ever see herself as worthless again.

The Starveling lunged at Finder and she screamed, running at the Starveling and bringing her knife down with all her strength. In one lazy motion, the Starveling caught her, lifting her into the air by her throat.

Larken choked, the knife clattering to the dirt below. She grasped the Starveling's wrist with both hands. She couldn't breathe, she couldn't think.

"Look at me, Finder," the Starveling hissed. "Watch your tithe die, just as I said she would."

Finder's eyes bulged as his own airway was cut off. Without a sound, Finder threw out a hand toward the Fomari. As one, the creatures fell to the ground.

Through her flickering vision, Larken struggled to process what had happened. Dead. They were dead. And Finder had barely lifted a finger.

Holy Twins. This was the power Etain had tried to goad out of Finder at the Spring Court. Finder had the power to make someone die with a single thought. The Fomari's eyes stretched wide in death, their bodies already growing withered and cold.

Like an autumn leaf fallen from a tree.

That is how Finder had annihilated the entire town when he had become Prince. Just like this. All of their lives had simply ceased to exist. Still, her heart pounded with some kind of strange excitement. She wanted *more*, to see Finder kill again with his powers. The golden thread of their life debt pulled taught inside her, linking them more strongly than it ever had before. Her eagerness for more bloodshed frightened her, but this must be how Finder felt. No wonder he hated his powers, if death made him feel this good. But he resisted, shut down this part of himself to protect others.

She was not afraid. Not of him.

The Starveling's eyes went wide. "Finally, the prince's powers reborn." He gave a low laugh. "How does it feel, using them after all this time?"

Finder retched. His eyes were wide with terror and pain now, his air cut off by the life debt's bond. Larken's lungs burned, unable to pull in enough air.

The Starveling made a *tsking* sound in the back of his throat. "You call me a monster, boy, but look to your own powers, Prince of Autumn. I punish those who wrong me, yes, but you have punished thousands of innocents. Murdered them in their beds."

No words the Starveling uttered would change her mind about Finder now. She had seen all parts of him, both good and bad. She had hated him. Trusted him. Knew his very soul.

"You are not a monster, Finder," she said, her voice barely a rasp. The Starveling shook her, squeezing her tighter, but she didn't stop. "I saved you that day in the woods because I knew there had to be some good in you. You showed me that I was right. I know you. I feel your powers. And I am not afraid. Don't let him change you. Don't let him win."

The last word came out as a mere wheeze, but she knew Finder had heard her. At least he'd heard her, before the end. She thought of Dahey and Saja, Madden and Finder. Mama, Papa, Rosin and Brigid. Remira and the Cynyadas. She smiled. Black spots swam at the edge of her vision, and she let go of the Starveling's wrist.

Fire blazed before her eyes as Finder's sword parted the Starveling's hand from his body.

Larken gasped, sucking precious air back into her lungs. The Starveling howled, clutching his stump. He snarled, advancing at Finder once more. Before he could reach him, a pulse of power rippled through the night air, moving in a wave that stemmed both from her and Finder.

The life debt had broken.

The two ripples of power struck the Starveling. He fell onto his back, impaling the tip of his scythe in the dirt.

Finder did not hesitate. He grasped the Guardian's dagger, raised it high, and his lips moved, forming the words the strange being in the ring of mushrooms had asked of him.

Then he plunged the dagger down into the Starveling's chest; into his heart.

CHAPTER FORTY

The Starveling hissed, then went still. Magic pulsed through the air, rippling as it surged out from the fallen king much like it had when Finder and Larken's life debt had been paid. Larken shivered and turned to Saja, who looked at her, concern flickering through his golden eyes. Larken knew he had felt it, too.

Finder turned back to the Starveling's corpse, slowly pulling the dagger free. In a flash of blinding light, he burst into a swirling pillar of flame. Finder became lost in the blaze, the liquid pools of fire coursing over his skin growing ever brighter. Larken could feel the heat raging from him where she stood by the altar, and sweat poured down her body.

Saja and Dahey looked on with horror as they beheld their prince. The two other court rulers fled. Finder still clutched the dagger in one fist, the strange blade visible through the flames. Larken knew he had to release it, or the power would consume him completely.

"He's not strong enough to hold onto it much longer," Larken cried, but Saja and Dahey were rooted to the spot, seemingly unable to hear her as they watched their prince die before their eyes.

"Finder!" Larken screamed. Finder gave no response, his eyes glowing white as the sun. "Let go! Let go of the knife!"

Larken would have thought he was already dead had she not seen the gentle rise and fall of his chest through the haze of heat.

He's alive, she thought, a tiny flicker of hope winding through her. She pushed away from Saja, stumbling toward Finder. She heard Saja and Dahey cry out behind her, but she ignored them.

Look nowhere else.

The heat burned her even though she was still several feet away from him. The life debt no longer protected her from the flames. She could feel the sinister heat, feel it aching to consume her. Finder looked at her with those blinding white eyes, so bright they formed black spots on her vision.

"Finder." She reached out a hand and hissed, pulling it back when her fingers burned so close to the flames.

"Finder, you have to come back. Please come back," she begged. Would he die if he held on too long? Or would the power turn him into something else entirely? She didn't know what to do. She couldn't get any closer. "You have to drop the dagger now. It's time to let go," she pleaded. Still, Finder did not move.

Look nowhere else.

He needed her. He was too far away, too far gone in that dark place. He had used his powers. The ones Etain and the Starveling had provoked him into using, the ones he had hidden so deep inside himself. His power over death. He couldn't hear her. Didn't even know she was there. He didn't want to come back from wherever he was.

She had saved him once. And she could save him one last time.

Look nowhere else.

She took the final step and wrapped her arms around the Prince of Fire.

At first, she felt nothing. Then she could feel it all. Her body panicked, trying to pull away from Finder, but she could not let go—it was as though she were chained to him. She couldn't let go, couldn't scream, couldn't faint, couldn't die. She was trapped, clinging to Finder like he was the only thing in this world keeping her alive, when he was the only thing in the world who was killing her.

A voice swam to her through the flames.

"Larken?"
Oblivion took her.

CHAPTER FORTY-ONE

Larken woke slowly, pulling herself out of some strange dream. She opened her eyes, blinking in the darkness. She bolted upright. She had to get home before the dawn.

"Easy," Saja said, placing a steadying hand on her arm.

"Finder," she began, but Saja stopped her.

"He's fine, Larken. You saved him."

Relief rushed over her. But if she saved him..."I'm not caught up in another life debt, am I?"

Saja chuckled. "No. Life debts can only happen once. Once they are broken, the bond is over."

Larken expected more relief to come from his words, but all she felt was a strange emptiness. Her bond with Finder was over. Forever.

Her clothes from the Warga lay beside her, and Saja averted his eyes so she could change.

"Is..." Larken hesitated, closing her eyes so she could avoid looking at her ruined body. "Is there much scarring?"

"No," Saja rumbled. "Finder was able to heal you completely." He glanced toward Finder's sleeping form beside them. "I can't believe, after everything he went through, that he had the power to heal you," Saja said. "The strength it must have taken... I can't imagine it. He must

287

have dug very deep inside himself. I do not know if it was the remnants of the knife's power that helped him or if some of his power was restored after the Starveling's fall, but it is a miracle, nonetheless." Saja regarded her with those luminous golden eyes, a small smile on his lips. "I'm glad you are all right. He cares for you, Larken, more than I have seen him care for someone in a long time. Thank you for saving him," Saja finished softly.

Larken blinked at him, running his words over in her mind. She placed her hand on Finder's back, letting it move with the rise and fall of his breathing.

"How is Dahey?" she asked.

"He's recovering as best he can. You two have only been out a few hours. He stayed to make sure you and Finder were all right, and then he took off. Riding to clear his head, most likely."

His face fell, his golden eyes pained.

"What is it?" Larken asked. Shouldn't he be relieved? It was all over, now.

He shifted slightly. "When the Starveling fell—" Saja broke off as Finder stirred. His golden eyes darkened, making a chill run up her spine. What was he talking about? "It might be best if Finder explained."

Saja stood, dusting off his pants. Casting one last glance at them with an expression that made her skin prickle, he left them alone.

Finder struggled to sit up, hissing as it stretched his bad shoulder. He had healed her before healing himself. Pressing a hand over the wound, his flesh began to heal. He sucked in a breath as the bloodied flesh came together, and then it was over. Not even the faintest line of a scar remained.

He caught sight of her, his eyes widening in disbelief. "Larken," he breathed. He reached out shaking fingers to touch her face, but then he stopped himself, his fingers hovering over her skin.

She took his hand and pressed it to her cheek. "I'm okay." She smiled.

"Our bond," he whispered. He stroked her cheek. "It's broken."

Larken tried to sort through her feelings as she stared into the eyes of the prince. She was relieved, of course, that their life debt was over, that she wouldn't be trapped here for another year. But her heart ached fiercely, yearning for that golden thread between her and Finder. Loneliness curled within her.

Finder released her, looking away. "There's something else I have to tell you," he said. "But I don't want to. Not after everything we just went through."

"What do you mean?" She frowned. "The Starveling is dead. We broke our life debt. It's not yet dawn, I can go home—we did it. We won." Part of her knew that Finder spoke of something else, she just didn't want to admit it.

Please, let all of this be over.

Finder stood and began to pace back and forth. Larken scrambled to her feet as well, bracing herself for what he was about to say.

"We were wrong." He looked at her, his green eyes filled with such fear she almost stumbled back. "So wrong. The Starveling was not our true enemy. We've been deceived."

Larken was sinking very fast, deep inside herself, trying to shield herself from Finder's words.

"Do you remember when I spoke of the war against the dark creatures, when we united with the Starveling and the Dark Priestesses to defeat our enemies and the tithe was born?"

Larken nodded. Finder and his *dornán* hadn't been able to finish the tale, as if their memory had failed them.

"I was wrong. The Starveling did help us banish the creatures. But he did more than that—he imprisoned their creator. This being...he was the one wreaking havoc in Airodion. He created a magical language, one that harnessed magic to words in ways previously unknown to our world. He gave this power to those he chose—innocent and evil alike. He created new creatures—spoke them into being. Something that should not be possible. He was the one who created the Fomari. The court rulers banded together to stop him, working with the Starveling. But the Starveling cursed us to forget. Forget the magical language, forget its creator so the language could never be accessed again."

Finder's words outside of the Guardian's prison drifted back to her, then. *Magic is not bound by words, but I fear something else is at play here. I recognized the language as if from a dream.*

289

"The Starveling worked with the Priestesses and the court rulers at the time to imprison him deep in the Wyld, and he could only be free when the Starveling was dead at the hands of a court ruler with a knife of power... and his magical language spoken once more."

Larken stopped breathing.

"The Guardian," she whispered. "We freed him."

The Starveling and the Dark Priestesses had deemed the Guardian so dangerous that they had cursed an entire population to forget him. It explained her companions' confusion about their history—the memory curse had addled their minds. But now the Guardian was free.

And it was entirely their fault.

Finder nodded. "And without the Starveling, there will be no way to imprison him once more."

Larken hugged herself. "How do you know all this?"

"The Starveling placed a failsafe in the magic that would alert the court rulers should the memory curse ever break. Only the court rulers know for now, but it is only a matter of time before that information spreads. I told Saja and Dahey after I healed you—before I lost consciousness, but soon enough the Guardian will begin searching for allies of his own."

Everything they had done, everything they had worked for, all of it had led to this. They thought they were ridding Airodion of a tyrant, and they'd only freed another monster.

Yet one part of the puzzle still didn't fit. "But if the Dark Priestesses helped the Starveling imprison the Guardian and create the memory curse, then why did one of the Priestesses give us the knife? Why did she lead us to him?"

"Givrain wanted him to be free," Finder said. "I fear they are working together."

Larken clenched her shaking hands. What would happen to the humans now that the Guardian was free?

"Will the bridge still hold?" she asked, holding her breath. Finder had said before that the bridge would remain even after the Starveling's death, but what if all that had changed because of the Guardian's language?

"The chasm and the bridge still stand."

The small sliver of relief she felt was drowned by her fear. "What are we going to do?" She looked at Finder, at his slumped shoulders, the sheer weight that pressed down upon him.

Finder glanced up. The sky was still dark, but the horizon was swirling into tones of grey. "You've done so much, Larken. This is not your fight any longer. You need to go home."

Larken shook her head. She couldn't leave. She'd had a hand in the Guardian's newfound freedom as much as anyone. She had to stay. She *wanted* to stay. Even if it meant remaining in Airodion for another year, she couldn't leave her companions to face this next evil alone.

"I'm staying," Larken declared.

Pride glimmered in Finder's eyes. "Your people need you in your world. I don't know what will happen once the Popes discover that the Starveling is dead, but if you aren't there to tell the truth then think what lies they could spread."

Larken bit her lip, contemplating his words. If she stayed, she would be trapped in Airodion for another year. Another year for the Popes to go uncontested, to spread new lies about the fey and Airodion.

Finder had his *dornán* to help him. The humans had no one. She had to let everyone know the truth about their history with the fey, the Starveling and the Guardian.

"I don't want to leave you," she whispered.

Finder's brow softened. "I know Larken. But—"

The sound of pounding hoofbeats tore through the woods. Dahey came barreling through the trees, Saja in close pursuit.

"Finder," Dahey gasped, his chest heaving. A white raven clung to his shoulder, cawing harshly. "They sent a raven. We must return to Shadeshelm. Now. There are rumors that the Spring Court is preparing to invade the Autumn Court now that the Starveling is dead. All the courts are preparing for war."

The blood drained from Finder's face. He turned to her—his beautiful, dear face frozen in stricken indecision. Larken chose for him.

"Go," she told him, and placed a steadying hand on his arm. He looked at her, eyes filled with agony.

"Go," she said again, pushing him away.

"Saja can escort her back to Ballamor," Dahey said. "You and I must return to Shadeshelm."

"No. I'm going with you," Saja said, fists clenched at his sides. Finder shook his head.

"Dahey is right. You take Larken home, then ride hard and join us in Shadeshelm after she is safely escorted to the bridge." Finder took in Saja's frown and added, "Please, my friend. I beg you."

Saja relented, bowing his head.

Larken merely brushed Finder's arm with her fingertips as he leapt onto Rhylla's back—the thought of anything more was too much. Her heart ached at the thought that she would never see him again. She had no idea what the following year would bring for either of them.

"Goodbye, Larken."

"Goodbye, Finder," Larken whispered, but he was already turning and galloping off into the trees. Dahey nodded once to her, then rode after his cousin.

Saja pulled her up onto Arobhinn's back. Tears stung her eyes as they rode hard for the bridge. Arobhinn's pounding four-step was the only thing that kept her from falling to pieces.

CHAPTER FORTY-TWO

Arobhinn's hooves ate up the ground, carrying them swiftly over the terrain. Guilt for leaving her companions and returning to the safety of the human world consumed her. But she knew she had to warn the humans about the Guardian.

They pounded through the forest, the leaves a blur of color against her vision. Such stunning autumn colors, so much brighter than the ones in the human realm. She would miss it.

Arobhinn snorted and stamped his hooves as they paused in front of the cliffs. The tiny pathway of the bridge stretched out before them.

Larken squinted. She couldn't see any members of the Black Guard. They liked to drink on the last night of their shift, celebrating the closing of the bridge—perhaps they had abandoned their posts early.

A series of clicks filled the air. The hair on the back of Larken's neck lifted. No, they couldn't be here...

She and Saja turned to see a pack of Fomari descending from the trees. They scuttled closer, clicking their beaks. Arobhinn backed up, stepping onto the bridge.

"Go, Larken." Saja pulled out his crossbow. "You have to be in Elle-vere before dawn."

Larken glanced at the lightening sky, worry pinching her gut. Why were the Fomari here? What did they want?

But she couldn't leave Saja to face five Fomari beasts on his own.

"I'm not leaving you." She unsheathed Madden's knife.

The beasts filed one by one onto the bridge, pushing Larken and Saja back. Stones fell away beneath Arobhinn's huge hooves.

But the Fomari didn't attack. They just pushed Arobhinn further back toward the human realm. Saja's face turned stricken.

"Come on!" Saja bellowed. "Fight!" He shot the first Fomari twice through the throat. Blood spewed. The creature fell, dropping over the side of the bridge and into the chasm below.

Do not let them leave, another hissed. *Master promised us flesh if we complete our bargain.*

The Guardian created the Fomari, so that must have been the Master they were referring to. But they had spoken of human flesh when Larken had first entered Airodion. Exactly what kind of bargain were they talking about? Why wouldn't the Guardian want them to leave the bridge?

Arobhinn took a step forward, his hooves clattering on the stones. One misstep from the huge stallion and they would all fall to their deaths.

One of the Fomari lunged at Arobhinn, swiping at him with wickedly sharp talons. Arobhinn lashed out with his front hooves, striking the Fomari in the head. The beast howled, and the other creatures rushed to his aid.

Saja fired his crossbow, but the creatures were nimble, clinging to the sides of the bridge with their long talons.

"Larken, you must go!" Saja pleaded, shooting at the Fomari to no avail. The bolts would hit home, and though the beasts slowed, they were relentless.

One of the Fomari hissed at her, crawling up from the side of the Bridge. Larken slashed at its outstretched claw with her knife, and the creature reared back. It lost its balance and fell into the chasm below with a shriek.

Two more. They had to get through two more and then both of them would be safe. She glanced toward the sky. She had a few more minutes.

Saja shot one of the Fomari through the eye. It collapsed upon the stones. The final monster launched itself at them, colliding into Arobhinn's chest. The horse whinnied. His hooves scrambled for purchase.

The monster snapped its beak, and Arobhinn reared, striking the Fomari in the head.

The Fomari screamed, opening its jaws wide, and Saja shot it through the mouth and into its skull.

In one swift movement, Saja hurled Larken from Arobhinn's back. She cried out, her hands slamming into the dirt of the human realm.

Just as the first rays of sunlight poured over the bridge.

AUTUMN'S TITHE

CHAPTER FORTY-THREE

Dawn broke, spilling light into the world like blood from a puncture wound.

"Wait, wait!" Dahey panted. He pressed a hand to his shoulder. "We need to stop. I was wounded by that bloody Winter Court Princess." He slid off his mare's back, falling to his knees in the dirt. His heart beat wildly in his chest, like a beast trying to claw its way out.

Finder dismounted, running a hand through his sweaty curls. They had been riding hard, slicing through the Autumn Court forest like a blade.

"You should have let me heal you before you took off into the woods," Finder admonished.

"I thought it was healing well enough on its own, but the riding must have torn it loose." Dahey gritted his teeth.

Just hold on a little longer.

Finder knelt beside him. Dahey stared into Finder's face, the face that looked so similar to his own. Since they were children, Finder had always been his other half. Finder was his brother, even if blood hadn't bound them. Finder's green eyes seemed darker in the early morning shadows. Dahey looked away.

Finder examined his shoulder, pulling Dahey's linen shirt aside to get a better look. "I don't see any wounds. Where—"

Dahey spoke the words the Guardian had taught him to sever the *dornán* bond.

And then he plunged his sword into Finder's chest.

CHAPTER FORTY-FOUR

Larken's head whipped toward Saja. He sat astride Arobhinn, completely still. The last Fomari hissed and shuddered on the stones, alive, but only just.

"Saja!" she cried. Her heart leapt into her throat. Arobhinn's back hooves were planted squarely in the human realm.

"How is that possible?" she breathed.

"Listen," Saja said. Arobhinn's ears were flicked toward Airodion.

"I don't hear anything," she said. And, at first, she didn't. Then she felt it.

The first time she had crossed the bridge and entered Airodion, she had been too terrified to think of anything but making it across alive and without attracting the attention of the Black Guard. But now, after spending so much time around the fey, she knew what magic felt like. She knew how to sense it.

The magic around the bridge was gone. By now, even with her human senses, she should be able to feel the rhythm, the subtle push-pull of the magic. But there was nothing. And in the forest before the bridge, she hadn't felt the glamour that had made her so relaxed when she had first entered Airodion.

Saja slid off Arobhinn's back, his muscles tense and alert. He walked to the other side of the bridge, taking a cautious step into Airodion. Larken sucked in a breath but—nothing. The bridge was open.

Larken followed him, making sure to avoid looking at the hideous drop on either side of her. She stepped into the faery realm. Fear pooled within her.

The Starveling created the bridge and the Guardian's prison with the court rulers and the Dark Priestesses. His death shouldn't have broken the spells.

This must have something to do with the magical language. The language must have had the power to end the Starveling's magic.

Dread spilled through her, freezing all her muscles in place. They had released something truly vile into Airodion. And while the Guardian might be searching for allies, he likely already had one— Givrain, the last of the Dark Priestesses. One of the most powerful beings in Airodion now that the Starveling was gone.

At least they had known what the Starveling was capable of. Not knowing what the Guardian and his language could do—this was far worse. Larken pressed a hand to her temple, overwhelmed by how little she truly knew about the fey.

And the humans…the humans were defenseless.

"If any of the fey can enter Ellevere, the humans are in danger." Larken gripped Madden's knife. She had to warn her people. She had to get Mama and Papa, and they needed to leave the North. They would find help, and then they would find a way to keep the fey out of Ellevere.

Saja stormed over to where the Fomari lay twitching. His bolt must have barely missed the creature's brain. Larken followed close behind Saja. The warrior pinned the monster's neck down with his boot.

"You said your Master sent you to keep us here. Why? Why would the Guardian want us to be trapped in Ellevere?"

We serve another Master, now, the Fomari hissed. Blood leaked from its beak.

Saja's hand flew to his chest, his eyes wide.

HANNAH PARKER

"What is it?" Larken placed a hand on his arm. Was he having another breathing attack?

"Something happened," Saja gasped. "Dahey's bond—it's been severed. Finder is wounded, but I feel—" Saja's eyes darted back and forth. He struggled to find words. "His heart is breaking."

Larken's heart leapt into her throat. "But *dornán* bonds can't be broken—not until death."

"I don't think Dahey is dead—it didn't feel like the severing that occurred when Madden died. It felt too... abrupt."

Larken gripped his arm harder. "Would Finder ever release him from the bond?"

Saja's eyes were filled with horror. "Not under any circumstances I can imagine."

Master's plan... has... succeeded, the Fomari said. Larken flinched when the voice scraped over her mind.

Saja's gaze whipped back to the Fomari. "What did you say?" he breathed.

We failed... but Master has triumphed. Soon, he will be King. And he shall reward us with all the flesh we desire.

"No," Larken whispered. The Fomari couldn't mean... their Master couldn't be...

Dahey, the Fomari hissed. Its head fell to the side. Dead.

Larken's mind reeled. Dahey would never betray Finder. He had sworn to serve him. Her thoughts flew to every moment she had spent with Dahey. How he had helped her during Madden's outburst of glamour, how he had started training her to see through illusions. He had even defended her against Finder.

Dahey's first loyalty has always been to his court. Dahey had challenged Finder at every turn. Accused him of not putting his court first.

"No," Saja growled. He grabbed the Fomari and shook it, but the beast was dead. "*No.*"

"He wanted the Fomari to keep us here so he could attack Finder," Larken realized. "But he couldn't have done that without breaking his *dornán* bond first." But severing the *dornán* bond was impossible. Or it had been, until...

"He used the Guardian's language," Larken gasped.

Saja screamed, kicking the body of the Fomari off the edge of the bridge. He fisted his hands in his curls.

Larken's mind whirled as she tried to fit the pieces together. Dahey's resentment toward Finder for never putting his court first. Dahey, encouraging them to visit the Priestesses, the beings he had just so happened to have visited before...

"It's been him from the beginning," Larken whispered. "It's been him all this time. He *planned* for the Fomari to kill Rosin. He was the one who cut her hand. I heard the Fomari in the forest. They said their Master had promised them human flesh."

She turned to Saja. "Dahey was the one who led us to the Priestesses. He'd been there before. They must have told him about the Guardian, then. Dahey doesn't just want to protect his court. He wants to be Prince. That's why he did all of this."

Saja shook his head. "There is no way for Dahey to force the magic to choose him. Even if he kills Finder, there is no guarantee."

"Maybe not before, but perhaps with the Guardian's language there is."

The language had powers none of them could have imagined if it had the power to destroy the magic of the bridge and the Guardian's prison. If Dahey knew about the Guardian, then he would know about the curse and how the Guardian needed a court ruler to free him by killing the Starveling and speaking the words. Dahey couldn't have done that himself, which is why he pushed Finder to go to the Priestesses in the first place.

Saja ran shaking hands through his hair. "He set Finder up to break the Guardian's curse, and now he will use the language to take Finder's crown."

Anger crashed through her. Dahey had been her friend, or so she had thought. But now all she felt for him was rage. How could he do this to them? He had been at their side throughout their journey. He had suffered as much as any of them. He had sent the Fomari here to keep them distracted, but what if the Fomari had killed them? Would he have felt any remorse?

And Finder…she bit her lip. He was hurt—Saja had felt it. Dahey had hurt him. But he hadn't killed him. Not yet, at least. Would he really kill his own kin? He and Finder had grown up together. Finder was like a brother to him. But he had done all this to get the crown. They had clearly underestimated the cruelty he was capable of.

Saja hauled himself onto Arobhinn's back. "I need to leave. Now."

Larken glanced back to Ellevere. To her home. Guilt twisted in her belly, knowing she was about to turn away from her parents again. She needed to tell her people what was happening, but she couldn't leave Finder. The Popes were a threat, yes, but her friends were in danger at this very moment. The courts scrambled for power, the Guardian walked free, and Dahey had betrayed them all by using a language that could cause irreparable damage to Airodion.

She would not leave her companions to face that alone, not when she had played a part in it. They would figure out how to stop Dahey and whatever plans the Guardian prepared.

Her soul had been tied to Finder's. When one had been cut, the other had bled. Their lives had been spun together, bound by that golden thread. Her heart ached where it had been cut, feeling as though it had lost a part of itself.

Their life debt might be over, but she and Finder would never be alone. She cared for him, deeply, fiercely; not because their lives were bound, but because he was her friend. She would never leave him alone to face this oncoming darkness.

And though the golden thread of their life debt had been cut, she felt a new thread form inside her. Not one forced upon her by magic, but one she willingly created. One that was real. She let it pull her toward Finder.

"I'm coming with you."

Saja didn't question her. He pulled her up onto the stallion's back, and they charged back into Airodion.

Larken and her companions had faced one great evil already. She knotted her fingers in Arobhinn's mane, steeling herself for the future. Whatever came next, Larken knew she was strong enough to face it. She would not leave her companions and Airodion to Dahey's greed and the wrath of the Guardian.

She would free Finder, and then they would turn all of their enemies to ash.

CHAPTER FORTY-FIVE

Dahey had to look away from the pain and betrayal in his cousin's eyes.

Saja would feel the pain through the bond, but the Fomari would
keep him occupied at the bridge so he would not be able to interfere.
Dahey repressed a grimace at the thought of those foul beasts. But they
were the Guardian's creatures, and the Guardian had taught him the
best way to make a bargain with them. All the Fomari asked in return
for their services was flesh. Preferably human, or at least fey. And Dahey
knew how to deliver that once their deal was done.

Rhylla snorted, pawing the ground with her hoof. "Quiet, you,"
Dahey snapped.

He pulled his sword slowly from Finder's chest. Finder cried out.
Dahey had struck him just beneath his right collarbone near his shoulder. A painful wound, but not a mortal one. Finder was powerful now,
and though he was weak from his battle with the Starveling, Dahey
knew he would heal quickly. If he waited until they were too close to
Shadeshelm, Finder might have healed enough to have the strength to
overpower Dahey, and he couldn't allow that to happen. This wound
would weaken him enough to get Finder back to court.

"Why?" Finder gasped, a crease forming on his brow.

"I had to, Finder," Dahey said, watching the blood pour from his cousin. Only a matter of time now. "I did not wish for it to come to this, but you abandoned your court, especially after Embryn's death, and now when you challenged the Starveling again. You never wanted to be Prince. I knew that it was time for the Autumn Court to have a new ruler—a ruler who truly understands what it is to lead, to sacrifice."

Finder groaned, his breath coming in ragged gasps. "Dahey, no... please—"

"When I discovered the Dark Priestesses, I asked them how I could become Prince. They led me to the Guardian, who knew his ancient language could help me, if only I would free him. I knew once your tithe was dead that you would jump at the chance to kill the Starveling." Dahey wiped his sword clean on the grass. "The Guardian assured me that the knife would overpower you and your magic would come to me. But things did not go according to plan, thanks to that bloody human girl's interference." Dahey hesitated, a tiny sliver of guilt pricking him. He had grown fonder of Larken than he had expected. But she had caused a rift in his plans, nonetheless. "I knew I had to separate the two of you and Saja—so I sent my Fomari to keep them at the bridge until I could incapacitate you."

Dahey glanced up at the sky. The sun had almost fully risen. "If Larken knows what's good for her, she'll go back to her world and stay there."

"You can't do this. The Guardian can't be trusted," Finder panted.

"Yes, I know the true events of the war, now, thanks to you." Dahey frowned. "It irritates me that the Guardian did not share this information with me from the beginning, but it changes nothing. I still need him to tell me the words that will force your magic to come to me."

"It doesn't have to be this way, Dahey," Finder said. "It's not too late. Shadeshelm will be under attack soon; we need to help our court."

Dahey shook his head. "There is no attack from the Spring Court. I'm taking you back to Shadeshelm to confess your crimes, and then you will be put on trial for treason. And once I take your powers, I will be a king."

"You swore to protect me," Finder's voice broke. "You're my kin, Dahey."

"This is for your own good," Dahey said sadly. "You don't need this burden of being a prince any longer."

Finder slumped to the forest floor. Dahey hauled his cousin up and threw him on his mare's back, climbing up after him.

The Autumn Court was about to enter a new age, and he would be the one to rule it.

ACKNOWLEDGMENTS

Reaching the end of this book was a journey five years in the making, and I've finally gotten to the part where I get to thank everyone who has made this book possible!

Vicky Galier, the Schmidt to my Nick, the Louise to my Tina, my best friend and roommate, I don't know what I would do without you. Our daily 4:30 phone calls keep me sane. You've helped me brainstorm villain names and let me complain endlessly about every aspect of publishing even when you had no idea what I was talking about. Looking forward to our TinFinity. I love you!

To Lauren Elliott, my oldest friend, I love you endlessly. We speak in a language others simply cannot understand: boom boom firepower, hey bud, oh honey, water balloon babies, my stomach hurts, step brothers, two failed trips to Bowdoin, why can't Hannah just go to space, macchiato. I would cross the bridge for you any day.

To my amazing editors, Sylvia Cottrell, Emily Martin, and Jennifer Rees, you all helped me turn this book into something I'm proud of. Thank you. I'm still convinced you know the characters better than I do.

To Camille, Annie, Pauline and Gabby—only one of you will ever read this book (Gabby) but I love you all anyway. You all got me through high school, college and now "real" life. I'm incredibly lucky to call each of you friends. To many more powerpoint karaoke nights.

Maddie Tomasko, one of this book's biggest champions, Toma is for you. Ally Jones, I'm so lucky to have you in my corner, thanks for all the long brainstorming phone calls. Sammira Rais-Rohani, nothing can describe the joy I get from your voice memos and paragraph texts. Jordan Roe, thank you for supporting Autumn's Tithe from the very beginning. To Réka Patai, my sweet and caring friend—love you! And to Caitlin Fuller, to all our Barnes and Noble dates talking about big dreams—thank you.

To everyone on bookstagram who has relentlessly supported and promoted this book, thank you!!

A very special thank you to all my friends and family who didn't bat an eye when I said I wanted to write fantasy books for a living. To my barn family, thank you for making the barn a home away from home.

To Happy and Lazio, the horses in this book are inspired by both of you. Happy, if we went to a magical faery world together you would immediately buck me off. I still love you. Laz, you put up with so much. Thank you for being my kind and steady teacher when I needed it most. Jinxy, you are the best therapy cat a girl could ask for. And to Tater the pandemic puppy, thank you for getting me through a tough year.

And lastly, to my parents. Words can never convey how deeply grateful I am for your unconditional love and support. Both of you have supported every single one of my crazy endeavors from selling tin foil sculptures door to door (why did you let me do that) to selling 300 pages worth of stuff I made up. I am so tremendously lucky to call you my parents. This book, and everything I do, is for you.

PRONUNCIATION GUIDE

CHARACTERS
Brigid: Bridge-id
Finder: Find (like kind) -er
Dahey: Da (like law) -hee
Saja: Sa (like law) -ja
Madden: Mad-in
Remira: Ree-meer-uh
Rosin: Rose-in
Imogen: Emma-gin
Ainsley: Ains (like gains) -lee
Etain: E-tane
Asphalion: As (like has) -fey-lee-on
Aleea: Al-lay-uh
Embryn: Em-brinn
Givrain: Give-rain
Toma: Tow-ma
Maeve: May-vuh

PLACES
Airodion: Air-row-dee-on

Ellevere: Ell-vere
Ballamor: Balla-more
Fomari: Foe-mar-ee

OTHER
Dornán: Door-nan
Laithnam: Laith (like faith) -nam
Cynyada: Sin-ya-da
Arobhinn: Arrow-vin
Rhylla: Ra-la
Bresel: Bree-sell
Basiog: Bass-ee-og

ABOUT THE AUTHOR

Hannah Parker was born and raised in Oklahoma. She holds a Bachelor's Degree in English Literature from Oklahoma State University, and her fiction won overall first place for the Katherine Paterson Prize for Young Adult Literature in the Journal *Hunger Mountain*.

When not writing, Hannah can be found drinking coffee, reading, or competing in the hunter ring with her horse. Hannah currently lives in Oklahoma with her cat, dogs, and horse.

CPSIA information can be obtained
at www.ICGtesting.com
Printed in the USA
LVHW042142160222
711307LV00018B/1905

9 781736 741429